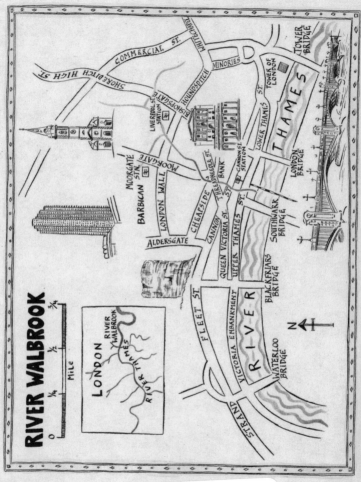

RIVER WALBROOK

Mile
0   ¼   ½   ¾

LONDON
RIVER THAMES
RIVER WALBROOK

N

COMMERCIAL ST.
SHOREDITCH HIGH ST.
WHITECHAPEL
HOUNDSDITCH
MINORIES
TOWER BRIDGE

BISHOPSGATE
LIVERPOOL ST. STATION
TOWER OF LONDON
LOWER THAMES ST.

THAMES

MOORGATE STN.
BARBICAN
MOORGATE
LONDON WALL
CHEAPSIDE
THREADNEEDLE ST.
BANK
CANNON ST.
CANNON ST. STATION
LONDON BRIDGE

ALDERSGATE
CANNON ST.
QUEEN VICTORIA ST.
UPPER THAMES ST.
SOUTHWARK BRIDGE

FLEET ST.
VICTORIA EMBANKMENT
BLACKFRIARS BRIDGE

STRAND
RIVER
WATERLOO BRIDGE

PENGUIN BOOKS

Thursday's Child

Thursday's Child

NICCI FRENCH

PENGUIN BOOKS

PENGUIN BOOKS

UK | USA | Canada | Ireland | Australia
India | New Zealand | South Africa

Penguin Books is part of the Penguin Random House group of companies
whose addresses can be found at global.penguinrandomhouse.com.

First published as *Thursday's Children* by Michael Joseph 2014
Published in Penguin Books 2015
002

Set in Garamond MT Std
Typeset by Palimpsest Book Production Ltd, Falkirk, Stirlingshire
Printed in Great Britain by Clays Ltd, St Ives plc

A CIP catalogue record for this book is available from the British Library

B FORMAT ISBN: 978–0–241–95035–7
A FORMAT ISBN: 978–1–405–91915–9

www.greenpenguin.co.uk

MIX
Paper from
responsible sources
FSC® C018179
www.fsc.org

Penguin Random House is committed to a
sustainable future for our business, our readers
and our planet. This book is made from Forest
Stewardship Council® certified paper.

He that has eyes to see and ears to hear may convince himself that no mortal can keep a secret. If his lips are silent, he chatters with his fingertips; betrayal oozes out of him at every pore.

Sigmund Freud

I

It started with a reunion and it ended with a reunion and Frieda Klein hated reunions. She was sitting in front of her fire, listening to its slow crackle. Beside her was Sasha, who was staring into the glow. Beside Sasha was a buggy. In the buggy was Sasha's ten-month-old son, Ethan, a blur of dark hair and soft snoring. A cat lay at Frieda's feet, faintly purring. They could hear the wind blowing outside. It had been a day of fog and swirling leaves and gusts of wind. Now it was dark and they were inside, hiding from the approaching winter.

'I've got to admit,' said Sasha, 'that I'm intrigued by the idea of meeting an old school friend of yours.'

'She wasn't a friend. She was in my class.'

'What does she want?'

'I don't know. She rang me up and said she needed to see me. She said it was important and that she'd be here at seven.'

'What time is it now?'

Frieda looked at her watch.

'Almost seven.'

'I don't know things like that any more. Since Ethan was born, I've forgotten what a night's sleep is like and my brain has turned into sludge. I don't even know what day it is. Is it Wednesday?'

'Thursday.'

'That's good. Almost the weekend.'

Frieda gazed back into the fire. 'Thursday's perhaps the worst day of the week. It's nothing in itself. It just reminds you that the week's been going on too long.'

Sasha pulled a face. 'That may be reading too much into it.' She leaned over the buggy and stroked her son's hair. 'I love him so much but sometimes when he's asleep I feel relieved and grateful. Is that a terrible thing to say?'

Frieda turned to her friend. 'Is Frank helping out?'

'He does his best. But he's so busy with his work. As he says, helping the guilty walk free.'

'That's his job,' said Frieda. 'He's a defence barrister and –'

She was interrupted by a ring at the door. Frieda gave Sasha a rueful look.

'You are going to answer it, aren't you?' Sasha said.

'I was tempted to hide.'

Opening the door, she heard a voice that seemed to come out of the darkness and was immediately enfolded in a hug.

'Frieda Klein,' said the woman. 'I'd know you anywhere. You look just like your mother.'

'I didn't know you'd ever met my mother.' She gestured towards the fireplace. 'This is my friend Sasha. This is Madeleine Bucknall.'

2

'Maddie,' said the woman. 'Maddie Capel. I got married.'

Maddie Capel put down her large embossed bag and unwound a chequered scarf from her neck. She took off a heavy brown coat that she handed to Frieda. Underneath she was wearing a maroon crossover dress with wedge-heeled leather boots. There was a thick gold chain round her neck and small gold earrings in her lobes. She smelt of expensive perfume. She stepped towards the fire and looked into the buggy.

'What a darling little thing,' she said. 'Frieda, is it yours?'

Frieda pointed at Sasha.

'Just the sight of it makes me want to have another,' said Maddie. 'I love them at that age, when they're like a warm bundle. Is it a boy or a girl?'

'A boy.'

'So cute. Is he walking yet?'

'He's only ten months old.'

'You just need to be patient.'

Frieda pulled a chair up, close to the fire, and Maddie sat down. She had long brown hair, artfully styled into shagginess and streaked with blonde. Her face was carefully made up, but this only emphasized the tightness of the skin over the cheekbones, the little lines around the eyes and at the corners of the mouth. Frieda remembered her from school, cheerful, laughing, loud, but there was always an anxiety: being in the

3

group or not in the group, having a boyfriend or not having a boyfriend.

'Should I give you some privacy?' said Sasha.

'No, no, it's lovely to meet a friend of Frieda's. Do you live here as well?'

Sasha gave a faint smile. 'No, I live with my partner. Somewhere else.'

'Yes, of course. Thank you, thank you,' she said, as Frieda handed her a mug of tea. She took a sip and looked around her. 'Such a sweet little place you have here. Cosy.' Another sip. 'I read about you in the newspaper, Frieda. About how you helped on that terrible, terrible case with all those girls. And you rescued one of them.'

'Only one,' said Frieda. 'And it wasn't just me.'

'How can people do things like that?'

There was a pause.

'What was it you wanted to talk to me about?'

A gulp of tea.

'I can't believe we've lost touch,' Maddie said. 'You know that I still live in Braxton. Do you ever come back?'

'No.'

'Some of the old lot are still there.' She gave a mischievous smile. 'I remember you and Jeremy. I used to be rather jealous of you. He was quite a catch. He left, of course. Do you keep in touch with him?'

'No.'

'I married Stephen. Stephen Capel. Did you know

4

him? We had some good years but it went wrong. He's remarried, but he still lives nearby.'

'When you phoned, you said there was something you needed to talk to me about.'

Another gulp of tea. Maddie looked around. 'Is there somewhere I can put this?'

Frieda took the mug from her.

'I've read about you in the paper.'

'You said.'

'More than once,' Maddie said. 'You've attracted quite a lot of attention.'

'Not by choice.'

'Yes, it must be difficult sometimes. But they said that apart from solving crimes . . .'

'That's not really . . .' Frieda began, and Sasha smiled again.

'No, but the articles mentioned that you're a psychologist.'

'I'm a psychotherapist.'

'I'm not very good on all the jargon,' said Maddie. 'I'm sure there's a difference. I don't know all the details, but from what I understand, people talk to you and you help them. Is that right?'

Frieda leaned forward. 'What is it you want?'

'It's not me.' Maddie gave a little laugh. 'If that's what you're thinking. Not that I couldn't do with some help. When Stephen left, I was crying for days and days. Weeks, really. I didn't know who to turn to.'

There was another pause.

'I know things like that are terrible,' said Frieda, 'but, please, why have you come to see me?'

'It'll sound silly. It's probably a waste of your time, my coming up all the way from the country.'

'Should I leave?' asked Sasha, again.

'No,' said Maddie. 'We're just old friends talking.'

'Tell me what you want from me.'

Maddie hesitated. Frieda had experienced this moment dozens of times with her patients. One of the most difficult, precarious moments in therapy was that first naming of the patient's fear. It was like jumping off a cliff edge into darkness.

'It's my daughter, Becky,' said Maddie. 'Rebecca. But everyone calls her Becky. She's fifteen, almost sixteen.'

'Has something happened?'

'No, no, nothing like that. It's hard to put into words. Becky was such a sweet little girl. When I looked at this little boy in the buggy, it reminded me of those days, when it was all so simple. I could just look after her. You know, when Becky was that age I thought I was going to have lots of children and I was going to be the best mother in the world and protect them from everything. I was so young when I had her, almost a child myself. And then . . .' she breathed deeply, as if she were trying to control herself '. . . I couldn't have another child. And then Stephen left. It was probably my fault. I tried to hide the way I felt from Becky but I didn't do a very good job. She was

6

only six. Little thing. And I was still in my twenties and all over the place.' Her voice wavered and she stopped for a moment. 'It must have hit her hard but I thought we'd come through it. I suppose I'd always dreaded the teenage years.' She glanced at Frieda. 'Maybe I was thinking of our own teenage years. We got up to one or two things that we probably regret now, didn't we?'

A voice inside Frieda was saying, What do you mean, 'we'? We weren't friends. We didn't get up to anything together. But she stayed silent and waited.

'In the last year or so she's changed. I know what you're going to say. She's just an adolescent. What am I worrying about? Well, I am worrying. To begin with, she was just withdrawn and moody and she wouldn't talk about anything. I wondered whether there were drugs or boys involved. Or drugs *and* boys. I tried to ask her about it. I tried to be sympathetic. Nothing worked.

'About a month ago, it got worse. She seemed different. She looked different. She stopped eating. She was on this stupid diet before, and was already rail-thin. Now I don't know how she's managing to stay alive. I've cooked everything I can think of, but she just moves it about on her plate. Even when she does eat, I think she makes herself sick. She misses school. She doesn't do homework.'

'Does she see her father?'

'Stephen's hopeless. He says it's just a phase. She'll get over it.'

'What do you want from me?' said Frieda.

'Can't you just talk to her? Isn't that what you do? Just have a word with her?'

'I'm not sure if you're clear about what I do. I see patients over extended periods of time in order to explore problems they have in their life. I wonder if your daughter ought to see a school counsellor or a teacher.'

'Becky won't accept it. I've tried everything. I'm completely desperate. I don't know who to turn to. Please. As a favour to an old school friend.'

Frieda looked at Maddie's pleading expression. She didn't like this woman from her past claiming to have been her friend and wanting something she couldn't really give. She felt bad about Sasha being there to witness it. 'I'm not sure I'm the right person for this,' she said, 'but if you bring your daughter here, I'll talk to her. I'll see if I can give you, or her, some advice. But I can't promise anything.'

'That's wonderful. I can be there too, if you want.'

'I'll need to talk to her alone. At least at first. She needs to know it's private and that she can say anything. That is, if she wants to say anything. She may not be ready to talk. Or, at least, ready to talk to me.'

'Oh, I'm sure she'll talk to you.'

Maddie stood up and fetched her coat as if she needed to get away before there was any possibility of Frieda withdrawing her offer. She pulled it on and wound the scarf back round her. Frieda felt she was watching someone put a shell on. In the doorway, after saying goodbye, Maddie suddenly turned round.

'You know, there's something in my daughter that frightens me,' she said. 'Isn't that terrible?'

'I'm only here to get my mother off my back.'

'Why don't you at least come in out of the wet?'

It was raining steadily, the sky a heavy unbroken grey and the leaves on the cobblestones sodden in the downpour.

Becky stepped inside, pulling the door shut. Her long dark hair was wet and sticking to her skull; her eyes, almost black, were large in her pinched face.

'She wouldn't even let me come here alone. I'm nearly sixteen, but she insisted on getting the train with me and coming all the way to Goodge Street. She'll be there now. Buying more *shoes* or something. She's got a thing about shoes.'

'Sit by the fire. Can I take your jacket?'

'I'm all right like this.' The girl pulled her thick woollen jacket more closely around her. Even though she was huddled inside it, Frieda could see how thin she was. Her wrists were tiny, her legs were as narrow at the thigh as at the knees, her cheekbones sharp. She looked malnourished, her skin stretched tight over her features.

'Can I get you some some tea?'

'No. Or do you have any herbal tea?'

'Mint?'

'Mint's OK.'

'Take a seat. Warm yourself. Biscuit?'

'Just tea.'

Frieda left her leaning towards the flames, her delicate fingers held out to their warmth, and went into the kitchen. She made two mugs of tea – mint for Becky, Assam for her. Becky wrapped her hands around the mug for warmth and let the steam curl into her bitter little face.

'It's always hard to begin,' said Frieda.

Becky drew her brows together in a frown and muttered something under her breath.

'There's no value in coming if you don't choose to be here. I'm not going to force things out of you that you don't want to tell, make you say things you'd prefer to keep secret. You're here because your mother is worried about you and she asked me to talk to you. But I don't want to talk to you or tell you what to do. I want to listen to you, if there are things you need to say to someone.'

Becky gave a violent shrug. 'I'm OK.'

'But you're here.'

'Only because she made me come.'

'How did she make you?'

'She said I only thought about myself. I was selfish. But that she was suffering too, and if I cared at all about anyone else, I could do this one small thing for her.'

'You know I'm a therapist.'

'So now she thinks I'm mad, as well as selfish.'

'She thinks you may be in some kind of trouble.'

'I know. Drugs. Or boys. That's all she can think of. Is that what she told you?'

'Are you in some kind of trouble?'

'I'm fifteen, aren't I? Isn't that what being fifteen means? Everything feeling rubbish and shitty?'

'Shitty. Is that how everything feels to you?'

'Is that what you do?' Becky lifted her fierce eyes and glared at Frieda. 'You take a stupid random word and twist it around and say, "Oh, how interesting, she thinks everything's shitty." Shitty, crap, disgusting. I can do that too.' She looked around her, her gaze resting on the chess table that Frieda had inherited from her father. 'You play chess. You move pieces around on a board. Is that how you think of life? Like a great game you can win at?'

'No. That's not how I think of life.'

'You're famous, aren't you? I Googled you, you know.'

'And?'

'It gave me the creeps. I'm not like those missing girls.'

'But you're not in a safe place right now, are you?'

'What do you mean?'

'You're angry and anxious and unsettled. I know you've been missing school and falling behind with work.'

'Oh, that's what it's about. I won't get my precious A stars.'

'And I can see you're not eating,' Frieda continued.

Becky glowered at her. 'Everyone I know is too fat or too thin,' she said.

'You won't confide in your mother.'

'She's the last person I'd talk to. I'd rather go to my friends' mothers than her.'

'Your school must have a counsellor.'

'I'm just working stuff out.'

'What stuff?'

'Just stuff. Don't look at me as if you can see through me. It makes me feel sick.'

'Why?'

'It makes my skin crawl.'

Frieda scrutinized Becky. Then she said, 'I know this will make you feel even angrier, but I want you to think a bit about your language.'

'What do you mean, my language?

'Rubbish, shitty, crap, sick, skin crawling.'

'So? They're just words. Everyone uses words like that.'

'It's a language of disgust.'

'So? Maybe I am disgusted.'

'Why?'

'Aren't you going to ask me about my dad?'

'Your father? Why?'

'Mum said you'd want to know about him. She says that's what it's all about. She thinks I blame her for their divorce and let him off too lightly. She says that I can be furious with her because I know she won't leave me like he did – because she's *stuck* with me, for better or for worse, and that's what motherhood is all about. Not being able to escape your nasty daughter. I didn't ask to be born. She says I can't face up to the fact that my dad went off with this other woman, but I know it anyway, and that –'

'Hang on, Becky.' Frieda held up her hand. 'I don't want to hear what your mother thinks.'

'Why not? You're only seeing me because you were best friends at school or something.'

Frieda opened her mouth to protest, then stopped herself. 'That's not the point at all,' she said. 'This is about you, Becky Capel, not about your mother and certainly not about the fact that she and I knew each other many years ago. You can tell me things and I won't pass them on to her or anyone. You can feel safe here and you can say things that you feel unable to say to other people, because I'm a stranger.'

Becky turned her face away. There was a long silence.

'I make myself sick,' she muttered.

'Do you mean that you literally make yourself sick?'

'Both.' She gave a choked laugh. 'What do you call it? Metaphorically, that's the word. My teacher would be proud of me. I literally and metaphorically make myself sick.'

'Have you ever told anyone that before?'

'No. It's disgusting.'

'Do you know why you do it?'

'Food's disgusting too. People taking gobbets of dead animal and bits of fish and mouldy cheese and dirty roots from the ground and putting them into their mouths and chewing them. And then swallowing so it all goes deep into their own bodies to rot away inside.'

Becky looked at Frieda as if to see the effect she was having. 'Apples are all right,' she continued. 'And oranges.'

'So you say you're starving yourself because food disgusts you?'

'I don't like plums. I hate bananas. And figs.'

'Becky . . .'

'What? I hate this stupid conversation. Who cares what I eat? They're starving all over the world and here one poor little rich girl is being sick because . . .'

'Because?'

'Because. Because nothing. It's just a phase.'

'And truanting from school.'

'It's boring.'

'School's boring?'

'Yeah.'

'So if school's boring, what do you find interesting?'

'I used to like swimming, especially in the sea when the waves are big. Swimming in the rain.'

Despite herself, Frieda felt the tug of an old

memory, the grey North Sea and breakers surging towards her, shingle shifting under her bare feet. 'But not any longer?'

'I haven't been for a bit. And now it's nearly winter. I hate being cold. I get cold to my bones.'

Frieda was beginning to reply, when there was a rap at her front door. Maddie was on the doorstep, standing under an open umbrella, her cheeks pink and damp, a shopping bag in one hand.

'Am I too early?'

'Early for what?'

'I thought the session would be over by now.'

'It's not a session, it's a conversation.'

Maddie closed her umbrella and leaned forward conspiratorially. 'What do you think?' she half whispered.

'I'm sorry?'

'What do you make of Becky?'

'I think she's a very intelligent young woman who's sitting a few feet away from us, probably able to hear everything we say.'

'But has she said anything?'

'I'll call or email you this evening. We can talk about it then.'

'She's going to be all right, isn't she? You are going to help?'

A few hours later, Frieda sat in her study at the top of the house, listening to the rain on the roof and the wind against the windows. She sat for several minutes in deep thought and then she picked up the phone. When Maddie answered, Frieda could hear the eagerness in her voice.

'I was hoping it would be you. Becky wouldn't tell me anything about her visit to you. I hope she wasn't surly.'

'No. She wasn't surly.'

'Did you discover anything?'

'I'm not sure what you mean by that. But I think your daughter needs help.'

'That's why I made her see you.'

'I saw her today in my house for a chat – because you asked me to see her. I think she needs professional help.'

'You make it sound so serious!' Maddie gave an anxious, grating laugh. 'I just need a bit of advice, someone to point me in the right direction. You can do that, can't you? Get to the bottom of her moods and put her back on track.'

'It's important to keep clear boundaries. She needs to see a therapist, not someone who – in her eyes – is connected to her mother.'

'You're a therapist, aren't you? As for being connected . . .' Her tone changed, grew chillier. 'We never really hung about with the same crowd, did we? So we needn't worry about that.'

'I'll see Becky for a proper consultation,' said Frieda. 'I'll make an assessment, and I'll tell you what

I think she needs, and I can recommend someone for her to see, although she would need to be involved in that decision.'

Maddie's tone became warm again. 'That's lovely. But what do you mean by a proper consultation? It sounds a bit intimidating.'

'It will be in my room in Bloomsbury. I'll give you the address. It will last exactly fifty minutes. I'll charge you seventy-five pounds.'

'You'll charge me?'

'Yes.'

'That seems a bit cold-blooded, I must say.'

'I saw Becky today because I know you,' said Frieda. 'Next time I'll see her as a patient. That means you must pay me, as if I were an electrician or a plumber.'

'You're being very stern. Is that how much you charge everyone?'

'It's an average fee. If you're not in the position to pay that much, I'll make a concession.'

'I've got plenty of money, thank you, Frieda. That's one thing Stephen did leave me with. It just seems rather odd, paying for a little favour.'

'It's not a favour any more. This is what Becky needs and this is what I do.'

3

Frieda took the Tube up to Finsbury Park. She needed to clear her head. She walked along the edge of the park, then turned off on the old cutting that was like a secret green tunnel through Hornsey to the foot of Highgate Hill. Once it had been a railway line but now it had been abandoned to the trees and the dog walkers and the foxes. The yellow autumn leaves were everywhere, soggy under her shoes, blown around her face. There was a dank smell of decay, of mushrooms somewhere, though Frieda couldn't see any. It felt like a time for change, for endings and beginnings. She was composing a sort of speech in her head when she was interrupted by the ringing of her phone. She looked at the screen. It was her old pupil, Jack Dargan. She answered.

'Oh, sorry,' said Jack. 'I'm always a bit shocked when you answer your phone.'

'I've discovered that not answering the phone is even more complicated than answering it.'

'I'll need to get my head around that one.'

'Is this about something?'

'Can we meet?'

'Has something happened?'

'There's something I need to tell you.'

Frieda felt a twinge of alarm. Jack usually rang her when he was in distress and he had periodic episodes of doubt about the whole idea of being an analyst.

'Is something wrong?' she asked.

'No, no. And don't start trying to guess.'

Frieda suggested he come round to her house later in the day but he insisted that he wanted to meet on neutral ground and named a pub, the Lord Nelson, that was just around the corner from her house. They would meet there in two hours.

Half an hour later she was sitting in a now-familiar upper back room of a Highgate terraced house, looking into the wrinkled, kind, shrewd face of her own therapist, Thelma Scott. Frieda took a deep breath and began the speech she had rehearsed on the walk over.

'I've always found two difficulties with therapy, and they're entirely different. One of them is starting, because you don't want it or don't think you need it, and the second is ending, because you're addicted to it or you just don't know how to bring it to a finish. It's difficult to say, "Enough, that's it."'

'And that's what you want to say today, is it?' asked Thelma, smiling but still grave. 'Enough?'

'Yes.'

'What makes you feel that?'

'We've been on a journey,' said Frieda. 'And I think

we've come to the end. Or *an* end. I'm grateful. I really am.'

'As you well know, Frieda, usually when patients end therapy, they do it gradually. It can take weeks or months.'

'I don't like goodbyes. Usually, I like to leave without saying goodbye at all.'

Thelma's face wrinkled again. 'If I was your therapist, I'd want to discuss that. Oh, hang on . . .'

Frieda couldn't stop herself smiling. 'You think I'm wrong?' she asked.

Thelma shook her head slowly.

'When you first came to see me – when was it? Eighteen months ago? – I wasn't sure what therapy could do for you. I'd never seen anything quite like it. When you called me up wanting to see me, I knew you'd been attacked and almost killed. You'd obviously been through a severe trauma and needed some kind of help. But then, just before we began, you were also involved in a terrible incident where a man was killed, a close friend badly hurt. You told me how you had walked all the way home, twenty miles, covered with blood.'

'It wasn't my own blood.'

'I remember you making that point to me, and I honestly wondered whether what you really needed was time in hospital.'

'I was on fire,' said Frieda, 'and I didn't know how to put myself out.'

There was a long pause.

'I think the image you used is about right. Not the one about being on fire, though that may have been true last year. I mean the one about being on a journey. You've got to a station and it might be a good time to get off.' She paused. 'For a while, at least.'

'Because it's only a station on the way?'

'We've talked a lot in this room and I think we've developed.' She stopped for a moment. 'I don't think you've shed all the pain of the episode that made you seek me out. I think you've absorbed it, made it a part of you, learned from it. But maybe what you can't put your finger on is that it involves all the things you never talked about with me: your past, your parents, where you came from.'

'When I see patients, they generally talk about their childhood and their parents, and also about their lovers. I know I haven't done that.'

'No.' Thelma regarded her. 'But you've talked a great deal about Dean Reeve.'

'It's true. For everyone else, Dean is dead. The police think he's dead. His ex-partner thinks he's dead. His body – what people took to be his body, rather than that of his poor brother Alan – has been cremated and the ashes scattered. He used to be the media's favourite villain but even that has faded. He's gradually becoming forgotten, but not by me. For me he's alive. He's like a ghost, but he isn't dead. He watches me, watches over me in a way. I feel like he's out there and he's waiting for something.' Frieda saw Thelma's expression and shook her head. 'He's not a figment of my imagination, not some kind of Freudian other. Dean Reeve is a murderer and he's out there in the world.'

'I don't know about him being in the world, but he's inside your head. He haunts you.'

'He does haunt me. But he's alive.'

'Alive for you.'

'No. He's alive. Therapy can help me with my feelings, my fears about Dean, but it can't help with that.'

'So, you're saying that you haven't talked about your parents and your lovers because Dean Reeve gets in the way?'

'I've actually been thinking about the past. The distant past, I mean. A couple of days ago a woman came to see me, someone who'd been in my class at school. She wasn't a friend, I hadn't seen her since we were sixteen years old, but she wanted me to talk to her daughter. I saw her yesterday, and I have this feeling about it. Something I can't put my finger on.'

'Try to put your finger on it.'

'It felt like my past has come for me.'

'Perhaps that's a good thing.'

But Thelma thought she saw a sadness on Frieda's face she hadn't seen before.

'I don't see how it can be.'

When Frieda arrived at the Lord Nelson, Jack was already there. He didn't notice her at first and she was able to take a proper look at him. He's grown up, she thought. She'd first met him as a young medical student, nervous, argumentative, self-conscious and insecure. Now he looked his own man, even if his own man was dressed like a gypsy, with a patterned jacket over a purple shirt, black and white striped trousers and a multicoloured striped scarf. His tawny hair – usually an unruly mess – seemed to be arranged in a kind of quiff. She blinked and advanced, and as she did so, he turned and noticed her, flushed and suddenly looked much more like the old Jack. He offered to buy her a drink but Frieda only wanted tap water. Jack grumbled and put a slice of lemon into it. 'That makes it a bit less boring,' he said.

He bought himself a half of bitter and led the way to a table in the corner.

'How's work going?' asked Frieda.

Jack shook his head energetically, like someone in a play shaking their head so that the people in the back row could see. 'I can't talk about anything like that,' he said. 'I had to see you face to face because there's something I've got to tell you.'

'So tell me.'

Jack looked Frieda straight in the eyes. 'I'm seeing someone.'

'Okay,' said Frieda, slowly. 'Clearly I should say I'm happy for you but why all the fuss?'

'Because the fact is, I thought I should tell you because it happens to be someone you know.'

'Someone I know?'

'Yes.'

Frieda felt slightly dazed, as if her brain wasn't working properly. She ran through a sort of mental address book. Who could it possibly be? And in any case, whoever it was, why the big drama about summoning her and telling her like this? 'All right, then,' she said eventually. 'Are you going to tell me or am I supposed to guess?'

'I think you need some sort of explanation, Frieda, just because –'

'For God's sake, Jack, who is it?'

'Frieda.'

She turned and saw her niece, Chloë, bright and cheerful. 'Chloë, what are you . . .?' But then she realized the truth and stopped.

'Hello, lovely,' Chloë said to Jack, and he got up and they kissed and Chloë gave a murmuring sound. 'So how is it going?'

'I was about to tell her.'

'Could you get me a drink?' Chloë said. 'A white wine.' She turned to Frieda. 'It's all right. I've got my ID.'

The two of them watched Jack start to push his way ineffectually through the crowd to get to the bar. Then they looked at each other.

'Chloë,' said Frieda.

'I know you're going to find this weird.'

Frieda started to speak but Chloë interrupted her.

'First, you're my aunt and you've known me since I was born, and then you were virtually my surrogate mother, since my own mum is a complete waste of space —'

'Chloë —'

'And you spent all that time helping me. You basically got me through my science GCSEs single-handed. I just wish you'd done the same for my A levels, but that's another story. And I've lived in your house and we've gone through all sorts of emotions together. And I know that Jack is like a son to you —'

'A student, in fact.'

'But people aren't like that with you, Frieda. Everyone becomes a part of your family.'

'I don't think that's right at all.'

'What I'm saying is that this probably feels almost like incest to you and it must be even stranger because, really, you were the person who brought us together . . .'

'Brought you together?'

'By which I mean it was through you that the two of us got to know each other, and I'll never stop being grateful to you for that because he's so lovely. As you know.'

Frieda couldn't immediately think of anything to say and when she was finally about to speak Jack arrived with Chloë's white wine and sat down.

'Is everything all right?' he said nervously.

'It's fine. We've sorted it out.' Chloë raised her glass.

'To all of us.' She took a gulp of her wine. Jack sipped his beer while giving Frieda a wary glance. Frieda left her glass sitting on the table. Chloë frowned. 'Is something wrong?'

'No,' said Frieda. 'I'm just surprised, that's all. I'm trying to take it in.'

'I know it's difficult for you,' said Chloë. 'You probably think of me as if I'm, like, twelve years old or something. But I'm eighteen. This is legal. We're not breaking the law.'

'There is a bit of an age difference.'

'All right, so we're six years apart. Is that such a big deal?'

'Well, nine years, if we're being pedantic.'

'Which we clearly are,' said Chloë. 'I'm sorry. I thought you'd be happy for us.'

Frieda forced herself. 'I am glad for you. It's just that you're two people I care a lot about and I don't want you to rush into something where someone will get hurt. I know even as I'm saying this that I'm sounding middle-aged and disapproving.' Frieda took a deep breath. 'I don't mean to. And it was good of you to tell me about it and not feel you have to keep it secret.'

'Good.' Chloë looked across at Jack with a triumphant expression. 'I told you it would be no problem.' She looked back at Frieda. 'Don't you want to hear about how it all started?'

'In the course of time,' said Frieda, who didn't.

'My own suspicion,' Chloë went on cheerily, 'is that Jack fancied me from when he first met me. It was one of those schoolgirl fantasies.'

'Which is completely not true,' said Jack.

'You came to a party at my house when I was sixteen.'

Frieda remembered that party – it was when she had first met young Ted Lennox, whose mother had just been killed and with whom Chloë had been besotted.

'That was different,' said Jack. 'We were just friends.'

'That's your version.'

'In actual fact, this has only just happened,' Jack hissed urgently to Frieda. 'I wanted to tell you right away. I was worried what you might think.'

'Don't be silly, Jack,' said Chloë. 'What are you talking about?'

Frieda suddenly had the horrified sense that she was going to be present for their first argument. 'Does Olivia know?' she asked.

'Mum wouldn't understand.'

'You ought to tell her.'

'I know how she'd behave: she'd get drunk and tell me I ought to be concentrating on my retakes.'

'Which, incidentally . . .'

'And then she'd say I don't know what I'm doing. And then she'd want to know all the details and then she'd tell me about her early sex life. Yuck.'

'You ought to tell her anyway,' Frieda said. 'I don't

like knowing things about you that your mother doesn't know.'

'Some time,' said Chloë.

Frieda got up. 'I've really got to go.'

Chloë stood as well. 'You're not angry, are you? Just say you're not angry.'

'I'm not angry and I have to go.'

'I'm going to come and see you,' said Chloë. 'I want to talk to you about my exams. Don't tell Mum, but I'm not sure that side of my life is going very well. And I've got so much else I want to talk to you about.'

'Yes, yes,' said Frieda, backing away, and she left the pub feeling she was escaping.

4

'Please sit down.' Frieda gestured to a chair and waited until Becky was sitting before taking up her own position in her red armchair. The girl stared around her. The room was orderly and plain. On the wall facing her was a painting of a dusty-looking landscape; between the two chairs was a low table, with a box of tissues on it; the lamp in the corner cast a soft light over the room, whose walls were grey-green. Becky noticed that there was a plant on the windowsill. Through the window, she saw a vast cratered building site, with cranes emerging from behind the high wooden barriers.

'This is a bit scary,' she said, turning back to Frieda, who sat upright in her chair, waiting.

'Beginning is always scary.'

'I mean, when I saw you before it was just at your house and you gave me tea and there was a fire burning and it felt quite homely.' She gestured at the room. She was wearing an oversized cable-knit jumper over baggy jeans – hiding her tiny body inside layers of clothing. 'This feels serious.'

'It's just a space where you can say anything.'

'I don't know. I never meant to go this far. I only

agreed to come here to get Mum off my case. And suddenly I'm sitting here and it seems horribly quiet, as if you're waiting to hear what I'm going to say.' She put a hand over her mouth, then took it away again. 'But I don't have anything to say. My mind's gone all blank and scratchy. It makes me want to run away.'

'That would be a pity, after just one minute.' Frieda smiled.

'Do some people sit here for the whole time and not say anything?'

'Sometimes.'

'So if I wanted, I could do that?'

'You'd probably find it uncomfortable. Staying silent can be harder than talking. But, in fact, what I want to do today is different, a kind of assessment. I'll ask you some questions and you answer them and then we'll see where we go from there.'

'And if I don't want to?'

'Then don't. You're in control here. It might not feel like it. You can talk or be silent, you can leave whenever you want. You can tell me things, and I'm not going to judge you or be shocked. I'm here to help you to say things that you haven't been able to talk about. Sometimes when you say things, acknowledge them, they become less frightening.'

'Why? They're just stupid words. They can't change anything.'

'It can be like shining a light into a dark corner. Or perhaps it's more like staring long enough at the darkness so that you become accustomed to it and can make out the shapes it hides. Fears that we don't have a name for have power over us. Think of this time here as an opportunity to gain some kind of control.'

'What's this about fears? Just because I've gone off food a bit.'

'This won't go away just by sitting it out. It's not getting better, is it? It's probably getting worse.'

'I don't even know what you're talking about. What do you mean, "it"?'

'Whatever it is that's stopping you eating, stopping you going to school, making you feel disgusted and bored, making you angry and withdrawn with your mother. And it's brought you here. You wouldn't have agreed to see me, however much pressure your mother put on you, if you hadn't in some way felt it might help you.'

'That's all you know.'

'Let's start by me asking you some very simple questions. You're fifteen, is that right?'

'I'll be sixteen in January.'

'And you live with your mother?'

'That's right. Just the two of us.'

'How old were you when your father left?'

'Six. He kept coming back for a bit and then he left for good.'

'Can you remember how you felt about that at the time?'

'How do you think?'

'I don't know. That's why I'm asking.'

'Upset.'

'Do you remember them telling you?'

'My dad told me. Mainly I remember arguments and shouting.'

'What do you remember about your father telling you?'

'He pulled me on to his lap and he started crying. That's what I remember, feeling his tears on the top of my head. I had to hug him to make him feel better.'

'Did you feel angry with him?'

'Not really. I just wanted him to come home. But then when he came home it was horrible, so I wanted him to go away again. Or her.'

'Your mother?'

'Yeah.'

'You felt angry with her?'

'I know it's unfair. She's the one who kept by me. But she irritates me. And she doesn't get me. She never has.'

'Does your father get you?'

'I used to think he did. Now he seems fed up when I'm not cheerful with him. He wants me to be his sweet little girl.'

'So you can't talk to them about what's going on in your life?'

'I wouldn't want to.'

'Tell me about your friends. Do you have friends you're close to?'

'I don't know about close.'

'Do you have a friendship group?'

'I suppose so.'

'At your school?'

'Mostly.'

'And do you have best friends?'

'That makes me sound like a baby. There's Charlotte, I suppose, or there used to be, and a girl called Kerry. I've known her since primary school. I used to talk to them about everything.'

'You used to – but not now?'

She pushed her hands into the opposite sleeves of her jersey and leaned forward so her soft dark hair fell over her face. 'I can't be bothered. Max is OK. I like him, but not in that way.'

'So you're less close to your friends than you used to be?'

'Maybe.'

'Have you been bullied at school?'

'No.'

'Never?'

'It depends what you mean by bullied. Girls can be bitchy and there've been times when I've been left out and it's horrible – but it happens to everyone, and I've done that to other girls as well, if I'm honest. It's like how everyone is. You're in and then you're out and that's how it works.'

'Are you in or out now?'

'It's not like that. I don't belong with them any

more. They've given up on me, or maybe I've given up on them.'

'This is just in the past few weeks.'

'Mainly.'

'The past few weeks when you've been truanting and starving yourself?'

'I'm just not hungry. I was thin anyway.'

'And food disgusts you.'

'Yeah.'

'Putting things into your body.'

Becky shrugged.

'So maybe recently you did something or had something done to you that has disturbed and frightened you.'

She shrugged again and looked out at the cranes swinging their gleaming arms across the skyline.

'Becky?'

'I have bad dreams.'

'Tell me.'

'I don't know. I can't remember.' She pulled one hand out of the sleeve and chewed her knuckles. 'I don't like going to sleep.'

'Because of the dreams?'

'I don't know.'

'Some people don't like to sleep because it's a bit like death.'

'I don't care about that.'

'Do you sleep in the dark?'

'I keep my light on. I *hate* the dark.'

'Always?'

'No.'

'You've recently started hating the dark.'

Becky shuddered.

'Something happened to you in the dark.'

'I want to go home now.'

'Becky. You don't need to look at me. You can look outside, or you can close your eyes if you want. And you can tell me what happened to you in the dark.'

Becky closed her eyes. The lids were purplish, almost transparent.

'You're safe here. Tell me. Were you alone?'

'Yes.' A tiny whisper.

'Go on.'

'I was in my bedroom asleep, or nearly asleep. I don't know.'

'Yes.' She mustn't put words in the girl's mouth, thoughts in her mind; she just had to wait.

'And then I was awake, or half awake, and I knew that someone was in my room.' Her eyelids fluttered open, then closed again. 'It was very, very quiet.'

'Tell me.'

'Can't you guess?'

'I don't want to guess. I want you to say it to me.'

Silence filled all the spaces of the room.

'I was raped. Someone raped me.'

Later, she cried, and Frieda – who never made physical contact with her patients – held her in her arms and stroked her hair away from her pale, streaming face. Then she brought her a tumbler of water and made her drink it while she called her next patient to say that she was running late and that he should arrive half an hour after his appointed time.

'We're going to talk about this properly soon,' she said, when she returned. 'But, first, there are practical questions. Did he use a condom and, if not, have you done a pregnancy test?'

Becky looked appalled. 'No, he didn't, and no. I didn't think, I mean.' She stopped.

'Have you had a period since?'

'I stopped having periods before all of this.'

'You need a pregnancy test and you need to get checked by a doctor.'

'I can't. I don't want to.'

'Just to make sure.'

'Oh, God. I might have Aids. You think I might be infected.'

'Just to make sure.'

'I don't want to!'

'You can go to either your GP or a clinic. I can give you numbers.'

'Can you come with me? I can't do it by myself.'

'You should tell your mother, Becky. She should go with you.'

'You can't make me.'

'I'm not going to make you, but you should tell her.'

'She'll hate me.'

'Something very terrible was done to you, Becky. Why do you think you'll be hated for that?'

'I can't tell her. Do you really think I have to tell her? I don't know how.'

'It's very hard. But you've said it to me, and now it will be a bit easier to say it to your mother.'

'When?'

'As soon as you can.'

'I don't know.'

'And she can go to the doctor with you. That would be best.'

'I don't know how to.'

'And, Becky?'

'Yes?'

'Did you never think of going to the police?'

'I'd rather die. If you tell them, I'll kill myself. I promise. I won't go to the police. I don't know anything. I don't know who it was, I never saw their face, and you can't make me tell them anything. You can't.'

'You're right. I can't.'

'Is it time for me to go?'

'You've been here well over an hour so your mother will be waiting. But you can stay as long as you want.'

'What shall I say to her?'

'Tell her what happened. Talk to her. Ask her to take you to the doctor. We'll meet again very soon.'

'You'll help me?'

'Yes.'

'I don't feel very well. I feel a bit sick.'

Frieda held out her hand and pulled Becky into a standing position. The girl's face was peaky and wan. She looked like a small child. She put her hands on Becky's shoulders. 'You've been brave,' she said. 'You've done well.'

5

Becky must have told Maddie that day, because the following morning Maddie arrived at Frieda's consulting room, pressing the intercom several times and asking with a breathless voice to be let up.

'What do I owe you?' she said, her cheeks flaming. 'Seventy-five pounds?'

'I'm sorry?'

'That's what you said, wasn't it? Seventy-five pounds a session.'

Frieda paused for a moment. This wasn't quite what she had expected. 'Yes,' she said.

Maddie was holding a cheque book in her hand, almost brandishing it. She looked around Frieda's consulting room but there was no table to write on except the low one between the two armchairs. She went to the window, rested it on the sill and wrote quickly. She handed the cheque to Frieda. Frieda looked at it.

'You've left off the date.'

Maddie gave a snort and snatched it back. 'Is it the sixth?' she said.

'The seventh.'

'All right.' She added the date and handed the cheque back.

'I'm slightly surprised,' said Frieda.

'Why?'

'When you rang and said you had to see me urgently, I didn't think it was because you were going to give me a cheque.'

'Really? What did you think?'

'Are you serious?'

'I am serious.' Maddie was breathing heavily, almost panting. Frieda couldn't tell whether she was going to shout or to start crying. 'When I phoned you and said I had to see you, what did you think I wanted to say?'

Frieda gestured Maddie towards the patients' chair, where her daughter had been. She sat opposite her in her own chair. 'If we're going to talk,' Frieda said, 'you need to tell me what your daughter told you.'

Maddie's mouth opened but she didn't speak at first. She looked even thinner and more drawn than before, as if she hadn't slept or eaten. 'I thought you were going to help her,' she said. 'Not join with her . . .' she seemed to be reaching for a word '. . . difficulty.'

'What did Becky tell you?'

Maddie shook her head almost fiercely. 'You said you were going to help her. If I had believed that you were actually going to make things worse for her . . .'

'Is that what you think I've done?'

'You should see her. I didn't want to leave her even for a single second but she insisted on going to school.

41

I didn't know what to do but I had to come here and tell you what you've done.'

Frieda held up her hand. 'Wait. I need to know what your daughter has told you.'

'Why? Why do you need to know that?'

'I can't speak to anyone else, even you, about what Becky said to me.'

'What are you talking about?' Maddie said angrily. 'The whole point of bringing Becky here was to find out what was wrong with her so that I can do something about it.'

'If you felt that, then I didn't explain it properly to you. What I do when I talk to a patient is for the patient, and the patient needs to know that they can say anything – or almost anything – to me in the confidence that it will stay secret. So, if we're going to talk about this, you need to tell me what you know about your daughter.'

'I'll tell you what I know about my daughter. She's an attention-seeker, she keeps secrets, she's been mixing with all sorts of people I don't know and she won't tell me about, she lies, she hides things. She seems to be angry with the world and especially angry with me.'

'But what did she tell you that made you come all the way here to talk to me about?'

Maddie gave Frieda a sullen, angry look. 'She told me what she told you. About the attack.'

'What kind of attack?' Frieda asked steadily. 'You need to say the words out loud.'

Maddie rubbed her fist around her mouth, as if she was trying to wipe something away. 'She says she was raped. There, I've said it. Does that make you feel better?'

'The question is, what does it make *you* feel?'

'I know what you're thinking.' Maddie became confrontational. 'You feel I don't care about my daughter. I'm not being sympathetic enough to her. If you don't mind my saying so, you don't have children and you can't possibly imagine what it's like.'

'I can't imagine what *what*'s like?'

'Sometimes in the last year it's been like living with my worst enemy. Someone who wants to hurt me, who knows all my weak points. But I'd do anything for her. I love her.'

'But do you believe her?'

Now Maddie thought for a long time. 'You met her yesterday,' she said finally. 'She looks like a young woman – except she's starved herself, of course – and she's got a sort of grown-up tone. What's the word for it? Streetwise?'

'She didn't seem very streetwise to me.'

'That's my point. When Becky goes and stays out all night and doesn't tell me where she is or what she's taking or who she's . . .' Maddie stopped for a moment and ran her fingers through her hair '. . . who she's with, she's playing with things she doesn't understand, things she can't control.'

'This isn't about being out all night and rebelling

43

and being confused. That is something to be talked about. I could talk about it with Becky, or you could. But this is different. She said she was raped. That is very serious. It's also a crime. You haven't answered my question: do you believe her?'

'Haven't you been listening? Becky has been living in this chaotic way, with God knows what drugs and awful people and sex and bad behaviour. She's still only fifteen. Isn't any sex wrong at that age?'

'That's not what she was talking about. Do you believe her?'

'I don't know what to believe. If you asked me is Becky capable of making up something like that or exaggerating it just as a way of frightening me or hurting me, then I would have to say that she is.'

'But she didn't tell you,' said Frieda. 'She tried to keep it from you. She showed symptoms of great distress, which alarmed you. And then, when you brought her to me, she was extremely reluctant even to mention it.'

'Perhaps because it isn't true. And even if it is true, at that age, couldn't she just be talking about something that went too far, something she did and then regretted?'

'That's not what she said. Your daughter told me and then told you that she had been raped. That was a big step for her and it took trust and it took courage. You need to think about how to respond to her. You also need to think about her going to the police.'

'No, no, absolutely not.'

'It's a serious crime.'

'That's easy for you to say. You wouldn't have to go through it all.'

'Do you mean Becky would have to go through it? Or that you would?'

Maddie looked up sharply. Frieda recognized a flash of the haughtiness she'd displayed when she'd first arrived at Frieda's house.

'I've thought about what Becky would have to go through,' she said. 'And I've thought about it as a mother, not as some kind of spectator. Imagine if she went to the police. She didn't report it when it was supposed to have happened. Nobody else saw anything. It's just the word of a fifteen-year-old girl.'

'Just the word of your daughter.'

'Yes, my daughter. And imagine what would happen if the police decided to proceed, and if Becky could be persuaded to reveal the name of the person who may have done such a thing. Becky herself would be on trial, her lifestyle, her sex life, her psychological state. Even the fact that she'd been seeing a psychiatrist, psychologist, whatever you are. That could be used against her. You've talked to Becky. Would you put her through all that? Do you think it would do her good to be in the newspapers?'

'She's underage,' said Frieda. 'Her name would be withheld in any proceedings.'

Maddie pulled a face and made Frieda think briefly of when they were fifteen years old themselves.

'I don't know much about modern technology but these things always get out. Everybody would know.'

'I think you've misunderstood me,' said Frieda. 'I don't tell people what to do. Well, not most of the time. I just wanted to lay out the options. The decision about what to do is yours and Becky's. My real concern is about Becky's state of mind. That's what you came to me about.'

'Exactly. And look what happened. You haven't exactly cured her.'

'Is that your reaction to what your daughter has told us? That I haven't cured her after two brief meetings?'

Maddie got up, walked to the window and looked out at the huge building site. 'I hate London,' she said. 'I could never live in a city. I can't even bear Ipswich or Colchester. When I'm here, I feel like I'm holding my breath until I can get out into the fresh air.'

'I've got pretty mixed feelings about it myself,' said Frieda.

Maddie turned round. 'We weren't really friends when we were at school, were we?'

'I don't know,' said Frieda. 'We were in the same class.'

'You were part of this group and I had a fantasy of being part of it. I used to see you together at parties. You probably didn't even know I was there, but I still remember them. There was Chas Latimer. There was Jeremy. Your boyfriend.'

'Briefly.'

'And Eva Hubbard. You were best friends. I was always the one wanting to join the gang.'

'I think everyone feels like that.'

'You didn't.' Maddie gave a strange smile. 'When I left school, I thought I'd be leaving all that behind, but it stays with you, even twenty-five years later. Don't you find that?'

'No, I don't.'

'Maybe I'm the one who should be coming to see you, instead of Becky.'

Frieda shook her head. 'I'm not sure I should be seeing Becky either. I told you I would assess her and decide whether she needed to see someone. She does need that, and I can find someone for her, someone good. But I'd like to see her again first.'

Maddie looked suspicious. 'What for? Are you going to persuade her to go to the police?'

'No. Not that. I had the feeling that Becky started to say something, but she didn't quite finish. Once she has said it, she should move on to someone else.'

Maddie turned away from Frieda and looked out of the window again. It was still dark when she left. 'I thought it was going to be simple,' she said, almost to herself.

6

'She doesn't believe me.'

'She doesn't know whether to believe you.'

'Do you really think that makes it any better? That she doesn't *know* whether to believe me?' Becky leaned forward in the chair, grasping its arms with both hands. Her face was screwed up in a grimace of anger and distress. She had a cold sore at the corner of her mouth and her hair was lank and unwashed. 'Because it doesn't. It fucking doesn't. She's my mother. She's supposed to be on my side. Now she looks at me as if I smell rank or something. I embarrass her. She speaks to me in this high, careful voice and can't look me in the eye. I wish I'd never met you. I wish I'd never told you anything.'

'Do you?'

'I was doing OK and you made me drag everything out in the open and now it's there and I can't hide it away again.'

'Your mother –'

'My mother thinks I made it up.' Becky gave a sharp sob. 'That it's a fantasy. What kind of person would have a fantasy like that?'

'People make things up all the time. All sorts of people for all sorts of reasons.'

'Don't you believe me either? Now that you've made me ruin my life?'

'I do believe you,' Frieda said steadily.

'Why? You don't know me. Maybe my mother's right and you're wrong. Maybe you're just too trusting and gullible.'

'I don't think many people would agree with that.'

'So why?'

Frieda paused, considering. 'You rang true,' she said.

'So you don't think I'm just trying to draw attention to myself.'

'I know you're telling me the truth. It must have felt terrible, Becky.'

Becky wrapped her thin arms around her thin body and stood in the centre of the room as if she was trying to protect herself or hide herself.

'Yes,' was all she managed. 'Yes, it did. It does.'

'Do you want to sit down?'

Becky sat, but on the edge of her chair, as if she was about to jump up again.

'She said I shouldn't talk about it to other people, that it would all die down.'

'What did you actually say?'

'Not much. I couldn't. It took all my courage to get the words out. I was sick – literally sick – before I went downstairs and told her. I just blurted it out.'

'So, no details of any kind?'

'No details.'

'You didn't tell her the circumstances?'

'I said it was at home, in my bedroom.'

'Do you remember it?'

'I don't know. I don't want to.'

'So you're trying to push it away into the darkness and bury it.'

'Yes. I have been since it happened. Until you came along.'

'You were raped.' Frieda paused, watched Becky intently. 'A terrible thing was done to you, and now you feel polluted and ashamed, as if it was your fault.'

'Maybe it was.' Becky's voice was a whisper.

'Why?'

'Like, I'd been asking for it.'

'Asking for it in what way?'

Becky was staring down at her knotted hands. Her face looked grey; old and babyish at the same time.

'I was in with a crowd of guys and I slept with one of them. Just a couple of times. But it was a bit out of control, really.'

'Was it one of them who raped you?'

'No. I mean I don't know, but I'd know if it was.' She had perspiration on her forehead. 'It was a man, not a boy. Wouldn't I know?'

'So you feel ashamed because you think it was some kind of punishment for what you'd done before?'

'I guess.'

'Listen.' Frieda's voice was strong and clear in the little room. 'This is very important. Many people who are raped feel that in some way or other it was their fault. Most of them, I would say. They feel that they led their rapists on, didn't struggle enough, didn't say no clearly enough or, like you, they have a feeling that they were getting what they deserve. It's not true.'

Becky gave a small murmur.

'Do you understand, Becky? It is not true. It was done *to* you but it doesn't define you.'

'I knew as soon as I woke up that something horrible was about to happen,' said Becky. 'I could have called out.'

'Go on.'

'I woke up and it was all quiet. Quiet inside the house and quiet outside as well. Dead quiet, but I could tell something was different. I thought maybe I'd had a bad dream, but I knew it wasn't a dream. I don't know how. I just lay there in the dark and I could hear my heart beating. My mouth tasted funny, as if I hadn't cleaned my teeth. I remember thinking that. Now I clean my teeth ten times a day.'

Frieda didn't speak.

'I thought of turning on the light, but I didn't. I just lay there. Then I heard someone move. It was like a creak and then a rustle.' She bent even lower in her chair so her dark hair hung over her face, like a curtain. 'I couldn't move. I couldn't even breathe.' She stopped, rocked forward and back, just once. 'There was a hand.'

'Where?'

'On my mouth. To stop me making a noise. It was warm and smelt of soap. I remember that. I remember thinking it was quite a nice smell. Maybe an apple smell. I can't.'

'You can't what?'

'I can't say it all.'

'You don't have to.'

'I opened my eyes but I couldn't see anything except a dark shape just above me. He pulled off the duvet. I was wearing pyjama trousers and a T-shirt and he put his other hand down my trousers and I could see his shape above me, but not his face. He was wearing something over his face.'

'It's all right, Becky.'

'Why doesn't she believe me?'

'It's complicated.'

'I didn't struggle properly. I didn't try to stop it happening. I was so scared. I thought I was going to die. I wish I had. I wish I'd died.'

Frieda handed Becky a tissue.

'I can't remember it all. I don't want to. It was just dark and nasty and silent and ugly and fumbly. I wanted to shout but his hand was still over my mouth. I could hear him panting but it sounded weird and muffled through the cloth over his face. He was just, like, this thing, and I was like a thing as well. It hurt.'

'I'm so sorry that this was done to you.'

'He kept trying to arrange me, like I was a doll.' Becky suddenly looked worn out by it all. 'It'll never go away, will it?'

'It won't stay the same. With work –'

'I don't want to work at it. I want it never to have happened.' Becky pulled a face that made her look like a toddler. 'I know, I know. It did.'

'It did, yes.'

'Mum's very angry, isn't she?'

'What do you mean?'

'With you. She's ashamed of me but she's angry with you. She says you've let fame go to your head.'

'Does she?'

'She says this is my last time here.'

'I'm going to recommend someone for you to see. I think your mother will agree.'

'Why not you?'

'Because I know your mother. I've got someone in mind. I think you'll like her, and if you don't, I'll recommend someone else.'

'But I want *you*!'

Frieda couldn't help smiling. 'I'm not the right person. But you do need to keep seeing someone, Becky. This is just the beginning of a journey for you, but you won't have to make it alone. You're strong and you're intelligent and you can come through this.' She leaned forward slightly, fixing Becky with her dark eyes. 'You will feel better one day.'

'Will I?'

'Yes.'

Just as Becky was leaving, Frieda asked her, 'Tell me, have you thought any more about going to the police?'

'No. They wouldn't believe me. Why should they if my own mother doesn't?' Her voice became flat and dreary. 'He was right.'

'Who was right?'

Becky made a visible effort. 'He said no one would think I was telling the truth.'

Frieda gazed at her. 'Is that what he told you?'

'He said it in my ear, in this muffled kind of voice, thick and lisping through the mask but I could make out the words. I think it was the only time he spoke, the whole time. I can hear him saying it, like he was saying something loving.' She shivered again. 'He said, "Don't think of telling anyone, sweetheart. Nobody will believe you." And he was right.'

7

After Becky was gone, Frieda stood for a moment, waiting. She walked to the window, looked down and saw the girl emerge on to the pavement. She put her hands into her pockets and started to walk away, looking small and lost. Was this right? What if something happened to her on the way home? Frieda caught her own faint reflection in the window pane. That was what she did. She dealt with people's problems in that room, then sent them back out into the world to fend for themselves.

Her thoughts shifted and the reflection in the glass seemed to shift as well. Just for a moment Frieda saw another face. It was her own, but from long ago, and she had the unnerving sense that the face was looking at her and calling to her across the decades. For years this room had been a sanctuary, a quiet place where damaged people could come and say anything, be heard and understood. Suddenly Frieda felt trapped there, as if she couldn't breathe. She pulled her jacket on and left the office, as if she was escaping something. She descended the stairs two at a time. She started walking east with no sense of any destination. She crossed Tavistock Square. This was where one of the bombs had gone off back in 2005. It was a London sort of terrorist atrocity. The bomber had got on the bus because there were delays on the Underground. Frieda had been half a mile away and hadn't heard a thing. Dozens of people had been killed but London just absorbed it and went on. London always went on. The driver of the bombed bus had stepped out of the wreckage, covered with blood, and walked home, all the way west across London to Acton. Frieda hadn't understood what this meant until the same thing had happened to her. When you face real horror, you need to walk home, like an animal crawling back to its lair.

She walked to the north of Coram's Fields, past King's Cross, along York Way until she reached the canal. From the bridge she looked along it to the east and mouth of the Islington tunnel. She was almost tempted by the idea of continuing east along the canal, through Hackney and the Lea Valley and out – somewhere, miles ahead – into the countryside. She could walk out of London and never come back. No. That wasn't right. She needed to go in the other direction, back into the centre. She walked down the steps on to the towpath on which she had walked many times. The landmarks were familiar to her: the strange garden in the barge; the neat little lock-keeper's cottage; the bright new plate-glass offices; Camden Lock. But Frieda remembered something else, with a shiver.

She looked at the rippling grey water. How long

ago had it been? Frieda had been a medical student when it had happened. A tourist had been walking here late at night, the way Frieda did. She had been attacked by a gang of young men. Raped. There'd been a detail she'd never been able to get out of her mind. They'd asked her if she could swim. She'd said she couldn't and – so – they had thrown her into the water and she'd swum across the canal and got away. She had lived to testify against them. Frieda had been struck by those two details: that last clinching bit of sadism, as if they hadn't done enough already. And the woman's ability to think clearly, to plan to fight for her life, even at such a time.

As she walked along the towpath, she thought about bombs on buses, a young woman thrown into the canal. Wherever Frieda walked in London she was haunted by these ghosts. She heard a sound and looked at the water that was starting to speckle with raindrops. As the canal snaked through Kentish Town and past the edge of Camden Lock market, the rain grew heavier and heavier, a grey curtain that turned the afternoon dark. Frieda was wearing a light suede jacket and within a few minutes her clothes were wet and cold against her skin. She almost welcomed it as a relief. It stopped her thinking. When the huge London Zoo aviary came into view ahead of her, she went up the steps, crossed the road and walked into Primrose Hill.

*

Reuben was making himself a sandwich. He assembled the avocado, rocket, sun-dried tomatoes, hummus, then took the focaccia bread from the oven and sliced it open. He arranged his ingredients in careful layers and ground some black pepper over the top. During the morning he'd been at the Warehouse, the clinic he had opened decades ago, and for the last hour, as he sat listening to the woman whose father had never loved her and whose husband was cheating on her, he had been imagining the lunch he was going to have. The question was, should he have a glass of red wine with it? He used to drink too heavily, during those terrible days of disenchantment and chaos. Nowadays his rule was that he never drank before six o' clock, but he frequently broke it, especially if Josef was with him. Josef was not there now, but there was an opened bottle of red wine on the side. Maybe half a glass.

Then there was a knock at his front door. He cursed under his breath and considered not answering. The knock was repeated and he sighed and went to the door.

Standing in the streaming rain, her hair plastered to her head and her clothes drenched, was his old friend, colleague and – long before that – his patient, Frieda.

'Bloody hell,' he said.

'Hello, Reuben.'

'You're fucking soaking.'

'I know.'

'Where's your umbrella?'

'I don't have one. Are you going to let me in?'

Five minutes later, Frieda was sitting in an armchair with both hands around a mug of tea and half of the bulging focaccia sandwich on a plate at her side. She was wearing a pair of Reuben's jeans and a bulky woollen sweater but she was still shivering. Reuben slouched on the sofa opposite, munching his lunch. He had decided against the wine.

'So, you walk through driving rain to get here. You don't ring ahead to check whether I'm in. You might have to walk all the way back in the rain. What's it about?'

'There's something I need to tell you. I'm telling you this because you're my friend. But also because you were my analyst.'

'Which is it? Analyst or friend?'

'Both. But if you hadn't been my analyst I couldn't tell you at all. You know, rules and all that.'

Reuben examined her as she sat before him, in her familiar upright posture. She looked fine, more than fine, better than she had done in months: calm, clear, alert.

'Go on,' he said. 'I'm listening.'

'I've just seen a fifteen-year-old girl. She comes from Braxton in Suffolk.'

Reuben's eyes narrowed. 'That sounds familiar.'

'I might have mentioned it in our sessions. It's where I grew up. Where I went to school.'

'Why are you seeing a patient from there?'

'She's not exactly a patient. Her mother was in my class at school. She suddenly got in touch and asked me to talk to her daughter. She was being difficult. The daughter, I mean. Acting up.'

'What happened?'

'She told me she had been raped.'

'How?' said Reuben, and then he corrected himself. 'I mean, in what circumstances?'

'A stranger broke into her bedroom at night. She didn't see his face. It was dark and he was wearing something over it. So she didn't recognize him.'

'Has she gone to the police?'

'She doesn't want to, her mother doesn't want to.'

Reuben lay back on the large sofa and ran his fingers through his long, greying hair. He was wearing a shirt with an intricate pattern in black and white. It almost shimmered. 'It sounds terrible,' he said. 'But why are you telling me this?'

'She told me that after it had all happened, the man had leaned close to her and told her that nobody would believe her.'

'Do people believe her?'

'I do. Her mother isn't sure. Or is scared to be sure.'

There was a long silence. When Reuben spoke he sounded tentative, as if he knew he was entering dangerous territory. 'That's a terrible thing to happen,' he said. He sat up and put the last of his lunch into his

60

mouth, chewed vigorously. 'But, again, why are you telling me?'

'Because twenty-three years ago I went through exactly the same thing.'

Reuben's features froze. 'What do you mean?'

'The same thing, the same words.'

'You mean you were raped?'

'Yes.'

'When you were a girl?'

'I was just sixteen.'

Reuben felt as if he had received a blow. It took an effort for him to speak calmly. 'I'm going to say two things. The first is that I am so, so sorry about this. And the second, I was your therapist for three years. Why didn't you tell me?'

Frieda thought for a moment. 'One of those things explains the other. I survived it. I got out. I didn't want your sympathy or anybody's sympathy. If I had told you, that would have given him power over me. It would have shown he was still in my head.'

'If that's what you feel, then I must have failed you deeply as a therapist.'

'I probably wasn't a good patient.'

'I don't know what a good patient is,' said Reuben, with a rueful expression. 'I probably learned more from you than you learned from me. But I wasn't able to help you. Or you weren't able to turn to me for help.'

'You did help me in so many ways, but I didn't

need that sort of help,' said Frieda. 'If by that you mean coming to terms with it. That's the old cliché for it, isn't it? I don't believe in coming to terms with things.'

'You felt a need to come here, walking through the rain. You didn't have a proper coat or an umbrella. I could say that you were punishing yourself, or scouring yourself.'

'I could say that it wasn't raining when I set off,' said Frieda. 'But that would be evasive. This girl was like a visitor from my past. Calling me back. I felt I had to tell someone.'

'I'm glad it was me.' Reuben turned his palm upwards in a summoning gesture that was familiar to Frieda, taking her back to the time when he had been her therapist. 'Can you tell me now?'

'I can try,' said Frieda.

Two hours later, Frieda was walking alone down Primrose Hill, with what felt like the whole of London laid out in front of her. She had told the story to Reuben, such as it was; she had said it out loud for the first time in twenty-three years. He had listened in a way that had taken her back to the old Reuben, shrewd, perceptive, entirely focused on the words she was finally uttering. Yet as she thought over it now, it wasn't something that could meaningfully be told as a story, narrated in words. It existed for her as a series of images, flashes lit by a strobe light.

The feel of her bed in the pitch darkness, the weight of her body, the smell of bath soap.

A movement. A creak of a floorboard. The heaving of the bed.

Light in her eyes. A shape behind the light. A blade against her neck. Something whispered. A mask. Woollen.

Duvet thrown back. The feeling of air on bare skin. Legs pushed apart. The weight on her. Gloved hands. Terror invading every part of her body.

Voices from downstairs. The television. Canned laughter. Life going on as it always did, careless of atrocity.

Trying to hold on to her thoughts, to her rational self. Saying, 'Please don't do this. I'm a virgin. Please please please.' And a snorting little chuckle coming from him.

A sensation of pain and the feeling – which Frieda had never forgotten – that it was happening to her yet she was separate from her body. The sudden warm wetness.

The flashing certainty that this might be the last moment of her life, the final thing she would ever experience. Waiting for the hands around the neck.

Warm, panting breath. Horrible intimacy. The last murmured, muffled words lisped into her ear: 'Don't think of telling anyone, sweetheart. Nobody will believe you.'

Lying in the dark, trying to believe he was gone and not coming back. The thought that it would never be safe to sleep ever, ever again.

8

Frieda sat in her little garret at the top of the house. From the skylight window she could see, across the rooftops of Fitzrovia, the old Post Office tower. Inside it was quiet and peaceful. A standard lamp threw a soft light over the room, and there was a jug of crimson dahlias on her desk. Her drawing pencils, her charcoals, were ranged neatly in front of her. She wrapped her hands around her large mug of tea and took a small sip. She felt calm. Her thoughts were clear. She opened the lid of her laptop and, ignoring new mail, pressed the message icon.

Dear Sandy [she wrote]

I have just returned from seeing Reuben. I told him something that I should have told him a long time ago, when he was my therapist and I was his patient. Now I need to tell you too. You don't have to say anything or do anything. I don't want help and this is not a confession, just a story of something that happened to me that you should know because I don't want it to be a secret. If it is a secret, then it has power over me still, and I don't want that.

When I was just sixteen, some months after my father killed himself, I was raped. A man broke into my room at night and raped me. I do not know who he was. He was never discovered. There are ways in which my life changed after this; I changed. I never spoke of it because I did not want to be defined by it. Now, however, the past seems to have returned to me. Perhaps it never left, after all.

I wanted you to know.

I really am fine, better than I've been for a long time. You don't need to worry about me. Not an hour goes by that I don't think of you and send you my love xxxx

Frieda sat for several minutes, sipping her tea, staring out at the blurred lights of London, before she pressed the 'send' button. It was gone. Soon he would know. She felt slightly vertiginous: for all these years she had kept the secret sealed away inside her; now in the space of a few hours she had told two people. And she knew that this meant she had other people to tell.

The next morning she phoned Sasha. Yes, it was important. Yes, it was almost an emergency. But nothing Sasha needed to worry about.

They walked together in silence until they reached Bloomsbury Square, Sasha pushing Ethan in his buggy. The winds were almost gale force and the trees were swaying in unison. Frieda was wearing her long black coat and her red scarf. She had to lean in close while she told Sasha what had happened to her; she saw her friend flinch.

When she had finished, Sasha hugged her. Frieda glanced around to see if anyone was watching.

'I'm thinking of when we first met,' Sasha said, her hair blown around her face by the wind. She looked as if she were on the deck of a ship. 'I came to you and told you about what happened with me and Dr Rundell. And all the time you'd gone through that. How did you keep something like that to yourself? Why did you never mention it before?'

'I've never told anyone. One of the reasons is that I didn't want that to be the way that people thought of me: the victim. I told you ten seconds ago and already you think it influenced the way I responded to you when we first met.'

'You didn't just respond,' said Sasha. 'You went straight across London and punched him in a restaurant and got arrested. Is that normal?'

'It seemed appropriate in the circumstances. So now you know.'

'What next?'

Frieda took her phone from her pocket. 'There are one or two more people I've got to burden with this.'

Josef was working in a large detached house near the canal in Maida Vale. Frieda noticed a smart white van parked outside. A suspicious Spanish cleaner admitted her and led her to an upstairs bedroom. Josef was up a ladder spreading plaster on the ceiling. A burly man with his hair in a ponytail and tattoos on his arms was stripping discoloured paper off the walls. Josef noticed her and slid down the ladder. He stepped forward to hug her, then looked at his smeared arms and stopped.

'It looks as if things are going well,' said Frieda.

'How?' asked Josef.

'I saw a new van outside. Hello, Stefan.'

The man with the ponytail stood up and held out his broad hand. He was Russian and from time to time he worked with Josef. Frieda was never quite sure what he did outside that.

'How is your bath?' Josef asked.

'My bath is fine, thank you.' She peered up at the ceiling. 'You're nearly done.'

Josef shook his head. 'Is shit.'

'No,' said Frieda. 'It looks really nice.'

'No, no,' said Josef, pointing upwards. 'Over there in room is toilet. They put wrong things down. It very, very bad. Three days ago, this room was like hell. And it smelt . . . Ooof.' He pulled a face.

'It looks fine now,' said Frieda.

'But you said you must see me,' said Josef.

Frieda looked at Stefan. 'Can we find somewhere private?'

Stefan grinned. 'I make tea. Or something stronger?'

'Tea's good.'

'I have custard creams.'

'Lovely.' She hated custard creams.

Stefan left the room.

'There's something I have to tell you,' said Frieda, 'but I can tell you while you're working.'

Josef climbed back up the ladder and started slapping on the plaster and shaping it flat, in broad sweeps with two trowels. It was oddly satisfying and soothing to watch and Frieda would have been happy just to lie on the floor and look as the ceiling was covered.

'I can't watch a ceiling without imagining you falling through it,' she said.

'A strange way for our first meeting,' said Josef. 'You could have watched me die. But what is it you have to say?'

So Frieda told him. After she had begun, Josef stopped his plastering and turned and sat on the steps, gazing down at her. Frieda felt that there was something incongruous about the whole scene, as if she was talking to someone sitting up in a tree. 'So,' she said finally. 'That's what I came to tell you.'

He stood up on his ladder, his head almost touching the newly plastered ceiling, and put a hand to his heart. 'Thank you, my friend,' he said.

'What for?'

'For telling me this.'

'You're welcome.' There was a pause and the two of them looked at each other. 'You need to finish your ceiling.'

Josef shrugged.

'I came to say what I had to say,' said Frieda. 'So I'll go.'

*

'Whisky with a dash of water,' said Karlsson.

They clinked tumblers and smiled at each other.

'You're tanned,' said Frieda. 'You haven't been using a sunbed, have you?'

Somehow, over the turbulent years that they had known each other, Frieda and DCI Malcolm Karlsson had become comfortable in each other's company. They had had fierce arguments; they had let each other down and had rescued each other; they had seen each other in danger and great distress. Now they could sit on the long, battered sofa, drink whisky and say what was on their minds.

'Spain,' Karlsson said. 'I was there for a long weekend.'

'Of course. How are your children?'

Karlsson's children were spending two years in Madrid with his ex-wife and her new partner. Frieda had seen how much he hated their going and how painfully he missed them.

'Brown, freckled, talking a language I don't understand.'

'Happy, then?'

'Yes. They seem very happy.'

'That's good, isn't it?'

'Is it terrible to wish they sometimes missed me a bit?'

'They'll be back in a few months, won't they?'

'Yes. I hope we can get back to normal.'

'Rather than what?'

'I make so much effort with them when I see them for these brief snatches, as if I always have to entertain them. I don't want to be their holiday, I want to be their home.'

'Perhaps you should trust them more.'

'You're probably right.' He smiled at her. 'You usually are.'

'I'll remind you that you said that. How's work?' They had first met each other through his work, which had come for a time to be hers as well.

'Nothing to interest you. No murders and missing children. No, I'm – what's the term Commissioner Crawford uses? – I'm facilitating a reorganization.'

'That sounds painful.'

He made a grimace of distaste. 'Resource limitations. Performance indicators. Streamlining. Making operations fit for purpose. This isn't what I went into the police force to do.'

'Are you laying people off?'

'I'm afraid so. Yvette's helping me. She hates it more than I do, which, of course, makes her like the poor old bull in a china shop. She charges angrily at it.'

Frieda smiled. 'Poor Yvette.'

'Don't feel sorry for us. We're the lucky ones.' He poured more whisky into both glasses. 'How are you, though, Frieda? You look well. This is a very nice surprise visit.'

'I wanted to see you for a particular reason. As a friend.'

Karlsson became slightly wary.

'I mean, as a friend who also happens to be a police officer.' She took a mouthful of whisky. 'I've only given the full version of this story to one other person. I've told Reuben. I'm allowed to do that because he was my analyst when I was training. I couldn't tell the full version even to Sasha or Josef but I can tell you because you're a policeman and this is about a crime.' She looked Karlsson full in the face. This had got his attention. 'I'll begin with the easier part. Over the past few days I've been talking to a girl – she's fifteen – who comes from the town where I grew up. I was at school with her mother.'

Karlsson nodded. He had never before heard Frieda refer to her childhood.

'She came to see me because she's in a bad way – truanting, self-harming, being withdrawn. She has now told me that several weeks ago she was raped,' continued Frieda. 'She was in bed, in the dark. She has no idea who it was and hasn't reported it to the police.'

'Do you believe her?'

'Yes.' Frieda's tone was sharp.

'What is it you want my advice about?'

'She is insistent she won't report it. Even more insistent now that she's told her mother, who isn't being supportive.'

'I see. And you want to know what you should do about it, as her therapist?'

'It's a bit more complicated than that.'

Frieda stood up and went to stand by the door that led out into the long garden. It was dark outside but she could see leaves swirling in the gusts of wind. There was a cat on the roof opposite. She turned back. 'There is a reason that I know she's telling the truth. You see, the same thing happened to me.'

Karlsson rose to his feet and Frieda looked into his face; she wanted to see how he would react. She waited for a slight recoil, an expression of suppressed horror. Instead, she found a strained tenderness that was hard for her to bear.

'Frieda,' he said, in a low voice. 'My dear Frieda . . .'

She held up a hand. 'It's all right,' she said reassuringly. 'It was a very long time ago. Twenty-three years ago. The eleventh of February 1989, to be exact. I've had plenty of time to get used to it.'

'You were just a girl. Christ, how awful.'

'I was a bit older than the young woman I've been telling you about. I was sixteen.'

'I'm so sorry. So very sorry.'

'That's not why I'm telling you.'

Karlsson sat down again.

'My mother didn't believe me,' she said. 'She thought I was an attention-seeker. But I did go to the police eventually. There was one officer who was kind to me, but I'm not sure some of the others took it seriously. The inquiry just petered out. A few years later, a man was arrested in the area for a series of sexual assaults.

73

His name was Dennis Freeman. He was the usual kind of suspect – well known to the police, a bit of a loner, lived in a hostel, drank, already had a suspended sentence. You know how it goes.'

Karlsson nodded.

'When I read about it, I thought it must have been him.'

'Did you go to the police?'

'And be put through it all again? I just assumed it must have been him. He died in prison a few years later. I thought it was all over, in the past, and anyway, I'd left Braxton by then, left everything.'

Frieda stopped, swirled the amber liquid in the bottom of her tumbler and finished it off in a gulp.

'But?' prompted Karlsson.

'It wasn't him. The girl I was talking to is fifteen. She was in Braxton – the town where I spent my childhood – in her bedroom, in the dark. He wore a mask. When the rapist left, he said something to her.'

'What?' asked Karlsson, after a pause.

'He said, "Don't think of telling anyone, sweetheart. Nobody will believe you."'

'I can see that's very frightening but –'

'I was raped in Braxton when I was sixteen. In my bedroom, in the dark, by a person who also wore a mask. When the rapist left, he said, "Don't think of telling anyone, sweetheart. Nobody will believe you."'

'Are you saying what I think you're saying?'

'Yes.'

Karlsson moved on to the sofa beside Frieda. 'How can I help?'

'A man who raped me has now raped someone else. He isn't in prison and he isn't dead. He's out there. I have to do something. Also, isn't it very unlikely he hasn't raped other young women? He wouldn't have waited twenty-three years, would he?'

'No,' said Karlsson, slowly. 'It's extremely unlikely – although it's not uncommon for rapists to wait several years between assaults.'

'So other women have been raped by him, and presumably other women will be, unless he's caught.'

Karlsson's face was grave. 'I won't lie to you,' he said. 'This isn't simple. You say the teenager you've been seeing is not willing to report the rape to the police?'

'She says she won't.'

'And even if she did, you say that it happened several weeks ago.'

'Yes.'

'So there will be no forensic evidence.'

'I suppose not.'

'Rape cases are difficult.'

'I know that,' said Frieda, wearily. 'But look at the situation. The girl won't go to the police because she thinks that they, like her own mother, won't believe her, and my own experience tells me she may be right. She feels that in some contorted way she deserved to be raped because she was – in her mother's words –

leading a disordered life and this was her punishment. She feels ashamed. Horribly, horribly ashamed and defiled. So the rapist gets away with it, because his victim has been made to feel guilty and utterly powerless.'

'Does she suspect anyone?'

'Not that I know of.'

Karlsson looked troubled. 'We can go back there together,' he said.

'You'd do that?'

'I can talk to the local force. But look at the situation from their point of view: no crime has been reported, there is no evidence and no suspect. There's another thing.'

'What?'

'Have you thought what all this will mean for you?'

'Yes, I have. But this man is still out there. I don't have a choice. Also, it's time.'

'What does that mean?'

'There are things I've run away from all my life. My father's death. My rape. Things that happened after. But it seems as though I've run in a perfect circle and I'm back with it again. In the thick of it.' She touched Karlsson on the arm. 'Don't look so anxious. In my profession, this is what we call progress. I'm all right – I can do this *because* I'm all right.'

'Is this all a problem for you?' said Chloë. 'Where's your corkscrew? Answer the second question first.'

76

'It's in the drawer on the left-hand side of the cooker,' said Frieda.

Chloë disappeared into the kitchen and there was a clattering sound. Frieda gently touched her temples. She could feel the beginning of a headache but at the moment it was even worse, like a little buzzing fly inside her skull. What she had told Karlsson was almost true. She had left his house with the determination to go home, get into bed and sleep, and if she couldn't sleep then at least she would get into bed. But almost immediately her phone had rung and Chloë was saying she needed to see her now, absolutely this minute: could she come straight over? This, Frieda thought, was the reason why getting a mobile phone had been a mistake, as was leaving it switched on. But she had always felt a duty of care to her niece, since she was a podgy nervous toddler, through her angry, chaotic teenage years. She was someone Frieda said yes to, and she did so again, with a sigh.

Barely five minutes after Frieda had arrived home, Chloë was at the door clutching a bottle of white wine. Now she re-emerged from the kitchen precariously clutching the opened bottle, two glasses and a small bowl. She placed them delicately on the table.

'I found some peanuts in the cupboard,' she said. 'Is that all right?'

'Fine,' said Frieda.

'You know, I've always pictured this,' said Chloë.

'What?'

'That one day it wouldn't be just Auntie Frieda giving me a science lesson and looking disapproving. We'd be two friends meeting for a drink.'

Frieda couldn't suppress a smile, even when Chloë poured much too much wine into the two glasses. She handed one to Frieda and raised her own. 'Cheers,' she said. 'I just saw a news story that made me think of you.'

'Does that mean it was some kind of murder?'

'No, not at all. But it was about the brain. There are these people who've been in comas for years, but worse than comas – what's that called?'

'A deep vegetative state,' said Frieda.

'They've discovered they're not complete vegetables, after all. They've managed to communicate. They ask them a question, and if the answer is yes, they should imagine they're playing tennis, and it shows up on a brain scan. Isn't that amazing?'

'Yes,' said Frieda. 'I've been following the research.'

'Isn't that the most nightmarish thing in the world? Being trapped in your own brain and unable to move or talk or do anything, but still being conscious.'

Frieda took a sip of the cold white wine that Chloë had brought and thought for a moment. 'A persistent vegetative state sounds quite restful. Maybe I could find a doctor who could put me into one.'

'Frieda! You don't mean that. Are you saying that for a joke?'

'Of course,' she said.

'So what is the answer to my question?'

'Which one?'

'The one about whether me being with Jack was a problem for you.'

'Why should it be a problem?'

'It might be like two of your little babies suddenly growing up and having a relationship. I don't know, it might seem like something incestuous.'

Frieda looked at her bright, restless niece, half girl and half young woman. She had watched her through her early years, through the turbulent adolescent ones. She had stepped in when her mother, Olivia, had seemed incapable of doing so. She had seen her in love with a tragic boy who couldn't love her back. She smiled at her reassuringly. 'I don't feel that at all.'

'Obviously, we met through you and it's really interesting meeting someone who sees you in a different way. It's quite funny, but Jack is so completely in awe of you. He's like some schoolboy with a crush on his teacher.'

'Chloë, you probably shouldn't tell me that.'

'He wouldn't mind. And there's nothing he's told me about you that should embarrass you at all.'

'I don't think I was worried about that.'

'That's great. It was really important to me that it was no problem for you.'

Frieda felt she couldn't let this go completely. 'As I said,' she began slowly, 'if I have any concern, it's that there's quite a big age difference.'

79

'Of course I've thought about that. You think about lots of things. That doesn't mean they're problems.'

'I trust you,' said Frieda. 'But I don't want you to get hurt.'

'Oh, that,' said Chloë. 'You're making too big a deal of it. That's why I wanted to come and talk to you about it. Obviously I can't talk to my mum.'

'Maybe you should.'

'It would be a complete and utter disaster. And most of my friends are too immature. I feel that you're the only person I can really talk to about something like this. The point is, you don't need to worry about us because so far we're really just having a good time. And it really is a good time. In fact, the sex with Jack has been just wonderful. I've never experienced anything like it.'

'Chloë . . .' Frieda began feebly. She felt a desperate need to shut Chloë up but she was finding it difficult even to speak.

Chloë took another gulp of wine. 'You clearly know that I'm not exactly a blushing virgin . . .'

'Chloë . . .'

'. . . but in the past, by comparison, it's really just been fumbling and groping and all a bit desperate, you know what I mean? With Jack it's something completely different. It's funny, because when you first meet him, he seems sweet and shy, but in fact he's amazingly uninhibited. He's really up for it, you know what I mean? It's not like some angsty, anguished relationship, if that's what you're worried about. Really, we don't talk that much at all at the moment. We spend most of our time in bed.'

'Stop,' Frieda finally managed to say, in a sort of gasp. 'Stop. Enough.'

'What?' said Chloë, with concern.

'I don't think I should be hearing all of this.'

'But isn't that what you do all day?'

'I'm not a sex therapist, Chloë. And especially not a sex therapist to my niece.'

'Well, I can tell you, if there's one thing we don't need it's sex therapy.' She suddenly looked puzzled. 'I thought you'd be the one person who would understand what I was feeling.'

'I would love you to tell me what you're feeling,' Frieda said delicately. 'It's just that I'm not sure I need to know what you're *doing*. Chloë, when I see patients in my consulting room, the deal is that they have the freedom to say anything at all, the things they've never been able to speak aloud. But the deal is also that what they say stays in that room. The same is true, maybe, about sexual intimacy. You can be free with someone because it stays as a secret between you and the other person. Not to be communicated to your aunt.'

'That's a bit boring,' said Chloë. 'With Jack I've just felt how sex with one person can be a completely different experience. I thought it was something we could talk about.'

Frieda leaned across the table and touched Chloë's hand with her own. 'Jack might not want you to talk about this with me.'

'You think you know Jack. But you don't know him the way I know him. He's not like you think.' She sat up straight and put her glass down on the table with such firmness that some of the wine spilled. 'Oh, well. If that's what you want. But don't you remember what it was like when you were my age? I bet the eighteen-year-old Frieda would have been a bit more unbuttoned about all this.'

Frieda put her own glass down. 'It's time for you to go. It's late.'

Chloë got up and pulled on her jacket. 'Well, that wasn't a great success,' she said.

'I'm sorry you think so.'

'If you reckon it's all a great mistake, you should just say so.'

'It's clearly not a mistake,' said Frieda. 'I don't see why it matters what I say.'

Chloë gave Frieda a last puzzled look. 'Of course it does. It matters more than anything.'

When Chloë had gone, Frieda washed the glasses and put them away. She looked in the fridge and found some blue cheese, past its best, that she sliced on to crackers. Then she made herself camomile tea and had a long soak in the wonderful large bath that her friend Josef had installed for her with Stefan's help.

Afterwards she got into bed and turned the light out. Instantly she knew that there was no chance of sleep, not for hours. In normal times she might have considered getting up and putting her clothes on, going out and walking somewhere through late-night London to wear her body out and still the voices in her head. But just now she didn't want to leave her house. She lay and stared at the ceiling and tried not to think of the events of the day, of what she had said to Karlsson, of what she hadn't said to Chloë. She thought of the eager, happy, ridiculous face as she arrived. However, she had no intention of having an intimate discussion about sex with her niece.

So she lay there for hour after hour of a raw night, somehow having dreams without sleeping. From time to time she would look at the clock on the bedside table and see that another half-hour or hour had passed. Some people said that what you felt at four in the morning was the bleak, spare truth that you couldn't face up to in the daytime. Others said it was just a symptom of low blood sugar and the feelings were sham and a delusion. For much of the night, though she was in a dark that seemed like it would never end, Frieda felt she was staring at the sun, a cold and joyless sun.

Somehow she must finally have slept because she was woken from uneasy dreams by a sound that seemed a horrible part of the dream, then turned into her front doorbell. She looked at the clock. A visit at this time of the morning could only be more bad news. She pulled a dressing gown around her and padded downstairs in her bare feet. She stood for a moment by the door, taking a deep breath, delaying whatever was there for a few more seconds. Then she opened it.

'Oh, my God,' she said.

A man was standing outside, wearing a leather jacket, with a large shoulder bag. He looked tired and slightly sheepish and very concerned. It was Sandy.

9

'This property,' said the woman, 'will be snapped up.'
She clicked her fingers expertly. Her name was Melinda.
She had vermilion nails, thick peppery-blonde hair and
natty brown boots, whose heels tapped briskly over the
bare boards.

Sandy looked non-committal.

'Prime location. Recently renovated.' Her voice followed them from room to room. 'Double glazing.
Concierge. En-suite bathroom. New boiler. No chain.'

Each room was bare and echoey, every wall freshly
painted white. Frieda stood by the window, gazing
out on to the street. It was drizzling, and people
passed below under their umbrellas.

'Are you buying together?' asked Melinda.

'No,' Sandy and Frieda replied simultaneously.

'It's just me,' added Sandy.

She looked uncertain, not knowing how to read the
situation. Frieda saw her eye dart to her wedding finger, bare of rings. 'Well, it's perfect for one person.
Do you have any questions?'

'I can't think of any,' said Sandy. He put his hand
on the small of Frieda's back. 'Shall we go?'

'Yes.'

'It was like a hotel room,' he said, when they were out in the street. 'Where next?'

Next was Hampstead, and tiny. The pictures on the website were misleading. It was a bijou first-floor flat cleverly carved out of an inadequate space. There was a miniature kitchen, like a boat's galley, and a shower room scarcely large enough to hold the shower. The chandelier of coloured glass and the capacious leather sofa gave the living room a claustrophobic feel. The bedroom was painted red and one wall was lined with mirrors.

'Horrible,' said Sandy, when the agent left them alone.

'Creepy,' said Frieda.

'And expensive.'

'It's Hampstead. Look, you can see the Heath from here.'

'Yes. You don't need to look like that,' said Sandy.

'Like what?'

'Anxious.'

'Was I looking anxious?'

'Yes.'

'I love you for coming back like this.'

'But?'

'But it feels as if I'm being given no choice,' said Frieda.

'You mean that you don't want my sudden return to force you into a commitment you might not want to make.'

She didn't reply, just stared out over the green wilderness in the distance.

'I know what I'm doing, Frieda. This is what I want. You're as free as you ever were. But this was my wake-up call.'

'But your job . . .'

'It's not a problem. There are openings here. What was I doing, living on the other side of the Atlantic from you? I realized what I always should have known – that there's no point being with you if I'm away from you. After all –'

'Done?' asked the agent cheerily, coming into the room.

'Yes.'

'Any questions?'

'No.'

The big basement flat in Bermondsey was well within Sandy's budget and, what was more, it had a garden that was large by London standards, with a little patio and a murky pond at the far end where they spotted a single mottled goldfish. But it smelt damp; the ceilings were high and the rooms dark, cold and comfortless.

'I like the brickwork,' said Frieda, trying to be upbeat.

'Yes.'

'And there's a fireplace you could open up.'

'I suppose so.'

'It needs work, of course,' Frieda added.

'It's not right.'

'You're sure?'

'I was sure the moment I walked through the door. You can weigh up all the pros and cons and practicalities, but first you have to fall in love.'

'I agree.'

'We did, didn't we?'

'Yes. We did.' Frieda touched him briefly on the cheek. 'I've been wondering. Where are you going to live while you're looking?'

'Don't worry. I'm not going to move in with you. I'll stay with my sister and spend time with you when I can. I'm going to buy a place, get a new job, and return to the life I shouldn't have left in the first place.'

'If you're sure.'

'I'm sure.'

'Where next?'

The flat in Clerkenwell was on the ground floor of a beautiful late-Georgian house. It was flanked by a few similar buildings, a fragment of a street that had otherwise long ago been bombed or bulldozed. As the young man showing them round explained, the owners had separated in the midst of renovating it. It felt as if they had just walked out, leaving their broken life behind them. Units were ripped from the kitchen floor; a partition wall had been half demolished; a cracked marble fireplace had been removed and was leaning against the wall. There were paint pots and brushes on a trestle table; a ladder in the middle of the living room; clothes spilling out of drawers in the bedroom; books in piles waiting to be claimed. But the rooms were large and light, with windows running almost to the floor and exposed beams. The back door led out to a tiny walled garden with a fig tree in the corner where the city suddenly felt miles away.

'It was their project,' said the agent, dubiously. 'It's got great potential.'

'I can see that,' said Frieda, half in love with the place.

'For someone else,' said Sandy, firmly. 'It would take years, and it's not what I want to be doing with my time.'

'What do you want to be doing with your time?' asked Frieda, a little later, sitting in a café a few streets away, eating a hot buttered teacake and looking at the increasing rain outside, the leaves blown past the window like yellow rags.

'Not plastering walls.'

'Do you know how to plaster walls?'

'I want to spend time with you.'

'I suppose we could plaster the walls together,' she said doubtfully.

'No. Other things need our attention.'

'Like what?'

'Like you, Frieda.'

She winced. 'That makes me sound like an emergency.'

They walked to the next property, which was between King's Cross and Islington. Although it was only mid-afternoon, the light was beginning to fail. There were still weeks to go before the shortest day of the year, and Frieda thought of her own house waiting for her, the shutters she would close against the dying day and the fire she would light. They passed a busker, his hair wet and an open violin case containing just a few coins on the ground beside him. He wasn't playing anything, but as they approached he passed his bow across the strings half-heartedly. Frieda threw in several more coins and he gave a small salute.

The property they were viewing – they'd unconsciously started to adopt estate-agent vocabulary – was tall and narrow, a green front door and steep stairs with a worn carpet. The flat was on the two top floors. The agent fumbled with the keys to open the door and Frieda and Sandy walked swiftly through the rooms; the owners would be coming back in a quarter of an hour and, anyway, they'd seen too much of other people's homes for one day. There was a living room with two big windows, a narrow kitchen leading off it. A study, just big enough for a desk and chair, that looked out over someone else's wet garden with a silver birch tree and a green bench in it. And upstairs, a bedroom with a roof terrace. Sandy and Frieda pushed open the warped door and stepped out on to it, the rain blowing in gusts against their faces. They gazed out across rooftops, cranes and spires, the glittering lights of the great city dissolving into a streaming grey sky.

'That's St Pancras.' Frieda pointed.

'This will do just fine,' said Sandy. 'We can drink coffee up here in the mornings. Now let's go home.'

10

The phone rang. It was Josef. 'Are you there?'

'Of course I'm here,' said Frieda. 'I answered the phone.'

'You are going out this evening?'

'What?' said Frieda. 'No, I don't think –'

'Good,' said Josef. 'We bring food.'

'We?' Frieda began, but the phone had already gone dead.

An hour later the bell rang. Frieda opened the door and Josef and Reuben were standing on the step. Both of them pushed past her. Frieda saw that they were carrying shopping bags. There was a smell of fresh bread, a clink of bottles.

'You're going to have to stop doing this,' said Frieda. 'We're grown-ups now. We make arrangements days ahead of time.'

Josef laid the bags on the table and turned towards her. Frieda saw that he was wearing a dark jacket and a tie. He stepped forward and hugged her.

'Hey.'

Josef and Reuben looked around and saw Sandy coming down the stairs.

'You are welcome back,' Josef said. He stepped

forward and hugged Sandy and Reuben hugged Sandy, then Frieda. She felt a sudden nostalgia for the days when men shook hands. Middle-aged men seemed to have turned into schoolgirls. Reuben produced a bottle of vodka from one of the bags and Josef disappeared into the kitchen, returning with four shot glasses.

Frieda gave a helpless shrug to Sandy. 'He knows my kitchen better than I do,' she said.

Josef filled the glasses and handed them round. Reuben looked at Josef. 'Say something.'

'No,' said Josef. 'You say.'

'No, you.'

'Oh, for goodness' sake,' said Frieda.

'I speak,' said Josef. He looked into his glass. 'I was proud that you came to me. It was a trust. I do not want to just say words. Words which make me feel better but not you feel better. You go now and have bath in the bath I put into your house.' He looked at Sandy. 'And you if you want also with her. Or if she wants.'

'Please, Josef . . .' said Frieda.

'We have food and drink and we prepare and in one hour we eat. But first . . .' he raised his glass '. . . for a friend. Frieda.'

Josef and Reuben drained their glasses. Sandy and Frieda took wary sips.

'I will have a bath,' said Frieda. 'Alone. And thank you for this, but can we say that, from now on, we'll plan these events in advance? With fair warning.'

Josef turned to Sandy. 'You relax. Drink. Go for walk. We prepare food.'

Frieda found it difficult to enjoy her bath because of the sounds below her of dishes and pans. Something broke and she heard male voices shouting. She had an impulse to run downstairs and deal with whatever crisis seemed to be unfolding but instead she sank briefly below the surface of the water. Perhaps whatever it was that had broken wasn't something of hers. And if it was, what did it really matter? After the bath, Frieda pulled on trousers and a shirt.

When she came downstairs, her living room was transformed. It was mainly lit by the flickering candles that had been placed between the dishes that covered the table. There was a bowl of thick red soup with dumplings, there was something wrapped in cabbage, large sausages, pickled fish, beetroot salad, chopped potatoes, an unfamiliar kind of little mushroom, a huge wheel of bread, small pastries, a whole duck, rolled pancakes . . .

'The wine isn't Ukrainian,' said Reuben. 'I thought Australian was a bit safer.'

'There is good Ukrainian wine,' Josef protested. 'But Reuben bought wine.'

He gestured Frieda, Sandy and Reuben to sit around the table and spooned large helpings on to Frieda's plate.

'Whenever you feel a strong emotion,' said Frieda, 'you cook the food of your home.'

'That is funny, no?' said Josef.

'No,' said Frieda. 'It's good to have food that is like a kind of memory.'

Sandy picked up a rough-textured rissole and nibbled at it. 'This is good. What is it?'

'I don't know,' said Josef. 'The woman in shop give me lots of choices. Pork, I think. Or sheep.'

Everyone started to eat. Occasionally Josef named a dish or described or said what was in it but there didn't seem the need to say much and Frieda liked that, or at least felt relieved. Reuben opened a second bottle of wine and started refilling the glasses. Frieda put her hand over her glass.

'You know,' said Reuben, 'when someone does that, I'm always tempted to call their bluff and just pour the wine and keep on pouring until they move their hand out of the way.'

'I'm so glad you didn't try that,' said Frieda, and then she noticed he was picking up his glass and looking reflective. 'You're not going to make a speech, are you?'

'Well, I'm going to speak. If that's allowed. First, I just want to say to you and Sandy that I'm sorry if we've ruined a romantic evening that you had planned.'

'No,' said Sandy. 'This is nice.'

He put his hand on Frieda's leg, beneath the table.

'It's not for me to say,' Reuben continued, 'but I suppose I'm someone who believes – in fact, whose life depends on the belief – that you deal with things by talking about them. But you, Sandy, when Frieda told you, you got on a plane and came over. And Josef brought food. It's like an offering, like something in the Old Testament. You know, Frieda, when you first told me, my first reaction . . .' He paused. 'No, my second reaction, was a kind of self-pity. I'd been your therapist, your supervisor, and you'd kept that from me. I don't know whether that says something about me as a therapist or you as an analys– . . .' Another pause. 'Analys*and*. I can't even say it properly. Or something about therapy. Sorry, this is becoming all about me. Again. But probably the best thing is to sit with friends, eat strange food, not say too much. Have you told anyone else?'

'I told Sasha. And Karlsson.'

'Good,' said Reuben. 'And that's the end of the speech.'

'But what will you do?' said Josef.

'Yes,' said Sandy. 'What *will* you do?'

Frieda looked down at her plate. The food was lovely, the sort of comforting food that, if you were hungry and if you had the right sort of mother, your mother would cook for you to soothe you and make you feel better.

'I don't know,' she said. 'What I planned to do is what I've done for twenty-three years, which is just to carry on, to stop him – whoever he was – having any power over me. Things feel different now. I know he's still out there. But I wouldn't know where to start.'

There was a silence and the men exchanged glances.

'When you start talking like that,' Sandy said, 'I have a feeling that something's going to happen.'

'Well, something *is* going to happen. I'm just not sure what yet.'

Sandy pushed his plate away. 'I'm busy tomorrow morning. Let's go in the afternoon.'

'Go?'

'To Braxton. I'll drive you.'

'Oh.' Frieda was startled. Sandy looked at her with bright eyes, waiting. 'But I need to make arrangements.'

'Why?'

'I can't just turn up.'

'I don't see why not.'

'And my patients —'

'It's the weekend.'

Frieda stared at Sandy. For more than twenty years this had been waiting for her. She should have known that she couldn't escape.

'We need to find somewhere to stay,' said Frieda.

It was the first time she had spoken for a long while. They had driven out of London in silence, Frieda looking out of the window at the landscape flowing past her: places that were both familiar and yet strange, like things seen in a dream. A year and a half ago, she and Sasha had visited the church where her father was buried, but that was because she believed that her deadly stalker, Dean Reeve, had been there. They had not gone to Braxton; she had not been back there since the day she had left, when she was not yet seventeen.

'So we're not staying with your mother?' said Sandy.

'Why would I stay with my mother?'

'Will you go and see her?'

'I don't know. I haven't made up my mind.'

'We'll find somewhere and then tomorrow you can go to the police station.'

'Tomorrow's Sunday,' said Frieda.

'I don't think crime stops at weekends.'

'No.'

'Are you going to tell me anything before we get there?'

'What do you mean?'

'Do you realize how little I know about your past?'

'What do you want to know?'

'Well, for instance, I know you have an older brother called David, because he's Olivia's ex and Chloë's father. Isn't there another brother?'

'Yes.'

'Well?'

'His name's Ivan.' Sandy waited, until Frieda added reluctantly, 'He's younger than me and he lives with his family in New Zealand.'

'So you never see him.'

'I never see him.'

'And you never see David either, though he lives near Cambridge.'

'No.'

'Or your mother.'

'No.'

'How long's it been?'

'About twenty years.' It had been twenty-three.

'Is she so bad?'

Frieda turned towards Sandy. Driving, he could sense rather than see her dark stare on him.

'I'd rather not talk about it at the moment.'

'All right.'

'I need to concentrate.'

'On what?'

'Just concentrate.'

She was looking at the fields and hedges, at the oak

tree that brought back a flash of memory, remembering the way the sky was so large out here, pocked now with the first pale stars. At the canal glimpsed from the road, like a secret path leading back towards the city, the farmhouse half hidden between trees, the church spire in the distance. A scattering of modern houses, windows lit up in the gathering darkness. Light-industrial units. Pylons marching across the horizon. Like a face long pushed out of the mind, she remembered it all and saw what had altered and what had remained the same.

As she gazed out of the window into the darkening landscape, she remembered faces, too, that she hadn't seen for decades, young, cruel, anxious, cocky, beseeching. She brought their names to the front of her mind, to make them seem more solid and real, less of a figment of her suddenly surging imagination. It's so strange, the things you remember, she thought: her first cheap cider, all the words of that poem by Robert Frost, the hairy legs of her biology teacher seen through her beige tights, Sallys Newsagent, whose lack of apostrophe had so irritated her father, one stickily hot sports day and the spring of the turf underfoot, the view from her bedroom window and ice flowers on the panes in winter, blowing on a grass blade held between her thumbs to make it whistle, swollen glands, someone crying. She saw her mother's face, ironic and unmoved. Something else darted into her mind, swift, fugitive – she couldn't hold it and it disappeared again.

Braxton lay in a shallow valley so that the whole of it was visible as they approached, the last straggle of lights blinking on the hilltop ahead. Frieda was astonished by how small it was. She'd grown used to the endlessness of London: it was impossible even to say where it began and where it ended. Braxton was defined by the tilted bowl of the valley that contained it, and the river that ran through it. It was surrounded by large fields and clumps of woods, farms and quarries. In the distance, the orange glow of Ipswich illumined the night sky.

'Stop,' Frieda said. Sandy braked.

'What is it?'

'I'd like to walk the last bit.'

'It's dark.'

'That doesn't matter. There's a moon. Then street lamps.' She smiled. 'I know the way.'

'Shall I come with you?'

She swallowed and made an effort to speak gently. 'I'd prefer to walk there alone. It will only take twenty minutes or so.'

'Where shall we meet?'

'Outside the church. You can't miss it.'

She buttoned her coat and wrapped her red scarf around her neck. Then she opened the door and stepped out into the windy darkness. Something about the smell – wet soil, fallen leaves, the faintest tang of brine – caught her in the throat and took her back again. She closed the door and waited until

Sandy had pulled away and his taillights had been swallowed up in the night, and then she started to walk.

'What will you have?'

Frieda looked at the menu, with its sashimi and crust coatings and drizzles of oil. And she looked around the dining room with its minimalist black furniture, tasteful abstract paintings, zoned lighting. This didn't feel like the place where she had grown up. In the 1980s it had felt like the 1950s or 1930s.

By the time she had arrived in the high street, Sandy had arranged everything. He had booked a room in a pub that Frieda had remembered as a smoky, dingy place but now had framed awards by the door and a restaurant. The harassed young woman at the front desk had said that it was almost full but she could get them a table if they could eat immediately. Sandy looked at Frieda, who just shrugged, and they walked straight through without even going up to their room.

'I'll have the oysters,' said Sandy. 'You know, when in Suffolk.'

'You know about the norovirus, don't you?'

'Yes, I do.'

'Projectile vomiting,' said Frieda. 'Without warning.'

'Yes.'

'And oysters feed on human sewage. And the norovirus isn't treatable.'

'But it doesn't kill you,' said Sandy, putting his menu down. 'And there's an *r* in the month, and we're just a few miles from the sea, and this is oysters we're talking about. So I'm having oysters, followed by the fish of the day, whatever it is, whatever it's eaten. What are you having?'

Frieda ordered two starters and a green salad. Sandy poured them both white wine. The oysters and Frieda's scallops with bacon arrived, and after a few minutes, Sandy looked down at his six empty shells. 'They didn't taste of norovirus at all,' he said.

'We'll see,' said Frieda.

'So what was it like, walking into Braxton? Did you recognize every tree?'

Frieda shook her head. 'It wasn't like that at all. When you left me and I started walking it felt like I was going into a completely strange town. They've built a new industrial estate and a petrol station and what looks like a giant housing estate. It could have been anywhere.'

'It sounds as if they were trampling on your memories.'

'I don't mind having my memories trampled on,' said Frieda. 'I've done quite a bit of trampling and stamping on them myself.'

The fish arrived and Sandy started on it while Frieda ate her risotto. He gestured around the room with his fork. 'Are these your people?' he said, in a subdued tone. 'Can you tell me all about them?'

Frieda glanced around. 'They're too young,' she said. 'Most of them were children when I left. Anyway, Braxton isn't some tiny village. It's a market town.'

After the meal they drank coffee and went upstairs. It was a little room at the back, overlooking the car park.

'It's not brilliant,' said Sandy, 'but we were lucky to get anything.'

Frieda had a shower and then Sandy had a shower. When he came out of the bathroom, she was lying on the bed, still wrapped in a towel, staring up at the ceiling. She raised her head. 'It looks as if America has been good for you,' she said.

'There was nothing to do there but work and run.'

'Nothing?' She smiled. 'Not in the whole of America?'

He lay down beside her.

'I'm sorry,' Frieda said.

'What about?'

'All of this. We should have been doing this for real – going away for the weekend, me taking you back to where I grew up. That's what proper couples do. Instead, we're here on this . . . well, what is it?'

'Something you need to do,' said Sandy.

Frieda ran her fingers over his shoulder, still smooth and damp from the shower. 'Sex is still allowed, you know.' She leaned forward to kiss him. 'I'm not some damaged, traumatized object that needs to be handled carefully in case it breaks.'

Sandy looked serious, then kissed her and kissed her down her body and took the towel off her. Even when he was inside her, she felt that she was being fierce and longing and he was being careful and kind. Afterwards, they got into bed and lay in the dark and didn't speak. Frieda was jaggedly awake. She could hear wind and rain outside, in waves against the window. There were voices, laughing, car doors opening, engines starting. She could hear the shallow breathing beside her but she couldn't tell whether Sandy was awake, like she was, staring into the darkness.

12

The next morning was cloudy and cold and the gutters were still full of water from the night's rain. Frieda and Sandy walked along the high street to the police station but she found it was no longer there. The solid brick building had been converted into a solicitor's office and a café, and a shop selling flowers and local chocolates. They were all closed. Frieda had to ask three people before she found a man who could tell her where the new police station was. Through the car park next to the bank, turn left, cross the road. A big new building.

'It's probably closed,' said the man. 'It being Sunday.'

It was closed. According to the sign, it was open on Mondays, Wednesdays and Fridays between one p.m. and three p.m.

'I don't believe this,' said Frieda.

'It's reassuring in a way,' said Sandy.

'But what happens if there's a crime?'

The two of them walked round the side and found a uniformed officer sponging the windows of a police car. He was thickly built, breathing heavily with the effort.

'I need to talk to a policeman,' said Frieda.

'Is it urgent?' said the officer.

'What do you mean?'

'Has something serious happened?'

'It's about a crime that happened years ago,' said Frieda. 'But it's important.'

The officer sniffed. 'You'll need to go over to Moreton. They'll help you there. It's a bit of a drive, it's –'

'I know where Moreton is,' said Frieda. 'Is it open?'

'It's open all the time. Twenty-four hours a day.'

'I thought all police stations were open all the time,' said Frieda. 'Like churches.'

'We're lucky to be here at all,' said the officer. 'There's talk of selling this, turning it into a supermarket.'

Sandy looked at Frieda quizzically.

'I suppose now that we're here,' she said. 'If you can bear it.'

'So tell me about Moreton,' said Sandy, once they were in the car and driving out of Braxton on to the bypass.

'It's bigger than Braxton,' said Frieda. 'It's got a market on Saturday. It's got a church that's quite famous. It's got a guildhall. Two women were burned as witches in the market square. That was quite a long time ago.'

'You sound like a guidebook,' said Sandy. 'What part did it play in *your* life?'

'I went to parties there a few times. At one, I sat with a girl I hardly knew called Jane Nichols while she was sick into the toilet. Is that autobiographical enough for you?'

'It's a start.'

They drove past fields and patches of woodland. There were tiny splashes of rain on the windscreen. You could see the spire of the church in Moreton from several miles away, but before they got into the old centre they drove past new housing estates, a hypermarket, stores for pet supplies and furniture, home lighting and frozen food. Sandy pulled up outside the police station. 'This looks more like the real thing,' he said. 'Shall I wait here for you?'

'Go and look at the church,' said Frieda. 'It'll give you an idea of what this area was like before it started to go downhill about four hundred years ago.'

'You sound like an angry teenager.'

'I must be having a flashback,' said Frieda. 'I'll call you when I'm done.'

As Frieda walked up the steps and the glass doors opened automatically to admit her, she really did feel – if only for a moment – that history was repeating itself. What had she felt like all those years ago? It was oddly difficult to remember.

She stood near the front desk. There was a sign asking queuers to stand behind the yellow line and give privacy to the person at the front. The woman at the front wasn't giving herself privacy because she was loudly telling the uniformed WPC behind the desk that her driveway was completely flooded and that the level of the water was a quarter of an inch away from entering her house and destroying it. The WPC tried, rather more quietly, to tell the woman that the flooding wasn't a police matter and that she should try the fire brigade but even they might not be able to do anything. Really, her property was her responsibility, and if there was no serious threat, even the fire brigade were not legally obliged to attend. The officer had to repeat this several times before the woman went away, muttering to herself.

'It's a disgrace,' she said to Frieda, as she passed her.

It took a patient explanation from Frieda and a whispered consultation with a colleague and then, five minutes later, she was sitting in a windowless interview room with a female sergeant. The room seemed also to serve as a cleaner's store space. There was a bucket and mop to the side of the chair Frieda sat in, a vacuum cleaner by the door, two brooms leaning against the wall, and a dustpan and brush on the table next to Frieda's untouched cup of tea; the dustpan had lots of dead flies in it. The officer, a thin woman with short dark hair, picked it up and put it on the floor without comment.

'I want to say that this must have been distressing for you.'

'The question isn't what I feel,' said Frieda. 'The question is what needs to be done.'

'I'll consult with colleagues,' the officer said. 'It's difficult because, this being a Sunday, we're not operating at full capacity. But I understand that there was an inquiry back at the time of the original event in February 1989.'

'February the eleventh. It was a crime, not an event.'

'I didn't mean anything by that. But, from what you say, the inquiry didn't progress and was discontinued. And from what you also say, with this new possible crime, the victim is unwilling to come forward.'

'She's worried that what happened to me will happen to her. She'll mark herself as a victim and then not really be believed. But another important issue is that this man is still out there and still a danger.'

'And this is based on a feeling you have?'

'It's clearly the same man.'

The officer picked up the plastic cup of tea, then remembered it was Frieda's and quickly put it down again. Some of it splashed on to the table.

'Obviously I have no knowledge of the case apart from what you've told me. All I can say is that if the young woman in question comes forward, we will take the case seriously.'

'That doesn't seem possible just at the moment,' said Frieda.

'That's a pity,' said the officer. 'As I said, I will talk to my colleagues, but I can anticipate what they'll say.'

'Which is to do nothing.'

'I don't want to be unsympathetic,' said the officer, 'but I'm not clear what there is to investigate.'

'It would mean going back to the original file,' said Frieda. 'That would be a start.'

'As I said, I'll discuss this issue, this difficult issue, with my superior. But he's not in until tomorrow morning. I'll contact you and let you know what he says.'

'Wouldn't it be better if I talked to him?'

'I don't think that will be necessary. For the present. If you just leave your details at the front desk so we know how we can keep you informed. Also, we can supply you with contact details so that you can obtain help. It can sometimes be very useful in cases like these to have someone you can talk to about it.'

'Can it?' said Frieda.

'Yes. It's sometimes very helpful to get these things out in the open and get advice on how to deal with it.'

'Thank you.' Frieda nodded. 'I'll consider it.'

Sandy was in the car outside. Frieda got in beside him.

'Well?' he said.

'Look at me. Look at me and tell me what you see.'

'I'm tempted to say the face of the woman I love. But I have a sense that might be the wrong thing, just at the moment.'

'I'm an idiot,' said Frieda. 'An idiot. And I don't know what to do.'

'Well.' Sandy spoke after a pause. 'How about going to see your mother?'

13

As if in a dream from which she kept expecting to jerk awake, Frieda walked along the high street. It was a cool, dim day, the low sun a blur. People passed her – a jostling group of teenagers, a woman pushing her small and yapping dog in a buggy, an old man weaving from side to side. She didn't look into their faces: she didn't want to recognize anyone or be recognized, although, of course, that was unlikely. It had been more than two decades. The bakery where she used to buy baguettes was still there, and the shop selling cheap booze and a strange assortment of DVDs. The only change was that it had once been a different strange assortment of videos.

When Frieda was in London, she often had the feeling of walking over the past: layer upon layer of other people's histories under her feet. She had always loved the sense of a great city's buried secrets and the mysterious way they could make themselves felt in fragments of old buildings, in street names, in the hidden rivers that ran under pavements. But in this small town she was walking in her own footsteps. Here, at the bend of the road, her father had come to meet her and taken hold of her small hand in his large, soft, white one; here she had stood at the bus stop with her face in a book. Here a figure had lurked in the shadows and she could feel her teenage heart pounding. She caught her reflection in the window of the newsagent and for an instant thought she saw a fierce young girl, her dark hair in pigtails, but the figure resolved into Dr Frieda Klein, composed and expressionless, walking briskly by.

She turned off the high street, by a tattoo parlour that used to be a second-hand bookshop, into the street where she had first learned to ride a bike. The grass verge was now a pavement; there were street lamps that hadn't been there before, and the phone box where she used to make secret calls was gone. The bus stop had a new shelter. She paused for an instant beside it, frowning at a memory, then letting it go. Down a smaller, narrower lane leading towards the edge of the town, past a tiny ancient chapel squeezed between two timbered houses. A scrawny expanse of newly planted grass – what had been there before? She blinked and saw a sagging wooden building with a rusted iron railing running in front of it. The lane rose steeply, under trees whose branches sent down damp flurries of leaves when the wind blew. The landscape seemed to darken; the air was full of unshed rain.

The cottage where old Mrs Leonard used to live with all her cats and no heating – she had worn strange turbans and stained slippers and would bang a metal dish in the garden, calling them home in a high-pitched croon, but she must be long dead. The mock-Tudor that had belonged to the Clarkes: there used to be old bikes in the garden, and a small trampoline, but now there was a decorative pond and a small weeping willow. Tracey Ashton's little house. It was a different colour now, yellowish, a bit queasy-making. There was a satellite dish on its roof. Frieda looked at the empty windows, then away. There was only room for one reunion.

Here, then, at last: a long, low house that seemed to have settled into the earth. Its walls bulged and its roof sagged. Rich red brick, large windows that were all dark except the one at the side, the porch where her father used to leave his boots. Frieda pushed the gate and went into the front garden. The holly tree was gone. There were large iron pots against the path, but the plants in them had withered into futile stumps. There was a single leather glove lying on the grass; Frieda picked it up and straightened it. Perhaps it was her mother's. Her mother, whom she hadn't seen for more than two decades. Dr Juliet Klein, the GP in a little Suffolk market town, the wife of a man who had hanged himself in the room whose window she could see from where she stood, the mother to a daughter who had run away from home and never returned until this day. Frieda narrowed her eyes: she would be in her late sixties now, presumably retired. Perhaps she didn't even live here any more. She stepped forward and knocked hard on the door that was moss-green now, not red.

How long did she wait? The door swung open. Her mother stood before her; she stood before her mother. There was a silence during which the two women stared at each other.

'Well, well,' said Juliet Klein at last, in her dry, precise voice. She always sounded slightly mocking, a touch ironic.

'Hello,' said Frieda. She realized she didn't know what to call her mother: Juliet? Mum? 'Are you going to invite me in?'

Juliet moved aside and Frieda stepped over the threshold and into the hall, which was warm and smelt slightly stale. The tiles had been replaced with wooden boards, but the grandfather clock was still there, a crack running down its glass face. There were photographs – of David and Ivan and their families; of Juliet as a younger woman; none of Frieda or her father – on the walls. There was an unopened bottle of red wine in the middle of the floor that Juliet walked around as if it were a permanent fixture.

'Is that my glove you're holding?' she asked.

'I found it outside.'

'I wondered where it was.' She smiled. 'What do you think? Do we hug each other and weep?'

'Maybe not.'

'That's probably best. Would you like some coffee?'

'Yes, please.'

'I can't offer you anything else. I wasn't expecting you. No freshly baked cake, I'm afraid.'

They went together into the kitchen. Frieda blinked. Nothing was the same. The old cooker was gone, and the wooden table, the dresser, the rocking chair. Now everything was stainless steel, state-of-the-art, spotlit, bare and gleamingly efficient, like a laboratory for cooking – except Juliet Klein had never liked cooking and wasn't even very interested in food. Through the window, she saw the long garden. No swing, no plum tree, no bird table. Everything seemed straightened and neatened. The long washing line had been replaced with a circular device from which hung several pairs of socks and nothing else.

'This is all new,' she said, feeling her mother's shrewd eyes on her.

'Sorry. Did you want me to keep it the way it was?'

'It was just an observation.'

Frieda looked at her as she made coffee. She was smaller than she remembered, but still very upright, as if standing to attention, and her dark hair was a peppery grey. Her face was pouchy and sallow; her clever brown eyes slightly hooded. She had toothpaste marks around her mouth and was only wearing one earring. The collar of her crisp white shirt was folded in on itself.

'I don't know if you take sugar or milk. Help yourself.'

'Thank you.' They took seats on opposite sides of the metal counter. 'Are you still working?'

'I retired three years ago.' Juliet Klein took a small sip of coffee; a few drops rolled down her chin but she seemed not to notice.

'You're probably wondering why I'm here.'

'You could say so, Frieda. I had made up my mind never to see you again. I certainly wasn't going to come looking for you.'

'I haven't come to rake things over,' said Frieda.

'Why not? You're a therapist, aren't you? Why not rake things over? Isn't that what you do?'

'I wanted to ask you something.'

Juliet Klein folded her arms, then tapped one hand against her shoulder. She made a sudden violent grimace of disgust, as if she'd put something bitter into her mouth. It was an utterly unfamiliar expression, childish and slightly wild.

'Yes?'

'Are you all right?'

'All right? Oh, yes. I'm fine. What do you want to ask?'

'The night that I was raped . . .'

'Oh, not that again.'

'The night that I was raped, I was here. In my bedroom. Do you remember?' Her mother didn't reply, so Frieda continued. 'I was supposed to be going to a concert but I had a row with Lewis. I came home, told you I wasn't going out after all but wanted to be left alone, and then I went upstairs and climbed into bed.'

'It's more than twenty years ago. How would I remember?'

'It's the kind of thing mothers remember.'

'You've suddenly come down from London, burst in here, for what? To say I wasn't a good enough mother?'

'This isn't about you as a mother or me as a daughter. I want to clarify a few things.'

'It's a bit late for that.'

'I've been thinking about that evening, trying to remember it. You were here too. Downstairs. I could hear the TV. Later, I came down and I told you. You remember that?'

'Yes.'

'And you didn't believe me.'

'We had this out twenty years ago.'

'Twenty-three years ago. Someone managed to get into my room without anyone noticing them. You were downstairs. Is there nothing you saw or heard?'

'The police asked me all of this.'

'I know. But now I'm asking you.'

'What are you trying to prove? Is this how you've spent your adult life, storing up grievances against me?'

'It's just a simple question.'

'I have a simple answer. I don't know. I didn't believe anyone raped you, and the police agreed. I think you were an unhappy, angry teenager and you made up a story that got out of control. That's why you ran away. What I don't understand is why you've come back.'

'You didn't go out at all, or fall asleep?'

'You always blamed me for Jacob's death. Is that what this is about?'

'No.' Frieda thought, but didn't say, that in fact she'd always blamed herself.

'And for recovering from it.'

'Did you recover?'

'Oh, for God's sake. I'm not your patient.'

'I think it was someone I knew.'

'What are you talking about?'

'The rapist. I think I must have known him. It wasn't just opportunistic. It couldn't have been. He knew where I was. He knew this house.'

Frieda looked at her mother's grey, weary face.

'Sometimes you just have to get on with life. That's what I've been doing.' She looked at her watch. 'I'm going out in a few minutes. With my bat group.'

'Bat group?'

'We look at bats. It's like birdwatching. But with bats.'

'I'll be gone by then. There's someone else I need to go and see.'

'Are you married?' Juliet asked abruptly.

'No.'

'No children?'

'No. Can I look at my old room?'

'It's my study now. You know the way.'

It had been twenty-three years. Not a trace of Frieda remained. Just a long narrow room, whose window overlooked the garden. There was a flat roof underneath; perhaps someone could have used that. Or walked in through the door and up the stairs while her mother sat watching television. Standing by her bed. Looking down at her while she slept. She frowned and ran a finger along the windowsill, collecting a thick ridge of dust. The study didn't feel used: it was too neat and the computer and anglepoise lamp were unplugged. On the desk there was a large pile of letters addressed to her mother, some handwritten, others utility bills. None had been opened. Frieda leafed through them, looking at the postage dates. They went back over six months.

She went downstairs. Her mother was in the hall, tying a scarf over her hair, fumbling clumsily with the knot, a puckered look on her face. She glanced at Frieda and her eyes seemed to flicker.

'How are you feeling?' Frieda asked.

'It's a bit late to start sharing feelings.'

'That's not what I meant.'

'I am a doctor,' said Juliet. 'I don't need to talk to another. If you count as a doctor.'

'Doctors make the worst patients,' said Frieda.

'Have you got what you came for?'

'Not really.'

'You know what you can't stand? You want to think you're like your beloved father, but really you're like me.'

14

When Becky opened her front door she gave a look of surprise that was almost comical.

'Have you come all the way here to check up on me?' she said.

'I come from here, remember?' said Frieda.

'But I thought you hated this area with a passion.'

'I'm just visiting. I'm showing a friend where I grew up. And while I was here I wanted to see how you were. I really expected to see your mother. I thought you'd be out with friends.'

'What you mean is that I *should* be out with friends.'

'I just wanted to say hello.'

Becky thought for a moment. 'Shall I make you a cup of tea or coffee?'

Frieda smiled and shook her head. 'I'll be five minutes and then I'll go.'

Becky led Frieda through the tiled hallway to a rustic kitchen with copper pans hanging from a rail above an Aga. 'Let's go into the garden,' she said. 'It feels easier to talk out there.'

At the back of the old Georgian terraced house there was a large walled garden, and behind the far wall, a wood rose away so that the house felt overshadowed. The beds were raked, the bushes pruned, everything stripped down and bare for the winter. Becky gestured vaguely around. 'If Mum was here, she'd tell you what all these bushes and trees are. She finds that sort of stuff interesting.'

Frieda looked at her. The girl was still pale, dark around the eyes, but there was more of a spark about her. 'How are you feeling?' she asked.

For the first time, Becky looked her full in the face. 'It sounds strange, but I'm a bit better.'

'I was going to say that you looked better. Except that I find it can be irritating when people say it to me.'

'Why would they say it to you?' said Becky.

'We all go through difficult times.'

'And why does it irritate you?'

'You're good at asking questions.'

'And you're really good at avoiding answering them.'

'You're right,' Frieda said. 'I think it's irritating when people pretend to know more about how you're feeling than you do yourself. And sometimes when people tell you that you're looking fine it's because they're not looking hard enough.'

'Well, I'm not fine, but I'm better than I was.'

'The fact that you can even say that is encouraging.'

'And there's one thing more. Well, two things. Even though I'm feeling a bit better, I'm going to talk to someone about this.'

'That's good.'

Now Becky paused, pushing her hands into the pockets of her jeans. Suddenly she looked hunched up, as if she were protecting herself against something. When she spoke it was in little more than a murmur. Frieda had to lean forward to make out what she was saying.

'I've been thinking of going to the police. What do you think about that?'

'Have you told your mother?'

'Yes.'

'What did she say?'

Becky pulled a face. 'She didn't seem to like the idea. But I want to know what *you* think.'

Now it was Frieda's turn to hesitate. 'I don't like giving advice.'

'I thought that was what you did for a living.'

'No. I try to help people be clearer about what they want. Look, Becky, I'm not going to lie. If you go to the police, things won't be easy. It's too late for any physical evidence. I'm not sure how much they'll be able to do. But the fact you're thinking of doing that is a positive sign. It shows you're taking control.'

Suddenly Becky gave a shiver, as if a cloud had covered the sun. Looking at her, Frieda almost felt cold herself.

'Taking control?' Becky said. 'That's the problem. I keep getting these thoughts, of him and me. I don't even want to say the words. You can't imagine what it's like.'

Frieda looked hard at Becky and thought, Would it be of any possible help to her to say, 'Yes, I can imagine what it's like'? No, she decided. It wouldn't be right. But it made it even clearer why Becky would have to find someone else to talk to about this.

'I'm proud of you,' Frieda said. 'Remember that you've got my number. You can ring me any time, if there's a problem. But let me know how things are with you.'

The two of them walked back into the house and Frieda heard the front door closing, a clink of bags and a bunch of keys being put down. Maddie came into the kitchen and saw her. She was still wearing her fawn overcoat. Her expression changed to surprise, then from surprise to anger. 'What are you doing here?' she said.

'I was in the area,' said Frieda. 'I dropped in to see how Becky was.'

'What are you playing at?'

'Mum –' Becky began.

'Leave this to me.' She jabbed her finger towards Frieda. 'I don't know what you've been saying to my daughter and I don't want to know. But I came to you for help and all you've done is fill her head with strange ideas and, frankly, stir up her hysteria rather than cure it.'

'I wasn't here to tell Becky anything,' said Frieda.

'Really?' said Maddie, her voice becoming louder. 'You just happened to pop by? I come and see you and ask you for help and you tell me that you haven't been home for twenty years. And the next time I see you, you're in my kitchen. What a coincidence.'

'I'm sorry you feel that,' said Frieda. 'I was just leaving.'

'Don't let me stop you.'

Frieda nodded a goodbye to Becky and walked out of the kitchen towards the front door. Maddie was behind her, still talking, and Frieda felt as if she was being washed out of the house by a strong current. As she stepped back out on to the pavement, she heard the front door slam behind her.

She had arranged to meet Sandy in the large old church that was in a square behind the high street. He had found a little local guidebook in a newsagent's. 'It's got a very old font,' he'd said. 'Thirteenth century. And a famous rood screen. Whatever that is.'

Frieda walked back towards the church, replaying the scene with Maddie in her head. She thought of Maddie as she had seen her in London – pleading, affectionate – and the angry woman she'd just left. She was so distracted by these thoughts that when someone spoke to her she didn't respond at first. But then she heard the voice again, saying her name. She looked around. A woman was standing beside her. She was in her late thirties, with pale freckled skin and striking red hair tied up in a messy bun. She was dressed in a long brown skirt, slightly ripped at the hem, sturdy walking boots and a large scarf draped around her like a blanket.

'Aren't you Frieda?' the woman said again. 'Frieda Klein?'

Frieda nodded but couldn't think of what to say.

'My God. Frieda! I can't believe you're here. Have I changed that much? I'm Eva. Eva Hubbard.'

And then Frieda looked at the woman: the wrinkles smoothed from around her eyes and mouth, her figure became slighter, her red hair shorter and spikier, and then she recognized her old school friend. Eva stepped forward, threw her arms around Frieda and hugged her.

'I can't believe this,' said Eva. 'For years I thought you'd vanished off the face of the Earth completely. And then I read some things in the paper about you, really amazing things.'

Frieda thought about those things: violent deaths, accusations of professional incompetence, kidnappings. 'You shouldn't really pay attention to what you read in the newspapers.'

'Even if one tenth of it is true, then it's pretty amazing. What are you doing here? Have you moved back?'

Frieda found it oddly difficult to answer. What, really, was she doing down here? 'I came to see my mother.'

'I thought you'd lost touch.'

'We had.'

'If you're here, why don't you come over to my place? There's so much to catch up on. I could give you dinner.'

'That would have been lovely,' Frieda said, 'but I'm literally just setting off back to London. Some other time.'

'Definitely. I've got a card.' Eva fumbled in her purse and took out a card that she handed to Frieda.

Frieda looked down at it. EVA HUBBARD. FIFTY SHADES OF GLAZE. POTS AND POTTERY CLASSES. 'You're a potter,' said Frieda.

'For my sins. But the next time you come down, you must absolutely come and see me. Promise?'

'Yes, I promise.'

'Lewis,' said Eva.

'What?'

'I remember you and Lewis.'

'I've got to go.'

When she met Sandy he was standing outside one of the church doors, looking up at a relief sculpture of a sheep over the archway.

'I like this,' he said. 'To be honest, I'm not sure why the rood screen was so famous. But this sheep I like. I've read about it in the guidebook. It's not so much the Lamb of God. It's the wool from the sheep that earned the money to pay for the church. But enough of that. How did it go?'

'We can talk in the car. I'm done here. But I need your help.'

15

Frieda was relieved to be back in London, with tar-mac and not mud underfoot, in a city where it was never dark and never quiet. But she wasn't there for long. On Monday morning she rose early, had break-fast at the café her friends ran, Number 9, and walked to her consulting rooms. She saw two patients. The first was a middle-aged woman called Sarah-Jane whose youngest son had jumped off a tall building nine months ago; she no longer wanted to be alive but she had two other children so felt she had no right to die, or even to want to die. The other was a violently sarcastic young man who had recently been referred to her. After he left, even the air felt bruised.

Frieda drank a tall glass of water, then checked her messages. There was one from Sandy: 'Hi, Frieda. Bobbie Coleman is free tomorrow at a quarter past eleven. Let me know if that's fine.'

'She sounds perfect,' Frieda said, when she called him. 'I'll cancel my patients and go down there.'

There was also an email from Becky, saying that Maddie had been very angry after Frieda had left, but that she was still intending to go to the police; she just needed a few days to pluck up courage. And she asked

Frieda for advice about a therapist she could see.

Frieda wrote back to her at once. She gave Becky three names, two women and a man (although she said a woman might be easier to talk to about rape), and their phone numbers. 'Mention me,' she wrote, 'and tell them that I'm very happy to talk to them about your situation if that would be helpful. Remember, Becky,' she went on, 'you mustn't see someone you would feel awkward with or don't take to. It's very important to be able to say no if necessary. These three people are good, but they might not be good for you. Call me if you need more advice, and do please let me know how things go.'

Then she rearranged her three patients of the following day and called her mother, telling her she was going to visit her in the morning, at about ten. A voice in her head told her that she was treating her mother like a child, trying to control her. She agreed with the voice, but ignored it.

She had two more patients that afternoon, then a longed-for evening at home. She had told Sandy she needed to be alone and, indeed, when she closed the door of her little house and stood in silence, the cat at her ankles purring, she felt a relief so strong it was as if a heavy weight had been lifted from her shoulders. She closed the shutters, lit the fire, boiled a kettle for tea, sat in her armchair by the flames with a book, loving the patter of rain outside and the warmth and comfort within.

*

Maddie Capel let herself back into her house, slightly tipsy and fumbling with the key. It was after midnight and she'd been away since the early morning, visiting a friend in Norwich. They had been on a shopping spree, then had a meal in a little French restaurant and drunk rather too much wine, flirted with the waiter and talked about errant husbands and difficult children. At first Maddie had been a bit anxious about going. She didn't know if she ought to leave Becky alone. But her friend had been insistent that she needed a break, and Becky hadn't seemed to mind. They had argued about her intention to report the rape to the police, and then about Frieda, and Becky had seemed almost relieved to get her mother out of the house. Maddie had to admit that she felt better, in spite of her headache. It was good to escape sometimes; necessary.

She left her bags of shopping in the hall. She would put them away before Becky got up in the morning. She didn't want her daughter to see everything she'd bought: the red shoes and the skirt that was probably too short for her, but who cared?; the cloche hat she'd fallen in love with in the shop but knew now that she would probably never wear.

There was a faint, unfamiliar smell lingering in the air. In the kitchen she saw from the empty dishwasher that Becky probably hadn't eaten anything. But, then, she wouldn't have eaten anything if Maddie had been there, trying to persuade her. Her daughter was a stubborn young woman. Stubborn and angry and wretched. Her friend had reassured her that it would pass. 'They don't understand what they put us through,' she had said.

The smell was slightly stronger as she went up the stairs. Becky's bedroom door was shut and the house was very quiet, just the drip of a tap coming from the bathroom. Maddie wasn't sure why she pushed at the closed door. It swung open with a small creak, then stopped against something. She put her head around the door and for a moment stood gazing into her daughter's room. She saw the soft toys heaped up on the windowsill, she saw the postcards pinned on the board and the bookshelves and the schoolbooks. And her daughter hanging from the beam, as thin and slack and dead as a person can be. One of her shoes had fallen off. Her eyes were open.

Maddie screamed. She crumpled to the floor, still screaming, hiding her face from the terror above her. She screamed until a neighbour who had a spare key woke with the noise and let herself in to see what the trouble was. Still she went on screaming, until her voice was hoarse, and until the blue lights and sirens came down the street.

The following morning, Frieda was up very early and at Liverpool Street station in time for the eight o'clock train, going east against the thick flow of London-bound commuters. She got a cab from the station in Braxton and well before ten was once more knocking on the door of her mother's house.

'Well, well,' said her mother. 'I should probably say something about buses.'

'I'm sorry?'

'You know – you wait for twenty-three years and two come at once. Except, of course, you're not two buses, you're one.'

'Could I have some coffee?'

'As long as you don't ask me any more questions about what happened here on a night too long ago to remember.'

'I won't.'

The wine bottle was still in the centre of the hall. The kitchen still gleamed. It looked as if nothing had been moved or touched since Frieda's visit on Sunday. Juliet Klein made coffee in silence. Outside, the day was grey and damp.

'So,' she said, putting a mug in front of Frieda. 'Why have you come back? Did you suddenly realize how much you've been missing me?'

'I've booked a cab to come and pick us up here at half past ten. You've got a hospital appointment at eleven fifteen.'

'No, I haven't.'

'With Professor Roberta Coleman. She's organized a brain scan for you.'

'I beg your pardon?'

'I think it's necessary.'

'Is this some kind of joke?'

'No.'

'Good, because it's not making me laugh. You've come here to take me to hospital because you think there's something wrong with my brain?'

'Sometimes changes of behaviour are easier for an outsider to notice.'

'Is this some kind of psychological revenge? Because if so . . .'

'It's just a precaution,' said Frieda.

'When your patients come to you saying they're unhappy, do you send them off for physical examinations?'

'If they need it. Are you unhappy?'

'I wish you'd never come back. David was right. I was better off without you.' She glared at Frieda, her mouth a tight, straight line. 'So, what are these changes in my behaviour?' she asked.

'They sound insignificant.'

'Remember, I was a GP for nearly forty years. You can't patronize me with your medical knowledge.'

'You drink out of the corner of your mouth. You make sudden facial expressions that I don't believe you're aware of.'

'That's it?'

'I noticed that you haven't opened your mail for several months.'

'Detective Klein. That falls into a different category.'

'Yes, you're right.'

'It probably makes you think I'm depressed – while

133

my tea-drinking and face-making makes you wonder if I have a brain tumour.'

'It's worth checking.'

She put her coffee down on the side. 'I don't think I want to drink this in front of you. You'll be scrutinizing the way my mouth works, or doesn't.'

'Will you come to the hospital?'

'Why not? A nice morning out with my daughter.'

It was hard for Frieda not to respond ironically to her mother's incessant irony.

'Good,' was all that she said. 'You should take off anything metal. That way you'll probably be allowed to stay in your own clothes. I've brought some earplugs with me. It gets noisy in the MRI machine.'

'Thank you, Doctor.' The tone was brittle but, just for a moment, Juliet Klein looked anxious.

'The cab will be here any minute.'

Frieda sat in the waiting room and read her book until her mother returned from her scan.

'All right?' she asked.

'Slightly unnerving,' her mother replied.

'When will you get the results?'

'They'll send them to my doctor in a day or two.'

'That's quick. You'll let me know?'

Juliet Klein tipped her head to one side and regarded her daughter. 'Perhaps,' she said. 'But you can go home now.'

'Really?'

'Yes. I think I'll do some shopping since I'm here. No need for you to hang around. I'm not dying yet.'

They looked at each other. Frieda nodded and lifted her hand in farewell, then walked from the room.

While she waited for a taxi to take her to the station, she turned on her mobile. She hadn't checked her messages since yesterday afternoon. Two texts pinged on to the screen. The first was from Becky, sent the evening before in acknowledgement of Frieda's email of the previous day. *Thanks!* it said, and there was a smiley face beside the word. The second was from Maddie, sent two hours ago. Frieda opened it.

See what you've done. I hope you're satisfied.

The air chilled around her. She stood quite still for a moment, frowning, and was about to call Maddie when she changed her mind. Instead she went to Google and entered Becky's name, staring fixedly at the screen until the words appeared.

Even before she clicked on the story, she knew it was bad. 'Teenage Girl Found Dead At Her Home,' she read. The full story appeared, by a local reporter. She scrolled down, taking in the bare facts: Rebecca Capel, aged fifteen, had been found dead at her home in the early hours of the morning by her mother, Mrs Madeleine Capel. There were no suspicious circumstances; Detective Craigie confirmed that the police were not looking for anyone else. The family were devastated by the tragedy. The head of Becky's school,

Briony Loftus, said she had been a bright, popular and talented student whom everyone would miss.

A taxi arrived and Frieda climbed into it. 'To the police station,' she said.

'The one on Wolsey Road?'

'If that's the main one, yes.'

Detective Inspector Craigie was in her early thirties, thin and strong, with dark curly hair pulled into a tight knot at the back of her head and heavy dark brows that gave her a forbidding look.

'How can I help you?' she asked.

'You're in charge of Rebecca Capel's case?'

'Yes.'

'I'm Dr Frieda Klein. I have information about her death.'

'Well.' DI Craigie raised her eyebrows. 'There will be an inquest, of course, but I'm not sure how you can help in what is a very tragic death. The case is closed.'

'The case needs to be reopened.'

Craigie looked at her for several seconds. 'Very well. I'll find a room for us and you can tell me what's bothering you.'

But there wasn't a room available. They were in the process of redecorating, she explained. So in the end she led Frieda outside, into an unexpected patch of green at the back of the station. It was in need of tending. There were thick brambles along the wall.

'It's where people come to have a cigarette,' Craigie explained. 'Have a seat.' She gestured at the shabby wooden bench.

But Frieda remained standing and so did the detective.

'Becky didn't kill herself.'

'It's difficult when a young person chooses to take their own life. Hard to come to terms with.'

'Becky did not take her own life.'

'Becky's mother mentioned you, Dr Klein.'

'I saw Becky as a therapist, but Maddie's probably told you that. She must also have told you that Becky had been raped and that she was very distressed.'

'Mrs Capel expressed some doubt about that. But there was no doubt about her fragile emotional state.'

'There is no doubt about the rape.'

'But she didn't report it?'

'She was going to.'

Craigie looked dubious. 'What makes you think there was anything suspicious about her death?'

'I spoke to her on Sunday and she seemed better.'

'That's not her mother's opinion. But go on.'

'She told me she had decided to go to the police to report her rape, and that she had also decided to see a therapist on a proper basis. She asked me to recommend someone, which I did, yesterday.'

'And?'

'Both those decisions are dynamic, assertive, forward-looking. They are not the decisions of a girl who is suicidal.'

'I'm sure you understand things like this better than I do. But, from what I've been told, Becky was very upset by her parents' divorce. She was anorexic, she was self-harming, she had got into trouble at school, she was truanting. Her mother says that she suspects she was using drugs. She claims to have been raped.' She held up her hands to ward off any protest. 'I'm not saying she wasn't. I'm simply stating the facts as I know them. According to her mother, she was vulnerable and hysterical.'

'That's not true. Becky wasn't hysterical. She was remarkably resilient.'

'Your impressions aren't evidence.'

'How did she do it?' asked Frieda, thinking of the thin, anguished girl, who had sat in her room and wept so bitterly.

'I can't tell you that. There's going to be an inquest.'

'She sent me a text yesterday evening. Look.' Frieda pulled out her phone.

'It's very common, as you must know, for people to feel guilty or in denial when someone they know kills themselves.'

'That is *not* what this is about.'

'I'm sure you had good intentions, but Mrs Capel says you encouraged her daughter in her fantasies and wouldn't let her move on from her distress. I know it must be difficult to lose a patient, but there it is.'

16

Frieda went straight to see Karlsson at his house. It seemed the only thing to do. He made a pot of coffee, then didn't get round to pouring it. It gradually got cold, forgotten, while Frieda sat at the table and told him the whole story. When she had finished, there was a long silence.

'I'm sorry,' said Frieda. 'You must feel like you're trapped. I came and told you the story before and now I've told it again. You're probably wondering what I'm expecting of you.'

'I was just trying to see it from the local police's point of view. I can understand why they aren't proceeding. From where they sit, it's far from clear that there ever was a rape committed. On the other hand, there's no doubt that this was a troubled young woman with a history of self-harm.'

'You're just repeating what they said.'

'I'm trying to say that there isn't an obvious way forward from here.'

'I didn't come to ask for your permission.'

At that Karlsson couldn't suppress a smile. 'I don't recall you ever asking for my permission, even when you bloody well ought to have done. So why are you here? Not that you aren't always welcome, of course, but if you're not asking for my permission, what are you asking for?'

'I don't know,' said Frieda. 'When I look back, I feel I've mainly caused you trouble.'

'What you've mainly done is help. There have been occasional hiccups on the way, but they've usually been worse for you than for me.'

'How are relations between you and the commissioner?'

Karlsson shook his head. 'Not good. But they were bad before I met you. It's probably more your area than mine. I think I'm the son he's always been a bit disappointed with.'

'I'm not sure I'd be the right therapist for him. But what I was trying to say is that I don't know what I'm going to do, but I do know that I'll need help. I don't know what kind. I also want to say that I'm not asking you to believe me. And I won't ask you to do anything stupid.'

'I'll be the judge of that.'

'It felt wrong to me even to begin to think about embarking on something like this without telling you.'

'Thank you for that,' said Karlsson. 'Because you haven't always done that. So what are you going to do?'

'I suppose I'll have to go back to Braxton and spend time there. It's the thing I swore to myself I'd never do.'

Karlsson hesitated. What Frieda was saying made him uneasy. 'If you need help, you have only to tell me and I'll see what I can do.' Frieda got up to leave. 'And if you get any crazy ideas, tell me in advance so I can talk you out of them. Or at least come along with you.'

Frieda touched his hand with hers. 'I will,' she said.

The next day, Karlsson had meetings, a case review; he supervised the interview of a witness to a robbery who seemed to remember nothing whatever about what he was supposed to have witnessed. He told old George Lofting that in three months' time he would no longer be a police officer. He called a halt to the refurbishments in the canteen. All the time, somewhere in the back of his mind, he was thinking of what Frieda had told him. It was a little piece of grit in his shoe, an annoying scratchiness he couldn't rid himself of.

Back home, he tried to Skype the children but they were out. He made himself a bowl of pasta and ate it with several glasses of red wine. He was just washing up when there was a knock at the door. He was sure it was Frieda. He was wrong. At first, he didn't recognize the tall, rangy, middle-aged man in the dark suit, the white open-necked shirt.

'Sandy,' said Karlsson. It was almost a question. 'Is Frieda with you?'

Sandy didn't return Karlsson's smile. 'She doesn't know I'm here,' he said.

'Is something wrong?'

'Can I come in?'

Karlsson led Sandy through to the kitchen. He was glad he'd cleared up, so it didn't look too much like the symptom of a tired middle-aged man missing his children. He picked up his glass of wine. 'There's more in the bottle, if you'd like.'

'I'm fine,' said Sandy.

'I can make tea or coffee.'

'I'll just be a minute.'

'I'm guessing this must be something important.'

'Frieda came to see you yesterday.'

'That's right.'

'She wanted your advice.'

'Not exactly advice.'

'What did you tell her?'

Karlsson took a sip of his wine. 'Can we go through to the living room and sit down?' he said. 'This feels a bit strange, like we're standing waiting for a lift to arrive.'

'All right.'

When they were sitting opposite each other, Karlsson on a wooden chair, Sandy perched at the end of the sofa, Karlsson felt even more awkward.

'Look,' he began, 'I don't like talking about Frieda behind her back.' He looked down into his drink. 'It's no good keeping secrets from her. She'll find out.'

'But you know about all that's happened?'

'Yes.'

'I came back because of it. And I went down with her to Braxton.'

'That was the right thing to do.'

'I wasn't asking for a compliment. What I mean is that I'm worried about the situation.'

'In what way?'

Sandy made a gesture as if he were trying to conjure up the explanation. 'Frieda had this trauma in her past. She hadn't told me about it. From what I understand, she hadn't even told her own therapist. And now all this has happened, the tragedy of this girl in Braxton. You know what she's planning?'

'Not exactly.'

'She's going back there to conduct some sort of investigation.' Sandy looked at Karlsson for a response but Karlsson was still staring into his wine glass, as if he had noticed something interesting. 'Even by Frieda's account, it's possible that this girl wasn't actually raped, and it's possible that she did kill herself. I mean, just because the police said it was suicide doesn't mean it's not true.'

At Sandy's sarcasm, Karlsson looked up.

'Even if it did happen,' Sandy continued, 'it must be overwhelmingly probable that it has nothing to do with a crime that happened twenty-odd years ago.'

'I don't know enough about the case,' said Karlsson.

'What I'm really saying is that Frieda has faced up

to this terrible thing that happened to her, she's talked about it, she's told her close friends. I can understand the feelings that have been stirred up but sometimes you have to accept that what has happened has happened. Now she needs to put this terrible thing behind her and move on.'

'What?' said Karlsson.

'I'm sorry. Have I said something strange?'

'This is Frieda we're talking about. And maybe moving on isn't an option.'

'What do you mean?'

'That's something you should discuss with Frieda.'

Sandy looked puzzled and angry. 'You think going down to Braxton in search of whatever it is she's in search of is a good idea?'

'What I think doesn't matter very much.'

'You're a true friend of Frieda's.'

'I'd like to believe so.'

'She trusts and respects you.'

'Oh, please stop,' said Karlsson.

'What I was hoping was that you'd join with me in telling her to abandon this. God knows she's been through some terrible experiences. What she needs now is to get better, get back to her work, to her patients.'

Karlsson shook his head. 'I don't know where to begin. You know Frieda. You love Frieda. You must understand that the best way to get her to do something is to tell her not to do it. The fact is that I never know what Frieda's going to do or why she's going to do it. You and I live in a world of pedantic reasons and black and white. Frieda isn't like that.'

'So you're saying we should trust her instincts, whatever they are?'

'Sometimes with Frieda I feel like one of those cowboys in a western who's being dragged by a stampeding horse. You just hope the horse knows where it's going.'

'I don't get it,' said Sandy. 'You're saying you believe her on this.'

'I'm saying it doesn't matter.'

Sandy glanced around him. 'When you suggested a walk, I was thinking more of a park or along the canal.'

'Don't you like it?' said Frieda.

Sandy looked doubtfully at the semi-industrial buildings, the shoddy office blocks. At first he couldn't speak because they had to step back as a large lorry reversed its way out of the small street. It was starting to rain, slowly but steadily.

'This is Shoreditch,' he said. 'And not even the nice bit of Shoreditch.'

Frieda's expression changed, as if she were seeing something in the far distance. 'I remember a couple of years ago, we were lying in bed and I told you about a walk we were going to do along a hidden river.'

'That's right. The Tyburn. You described every detail. Down through Hampstead and Regent's Park and under Buckingham Palace to the river. We never did that walk.'

'We're doing this one instead.'

'This is a river?'

'This is my favourite one of all.'

'I would never have thought it,' said Sandy.

'What did you expect? The sound of rushing water?'

'Maybe some sort of valley, the shape of the old riverbank.'

'This river disappeared too long ago for anything like that.'

'What's it called?'

'The Walbrook.'

'Never heard of it.'

'Nobody has,' said Frieda. 'But it's there somewhere, about thirty feet down, still trying to get to the Thames. This way.'

They walked a few yards and crossed a busy road.

'Holywell Lane,' said Frieda. 'It's like a little whisper of memory that there's water somewhere underneath. So, you talked to Karlsson.'

'How did you know?'

'I talked to him and he told me.'

'I was going to tell you.'

'It doesn't matter.'

'I really was going to tell you. I talked to him as a friend of yours.'

Ahead, as they skirted the edge of Liverpool Street station, they could see a vast construction site, with cranes and bulldozers and lorries.

'Shall we have a look?' said Frieda. 'Maybe we can see what they've dug up.'

They made their way towards the edge of the giant pit but a man in a yellow coat intercepted them. 'It's a building site,' he said. 'You can't come here without a hard hat.'

'We just want a quick look,' said Frieda.

'You'll need to go to the site office.'

'It's all right.' They walked towards a small path that led around the site. 'This was built in the eighties and it's already gone. Five hundred years ago, this was all fields and marshes and there was a pit for victims of the plague. Dying people threw themselves into it.'

'And there was a river,' said Sandy.

'Yes, a river running through it.'

They crossed London Wall.

'We're in the old city of London now,' said Frieda. 'The river's gone, but whenever they dig here to build another headquarters for a bank, they find the sort of stuff that you get with rivers – bones from the old tanneries but also temples, statues of gods. Rivers are special. They come from another world.'

'You never step into the same river twice,' said Sandy.

'You don't think I should go back to Braxton,' said Frieda.

'I want us to discuss it.'

'You think I should put it behind me. You think I should move on.'

'You make that sound like a bad thing.'

'Look,' said Frieda, pointing at a street sign. 'Walbrook. We must be on the right track.'

'When was it covered up?'

'Five hundred years ago. People were complaining about the smell a thousand years ago. We're almost at the Thames.'

'It's a short river.'

'It was the main river running through the old city. Even the old Roman city. And now it's gone.'

They walked along the vast brick walls of Cannon Street station and arrived at a set of railings. In front of them was the Thames. There were vast barges tethered close to the bank. It was now raining more heavily and it was cold. They were standing next to a riverside pub. Sandy nodded at it. 'Would you like a coffee?'

Frieda shook her head. 'Follow me,' she said. They walked down some steep steps on to the gravelly bed of the river, exposed at low tide. 'The river is meant to come out of a pipe somewhere here but I've never been able to see it myself.'

'It's funny to think of it still flowing after all these centuries,' said Sandy.

Frieda looked up and down the river, then turned to Sandy and stared at him full in the face. 'When I was a teenager in the town that you don't want me to go back to –'

'I didn't mean –'

'Wait. My first boyfriend, I mean the first boy I ever slept with, was called Jeremy Sutton. We were obsessed with each other. Gradually that madness abated and, after a while, it just went wrong. I don't really know why. We bickered and drifted apart and drifted back together and scratched at each other. We sort of broke up and saw other people. It was my first glimpse of what two people can do to each other.' She paused. 'Well, not quite my first. But I couldn't believe how ugly it was, how shaming.'

'Frieda . . .'

'I swore to myself that whatever else I did I would never again go through that lying and pretence and evasion.'

'And?'

Frieda took Sandy by both hands. 'When you came back to London and when you accompanied me to Braxton, those were good things. I'll always be grateful.'

'Grateful?' His eyebrows rose and his face took on a pinched look.

'Yes.'

He took his hands from her grasp. His mouth curled in the wolfish smile she'd seen him turn on other people but never on her. 'You sound like a fucking chief executive who's letting someone go.'

'I don't mean to. But, Sandy, it's over.'

There was a long pause and still she looked him full in the face.

'I came back from New York. I gave up a prestigious job. I bought a flat near enough to you to be close, far enough away not to crowd you.'

'I know. I didn't ask you to,' she added. 'You chose to come and that was an act of generosity I will never forget.'

'It's because of that, isn't it? It's because you feel beholden.'

'I don't feel beholden.'

'You do, and you can't bear it.'

'No.'

'And because I know things about you that you wish I didn't. Your rape. As soon as you told me, the clock was ticking.'

'It's not that.'

'Yes, it is. Be honest with yourself at least. You owe me that.'

'All right.' Frieda took a deep breath. 'I feel the urgent need to be free and on my own. We have had a very wonderful time together, you and I. But I already feel that our relationship is in the past and we're just trying to rekindle something that is finished.'

'I don't accept it.'

'You have to.'

'You're wrong there. I don't have to. I don't believe you. I don't think you mean it.'

'I mean it.'

'You've done this before, remember?'

'Yes. But this time there's no going back.'

'You want me to take it in a civilized fashion? You've decided and I'm supposed to kiss you on both cheeks and say, "Good luck with the rest of your life."'

'No.'

'I love you.' His voice split. He took her by the shoulders, gripping her. 'And you love me.'

She pushed off his hands and stepped backwards. 'I do love you. But it's over, Sandy.'

'I wanted us to have a child.'

'That's not what I wanted.'

'Is it Karlsson?'

'Don't,' said Frieda, sharply. 'Don't even think of saying something like that. Not to me. Not about us.'

Sandy stared at her. 'That's it? After everything, we just go our separate ways?'

'You can walk up to Bank and catch the Tube. I'm walking home.'

'Frieda, let me come with you. It's raining. It's cold.'

'I know. I'm glad.'

17

There was an angry woman in Frieda's consulting room, who shouted about her father, about her husband, about her children and about Frieda herself, who, she said, was cold, smug, uncaring. And then, after she had left, stalking out into the rain without a coat, there was an angry woman on the phone.

'Congratulations,' she said.

'Who is this?'

'Oh, sorry! I forgot to introduce myself. I'm your mother.'

'Are you all right?'

'Congratulations are in order.'

'What do you mean?'

'You were right. Clever girl.'

'You've heard from your doctor?' Frieda still didn't know what to call Juliet so avoided calling her anything.

'She invited me to the surgery to talk. I should have known. I've done it enough times myself. When it's bad news, it has to be face to face.'

'And?'

'A very grave, concerned face. "Won't you sit down,

Mrs Klein?" She's had too much training in the right bedside manner.'

'What did she say?'

'Apparently I've got a jellyfish in my brain. Or was it an octopus? I forget now. When they do things like this, it's as if they're talking to a six-year-old child and it's all animal stories. It must have been an octopus. Tendrils, you know.'

'You have a brain tumour?'

'Inoperable. Stage three. That's where the tendrils come in. To cut it out they'd have to cut out my brain.'

'I'm sorry.'

'Why? You were right!'

'How long do you have?'

'Good. A nice precise question. But I don't have a precise answer. With patients at my stage, fifty per cent are alive at six months.'

'That sounds quite precise.' Frieda stared out at the building site and the grey November sky. Winter was coming, light closing in. 'Have you told David and Ivan?'

'Not as yet.' Still the tight, jocose tone. She could picture Juliet's furious face. 'I had to tell you first.'

'You should tell them. I'll come and see you soon, in the next couple of days. I'll let you know.'

'You'll come back?' For a moment, there was a tiny wobble in her mother's voice, but she recovered herself. 'It seems like you returned just in time.'

'It's frightening,' said Frieda. Of all things, there was a heron in the wasteland and she watched as it picked its way through the churned-up mud.

'It comes to us all.'

She rang her brother. She thought it was going to be a difficult conversation, but it wasn't. So far as Frieda knew, David had largely lost touch with their mother as well and he responded with nothing more than a mild interest.

'How did our family become like this?' Frieda said.

'I can't believe it. You finally want my opinion about something.'

'You sound just like Juliet.'

'This is great,' said David. 'It reminds me of when we were children.'

'Can you tell Ivan?'

'If you want. Do you think I should tell him to fly over? We can all meet at the bedside. How long does a flight from New Zealand take?'

There was a message on her voicemail from Sandy. She listened to it, then erased it. Her mobile rang and she saw it was her sister-in-law, Olivia. After a few moments' hesitation she decided to answer: it might be some new crisis over Chloë.

'Frieda?' Olivia sounded breathless. 'Are you OK?'

'Yes. Why?'

'I've just heard.'

For a moment Frieda wondered if she knew about Juliet's brain tumour, but decided that was impossible. 'Oh,' she said drily. 'News travels quickly.'

'You should have told me.'

'Why?'

'I wouldn't have known, except Sasha told Reuben and Reuben told Josef, and Josef is here bleeding the radiators.'

'I see.'

'Do you want to talk about it?'

'No.'

'Because if there's anything I can do, you know you have only to say.'

'Right.'

'Sandy was such a gorgeous man, Frieda.'

'He still is. He's not dead.'

'So I can't understand why on earth you would end it.'

'I've got to go, Olivia.'

'It must be such a painful time and –'

Frieda ended the call and turned off the phone.

Frieda had a late lunch of mushroom soup and crusty bread at Number 9, then walked home. The warmth and silence of her house soothed her. Just her and the cat and the open fire. There were still signs of Sandy everywhere – a couple of his shirts in her wardrobe, his toothbrush and razor in her bathroom, a book of essays he had been reading on the arm of the chair by the hearth, his vitamin tablets and the cereal he liked for breakfast in the kitchen – but bit by bit they would disappear.

She sat by the fire with a mug of tea and closed her eyes. She thought about her mother and she thought about Becky. She thought about herself as a teenager. She went over Becky's account of her rape and she let herself remember what had happened to her, so many years ago. She remembered the prickle of fear on her skin, lying in the darkness, and the unfamiliar smell. She remembered the heaviness on her body, the muffled words breathed into her ear, the television downstairs. The pain. She remembered the pain and she remembered that it didn't just hurt between her legs but everywhere, obscenely: her breasts and her stomach and her limbs and her face and her eyes and her head and her heart. She thought again of Becky. Two of them, bound by the same sick terror.

She knew that she and Becky had been raped by the same man. She knew that man had killed Becky. She knew that she was going to track him down.

She took her wallet from the bag by her feet and extracted a card. EVA HUBBARD, FIFTY SHADES OF GLAZE; she dialled the number.

Karlsson came to her house after he had finished work. He loosened his thin red tie and undid the top button of his shirt. Frieda handed him a glass of whisky, with just a dash of water in it, and he lifted it in a silent toast.

'Well?' he said. 'You told me you had a favour to ask.'

'Yes.'

'Go on.'

'I need to see my file.' He didn't look surprised. 'I asked for it, of course, when I was there, and the following day I was called by an officer who told me very politely that I could apply under the Data Protection Act, for a fee, of course. And it could take up to forty days, maybe even longer, and might be turned down under an exemption clause.'

'So you want me to get hold of it for you?'

'Could you?'

'I could try.'

'Thank you.'

'You're going back there?'

'My mother has a brain tumour.'

Karlsson lifted his head and stared at her. 'I thought you never saw your mother.'

'She's dying. I've decided that for two or three days every week, on the days I'm not seeing patients, I'll stay in Braxton.'

'With your mother?'

'No. With an old school friend who's a potter. She has a shed in her garden that she rents out.'

'A shed.'

'A very comfortable shed, with electricity and

running water and a small shower. She thinks I'm going down just to be with my mother.'

'It's all decided, then.'

'I'm going to find out what happened to Becky.'

'And what happened to you?'

'Yes.'

'I'll make some calls tomorrow.'

'Thank you.'

He suddenly seemed uncomfortable, rubbing the side of his face in that way of his, then staring into his whisky. 'Sandy called me.'

'When?'

'Yesterday evening.'

'He shouldn't have done that.'

'He was angry.'

'I'm sorry you were dragged into it.'

'Frieda, is it really over?'

She looked at Karlsson in puzzlement. 'Do you think I would have done this if I wasn't sure?'

'He doesn't think it's over.'

After Karlsson had left, Frieda sat at her desk in her garret study and wrote emails to the patients she saw on Thursday afternoons and Fridays, asking if it would be possible to rearrange their sessions for earlier in the week. She said that she could see them in the evenings if that made it easier. Then she went to her room and packed a bag to take to Eva's. She would go the next day, after her last patient. In Suffolk, the wind sweeps in from the east. She put in warm tops and extra socks and a hot-water bottle, walking boots and a fleecy jacket. She remembered to add a box of the tea she liked, as if they didn't have real shops in Braxton. She put in a tin of soft-leaded pencils and sticks of charcoal, and a sketch pad. Then she considered the cat: was it all right to leave it for two nights, with the food and water topped up? She decided it was. Cats can look after themselves, unlike many people.

18

Eva was in her clay-spattered work clothes when Frieda arrived. There were grey flecks on her cheek and in her hair; there was even a daub on the glasses that hung round her neck on a chain. She hugged Frieda, transferring some of the clay, and led her around the side of the house and through the garden, past the vegetable patch to the shed at the end. She showed Frieda the bed and the towels, how the radiators worked, where the hot water switched on, a drawer and a cupboard that Frieda could use. There were pots lining the shelves, waiting to be fired. There was also a tiny stove and a kettle, but she said that Frieda could use her kitchen whenever she wanted. They could eat meals together, she said. At the same time she told Frieda how lucky it was that the space was free. Until a few weeks ago it had been occupied by a German student – a lovely girl, really gorgeous – but she had met someone and now they had moved in together. It was all a bit quick. Kristina had seemed so young, almost a child. As she said this, she sounded melancholy.

When she had finished and the two of them stepped back outside, Eva looked at Frieda appraisingly. 'I can't believe I'm here with you again,' she said. 'I thought you'd gone for ever.'

'I thought so too,' said Frieda.

Frieda was finding it hard to see Eva clearly – her younger self kept getting in the way. A skinny, tomboyish scamp, with bright red hair that at one point she had cut into tufts and spikes. She'd loved climbing trees, Frieda remembered, and could scramble through branches with amazing agility. She had a sudden flash of recall: Eva's narrow face grinning down at her between green leaves, and a thick worm of blood on her bony knee. Of course, later she'd put on skirts and makeup and entered the teenage world, but even so, something of that unruly girl had remained.

'Do you still climb trees?' she asked.

'You remember. It was fun, wasn't it?'

'I think I stayed on the ground.'

'No, you didn't. You came with me. Surely you came with me.' She frowned. 'Weird what you remember and what you forget,' she said dreamily.

'It is.'

'I don't have kids myself, but I have a niece and she's a tree-climber too – maybe it's in the blood.'

'You used to do headstands as well.'

'I did, didn't I? I haven't done one of those in years. Maybe I'll try later, when I'm wearing trousers. It's very good to see you, Frieda. I missed you, you know. Where did you go?'

'Nowhere very glamorous.'

'We all talked about you for ages. What happened to Frieda? Every so often I thought of trying to get in touch with you but I didn't dare. I don't know why.'

'You should have done. I wasn't so far away.'

'Now you've come back.'

'Yes.'

'It feels like you've come at exactly the right time.' Suddenly her expression changed and her pale skin flushed red. 'I'm sorry, I know it's terrible news about your mother. I didn't mean . . .'

'That's all right. It's good to see you. But what do you mean about me coming at the right time?'

'Did nobody contact you about the high-school reunion?'

'What sort of reunion?'

'It's an anniversary. The eightieth or something like that. It's in a couple of weeks' time, maybe three. There was one about ten years ago,' said Eva. 'It was a bit strange. I remember wondering if you were going to be there. I kept thinking I'd see your face.'

'Nobody had my address.'

'I bet you wouldn't have come.'

'I'm not sure I'll go to *this* one.'

'Why wouldn't you want to see what's happened to people you were at school with?'

'I suppose because they're a group of people I didn't care enough about to stay in touch with.'

Eva pulled a hurt face. 'That's telling me.'

'I didn't mean you.'

'You did because you didn't stay in touch with me either. But they're a part of your past,' said Eva. 'They – *we* – are part of what made you who you are, even though you did run away from us all. Come on inside and let's have some coffee. I'm going to convince you that reunions are a good idea.'

'I can't,' said Frieda. 'I've got an appointment.'

'I'm sorry,' Eva said. 'You're suffering this tragedy with your mother and I'm just rabbiting on about things.'

'It's not my mother. I've some unfinished business to deal with.'

'Are you up to something mysterious?' Eva sounded jovial, but Frieda shot her a look. Her tone changed and she said that she needed to get on with her work but that maybe she'd see Frieda later. As she talked, she was tying her hair back more firmly, rolling up her sleeves. A purposeful expression came over her face. Frieda thought about how people are different at work: this was an Eva she had never suspected, no longer vague and flyaway but expert and sure of herself, mistress of her own world.

The young officer behind the front desk at Braxton police station had difficulty understanding what Frieda wanted, and when Frieda explained again, she didn't seem to believe it. In the end she had to fetch a sergeant and the sergeant had to go away to make a phone call while Frieda sat on a bench by the front door. When the sergeant returned, he still seemed suspicious but he buzzed her through the re-inforced door. He was a heavy-set, florid-faced man, who didn't look as if he'd be much use in a chase, and he seemed discontented.

'You'll need to leave your phone at the desk.'

'Why?'

'Security.'

Frieda took it from her pocket and placed it on the desk. The sergeant led her along a corridor and into an office. There were two desks, phones, a wall of box files. A safety leaflet and several picture postcards were pinned on a corkboard. There was a large window but it only looked out on a yard with a high wall at the end.

'Apparently you've got a friend,' said the sergeant.

'He's a detective. Can I take the file away?'

'There's more than one and, no, you can't. You can sit here.' He steered her towards the desk by the window. Frieda sat down and he brought a small pile of faded blue cardboard files, three of them, and placed them in front of her.

'This is about you, isn't it?'

'That's right.'

'What do you want to go through it all again for? It's a long time ago.'

'It doesn't feel like that.'

She took a pen from her pocket.

'You're not allowed to take notes,' said the sergeant, removing it from her.

'What?' said Frieda.

'No notes or recording devices.'

'Is that a real rule or a made-up one?'

'If you have a problem with this, we can stop now and you can make a query. In writing.'

'What's your name?'

'Are you thinking of making a complaint? Breedon. B-R-E-E –'

'There's no need to spell it out. I don't have a pen.'

'Just so you'll remember it. And I'll stay here while you're doing what you need to do.' He looked at his watch. 'We'll have to be done in half an hour.'

Frieda opened the first file. She saw a typed page, the paper so thin that the page beneath showed through. At the top was a date: 15 February 1989. And she saw a name: Frieda Klein. She stopped for a moment, almost dizzy at the thought of it. Her name and, below her name, her words. They had been on this paper and the paper had been in the file and the file had been in a cabinet or on a shelf somewhere for all these years. She looked up. Sergeant Breedon was seated at the other desk. He was staring at her.

'Could I get a glass of water?' she said.

'I can't leave you alone with the file. I can accompany you to the bathroom.'

'Forget about it.'

She returned to the typed statement and started to read, running her forefinger down the right margin.

*

Exactly half an hour later Frieda came down the steps of the police station and walked briskly along the pavement, almost breaking into a run. With what she had in her head, she felt as if she was holding her breath and that, if she was careless, everything she had read and seen in the file would be lost. It would be like those mornings when she woke from a vivid dream and could almost see the dream flowing away, being irretrievably lost and forgotten. She needed somewhere to sit.

On the high street she passed a dentist's, a kitchen-ware shop, a fish-and-chip shop, then found what she was looking for. There was a gallery that doubled as a coffee shop. She walked inside and sat as far away from the front window as she could, at a tiny table. She opened her notebook and began writing. She started with the names, the hooks that the memories would hang on: me, Jeremy, Lewis, Ewan, Chas. Then there was Dennis Freeman, the loner who had died in prison and whom she had assumed until a few days ago was the man who had raped her. And another one. Carrey. Michael Carrey.

'Yes?'

Frieda looked up. A woman was standing in front of her: mustard-yellow sweater, short dark hair, early thirties. 'Sorry?'

'What can I get you?'

Oh, yes. This was a café. 'Coffee. No milk.'

'Pastries? Carrot cake? Bakewell tart?'

'Just coffee. Thank you.'

Frieda went back to her list and began to fill in the memories, starting with herself. She turned to a new page and wrote 'Me' at the top. What she mainly remembered from the transcript were not her answers but the officer's questions. As she wrote them down, it brought the scene back to her, almost as if she were there again. Two male officers. They had seemed old to her, but were probably no more than forty. They had sat too close. One of them had done almost all the talking, as if he were in charge. Detective Tom Helmsley, it had said on the file. She hadn't known his name was Tom but she certainly remembered him. Tall and bulky, with thick blond hair that he pulled at, and a round, doughy face, slightly sweaty. He dabbed at it occasionally with a handkerchief and didn't look directly at her. Occasionally he had smirked, and now she thought that perhaps he had been embarrassed, although at the time she had seen him as indifferent to her and almost amused.

Did you resist? What did he do? Were you naked? Did he ejaculate? Why didn't you scream? Why didn't you report it straight away? Were you a virgin? Do you have a boyfriend? Had they had a row? Where was he? Why wasn't she there?

They were at the concert. They all were. Except for her.

Reading through the statement, she had seen herself through their eyes: resistant, troubled, broken home, dead father. Sexually active.

And then there was her mother's statement. Frieda jotted down the phrases 'going through a bad patch', 'highly strung', 'confrontational when challenged', 'vivid imagination', 'self-dramatizing'.

'Here's your coffee.' The woman placed a mug on the table in front of Frieda. 'Getting some work done?'

'Just a few notes.'

'Are you a writer?'

'No.'

'Have you been looking at our pictures?'

Frieda glanced around at some blurry, smudgy seascapes, trees, clouds and then some brightly abstract designs, like Turkish carpets fashioned in neon.

'They're all local artists,' the woman said. 'Are you here for a break?'

'I'm sorry,' said Frieda, gesturing at her notebook. 'Could you give me a minute?'

The woman's face fell and she withdrew. Frieda returned to her notes. She started with the two names of people she hadn't known. Dennis Freeman was the man she had heard of. Michael Carrey was new to her. Frieda assumed that he, like Freeman, had some relevant sexual history. The interviews were short. They'd been asked if they knew Frieda Klein. Neither of them did. Or admitted that they did. They were asked where they had been on the night. Freeman said he had been out drinking. Carrey said he'd spent the evening at home. He'd been ill. Frieda had seen nothing in the file about whether the claims had been checked.

Then there were the boys. They'd all been interviewed although they hadn't been told why. Frieda remembered how afterwards everyone seemed to think there had been an attempted burglary or something like that, and she certainly hadn't said anything to disabuse them. She jotted down phrases she recalled from the statements. It had been a bit like reading her own obituary, discovering what people felt about you, or what they said they felt about you, or what they told the police they felt about you. What would she have thought, aged sixteen, if she had heard Chas Latimer telling a grown-up that, although they were in the same friendship group, he didn't know Frieda Klein that well, that she was 'a bit weird', that she kept herself to herself, that they'd never had any kind of relationship, that, no, he'd never wanted one, she wasn't his type.

As she quickly wrote in the notebook, filling page after page, she had vivid flashes that weren't even like memories. It was as if she were there, the sights and sounds and touches were so vivid: Chas, in a group of people, always at the centre, suddenly catching her eye, giving that collusive smile; Ewan, clumsy but sweet and well-meaning; Jeremy, the smell of his hair, the smooth skin of his chest and back, almost like a child's, but whenever she thought of his face, it wore the expression of dismay and disbelief and anger that it had when she'd broken up with him. When she thought of him, that was what it mainly was: an endless parting. And Lewis, it was the smell of cigarettes: even when she remembered his full, almost swollen lips, it was with a cigarette between them; even his tongue, pink like a kitten's, she thought of it dabbing against the end of the filter.

When she had written everything she could think of, she paused. Her hand ached with the effort. But then she remembered. There was something more. Someone had clearly read through the file, pencil in hand, and marked it the way people did with lines down the margin and even under certain phrases. There had been faded underlinings and question marks. After a bit, Frieda had started to see their point. They had emphasized anything doubtful or problematic, especially about Frieda herself, what people thought of her, how much they trusted her. At the end of her own statement the word 'NO' had been written in large capital letters followed by a dash and the initials 'SF'. Frieda wrote them at the end of her notes and drew a circle around them.

'Can I get you more coffee?'

The woman had reappeared, like an animal that had been scared away but was now edging back.

'Yes, please.'

'So, you're not a tourist?'

Frieda looked up at the woman, wondering whether she should recognize her. Was this someone she had been at school with? Or the sister of someone she had been at school with? 'I grew up here. But now I'm a tourist.'

19

Before going back to Eva's shed, Frieda went shopping in the supermarket that stood where the swimming pool used to be. For herself, she bought ground coffee, milk, bread, butter, marmalade and six eggs. For her mother, she bought a bunch of dahlias, a packet of ginger snaps, some runny cheese (always a favourite of Juliet Klein's), with crackers to accompany it, and two bottles of red wine.

The front door to her mother's house was unlocked, and after she had rung the bell and got no reply, she opened it and went in, intending to leave the shopping in the hall. But she heard a noise coming from the living room: the television was on. Frieda put her head round the door. On the plasma screen a chef – whose face was vaguely familiar – was making something with noodles. They were heaped on a plate, looking like a nest of worms. Juliet was sitting on the sofa, her stockinged feet up on a small stool, her head tipped back and her eyes slightly open. She was snoring. One of the buttons of her shirt had come undone so Frieda could see the edge of her bra. A tiny thread of saliva ran down her chin. Frieda watched her for several seconds, frowning. As quietly as she could manage, she put down the shopping and left the house, pulling the door to with a small click. Her mobile vibrated in her pocket and, taking it out, she saw that Sandy was calling. She let it to go to voicemail.

In her shed, she made herself a mug of tea. There was a little table that acted as a desk at the window and she sat at it and took out her notebook. She was looking out over Eva's garden and could see straight into the kitchen. In fact, as she sat there, Eva came into view, running her hands through her hair. She started watering the plants on the windowsill.

Frieda moved the table away from the window. Now all she could see was the wall. She read through her notes and then she made a list:

People to Contact

- Detective Tom Helmsley (ask Karlsson to help?)
- Dennis Freeman (find out who/where he is from TH)
- Michael Carrey (ditto)
- SF: who is he? Ask TH
- Chas Latimer
- Jeremy Sutton
- Vanessa Bussock
- Ewan Shaw

- Lewis Temple
- Head of Braxton High (find out who Becky's closest friends were)

She looked at it, considering. She drew a tree down one side. Another name came to her – a man standing by the whiteboard, his poster-boy face and flashing smile, hair down to his collar. She added his name: Greg Hollesley, history teacher and head of her year in 1989. She added leaves to her tree.

Apart from asking Karlsson to help her track down Tom Helmsley, she had little idea of how to find these people who had once been so important to her. She typed Chas (Charles) Latimer into Google and a stream of names filled her screen: Chas Latimer the actor and Chas Latimer the businessman and Charles Latimer the sculptor and Charles Latimer the dietician, who could help you lose a stone in a fortnight, Charles C. Latimer the yachtsman … None of the photographs seemed right – but what would Chas look like twenty-three years later? Would his smooth face have become jowly, his knowingly charming smile faded into something more sober, his blond hair greying, receding? She stared at the list of names: none of them was uncommon enough to find by a simple search.

A message pinged on to her email from Chloë. Its subject was 'Help!!!!!!!' She opened it. 'Aunty Frieda!' it read. 'I think I have genital warts! What should I do?' Frieda made an exasperated face at the wall. 'Go to your GP or a sexual health clinic,' she wrote. 'They're contagious and very common.'

Then she stood up and went into the garden, where the light was fading into dusk. Eva waved at her from the kitchen, then came out to join her. 'Have you got everything you want?' she asked.

'Yes, thank you. What do you grow?' She gestured at the vegetable patch, bare except for some winter cabbage and a couple of butternut squashes, uprooted but lying on the soil.

'Oh, all sorts. Beetroot, potatoes, broad beans, sugar snaps, artichokes. And chillies in the greenhouse,' she went on enthusiastically. 'I've become a chilli obsessive. Gardening's good for the soul.'

'I can imagine. But isn't pottery as well?'

'And making bread. Whatever else happens, at the end of the day you can say you've made something.'

Frieda looked at Eva. Her hair was loose and slightly wild, the glorious red faded into something more subdued; her freckles, which had been so pronounced when she was a teenager, had become faint splotches on her pale skin. The hem of her long skirt was torn and muddy. 'That offer of dinner,' she said. 'Is it still on?'

A smile illuminated Eva's face. 'I'd love that. There's nothing I like more than cooking for other people. I can't quite believe you're back, Frieda.'

'I know the feeling.'

'Come and knock at the door at seven thirty,' said Eva. 'I'm vegetarian, just so you know what to expect.'

When Frieda arrived at Eva's back door with a bottle of red wine, the kitchen was full of fragrant steam. Eva, wrapped in a white apron, with pink cheeks, greeted her exuberantly – as if somehow this dinner put them on a different, more intimate footing. She'd clearly been busy. There were pans bubbling on the hob, and on the table three different salads, in brightly painted bowls that Frieda assumed Eva had made.

'Carrot and walnut with a spicy Japanese dressing,' she said, pointing. 'Beetroot and celeriac with horse-radish. Green salad.'

'Lovely,' said Frieda, made oddly melancholy at the effort that had gone into the evening.

Hanging from the beams were strings of chillies, evidently grown in Eva's greenhouse. There were jars of home-made preserves and pickles on the shelves. Eva saw her looking around and grimaced. 'It's what I do,' she said. 'I make everything, as if my life depended on it. I make my own pots. I make most of my clothes, as you can probably tell. I cook enough food and grow enough vegetables to feed a large family, except, of course, I don't have a family.'

'Did you want to?'

'Same old Frieda. No nonsense. Yes, I think so. You don't have children, do you?'

'No.'

'Did . . . ?'

'No.'

'Anyway, it's not too late. Let's have some of that wine.'

She uncorked the bottle and poured a generous amount into two glasses. 'To reunions,' she said, raising hers.

'Talking of which, I might just go to the school one, if I'm around.'

'That'll be such fun. Imagine all their faces when you walk through the door.'

'I don't want to. That might stop me going.'

'We'll go together. It's always a bit nerve-racking, arriving on your own.'

'Who do you think will be there?'

'Who knows? The weirdest people turned up at the last one. Actually, I know who knows. Vanessa's one of the organizers.'

'Vanessa? You mean Vanessa Bussock.'

'As was. She married Ewan.'

'Ewan Shaw?'

'Yes.'

'They were going out together, but I had no idea they were married.'

'Well, how would you?'

'Do they live round here?'

'They certainly do. They have a house on the road towards Bybrook. I see them from time to time. She's got all mumsy, he's lost some of his goofiness, though not so much, but otherwise they seem pretty much like they always were.'

'Maybe I'll get in touch.'

'Really? Well, I can give you their details.'

'Who else do you see?'

'There's Maddie, of course.' Her hand flew to her mouth. 'Oh, God, did you hear about Maddie? Her daughter killed herself.'

'I did hear that,' said Frieda.

'Isn't that the most awful, awful thing?'

'Yes.'

'Becky. Apparently she was going through a rough time, but it was so terrible. She wasn't even sixteen. The whole school's in shock. The funeral's next week, I think.'

She poured them more wine, then got up to ladle garlic mushroom soup into green-glazed bowls.

'Who else still lives round here?' asked Frieda.

'There's Lewis. Your boyfriend. After Jeremy, of course.' Her voice became wistful. 'I haven't seen him for ages.'

It felt like Frieda's old memories were being dragged out into the light and trampled on. When she spoke, she had to control her voice. 'Do you know what he does or where he lives?'

'He was an electrician, last time I heard, with a company in Oxley. He's got a small flat on the edge of Braxton near the old barracks, or had. He had a son but doesn't live with the mother.' Eva stirred her bowl of soup, then said suddenly, 'I had a thing with him.'

'With Lewis?'

'After you disappeared.'

'That's all right.'

'I felt awful. I think he did too. It was like we were both cheating on you, even though you had gone without a word.'

'It doesn't matter, Eva.'

'It does. You were my best friend and I slept with your boyfriend.'

'He wasn't my boyfriend by then. We'd split up.'

'It felt like he was. He was besotted with you. He was only with me because he was so angry and upset and confused. You've no idea what he went through but it still doesn't make it right.'

'Twenty-three years ago you had a fling with my ex-boyfriend, after I'd left. It doesn't matter.'

'Every so often I get this flush of shame.'

'What are you ashamed of?'

'It felt like I'd betrayed you. Though, mind you, you betrayed me, too, by going off like that.'

'Maybe that's why you did it.'

'No. It was because I'd always fancied him rotten. Didn't you know?'

Frieda thought back, trying to part the layers of the past to see that time more clearly. 'I don't think so.'

'God, the intensity of the young,' said Eva. She

gave a small laugh but still looked sad. 'Nothing's ever like it again.' She shook her head. 'I haven't seen him for ages. I think he went off the rails.'

'He was already going off the rails when I knew him. Maybe we all were, without knowing it.'

Eva cleared the bowls and put an aubergine and red pepper flan on the table. 'Help yourself,' she said, gesturing. 'And to the salads. I've made too much of everything, as usual.'

Without asking, she topped up their glasses. 'So you're a therapist,' she said.

'Yes.'

'You must hear some strange stories.'

'Strange stories, everyday stories.'

'Do you help?'

'I do my best. I try to help people take control of their own lives, to find their own voices again. That's something.'

'Do you still ride?' Eva asked suddenly.

Frieda was taken aback. She hadn't sat on a horse for twenty-three years, and felt slightly unnerved by being with someone who knew these things about her. She had become used to living among people who had no access to her old self, and now it felt to her as if she had left a front door unlocked, a window wide open. 'No. I don't ride.'

'You used to love it.'

'I live in London now,' Frieda said, as if that was the end of the matter. 'This is delicious, by the way.'

'Good. Chas Latimer.'

'What about him?'

'Vanessa said he might be coming. Wouldn't that be odd?' She gave a giggle, followed by a delicious shiver.

'Very odd,' Frieda said drily.

'I seem to remember you weren't so keen on him.'

'No.'

There were bright stars and a low moon that looked bigger than usual, though Frieda knew that was only an optical illusion, and the wind gusted through the trees. She had forgotten how dark it was in the countryside, and how quiet. She let herself into the shed. There was another message from Sandy on her phone, but again she ignored it. Instead she phoned Karlsson.

'Frieda? How's it going?'

'I think I'm homesick,' she said. 'There are no street lamps and no buses. Can you do me another favour?'

'All right.'

'Before knowing what it is?'

'What is it?'

Frieda told him, and he said that he would find out about Tom Helmsley first thing in the morning.

Then she listened to her messages from Sandy. In the first, he just said her name a few times, interrogatively and leaving pauses between each word as if she could hear him but was refusing to pick up. In the second, he said, 'We have to talk, Frieda.' She could hear the distress in his voice and also the rumble of traffic in the distance, and pictured him standing in some doorway, cold and wretched. She could see his face, grim with grief. 'I love you,' he added, sounding almost angry. 'It can't end like this. Please call.'

She rang but it went to voicemail and she didn't leave a message. What was there to say?

20

'Frieda? My God, it is! Frieda Klein!'

Vanessa – now Shaw, but it was hard not to think of her as Vanessa Bussock, fifth in the school register, which Frieda could still hear, like a kind of jingle, in her head – stood in the doorway, her face and indeed her whole body expressing comic surprise.

'Hello, Vanessa.'

Frieda had got up early that morning – well before the lights in Eva's house had gone on – and, after a mug of coffee, had walked to the Shaws' house, a small cottage with a fraying thatched roof on the edge of town. Eva had told her both of them worked and she wanted to catch them before they left.

'Frieda Klein,' Vanessa repeated, in a wondering tone and then, all of a sudden, pulled Frieda against her squashy body, as if she was her mother, cooing something indistinguishable. She smelt of soap and of baking. At last she left off and took a step back to examine her. 'I never thought I'd see you again. But I would have recognized you anywhere.'

Frieda wasn't sure she would have recognized Vanessa. She used to have glossy brown hair, worn long and layered; now it was short and turning grey.

She used to be curvy; now she was comfortably plump, in a knee-length dress and a slightly baggy grey cardigan. Only her eyes were the same: round, blue, warm, perpetually surprised. And underneath the left eye was a tiny smoky birthmark, like a tear running down her cheek; Frieda had forgotten that. Suddenly Vanessa twisted round and called out, 'Ewan! Ewan! Come here! You'll never guess who's standing in front of me!'

She took Frieda by the arm and practically pulled her over the threshold. 'Coffee?' she said. 'Or tea? Breakfast? I've got to leave for work in about fifteen minutes, but I could get you something. How lovely! But why are you here? My God. Has something happened?'

'Coffee,' said Frieda. 'Please.'

'I've *read* about you!' She looked at Frieda smilingly. 'You're famous, aren't you? Ewan! Ewan, come here *now*.'

She led Frieda into a kitchen. Two teenage girls were sitting at the table; the younger one, who was plump and brown-haired and reminded Frieda of the Vanessa she used to know, was eating a bowl of cereal, holding it to her mouth and spooning in mouthfuls as rapidly as she could; the other was scrolling through Facebook messages on her laptop. She was blonde, slender, listless-looking and rather beautiful.

'Amelia, Charlotte, this is Frieda.'

The girls looked up. Frieda nodded at them.

'I used to go to school with Frieda,' said Vanessa, putting the kettle on, shaking coffee grounds into a cafetière. 'But I haven't seen her for over twenty years!'

'Wow,' said the older one, Charlotte, but apathetically.

At that moment, Ewan bounded into the room. He had always bounded. He was quite tall and bulky, with a shock of chestnut hair that as a teenager he had worn long, curling to his shoulders, but was now collar-length. He was wearing a grey suit and a dark blue shirt but didn't manage to look neat. There was something about him that was slightly shambolic.

When he saw Frieda he did a cartoonish double-take, his eyes opening, then blinking, his mouth opening, then shutting. 'Is it really you?' he asked, taking a step towards her and stopping again.

'It really is.'

Ewan reached her at last, and gave her a hug that almost lifted her off the floor. 'Welcome,' he said, as he let her go. 'Whatever it is you're doing here, we're very glad you've come.'

'Thank you.'

'Dad, we're late,' said Charlotte, closing her laptop. 'Again.'

'Is that the time?'

'It's worse than that,' said Vanessa, putting a mug of coffee in front of Frieda. 'The clock's six minutes slow.'

'God,' he said again, half comically. 'They'll write

my name in a little book.' He turned to Frieda. 'I work for the council and they're – what's that horrible word? *Rationalizing*.'

'You go,' said Vanessa, giving him a little push. 'I'll make a proper date with Frieda.'

'Right. Kids, we're off.'

He put on his coat, patted his pockets for keys and phone, looked around the room as if he was forgetting something, then left.

'I've come at a bad time,' said Frieda.

'No! Or, at least, yes, but no, it's fine. More than fine. What are you doing here anyway, if you don't mind me asking?'

'My mother's dying.'

'I'm so sorry. I didn't know.'

'We've only just learned. I'm staying with Eva. She mentioned that you and Ewan were married and living in Braxton.'

'And you just thought you'd pop in for a cup of coffee?'

'In a way.' Frieda had been thinking about what she would say to the inevitable questions. 'As you know, I left quite suddenly –'

'I'll say.'

'Without even a goodbye.'

'Yes, it was very mysterious.' There was a little snap of hostility in Vanessa's voice. 'We thought we were your friends. You know, sharing secrets, confiding in each other.'

'So I wanted to make contact again, find out what had happened to everyone,' Frieda persevered.

'Well, I'm not so interesting. I've moved about one and a half miles, I've put on several pounds, my hair's turning grey, and I've married the man who was my teenage sweetheart.'

'You're wrong. It's very interesting,' said Frieda. 'And impressive. That kind of commitment.'

'Really?' Vanessa softened. 'It's odd, isn't it? The first person I ever fell in love with, and here we are.' She made an expansive gesture.

'With two daughters.'

'Two *teenage* daughters – the oldest of whom is now about the same age as I was when I started going out with her father and as you were when you left. Imagine that! We didn't hang around, though of course we didn't have a clue what we were doing at the time. You only realize later. It's a war zone.'

'Did they know Becky Capel?'

'Oh, God, that was tragic. Poor Becky. She was a sweetheart. I knew her quite well. She was a friend of Charlotte's. They were in the same year at school. It's been devastating for her. So young.' There were suddenly tears in her eyes. She dragged a sleeve across them. 'Such a waste.'

'Yes.'

'Maddie's in tatters.' A little gleam came into her eyes. 'Hang on, didn't I hear something about . . . ?'

'I met Becky a couple of times,' said Frieda, calmly.

'On a professional basis. Because Maddie was worried about her.'

'Yes,' said Vanessa, musingly. 'That's right. I knew I'd heard something.' Her manner had shifted slightly. 'Listen, I've got to rush off in a minute. I'm due at work. I'm a dental hygienist, not quite as glamorous as being a famous therapist, but sometimes I think healthy teeth are as important as a clear conscience.' She picked up her coat. 'One minute, though – Ewan will never forgive me if I don't make a date. When are you here until?'

'I'm going to be staying three days or so a week. For my mother. I'll text you my email and you can suggest days. How's that?'

'Great.'

Vanessa picked up a used envelope and wrote her number on it. She handed it to Frieda.

'Do you have contacts for other people?' Frieda asked.

'Like?'

'Oh. Chas, Jeremy. Lewis,' she added, and saw a little smile appear and then disappear on Vanessa's face.

'As a matter of fact, I do! I'm helping to arrange a reunion.'

'Eva mentioned something about that.'

'You must come. It will be my coup. The famous Frieda Klein.' Again, that undertone of resentment. 'Anyway, I'll mail you their details once you've sent me that text.'

'Thanks.'

'And now I've got to run.'

'Of course.'

She stood up, putting her mug in the sink, pulling on her coat. 'Can I offer you a lift?' Vanessa asked at the door.

'No, it's fine. I'd like to walk.'

'You haven't changed one bit, you know.'

'Oh, I probably have.'

When Frieda reached the lane at the end of the drive, she switched on her phone. There was a message from Karlsson. She rang him straight back.

'I've found him,' he said.

'Is he still in the police force?'

'He's done quite nicely. He's a detective chief inspector.'

'Do you think he'll talk to me?'

'I rang him. He's expecting your call.'

'Where does he live?'

'He still in the area, somewhere up near Norwich.'

'That's forty miles away.'

'It's still East Anglia. Doesn't that count as the same area?'

'I don't know. Around here there are people who think the next village is a foreign country.'

'Are you going to see him?'

'If I can.'

'And you'll just talk to him?'

'What else would I do?'

'You've been known to do other things. Remember it was me who put you in touch with him. I'm vouching for you.'

'Thanks, Karlsson. I'm really grateful. I wish there was something I could do back.'

'That's not how it's meant to work. Just don't do anything reckless. At least, not without telling me first.'

'I'd better go,' said Frieda. 'I need to make some calls.'

Three hours later, Eva knocked on Frieda's door. 'A van's arrived,' she said. 'A man says he's here to see you. He sounds Polish.'

Frieda pulled her jacket on and stepped outside. 'He's a friend of mine,' she said. 'From Ukraine.'

'Oh, no, before I forget, someone left you a letter.'

'Here?'

'Yes. It was on the doormat when I came in. Probably someone who'd heard on the grapevine that you were back.'

Eva held out an envelope and Frieda pushed it into her bag. She would read it later.

When she stepped out into the road, Josef's head was hidden inside the open bonnet at the front of the van.

'Is everything all right?'

Josef's head appeared. He took a rag from his

pocket and wiped oil from his hands. 'Is hot. But is OK, will get us to your man.'

They got inside and the van started with what sounded like a long, spluttering chesty cough.

'So where?' said Josef.

'I'll guide you.'

'You will not guide. You tell me address, I put in machine, we don't think any more.'

'It's a town called Rushton. It should take about an hour.'

Frieda spelled the name and Josef tapped it into his satnav. 'It is an hour and a quarter.'

'Sorry.'

'Is the little roads.'

'Yes.'

'But pretty.'

'Some of them.'

Frieda looked out of the window. They were leaving Braxton and turning on to the bypass. The sea glinted in the distance.

'This where you grow up?' said Josef.

'That's right.'

'Every tree is a memory?'

Frieda turned to Josef to see if he was joking but there was no sign of it on his face. 'In a way,' she said. 'Josef, I know that when I say thank you, you'll say that I don't need to say it. But I do need to say it. Thank you.'

Now Josef did break into a smile. 'Is too complicated for me.'

'No, it isn't. Your heart must have sunk when you heard me on the phone.'

Josef shook his head. 'I was nearly ringing you.'

'What . . .?' Frieda began. 'You've been talking to Karlsson.'

'He says to check on you.'

'Mad woman on the loose?'

'No,' Josef protested, in an aggrieved tone. 'A friendly look-after.'

'You know, Josef, when I think of you and me, I think of you helping me when I'm in trouble and me almost getting you killed.'

'And building you the new bath.'

'Without me asking for it. But it's a lovely bath,' Frieda added hastily. 'I'm just saying that friendship with me comes at a price.'

'No, no,' said Josef. 'There are many of the people I work with. The builders and the plumbers. They are from Ukraine and Russia and Poland. They sleep in the hostels and in the van and in the sheds. Is different for me. Because of you, I have a home, friends.'

'It's different for me as well, Josef.'

The rest of the journey passed mostly in silence. That was good as well. With Josef there was no compulsion to talk where talk was necessary, none of that asking how you are, without really wanting to know, or really needing to know. She just stared out of the window. Josef had been right. The landscape almost spoke to her. That woodland where they used to be taken for walks on Sunday mornings. The rectory you could just see from the road where she had been for Virginia Clarke's fourteenth birthday party. As they drove, the memories thinned out and the landscape grew less familiar, then not familiar at all.

They stopped once for petrol and Josef checked the engine again. 'When you have your meeting, I will sort it,' he said.

When Frieda had rung ahead to confirm the meeting, Helmsley had told her to come to the Duchess of York. It was in the main street of Rushton and, because it was lunchtime, the saloon bar was crowded. The room was decorated with aged photographs of solemn, moustached men standing in front of horses and traction engines. In the far corner a man was sitting at a table alone, reading a newspaper. He was dressed in the grey suit and discreet tie that were the uniform of insurance salesmen and police detectives. When he saw Frieda standing in front of him, he folded his paper and stood up to greet her.

She tried to see something of the young officer she had met almost twenty-three years earlier. He was heavily built, jowly, with hair cut so short that it was really little more than a fuzz around the edges of his large head.

'Dr Frieda Klein?' She nodded and they shook hands. 'Have you eaten?'

Frieda said she wasn't hungry. She bought drinks for the two of them, a fruit juice for the detective and water for herself. 'It's good of you to see me,' she said.

'When a colleague gets in touch, we like to help. This DCI Karlsson, he's a friend of yours?'

'That's right. Did he tell you what this is about?'

'He left that up to you. He said you wanted some information.'

'We've met before,' said Frieda.

Until then Helmsley's manner had been affable but now he looked apprehensive.

'I'm sorry. I don't recall . . .'

'It was a long time ago. In February 1989, you were working in Braxton down in Suffolk.'

'That's right. It was my first posting.' He spoke slowly, as if he was worried about committing himself.

'You interviewed me.'

'I did?' His expression was wary. What was coming?

'I was fifteen years old and I reported that I had been raped by a stranger in my own house. I was interviewed and some other people were interviewed as well. I don't expect you to remember it.'

Helmsley was frowning with concentration but then his expression changed. He became paler. 'Yes, I do remember it.'

'What do you remember?'

He sat back in his chair and folded his arms tightly across his chest so that his suit ruffled up and suddenly seemed too small for him. Frieda recognized it as a gesture she often saw in her patients. It was sometimes interpreted as a way of fending off the outside world, of refusing intimacy. But Frieda also saw it as a sign of vulnerability, as if the person was trying to construct a feeble, useless hiding place, with their own arms.

'First,' Helmsley said, 'where are you going with this?'

'If you've any worries about me, you can phone Karlsson back and check with him. You can do it right now, if you want. This isn't about you or the investigation. I just want some information. But when I mentioned the interview and you remembered it, it didn't look like it was a happy memory.'

'It must be worse for you,' said Helmsley.

'I'm not here as a traumatized victim. Just tell me what you remember.'

'I've done courses. That's what you do as you work your way up the ladder. You go on courses, away days, lectures. Some of them are a waste of time and some of them aren't. A few years ago we had one about the handling of sexual-assault cases. We heard from some specialist officers, a psychologist and a victim. *Two* victims. A lot of things were said, some of it not what you'd expect.'

'About what?'

'About post-traumatic stress disorder, about the interviewing of complainants. In the middle of one of the PowerPoints, I suddenly remembered that case. I mean, your case. It was the first of its kind I ever dealt with. And what I felt, what I mainly felt, is that I can't believe they let us loose on it. We were just a couple of kids, me and Jeff. That's the other officer who interviewed you.'

'What do you mean by that?'

Helmsley looked at Frieda more carefully, as if he were sizing her up. 'If you're planning some sort of legal action, then this conversation is probably a bad idea. From my point of view, I mean.'

'I promise you, I'm not after anything like that. So . . .'

'I have a feeling, and I might be wrong about this, that we didn't handle the interview the way we should have.' He seemed to be waiting for Frieda to say something but she stayed silent so, after a pause, he continued. 'I thought you were this confident – what's the word? feisty? – teenage girl. That's probably the way teenage girls looked to me when I was that age. It was only all those years later that I thought what it must have been like from your side of the table, what it must have been like for a child to go into a police station and say what you said. And then when you'd said it, you were hauled into an interview room and treated as if you were the criminal. I can't remember all the details.'

'I just read the file,' said Frieda.

Helmsley's pale face grew even paler. 'So we probably asked you about things . . . well, you know . . .'

'Like my sex life?' said Frieda. 'Whether I was a virgin? Whether I had a boyfriend? Was I on the Pill?'

'Sorry.'

'And then the investigation went nowhere.'

'Most of them do.'

'You mean rape investigations or any investigations at all?'

'Both, I guess. But . . .' He seemed to struggle as if the word was difficult to get out. 'Rape is always going to be a special case.'

'Because it's one person's word against another.'

'That's one reason.'

'This particular case got stopped especially quickly.'

'Is that right?'

'Well, I'm not an expert, but it didn't seem to proceed beyond some very preliminary interviews.'

'I only remember my interview with you.'

'What I noticed,' said Frieda, 'as I read through the report was that someone else had gone through it, commenting and underlining. He didn't seem very positive about the investigation. He signed with the initials SF. I was curious about who that might be.'

Helmsley picked up his fruit juice and took a slow sip. He put the glass back on the table. 'When I first joined the force, my life wouldn't have been worth living if I'd been spotted with a Britvic. It was whisky and beer. Whisky with beer. Christ, I don't know how we all survived it.'

'The good old days,' said Frieda.

'There was something to be said for them.' He looked down at his drink as if he was considering whether to pick it up. 'Stuart Faulkner.'

'What?'

'That's your SF. He was the DCI, doing the job I do now.'

'Do you remember his role in the case?'

'You saw the file. As far as I remember he wasn't really involved. He was probably on another case. We did the early interviews, then he turned up, read through the file, had a word with us and told us to drop it.'

'Why?'

'I don't want to keep saying this but rape isn't like other crimes. With burglaries, assault, it's about catching people, building a case. With rape, before anything else, you have to decide whether a crime has actually taken place. Once you've decided that, you can set about finding the perpetrator, assembling the evidence.'

'And your boss thought a crime hadn't been committed?'

'It sounds bad, saying it to you.'

'But he thought I'd made it up.'

'I can't speak for the actual details.'

'When I read his comments, I thought they seemed to come from someone who had made his mind up from the beginning that the case didn't amount to anything.'

'That's the job. Sometimes you get it right, sometimes you get it wrong.'

'Stuart Faulkner,' said Frieda.

'Yes.'

'Do you know where I can find him?'

He started to speak, then hesitated. 'Probably. It's just . . .'

'I'm not angry about this. Do I strike you as someone who's out for revenge?'

'I don't know what that would look like. I'll see what I can do and then I'll call you.'

'Thank you.' Frieda was going to get up, and then a thought occurred to her. 'Do you know how old he would be now?'

'I don't, really. Early sixties, maybe.'

'Are you in touch with him?'

'I haven't seen him for twenty years. He wasn't a bad guy. Old school.'

Now Frieda stood up and held out her hand.

'I'm sorry. If we let you down.'

'I'm sure you did what you had to do. But what I really need is that number.'

When Frieda came out of the pub, Josef wasn't there and she had to phone him. Unfortunately, there was a problem with the van.

21

When they finally started on their way, the van still wasn't right. It kept hiccuping, lurching Frieda and Josef forward in their seats.

'Is block in petrol supply,' Josef explained cheerfully.

'Will we get back all right?'

'Oh, yes.' He patted the steering wheel as if it were a horse that was spooking. 'All good.'

They jerked their way back towards Braxton under dark, rolling clouds. The sky looked heavy, and soon large drops were landing on the windscreen. Josef turned on the wipers, whose frayed rubber edges made squeaky, unsatisfactory attempts to sweep the water away. He leaned forward to squint through the clear patches, seeming unperturbed.

As they entered Braxton, Frieda touched his shoulder. 'Would it be possible for us to call in on my mother?'

'Mother?' The van hiccuped.

'Yes. She's ill.'

'You have an ill mother in this place?'

'Yes.'

'We must see your mother,' said Josef, excitedly. 'At once. Is she bad?'

'She's dying.'

'Dying? Your mother is dying here?'

'Yes.'

'Frieda,' he said, his face shining with solemn fervour, 'I do anything.'

'Just take the next left,' said Frieda. 'We won't be long.'

'However much time is OK.'

They stood together in the driving rain, Josef at Frieda's shoulder peering expectantly at the entrance where Frieda's dying mother would appear. But there was no reply. Frieda rang the bell once more, then took out the key she'd had cut for herself and opened the door. They stepped into the hall. Junk mail lay on the floor, along with a postcard and a bill. She stooped and picked them up. There was a strange smell, sweet and slightly rancid. Going into the kitchen she saw that the flowers she had left the last time she was here had been put into a glass vase, but without water, and now they had withered and died. An opened tin of tuna stood on the side, letting out a greasy, fishy smell. She picked up flowers and fish and dropped them into the bin. It was no longer gleamingly neat and tidy in there. There were dirty plates on the table, half a carton of milk. Frieda sniffed it. It was sour. The sink was filled with cold brown water. There was a scrap of paper on the side that was headed 'Things to Do' in her mother's handwriting. Underneath, there was nothing.

'Wait here,' said Frieda to Josef.

She went into the living room. The television was on with the volume turned down. She went up the stairs and into Juliet's bedroom. There was a smell of abandonment and neglect. Juliet was lying in bed, her hands gathered beneath her throat, her hair awry, her usually immaculate face smudged with old makeup. She was awake, staring glassily at the ceiling.

'Hello,' said Frieda.

Juliet didn't answer. She gave a single dry blink. Frieda could almost hear the brush of her lashes on her cheek.

'Are you all right?'

She gave a laugh that was almost a gasp, but she still didn't take her gaze from the ceiling. 'That's funny. I'm dying, or had you forgotten?'

'How are you feeling?'

'I have a growth in my brain.'

'I know.'

Juliet turned her face and fixed Frieda with a harsh, bright gaze. 'Why did you come back?'

'We can talk about that later. Tell me what's wrong.'

'I was all right before you came. Now I'm dying.'

'You were dying before I came,' Frieda began, but then stopped. What was the point? 'Are you in pain?' she asked instead.

'Sometimes,' Juliet said, in a fierce, low voice.

'Sometimes, Frieda, it's better not to *know*. Not to know about your brain tumour, or your husband, or what your friends think, or what happened to your daughter when she was sixteen. I *don't want to know*.'

'But –'

'I don't want to. Rubbing my nose.' She looked a bit startled by the phrase. 'I'll start dribbling soon,' she said, 'and talking gibberish.'

'I'd like to talk to you about your health regime and what the doctors have told you –'

'I don't want to.' She cut Frieda off. 'I don't want to talk about it and I don't want to talk to you. You just trail disaster in your wake.'

That was so close to what Frieda thought about herself that she didn't respond, just pressed the base of her nose between her finger and thumb and waited for her feeling of helpless anger to subside.

'Go away,' said Juliet. She gave a half-sob, like a retch. And then she said, in a voice that sounded unlike her usual one, 'Fuck off and leave me in peace.'

Frieda stared at her in astonishment: she had never heard her mother swear. Juliet herself seemed surprised.

At that point, Frieda's phone vibrated in her pocket. She took it out and saw it was an unknown caller.

'Answer it,' said Juliet.

She heard a hoarse voice she didn't recognize.

'Frieda?'

'Yes.'

'It's Lewis. Lewis Temple.'

Frieda spun on her heel away from her mother's eyes, and looked out of the window now where the rain was splashing against the panes.

'Someone told me you were back,' he said. Back, as if it had always been her destiny to return one day. 'And that you'd asked after me. So I got your number from them and thought I'd ring.'

Eva, thought Frieda, wryly. Or maybe Vanessa; even Ewan. Although Lewis hadn't been strictly a part of their group (he was older than all of them, druggier, poorer), this was Braxton, where everyone knew everyone else and where news was blown around the town by the hot wind of gossip.

'Can I call you back in a couple of minutes?' Frieda asked.

'Why not? It's been twenty-three years, what's a few minutes more matter?'

Frieda switched the phone off and turned back to her mother. 'Can I get you something?' she asked. Juliet shrugged. 'Some tea, perhaps. And when did you last eat?' Again, the shrug and the hostile stare. 'I'll get you some tea and toast then.'

'Go away, Frieda.'

'Is that what you want?'

'Yes.'

'All right.'

She went into Juliet's small study and called Lewis back.

'So,' he said. 'What happens now?'

'Do you want to meet?'

There was a silence. She heard a match rasp against its box, his deep intake of breath, and could see him drawing smoke deep into his scorched lungs, his cheeks hollowing, flakes of tobacco on his lower lip.

'Why not?' he said. 'When?'

'What are you doing now?'

'I'm on my way to a call-out. But I can always make a diversion. For old times' sake.'

Downstairs, she found Josef standing at the sink, washing dishes. He looked contented and at home.

'We're going,' said Frieda.

'We only just come now.'

'I know. But she doesn't want me here. And there's something I need to do. Someone I've arranged to meet. You can drive back to London. I'm really grateful, Josef.'

He shook his head. 'I stay.'

'There's no room in my shed. It's tiny, for one person.'

'I stay here.' He gestured at the kitchen. 'Make things nicer for your sick mother.'

'She's not in a good mood, Josef.'

'I stay and cheer her. Make soup with barley. You come back later.'

'But you've never even met her!'

'I stay,' he repeated.

Frieda gave up.

She had arranged to meet Lewis in the coffee shop that she had gone to after her visit to the police station. It wasn't really Lewis's kind of place. He would hate the chocolate-box landscapes on the walls, and he had never been one for tea and scones. She arrived before him. The woman who had served her before was there again and recognized her at once. Frieda ordered a pot of tea and cake to go with it.

Three women bustled through the doorway, carrying shopping bags, their hair damp from the rain. Then a gaunt man with peppery hair and a pale face meshed with lines entered, letting the door slam behind him. He was wearing a long overcoat and had a scarf wrapped several times round his neck. Frieda thought he looked like a cross between an artist and a homeless person. He glanced around him, his eyes flicking from table to table until they came to rest on Frieda. Then he smiled.

Later, Frieda tried to separate out the emotions that had run through her when she understood that this stooped, meagre man was Lewis. She felt a kind of sorrow at what the years had done to him. She remembered him as he had been the last time she'd seen him, strong and gorgeous with his shock of hair and his white teeth, his dandyish second-hand clothes. She saw herself through his eyes, middle-class, well-off, entitled Frieda Klein, sitting in this comfy little establishment with a cup of tea in her hand. She tried to keep her expression neutral. 'Thanks for coming out like this. You must be wet through.'

'Are we going to talk about the weather?' He raised his eyebrows mockingly at her and sat down, not taking off his coat or scarf and stretching out his legs in their balding corduroy trousers. She felt he was making a self-conscious display of his shabby clothes, his creased face, his poverty, and daring her to react.

'How have you been?'

'You mean, since we last met?' He gave his laugh again. She could practically hear his lungs crackling. She wondered what drugs he took now. When she had known him he'd experimented with anything that came his way; an oblivion-seeker. His recklessness had, she supposed, been part of his glamour. Now he just looked worn out, bashed about by life.

'I suppose so.'

'You first. Though you look as though you've done just fine.'

'I'm a psychotherapist now.'

'I'm an electrician.'

'You were always good at science. I live in London.'

'I live here, nearby.'

'So you never did get to leave?'

'Not yet.'

Frieda beckoned the waitress over. 'Tea?' she asked Lewis.

He grimaced. 'OK.'

'Cake?'

'No cake, Frieda.'

The way he said her name brought his young self back to her. For a moment she sat in the dazzle of memory.

'My mother is dying,' she said.

'Is she? I'm sorry. How she hated me, though.'

'She thought you were leading me astray.'

'Ah, well, maybe I was. Though I always thought you were the leader. I just followed you, anywhere.'

They smiled at each other suddenly. It was odd, thought Frieda, how she felt more comfortable with this damaged man than with the other characters from her past.

'I'm going to be here on and off,' continued Frieda. 'I wanted to make contact with people I used to know.' She didn't like misleading Lewis, but thought of Becky and pressed on. 'There are things in the past that trouble me.'

'Unfinished business.'

'What do you mean?'

'Why did you run away?'

'It's complicated.'

'Who did you run away from? Your old ma? Your dead dad? Me? Was it me?' He lifted his eyebrows. She saw he had a miniature puckering scar running down from the corner of one eye. A fight, perhaps; a fall.

'Maybe from all of those.' And more, she thought.

'You never explained.'

'I don't think I had the words.'

'So you went your way and I went mine.'

The tea arrived and they waited until the woman serving them had gone away again.

'Things had unravelled a bit,' said Frieda, carefully.

'Whatever that means.'

'I've been wondering.' She could think of no way to approach this subtly. 'Shortly before I went away, someone broke into our house.' She couldn't recall exactly what the pretext had been for the police investigation. 'Do you remember?'

'No.' He shook his head. 'I don't think so. Or, at least, I have a dim memory. But, then, I've had a few run-ins with the police over the years.' He smiled; his teeth were crooked. 'Maybe it's all merged. What kind of break-in?'

'Someone got into the house,' Frieda said. Footsteps in her room, the breath on her face, the television downstairs.

'What's that got to do with you leaving?'

'I wanted to know if you remembered. I've been thinking about everything, trying to get things clear. That concert everyone went to: Thursday's Children.'

Lewis looked at her vaguely. 'It's no use asking me to remember little things like that,' he said, self-mocking. 'How do I know what I was doing twenty-something years ago? I've destroyed most of the brain cells I used to have.'

'You used to love that band.'

He broke into a little hum that Frieda supposed was from one of their songs, then stopped and frowned at her.

'I was going to go with you,' she continued. 'It was the biggest thing to happen in Braxton since, well, since the witch was burned probably. But we had a violent row just before.'

'We had lots of those.'

'This was the worst.'

'What was it about?'

'I can't remember. I know that we said terrible things to each other.' She had a sudden flashback: Lewis standing opposite her, his fist clenched and his boy's face contorted with fury and distress. 'So I stormed off and went home to bed.'

'And I went to the concert without you.' He was suddenly subdued, almost wretched. 'I remember that like it just happened.'

'Do you remember the concert itself?'

'A few bits, but it's all tangled up. I remember you, though. Little things. That bike ride we went on. You made jam sandwiches with stale white bread and we climbed up a rock and looked out over the sea and ate them, and I rolled a joint and there were seagulls diving down at us. It was nice. One of those nice days that stay with you.' He gave a little shake of his head, like someone getting rid of an unwelcome thought. 'And I remember you saying to me once that nobody's meddling could come between us. We were stronger than that.'

'Did I?'

'Then you buggered off.' He snapped his fingers in the air. The three women looked up from their table curiously. 'I remember that too. One day you were kissing me in the cemetery, and then you were refusing to have anything to do with me, for no reason I could understand, and then you were gone. You could have been a dream, except I kept one of your shirts. I used to smell it and think, Where the fuck are you, Frieda bloody Klein?'

'I'm sorry,' said Frieda. She was gazing at him steadily.

'Then, bit by bit, you faded. And now here you are. I've no idea why you wanted to see me again.'

'I've been thinking about the time before I left and I wanted to work out what happened exactly. What did you make of my friends?'

He stared at her. 'What is this? I was eighteen, nineteen. You were, what? Sixteen? I hope you were sixteen.'

'When I left I was.'

'Did I like your friends?' He mimicked her voice; his tone had turned hostile. 'Not much, if you want to know. Jeremy from the posh school, who was still in love with you and glowered at me as if he wanted to do something terrible to me, that creep Chas whatever-his-name-was.'

'Latimer.'

'That's the one. What kind of name is that? And that other one, clowning around.'

'Ewan?'

'Ewan. Yeah. And that girl he was with. God, it's all coming back to me. And Maddie – was that her name? Always trying to get the boys to fall in love with her. Big eyes, nice tits.' He wanted to anger her, but she didn't react. 'She didn't like you much, did she?'

'Probably not.' And even less now, she thought.

'And ginger Eva,' he said. 'But I liked Eva.'

'She told me.'

'Did she?' That laugh again: it made him seem sad and run down. 'If she could see me now! Poor Eva.'

'Why do you call her that?'

'She loved me, God help her, or thought she did, and I loved you, and you – well you didn't love anyone, really, did you?'

'I don't know.'

'You loved your dad, that's what. None of us really stood a chance.'

Frieda looked at the abstract picture opposite her, the one that looked like a Turkish rug. Was that true?

'I should go,' he said. 'Things to do. Sockets to fit, circuits to mend.'

He shifted in his seat, patted his pockets as if he was checking for his phone, his keys.

'Did you marry?'

'Yes. And then I did it again.'

'And now?'

'I wasn't much of a husband, as it turned out.' He wasn't smiling any more, but looking at her through narrowed eyes. 'Every time I got something I wanted, I destroyed it.'

'Do you have children?'

'A boy. Fifteen. I was just a kid when his mother got pregnant and she was even younger. It was all a mistake but, God, I fell in love with him when he was born. I don't see him as much as I want. His mother won't let me.'

'Why?'

'You know. The usual stuff.'

'Drugs?'

'And my general badness of character. Though I don't think I've ever been like that with Max. He was always my second chance. But she was angry and wanted to punish me and I don't blame her. You know how it is.'

'Sorry.'

'Ah, well. Life.' He shrugged his shoulders, thin under the heavy coat. 'And you're on your own.'

'Why do you say that?' said Frieda, thinking of Sandy's face when she was telling him that it was over.

'You've got the look. Maybe you always did.'

Lewis stood up and so did she. She didn't know how to say goodbye to him. He gave her a nod.

'See you then,' he said, nonchalant. Then, as he was

leaving, he said, 'I used to dream about you and wake up crying. I hope that doesn't start again.'

When Frieda stepped into her mother's house she had a shock: it was as if she had stepped into the wrong room. The reek of illness and neglect was gone. The surfaces looked not just cleared and ordered, but scoured. She walked through to the kitchen. The plates were stacked in rows by the sink. There was a smell of lemon and disinfectant. And she saw the lower half of Josef's body, the faded jeans, the scuffed heavy work shoes. The upper half was in the cupboard under the sink. She nudged his foot. Josef edged his way out, stood up and rinsed his hands under the tap.

'Now the water goes through,' he said.

'I thought you were just going to make some soup.'

'Is problem?'

'No, it's good. It's what her children should have done.'

He pulled a dismissive face. 'Just while I was waiting.'

'Now it's time to go.'

'But first you say goodbye to your mother, no?'

Frieda felt like she was fifteen years old again. 'All right.'

Her mother was in bed, half asleep. But the clothes had been folded and arranged; even her hair had been brushed. Frieda leaned close to her mother's face.

'I'm going,' she said. 'I'll be back in a few days.' Her mother murmured something. 'What?'

'That man. That Russian.'

'What about him?'

'From the council.'

'He's not from the council. He's a friend of mine.'

'He comes every day. He takes things.'

'I don't think so.'

'He's stealing.'

'I'll sort it out,' said Frieda. She stood up and left the room.

In the van, Frieda suddenly remembered the envelope that Eva had thrust into her hand as she was leaving. It was square and pale pink and had spidery looped writing on the front, like an old woman's. She didn't recognize it.

She unstuck the gummed flap and slid out the glossy greetings card inside. There was a picture of lilies on the front. She frowned and opened the card, her eyes drawn first to the card's message, written in baroque font. 'With deepest sympathy', it read. Under this, in the same spidery, precarious writing as was on the envelope, she read:

Frieda, soon you will be an orphan. But, my dear, do not grieve too much for your mother. The end of life is only the beginning of something else. She is coming to join me. It is her time. But not yours, not yet. Yours always, Mary Orton.

She read the message again, very slowly. Then she closed the card and stared for a moment out of the window as the countryside sped by in a blur of dun November colours.

This was a card signed by Mary Orton. But Mary Orton was dead. She was a woman who, long ago, Frieda had tried to save but had arrived too late. She would always be haunted by the old woman's face as she lay dying. She herself had nearly died but had been saved – violently and bloodily saved – by Dean Reeve.

She opened the card once more and stared at the words. She stared at the writing. 'Pull over,' she said to Josef, and as soon as the words were out of her mouth he swerved to the side of the road and shrieked to a halt. Horns blared.

'Yes?' said Josef, not seeming to notice.

'Look at this.' Frieda showed him the card. 'Do you recognize the writing?'

Josef took the card and held it very close to his face, then away. 'I do not know. Perhaps.'

'Does it remind you of Mary Orton's?'

'Perhaps, Frieda.' His voice was solemn. He had known Mary Orton well and he had certainly seen her handwriting several times

'Or someone imitating it.'

'I do not understand.' He looked both baffled and wretched.

'But I think I do.' She took her mobile from her bag and rang a number. 'Karlsson, it's Frieda. I need to see you.'

22

Sian Raven had broken up with her boyfriend after four years. She had moved out of the flat they had shared, she had lost her job, she had attempted suicide. But, as she sat opposite Frieda in her consulting room, she was smiling.

'I'm really feeling better than I've felt for a long time. Really ever. What I'm doing is curing myself. That's what we all have to do in the end, isn't it?'

'How are you curing yourself?' Frieda asked.

'I run every day for a whole hour, pushing myself all the way. Afterwards I feel this complete high. You can't imagine it. And then, for the first time in my life, I've been thinking about my diet, stripping it down to absolute basics.'

'Basics,' said Frieda. 'What does that mean?'

'Fruit.'

'Fruit?'

'I don't want to leave a footprint of any kind. I won't kill anything to eat and I don't mean just animals. I won't eat anything if it means killing the plant. You know we all eat far too much.'

Frieda looked at the young woman in front of her

and her flickering smile. 'Shall we talk about your footprint?' she said.

Karlsson and Yvette were in his office when Frieda arrived. They had spent a thoroughly bad-tempered couple of hours with the commissioner, going through the list of potential cuts. The only person Crawford insisted on keeping on full pay with no limitations was Hal Bradshaw, the psychological profiler whom Karlsson despised and Yvette loathed. At this point Yvette had stormed out of the room, and knocked against a harassed constable holding a tray of tea, which had fallen to the floor, creating far more mess and noise than she had imagined possible. She was still feeling angry and embarrassed and, what was more, there was a damp patch on her trousers.

'Yvette,' said Frieda, holding out her hand. 'How are you?'

'I've been better.'

'That bad?'

'Worse.'

Frieda turned to Karlsson. 'Is this a bad time?'

'What do you need?' he said.

Yvette looked questioningly at Karlsson, then at Frieda, then back at Karlsson.

'I'll leave you two alone, then,' she said.

Karlsson was holding the card delicately between forefinger and thumb.

'So you think this is Dean Reeve writing as if from Mrs Orton.'

'Yes.'

'It seems a bit elaborate.'

'He wants to tell me he's still here.'

'And in Braxton.'

'Yes.'

Karlsson stood up and looked out of his window.

'Tell me if you want me to go away,' said Frieda, softly.

'I don't want that.'

'I know that this is the last thing you need. But I felt I had to tell someone. No.' She corrected herself. 'I had to tell you.'

'All right. Let's go through all that you're telling me. First of all, that Dean Reeve – who kidnapped Joanna Teale and then Matthew Faraday and who killed the young research student Kathy Ripon, and whom we all believed to have killed himself over three years ago – is alive.'

'Yes.'

'And that he killed Beth Kersey in order to save you.'

Frieda nodded.

'You're telling me he told you as much by sending a little girl with daffodils and a message.'

'"It wasn't your time."'

'Right. And that Dean Reeve was also responsible for burning down Hal Bradshaw's house, also on your behalf.'

'That's how he would have seen it. Or wanted it to be seen.'

'And this time he sent you lilies.'

'A picture of them. Yes.'

'And now he's in Braxton.'

'He went there once before. He sent me a drawing of my father's headstone.'

'Now he's sent you this card.'

'Yes.'

Karlsson sat for several moments in a silence that Frieda made no effort to break. She looked at his intent face, then at the photograph of his little children, Mikey and Bella, that he always had on his desk.

'All right,' said Karlsson, at last.

'What does that mean?'

'I'll talk to Commissioner Crawford about reopening the case.'

'Really?'

'But it won't be straightforward. As far as Crawford is concerned, and the rest of the world, Dean Reeve is dead. Plus . . .' He hesitated.

'Plus he thinks I'm crazy.'

'He doesn't appreciate your finer qualities.'

'Do you believe me?'

Karlsson looked at her and, for a disconcerting moment, Frieda felt that he was looking not at but into her.

'It's worth investigating,' he said eventually.

*

Later that day, in the early evening, it was turning cold and there was a feeling of rain in the air, but Frieda had no intention of taking the Tube or getting on a bus. Arriving back from the country lanes, the blank, sodden fields, the silence, the darkness in the evenings, she felt as if she had surfaced and was able to breathe again. It was going to be a walk of a mile or two but that would be fine. She needed the noise, the traffic, the fumes. It felt soothing to be walking through crowds of people with no chance whatever that any of them would know her or her family or her history. When she reached Tottenham Court Road, she stopped for a moment, orienting herself, thinking of this or that landmark, this or that possible route. Then she plunged across into the streets around the university and past the Inns of Court and then to the old meat market almost without seeing them but instead just feeling their presence, smelling them, hearing them.

As she approached the City, the buildings changed. They were larger, taller, there was more metal and glass, but in her current mood Frieda found them welcoming, almost human. Frieda had never really understood the way people thought about the countryside. What she saw were fields that you couldn't walk across, green spaces in which every possible living thing had been sprayed and poisoned out of existence. Cities were for walking through. Things could survive in cities.

Frieda stopped and looked around her. A vast construction of grey steel and dark glass loomed over her under which nothing could survive. She took a piece of paper from her pocket. It seemed to be the right address. There was a grand main entrance with the logo of a bank above it. She walked inside. Two women were sitting behind a reception desk like that of a hotel. They were deep in conversation, and when Frieda approached them, they looked at her as if she were interrupting something important.

'I'm looking for the Clouds Bar,' said Frieda, doubtfully.

'It's round the side,' said one of the women. 'You take the lift.'

'Which floor?'

'There's only one. That lift takes you straight to the top.'

The street entrance was surprisingly small, as if it were meant only for people who already knew about it. Inside, a man in a commissionaire's uniform gestured her towards the lift. As she ascended, it felt like an improbable joke, but when the doors opened, she saw a large plate-glass window and lights out in the darkness. She was in a small lobby that led into the bar. A man stepped forward and asked for her coat.

'It's all right,' said Frieda.

A brief discussion followed. Coats were not allowed. It seemed that there was a problem with sightseers coming for the view and not buying drinks.

Frieda was going to ask about sightseers without coats but she gave up and handed over hers. As soon as she stepped into the bar, she heard her name being called. A middle-aged man was sitting by the floor-to-ceiling window that ran the length of the room. She walked over and sat down at the table. He smiled broadly.

'Frieda. I can't believe it. You haven't changed a bit.' He held up his hands. 'It's all right. You don't have to be polite. I don't expect you to say the same thing back to me.'

Frieda couldn't possibly have said anything like that. Her first feeling was one of shock. It wasn't so much that Jeremy Sutton had changed or that he had simply grown older: she felt as if the old Jeremy had been snatched away, disposed of and replaced with someone different in every way. The fifteen-year-old she had known had been rake-thin, with long, dark brown hair that he was always pulling away from his face. It was a face that she remembered with a permanently ironic expression. He was as derisive about himself as he was about everything else. He'd been at Fearnley College, the expensive private school that occupied a vast set of Georgian buildings overlooking the estuary. Jeremy had mocked its uniform and its pretensions and his rich, entitled schoolfellows.

Frieda remembered another expression as well –

or, rather, a set of expressions. The disbelief and the distress and the anger when she had told him that she wanted to break up with him. He'd bombarded her with questions, face to face, on the phone and even in a series of letters. Why? What did I do? Is there someone else? Why didn't you tell me something was wrong? Can't you give me another chance?

She could find almost no trace of any of that in the man sitting in front of her. He was armoured in a dark grey pin-striped suit. He was largely bald, which made his face seem oversized. She had been expecting to meet a man who looked like Jeremy's father, but this man was more like his grandfather.

'It's been a long time,' said Frieda.

'You like this place?'

Frieda glanced around at the rows of leather seats, the bar with its rows of single malt whiskies arranged against an illuminated background, at the groups of men and women in suits. 'I like the view.'

'Same old Frieda. You think you're too good for these people.'

'You sound like we're in a soup kitchen.'

'We're all just doing a job. You probably don't want a lecture from me about how the British economy depends on people like us.'

'You're right,' said Frieda. 'I mean, about my not wanting a lecture from you.'

'I could have invited you to my office. You'd have found that even more ludicrous.'

'Can I buy you a drink?' said Frieda. 'Since I'm the one who asked you here.'

'Don't be ridiculous. You're in my territory now. Shall I get a bottle of wine?'

'I'm on medication at the moment,' said Frieda, truthfully but irrelevantly. She couldn't face a negotiation on what to drink. 'Water will be fine.'

Jeremy went to the bar and returned with water for Frieda and a glass of wine for himself.

'I got you sparkling,' he said. 'In honour of the reunion. Twenty-three years. I calculated it on the way over.'

They both sipped their drinks.

'Are you going to ask me how I am?' said Jeremy.

'How are you?'

'I mean, you're the one who contacted me out of the blue and now you're sitting there looking at me disapprovingly. I know this is meant to be a big nostalgic occasion, but that's more of a flashback than I wanted. How am I? I'm married to a lovely woman called Catrina. We've been married for thirteen years and we have two daughters: a nine-year-old and a seven-year-old.'

'Congratulations.'

'You might even know her. She went to Braxton High.'

'Really?' Frieda was taken aback.

'Catrina Young. Long dark hair. She was in the year

below you. I went out with her in my last year, and we got together again after university.'

'I don't remember her.'

'She's going to this reunion thing. I said I'd go with her. Will you be there?'

'Perhaps.'

'I know what you're thinking. You're thinking that I've become middle-aged.'

'We're still too young to be middle-aged.'

'I've read about you,' said Jeremy. 'That's what Google was invented for. You've had a dramatic time.'

'Things get exaggerated.'

'And you've become a figure of controversy. So, are you here about a criminal case? Is this part of an investigation?'

'I went back to Braxton.'

'In search of your roots?'

Frieda put her drink down and looked out of the window. She felt the view should interest her more than it did but it made her feel as if she was watching London on television. Then she turned her attention back to Jeremy. 'Everything you've said so far has been sarcastic or prickly and I don't know why.'

'I'm going to get another drink.'

'You haven't finished your first.'

Jeremy drained his glass, went to the bar and returned with a full one.

'When I arranged to meet you, I promised myself there was something I wasn't going to say and now

I'm going to say it. You were my first love and I've not felt the same about anyone since then.'

'We were fifteen years old.'

'Are you saying that fifteen-year-olds don't have real feelings?'

'They have lots of them. But they're for learning, for trying things out.'

'So I was one of the things you tried out.'

'You told me yourself, you have a wife and two daughters. That's something to be proud of.'

'You don't know anything about my life. I don't think a day has gone by without me thinking of you. You probably don't understand what that even means. I bet you never Googled *me*.'

'Of course I did. That's how I found you.'

'I mean over the years.'

'I left my Braxton life behind. All of it.'

'That's just another way of being obsessed with it.'

'You're probably right. But I've gone back. My mother's ill.'

'I'm sorry. I liked her very much.'

'Yes,' said Frieda. She remembered how, after the break-up, Jeremy had not just phoned her but phoned her mother as well. 'But I want to talk to you about something else.'

'What?'

'Do you remember the Thursday's Children concert?'

'The one at the Grand?'

'Yes.'

A smile spread across Jeremy's face. 'Those were the days. Why are you asking? Do you remember dancing in the aisles?'

'I wasn't there, but you were. There was an incident. Involving me.'

'I don't remember that. We weren't together by then, remember?'

'We weren't together, but you do remember it. The police interviewed people. Nobody forgets being interviewed by the police.'

'I remember being asked a few questions. But nothing came of it. What's this about?'

'I want to talk to you about that evening. What you did. Who you were with.'

Jeremy took a drink, more slowly now. 'I had a fantasy about this evening. I thought we might order champagne and you'd see in me what you saw when I was fifteen.'

'I remember some of what we saw in each other when we were *fourteen*,' said Frieda. 'But things change. I'm asking for your help now. If you can't do that, then just say so.'

Jeremy drained the last of his wine. He took a twenty-pound note and coiled it slightly so that it could fit into the glass. 'I need to think about this,' he said.

'What's there to think about?'

'I need some time. You'll have to come to the house. I'll phone you.'

His expression had changed. Frieda had a sudden sense of what he must be like in the office. It was clear that the meeting was over.

23

Frieda sat by her fire, the cat curled at her feet. She was thinking about Jeremy, his oversized head and his expensive suit. She tried to connect them with the boy she'd known and – yes – loved in a way, although it seemed impossible to imagine that now. It was a distant, tarnished dream. Jeremy had told her he had never felt so intensely about anyone since, but that was because they had been each other's first love. He was nostalgic for the fresh wonder of the time. Sitting in some high-up office, at a desk that was probably as shiny and large as a grand piano, he was remembering his fifteen-year-old self with yearning. But even when she'd looked into his eyes this evening, she hadn't seen that boy. Where had he gone?

She stared into the flames until at last what she was seeing wasn't flames, but faces. Their faces, twenty-three, twenty-four years ago. They were all sitting in a circle on the wide swathe of grass by the river in Braxton and it was spring. Frieda remembered the stencilled shadows of leaves on the ground, the warmth in the air, the sound of the river as it eddied past. She could almost feel her own body as she sat, cross-legged, bare-footed, her hair loose about her face. Yes.

Opposite her was Chas Latimer, with his long fair hair and his pale blue eyes with their uncannily small pupils that gave him the look of some kind of animal. A predator. He had a joint in his hand and was smoking it solemnly, as if they were involved in a religious ritual and he was the high priest, before passing it to the person on his left. Who was that? Yes, Vanessa Bussock, now Vanessa Shaw, of course. Her shining brown hair fell in a curtain over half of her face; she was wearing tight shorts. She took the joint nervously, not really knowing how to do it but not daring to say no, trying to imitate the way Chas held it and cupped it; coughing, gulping the smoke into her mouth and holding it there, not inhaling, passing it on, too quickly, to Ewan who sat beside her. Ewan made everything all right by laughing at his own clumsiness and his unabashed greed for experience. He didn't mind looking foolish, the way he spluttered, couldn't manage cool. He turned and smiled at Frieda, who was sitting beside him; an eager, boyish smile. She shook her head. It wasn't that she didn't want to smoke, more that she hated the way they were all supposed to join in and would feel embarrassed to refuse. She met Chas Latimer's mocking blue gaze, held it until he shrugged and dropped his eyes.

Jeremy was next to Frieda. She could feel his body

heat, feel his eyes on her. He smoked with practised ease. He was not part of the group, only there because of her, but was definitely one of the cool ones: thin, handsome, grungy, confident. His hand, the one that wasn't holding the joint, slid across hers. Who was next? Yes, Eva. The sun had brought out her freckles, and her red hair gleamed. Everyone liked Eva, the tomboy. There was something innocent about her that made her infinitely sympathetic. Everyone used to think that she and Ewan would get together: they had seemed so well suited.

Someone was next to Eva, taking the joint with a faint lift of her eyebrows, as if to say, Oh, well, why not? Who? Frieda frowned into her past, trying to see. Maddie? No, Maddie had never been one of their crowd. A girl with dark curly hair, rather shy but with a wide smile that brought dimples to her cheeks. Sarah May: the name dropped suddenly into Frieda's mind. Of course. How could she have forgotten her? Brilliant at languages. She liked horses, too, as Frieda had, so long ago. They had ridden together a couple of times, in the meadows. She had a little flash of memory: riding through a bluebell wood in spring, Sarah May beside her on a shaggy, short-legged piebald.

On an impulse, Frieda pulled out her phone and rang Eva. When she answered her voice was slurred. She sounded drunk, but cheerfully drunk.

'What happened to Sarah May?'

Frieda immediately felt Eva's mood change.

'Didn't you know? Didn't you ever hear? She died.'

'I never heard,' said Frieda.

'It was horrible, just horrible. So young.'

'How young?'

'Just eighteen.'

'How did she die?'

'That was what was so terrible, Frieda. She killed herself.'

'Why?'

'Nobody knew. Nobody had any idea she was depressed. She must have been, though.'

'How did she do it?'

'She hanged herself.' Like my father, thought Frieda. And like Becky was supposed to have done. 'Just before her A-levels. People thought that must have had something to do with it. It was completely senseless.'

'Yes.'

'I was quite close to her, after you left. She was your replacement in a way. But I had no idea. I've often thought about what I could have done.'

'People always feel like that when someone kills themself. They look back and try to see how they could have prevented it. Usually they couldn't have done, but that's no comfort.'

'The school has a prize in her name: the Sarah May Prize for Languages. Vanessa and Ewan's Amelia won it last year. It made me feel so strange when I went there, to see the Sarah May Prize on their mantel-piece.'

Someone was ringing the bell. Frieda left the fire, still holding the phone to her ear, and went to the door. Jack and Chloë were standing outside, arm in arm, and on their faces almost identical grins of embarrassed hopefulness. Chloë had shaved one side of her head, she noticed, and Jack's hair was in an exaggerated quiff. He looked like a nervous cockatoo. Frieda gestured them inside.

'Are her parents still in the area?' she asked Eva, shutting the door, noticing that Chloë didn't wipe her muddy shoes on the doormat and let her coat slide on to the floor. She never saw the mess she created.

'She only had a father. Her mum died when she was eleven – do you remember?'

'That's right,' said Frieda, slowly, walking into the living room after Chloë and Jack. 'It's coming back to me.'

'I think he went to pieces after. His wife and then his daughter. Last I heard, he's in that home near the sea. Something-view. He was much older than other parents, almost like a grandfather, so he must be ancient now.'

'What's coming back to you?' asked Chloë, brightly, when Frieda ended the call. She looked hectic with nervous excitement and clung to Jack as if she couldn't stand upright without his support.

'The past.' Frieda looked into the flames. 'The past is coming back.'

The next day was more than usually filled with patients, several of whom she had moved forward because of her days spent in Braxton. Her last two were Jane, the middle-aged mother whose son had killed himself, and then Joe Franklin. Over the years, Frieda had become very attuned to Joe. He had only to walk through the door and she could sense his mood. Sometimes he seemed heavy, his shoulders stooped, his eyes cast down, and at others he stepped lightly, looked directly at her with an open countenance. She noticed how his laces were tied, his buttons done up, his hair brushed, whether his clothes were dirty or clean. Often, sitting opposite her, he was silent, and Frieda attended to the silence. There were days when it was sore and full of a despair that pressed down on them both, and others when it was pensive, even restful. Today he was calm and weary. He was a battleground for the depression that raged through him, retreating, then gathering force again.

Joe left at four, and Frieda waited only a few minutes before leaving too. She would write up his notes later in the evening. She walked rapidly to Holborn Underground station, then took the train to Bethnal Green. Perhaps he wouldn't be there.

She had Googled Greg Hollesley the evening

before and found that he was now the head of a secondary school midway between Bethnal Green and Mile End. It was a large school in a poor catchment area and had a troubled past. But, she read, the new and dynamic head seemed to have turned it around. She skimmed through articles that mentioned or quoted him and looked at recent photographs of him: standing on a podium at some conference; posing with his students on A-level results day, with a smile on his undeniably handsome face. He was only a decade older than she was, and looked youthful and vigorous.

Greg Hollesley: history teacher, her form tutor during that last year, the school heart-throb. His name had been carved into a hundred desks and tables with the points of compasses by smitten schoolgirls. The boys liked him, too, because he didn't seem to care what the pupils thought of him; he was athletic, funny. Frieda remembered him now, standing at the front of the class, or sitting on the table with one leg swinging, somehow managing to be both relaxed and theatrical. He always wore suits with open-necked shirts or T-shirts underneath, soft leather shoes and a leather band on his wrist. He had thick, dark, collar-length hair and his cheeks were stubbly. He came from Dublin, and the way he softly rolled his words gave him an extra touch of glamour; his voice remained soft even when he was angry, which made him more intimidating. The number of students taking history had soared during his time at the school.

As she walked towards his school, Frieda tried to recall the time she had last seen him but she couldn't. She had a faint, perhaps false, memory of his smell of smoke and spice, and of the way he had laid his hand on her shoulder after her father had killed himself. He had said that if she ever wanted to talk, he was there. But she hadn't wanted to talk – and certainly not to Greg Hollesley, with whom all her friends wanted to claim some kind of special relationship.

The school was a neo-brutalist edifice that looked like a small town. Most of the students had gone home, though some still loitered in the playground and clusters stood at the gates, talking and smoking. A receptionist buzzed Frieda through and she asked if Greg Hollesley was available to talk to.

'Is he expecting you?'

'Could you tell him that Frieda Klein is here and would like to see him for a few minutes? Frieda Klein from Braxton,' she added. But perhaps he wouldn't remember her, even so.

The woman pointed a finger at a chair a few yards away. Frieda didn't sit down. She looked at the artwork that had been put up in the entrance lobby, and the security notices, and nodded through the window at a very fat boy standing on the other side of the glass.

'Mr Hollesley can see you,' the receptionist said. She sounded disappointed. 'Come this way, please.'

Together they went through double doors and down a corridor. The air smelt faintly of stale sweat. At a green door, she knocked.

'Enter,' called a voice.

And there, after twenty-three years, was Greg Hollesley, sitting at a cluttered desk in a large, well-heated room, smiling in welcome. The past and present slid together; he seemed to have barely changed. Jeremy Sutton had got bald and large; Lewis had become gaunt and raddled; but Greg Hollesley had remained slim, dark-haired, white-toothed, handsome. Frieda took in his grey-green suit, the wedding ring on his left hand, the framed photograph of two small boys on the shelf behind him, the flecks of silver in his hair and stubble.

'Hello,' she said, advancing.

He stood up in one supple movement and held out both hands. 'Frieda Klein,' he said, in a familiar smooth tone. Everyone, thought Frieda, seemed to call her by her full name when they saw her again for the first time – as if that made her return more momentous. 'Who would have thought it? Dr Frieda Klein.'

'Thanks for seeing me, Greg.' It was absurdly difficult to call him that. At Braxton he had always been 'Mr Hollesley'.

'I was hardly going to turn you away. Here.' He

came round from behind his desk. 'Let's sit down, shall we?' He gestured at the two armchairs. 'Let's have tea.' He pressed a button on the phone on his desk and said, 'Dawn? Can we have two teas? In mugs, not cups. Thank you. And some biscuits?' He smiled across at Frieda.

Frieda took off her coat and they sat in the chairs, facing each other. Their knees were almost touching.

'How long has it been?' he asked.

'Nearly twenty-three years.'

'Twenty-three years,' he repeated. 'Well, time's a funny thing. Does it feel longer or shorter than that?' He wasn't asking her but himself, with a frown that left two vertical grooves above his nose. He looked at her and gave his famous smile. 'A lot has happened to both of us in that time, Frieda. I remember you very well, you know. And I've seen your name since, of course.'

'I probably remember you better.'

'You'd be surprised. You and your friend with the red hair. I can see you now. You were quite scary, you know.'

'I don't think so.'

'Clever and gorgeous.'

Frieda fixed him with a cool stare. She was irritated by people who knew they were charming. 'A teenager and troubled,' she rejoined.

'Of course. Your father. That was tragic.'

The door opened and a very tall, very thin woman came in with a tray that she put on the low table.

'Two teas,' she said. 'And your favourite biscuits, Mr Hollesley.'

'When did you leave Braxton?' asked Frieda, when the door had closed again.

'July 1991. I took up the deputy-headship at a school in Cambridgeshire, then was head of a middle school and then came here. But that's not why you've come to see me.'

'No.' She had been thinking of what to say. 'You're right. I didn't just pop in after twenty-three years to catch up.'

'Nice as that would have been.' He picked up his mug but didn't drink from it. 'How can I help you?'

'I left Braxton rather suddenly.'

'I remember.'

'I've been back recently and I'm trying to clarify memories. For my own peace of mind as much as anything,' she added. 'Do you ever go back there?'

'I do. My father's in a home nearby so I'm actually there a fair bit.'

'It's a strange experience, returning after all this time. I've met people I used to know and I'm trying to piece things together. Particularly round the time I decided to leave.'

'I don't see what I can do, Frieda, though I perfectly

understand your wish to come to terms with your past.'

'I had a group of friends that I entirely lost touch with. Do you remember any of them? You've already mentioned Eva – the red-headed one. Then there's Lewis Temple, Ewan Shaw, Vanessa Bussock, Chas Latimer.'

'I remember him at least.' Greg gave a small laugh.

'Why?'

'He was the blond, arrogant one?'

'I suppose that describes him.'

'The staff used to say he would become the leader of a cult.'

'Really?'

'What did become of him?'

'I don't know yet. But you're right, he liked power. Looking back, I can see how dysfunctional our group was. Did that occur to you at the time?'

Greg shrugged. 'You were kids,' he said amiably.

'Then there was Sarah May,' said Frieda.

She knew she wasn't mistaken. She saw a tiny, almost lascivious smile on his face, followed instantly by wariness, a shutter coming down between them. So: something had happened between Greg Hollesley and Sarah May. Poor, innocent, dimple-cheeked, long-dead Sarah May.

'I don't remember her.'

'Surely you must.'

His voice had become softer, slower. 'It was a very long time ago.'

'She killed herself in the month that you left.'

'That was Sarah May, was it? I remembered that something tragic happened but I forgot the name. Poor girl. A terrible waste of life.'

'Was it ever discovered why?'

'I don't think so. But, then, I'm not the person to ask.'

'You were her form tutor.'

'Was I?'

'Yes.'

'I don't know why she killed herself. These things are often very mysterious. But you know that, in your line of work.'

'Eva said it was exam stress.'

'That's always possible.'

'Did you ever see her out of school?' she asked.

He stared at her. Neither of them dropped their eyes and a feeling of hostility gathered in the room, almost tangible.

'No.'

'She was just another student?' She saw the knuckles on his hands whiten around the mug of untouched tea.

'None of my students is ever "just another student".'

'Even at fifteen, she idolized you.'

Frieda now saw a coldness in his expression.

'I'm very sorry about what happened to her, but teenage girls often have crushes on their teachers.'

Greg Hollesley stood up. The meeting was clearly over. She could see him wondering if he should hold out his hand, then deciding not to. Good. She put on her coat and buttoned it up.

'I hope it won't be another twenty-three years,' said Greg, opening the door for her.

'It won't be.'

'Take care, Frieda.' He made it sound like a caress and a threat.

24

Reuben only cooked four or five dishes and he served them in rotation. Frieda had eaten them all, over and over again. There was chilli con carne, lasagne, baked potatoes with sour cream and grated cheese. And tonight it was pasta with the pesto that he bought from the local deli. Frieda was only at Reuben's house because he had blackmailed her. When she had said she couldn't come, Reuben said, in that case, they would all come round to her house and bring the food and wine with them. 'You know I'll do it,' Reuben said. Frieda did indeed know that Reuben would do it.

So she sat at Reuben's table and ate the pasta and drank the red wine and looked at the photos of the baby on Sasha's phone and listened to Josef talking about the flat he was working on over in West Hampstead, and Reuben opened a second bottle of red wine, then a third. A phone rang and everyone looked around and she realized it was hers.

'Sometimes I leave it on by mistake,' she said. She took the phone out of her jacket pocket and saw Sandy's name. 'I'll just switch it off.'

'Answer it,' said Reuben. 'It'll be good practice for you.'

She walked away from the table and into Reuben's living room. A window looked out on the unkempt back garden.

'Is this a good time to talk?'

'I'm at Reuben's.'

'With the gang?'

'Why are you calling?'

'It can't end like this. You can't just click your fingers and eject me from your life.'

'I know that we need to talk, but not now.'

'I've been going over and over everything. Was something going wrong that I wasn't noticing? Was it something I did? Was I crowding you? Did you get scared of the intimacy?'

'This isn't the right time.'

'It seems the right time to me. We're actually speaking to each other at least. I've been trying to call you for days.'

'We can't do this over the phone.'

Sandy started to say something angrily, and after a few seconds of hearing his bitter, recriminating words, Frieda took the phone away from her ear and ended the call. She found herself looking at an Escher print on Reuben's wall. It was a drawing of an impossible building in which people who were walking upstairs found themselves going down and people going downstairs found themselves going up. She took a few moments to compose herself, then went back into the kitchen. She found them talking, but they were like bad actors pretending to be talking. Frieda sat down and picked up her wine glass. Josef looked at Sasha. Sasha looked at Reuben. Reuben gave a shrug.

'All right, everyone,' said Frieda. 'Say what you've got to say.'

Josef looked puzzled. 'Is nothing.'

Frieda stared accusingly at Reuben.

'Look,' he said, 'the point of an evening like this is that you can be with friends and eat good food, or at least some kind of food, and you don't have to be hassled by people asking how you are.'

'Which suits me.'

'But this is ridiculous.'

'Reuben . . .'

'Hold on.' He gulped his wine, as if he was taking on fuel. 'Let me list just some of it. This is a group of your friends, by the way. First, you've told us that when you were younger, you were the victim of a serious sexual assault.'

'I don't like the word "victim".'

'I'm sorry about that. And, also, you never even talked about this to your own therapist, i.e. me. There's also . . .' Reuben remembered himself. 'Well, other things.'

'What other things?' Sasha asked.

'I can tell you now,' said Frieda. 'Since she's dead.' And she told them about Becky.

'Oh, my God,' said Sasha.

'And now,' Reuben continued, 'you've suddenly broken off with a man who was devoted to you. Have I left anything out?'

'My mother's dying. Josef might have told you something about it. She's been diagnosed with a high-grade inoperable glioma, which is as bad as it sounds, and probably has no more than a few months to live. But it's all right because our relationship broke down years ago. So there you are, you have all the information.'

There was a brief silence.

'It sounds worse than it is.'

'That can't be true,' said Sasha.

'Well, actually, it is true. A year and a bit ago, I was not in a good place. You all rallied round and I was, am, grateful. Now I'm feeling strong. Everything you say – about the rape, about Becky's death, about Sandy, about my mother dying – is true. But it doesn't have power over me.' She took a large mouthful of red wine. 'I feel I have power over it. That I am at last in control of something that I should have confronted years ago.'

Now Frieda looked at Josef. 'So what do *you* say about this?' For some reason, his opinion mattered the most.

'Is your mother,' he said. 'That is the big thing.'

Frieda paused for thought. 'Is it? I ran away from her and all of that years ago. And now it looks like I've gone back. For years I didn't care whether or not my mother was alive and now I suppose I'm going to watch her die. I swore I'd never go back to Braxton and now I'm there. When he did that to me, all those years ago, he couldn't get at me, not really. He must have thought he had power over me, but he didn't. Not really, not in an important way.'

'But you left,' said Reuben. 'And you never went back.'

'Yes.' Frieda sounded almost puzzled, as if the idea had occurred to her for the first time. 'That's right. I felt I had to leave and now I feel I have to go back.' She looked at Sasha. 'Does that make sense?'

When Sasha spoke it was mainly to Josef, as if there were something that needed explaining.

'My first therapist was a man,' she said. 'He made me feel connected in a way I hadn't felt for years. So I slept with him. That was when I met Frieda. She rescued me from that.'

A slow smile appeared on Josef's face. 'I hear that. You hit him with the fist.'

'Well . . .' Frieda began.

'And go to prison.'

'Not exactly prison. It was a police cell. And only for a few hours.'

'The point is,' continued Sasha, as if there'd been no interruption, 'if Frieda says she has to do something, well, she has to do it.'

'No hitting,' said Josef.

*

At the end of the evening, Reuben wanted to call Frieda a cab but she said, as she always did, that she wanted to walk. He came out on to the pavement to say goodbye. As they hugged, Frieda couldn't avoid the look on his face. 'What?' she said.

'I understand what you said in there. But are you sure you're not just someone running into a burning building?'

'Someone has to run into burning buildings.'

Early the next morning, she got a text from Eva: *Becky Capel funeral on Friday 11 a.m. Coming? xx*

Frieda stared at it. She had a sudden flash of the memory of Maddie Capel standing in her front room just a few weeks earlier. It was so vivid that she could almost smell the perfume. Maddie wouldn't want her at the funeral. But then she remembered Becky, her pinched and anxious face, her pleading voice, her courage.

'Yes,' she said aloud. 'Yes, I think I must.'

Karlsson and Yvette were sitting in Commissioner Crawford's large office, facing him across his large desk. His face was red and Yvette's face was red as well. When Karlsson was angry he became stern, controlled and quiet; when she was angry, she was abrupt and inarticulate. Her flush had left a tidemark on her neck. Karlsson could see that she was sweating. The commissioner's words flowed past him – performance indicators, dwindling resources, the public face of the police – but her almost palpable distress touched him. She was like a clumsy child, her own worst enemy.

'That's all for today,' said the commissioner, suddenly. He'd had enough. It was nearly lunchtime. 'Get me the list by tomorrow, Yvette.'

'There's something else we need to discuss,' said Karlsson.

The commissioner looked suspicious.

'There's a case we need to consider reopening.' Karlsson lifted his leather briefcase on to his lap and slid across the folder of notes he had painstakingly made. 'It's all in there. I think you'll find it convincing.'

Crawford waved the folder impatiently away. 'Give me the gist, for God's sake. What case?'

'The case of Dean Reeve.'

His face darkened. 'The Dean Reeve who died?'

'There's reason to believe that he isn't dead.' He sensed Yvette shifting beside him. She knew of Frieda's belief that Dean had not died, but had killed his identical twin, Alan, although she had not realized Karlsson had decided to believe her or that he was going to pursue it officially. He should have told her, but it was too late now.

'What reason?'

'It is possible,' continued Karlsson, carefully, 'that he faked his death and is still at large. In fact, there are several things that point to such a conclusion. The widow of his brother, Alan, believes that it was her husband who died. Also, there are question marks over the death of Beth Kersey, the arson attack on Hal Bradshaw's house, the . . .'

'My God,' said the commissioner. 'My God, it's that fucking woman again.'

'Beth Kersey?'

'Not fucking Beth Kersey. Fucking Frieda Klein. Is she meddling again?'

'Dr Klein has convinced me that we need to re-open the case. That we would be failing in our public duty if we did not do so. It's all in the folder.'

'This is a woman who assaults her own colleagues as well as innocent members of the public.'

'No,' said Yvette indignantly. 'That was –' Karlsson put a warning hand on her arm and she subsided.

'She actually killed a young woman, allegedly in self-defence. We'll never know the truth of that. She was even connected with burning Hal Bradshaw's house down.'

'She wasn't connected in any way to that,' said Karlsson, but Crawford only snorted. 'She was crucial in solving the Robert Poole case and the case of those missing girls.'

Crawford impatiently waved away Karlsson's words. 'She may have made a certain contribution and it has been duly acknowledged. But haven't you been paying attention? You sit here protesting about resources and in the same breath you want to reopen an investigation into a case we closed years ago. We are rightly held to account by the public and the public need to feel assured that their money is being spent responsibly. Here you are, taking a good indicator and turning it into a bad one.'

'But if Dean Reeve is alive . . .'

'I am not going to reopen a case that is closed. Now go – and take your ridiculous file with you.'

When Frieda arrived at the church, the mourners had gone inside. There was just a line of black cars along the high street. A group of men in dark suits were clustered by one of the vehicles. Frieda heard the sound of laughter. Two of them were smoking. As she walked inside, an usher handed her a card.

'Are you family?' the man asked.

Frieda just shook her head and edged along the row of pews right at the rear, on her own. She felt as if she was there and not there, observing without being seen, a kind of ghost returning to the scene of . . . well, what? She looked down at the card. Hymns, poems, pieces of music. Becky was too young to have arranged her own funeral. These would have been chosen by others. What Becky would have liked. Would have: the tense of the dead. There were good funerals, funerals that were the acknowledgement of a life fully lived, but not this one. The death of a teenage girl.

As a vantage point, her position was not particularly helpful. One reason Frieda had come was to see who else was there. What she could mainly see was the back of people's heads. Little bald patches, glossy young hair, lots and lots of hats, rippling as if in a breeze. Suddenly there was organ music that seemed to come from every direction and the congregation stood up. She sensed a movement to the side of her and, with a shock, she saw that it was the coffin being carried down the aisle. The actuality of it, the presence of it, the sheer thingness of it, hit Frieda like a punch: the honey-coloured wood of the coffin and what she knew was inside, the frail dead body.

As the coffin moved to the front on the shoulders of the six death-suited men, she heard something else, beneath the organ music. At first she wasn't sure what it was but then it became clear. It was crying, but it wasn't the normal, English crying of discreet gulping sobs. Frieda now saw and heard that the church was full of young girls, rows and rows of them. They must have been Becky's school companions, and they were crying in a chorus that was like nothing she had ever heard before. It was more like the sea or the wind than something human and it didn't stop. It seemed to feed on itself. The music ceased and a priest at the front coughed and called for silence but the swirling noise continued. A hymn was announced and sung but the crying was sustained throughout and afterwards, while the service continued. It wasn't moving exactly. Frieda kept thinking that all of these howling girls couldn't have been Becky's friends, and that they were drowning the authentic grief of the real friends and family. For some of the girls it proved too much and from time to time one or two of them, faces streaked with running black mascara, were led out. The ceremony passed in a haze. 'Abide With Me', 'Jerusalem' and the Lord's Prayer. Her father, a solid man with a tanned face, read out some memories of Becky, her love of life, her sense of humour, her dreams. It sounded like a teenage girl downloaded off the Internet. An uncle read a poem, but Frieda couldn't really make it out. She just saw his shaking hands and his red, damp eyes.

And then it was over. The coffin was carried out for a private cremation later, the family filed after it, then the congregation stood up and turned to make their way out as well. Frieda started to recognize people. There was Eva, in a battered straw hat, who smiled and waved at her. Her expression turned to shock and sombre distress as she remembered where she was. There was Lewis, in a faded blue jacket and open-necked shirt. He looked as if he was on his way to the pub. He whispered to someone and Frieda saw it was a teenager and that he looked like Lewis. In fact, he didn't just look like Lewis, he looked more like the Lewis she had known and once even loved than the real Lewis did. Beside his son, the father now seemed a faded carbon copy of himself.

And there were Vanessa and Ewan Shaw, both of them strained in formal clothes that were slightly too small for them. Each had an arm round a loudly sobbing daughter.

Frieda had hoped that she could slip away through a side door, but this church didn't seem to have one. She joined the last of the group, who were queuing to get outside. As she emerged from the church she saw that the queue led past Becky's father and then, a few rigid inches from him, Maddie Capel and an old woman, who was clearly Maddie's mother. There was no escaping it. When Frieda found herself opposite Maddie, she gave a helpless shrug and said, 'I'm so sorry.'

Maddie's eyes narrowed slightly into what was almost a smile. She leaned towards Frieda, as if they were in a noisy, crowded room and there was a risk of not being heard. 'How dare you?' she hissed. 'How dare you?'

'I had to come.'

'You're not welcome here. You should never have come.'

'You brought me.'

'It's OK, Maddie.'

Frieda recognized the soft voice before she turned and saw Greg Hollesley. 'I'm just going,' she said.

'That's best, under the circumstances.' Greg stepped forward, took Maddie in his arms, and she pressed her face against his lovely jacket. He stroked her hair and murmured something into her ear. She lifted her head and he pushed her hair back and smiled at her. Smiled at her the way a lover does, thought Frieda, feeling suddenly queasy.

Frieda didn't follow the other mourners. There was a reception in the church hall, but she couldn't possibly go there. Instead she turned into the graveyard that surrounded the old church. She felt she needed to calm herself after her encounter with Maddie. She wandered along a row of small graves that she remembered from her childhood. This section was devoted to sailors who had been stationed on the nearby coast. Most of them were from just three or four ships that had been sunk in 1941 or 1942. Once, the sailors had been a few years older than her; now they were twenty years younger. She was looking at their ages, twenty, twenty-two, nineteen, eighteen, when she heard a voice behind her.

'Frieda,' it said. 'Frieda Klein.'

She turned and was confronted by a tall man of about her own age. He had curly grey-blond hair, heavy-framed glasses, and wore a dark suit that almost smelt of understated money.

'Hello, Chas.'

'Someone told me you'd come back, but I didn't believe it. And now here you are.'

'Here I am.'

'People are wondering why. Which means that we should talk.'

25

They drove to Chas's house in Chas's car, which purred expensively along the Suffolk lanes and smelt of leather and money. She thought of Josef's old van with its rattling windows and wheezing engine and, for a moment, let the old homesickness for her London life fill her. Then she pushed it aside and glanced across at Chas, who looked like his car.

His house was on the seafront. It was a grand, red-brick, symmetrical Georgian building, with windows reaching almost to the floor, and an imposing porch. He led Frieda through the echoing hall and into the huge kitchen. Through the double doors, she could see a garden whose wrought-iron gate at the far end led on to the shingle beach. It was covered with yards of decking and copper bowls full of shrubs, and to one side was a built-in barbecue, an elaborate affair that could have fed thirty guests. Frieda took a seat. On the other side of the window was an abstract bronze sculpture that looked, she thought, like a vagina: was that its point? Beyond the wall and the gate lay the sea, which today was flat and grey, fading into the flat grey sky

'The house was a wreck when we bought it. Stuck in the fifties. We gutted it and started from scratch.'

He waited for Frieda to say how beautiful it now was. She said nothing. He offered her wine but she asked for a glass of water. He put it in front of her, then took off his suit jacket and hung it on his chair, carefully smoothing out creases. His shirt was pale blue and beautifully ironed.

'I'm sorry you can't meet my wife. She works part-time for an events company down the coast. Keeping her hand in.' He spoke of it with amusement, as if it were her hobby. 'And, of course, my kids are at school.'

'How many do you have?'

'Three. And you?'

'None.'

'Are you married?'

'No.'

He raised his eyebrows so they appeared above the thick frames of his glasses. His eyes were still that strange pale blue, with tiny pupils. Then he said, 'So, you're back.'

She was getting tired of people saying that to her. 'For the time being.'

There was a shimmer of hostility in the air. She was sure that Chas could feel it too. It had always been there and time hadn't changed it. Chas liked power over people. As she sat in his spectacular kitchen, she found herself wondering yet again why, as a teenager, she had spent so much of her time with a group of people very few of whom she had actually liked. Chas she had disliked and had resisted. However hard he had tried to win her over through flattery, complicity, exclusion, derision, she had been unmoving, and he had never forgiven her for that.

'Why are you here?'

'Various reasons. My mother's dying.'

'I'm so sorry,' he said, in his uninflected voice, with no hint of sincerity in it. 'What are the other various reasons?'

'I've been thinking about the past.'

'That's what I heard.'

'Who from?'

'You forget how quickly word gets around in Braxton.'

'This isn't Braxton.'

'It isn't London.'

'Why did you stay here?'

'Not everyone needs to run away.'

His voice was so neutral that it took Frieda a few seconds to understand he was insulting her. She was oddly cheered by his rudeness: it made her job much easier.

'We were never really friends, were we, Chas?'

'Perhaps we're too alike.'

'I don't think I'm like you at all.'

'I remember you vividly. When you disappeared, you left a hole. A Frieda-shaped hole.'

'We were an odd group. I even can't work out why we *were* a group.'

'Is that why you're back?' His eyebrows went up again, over the top of those glasses. 'To work out why we all hung out together when we were kids?'

'When I look back on it, I think you wanted to control us.'

'Golly, Frieda.' He made the babyish word sound obscene. 'You're the same as you were twenty-three years ago. Really, it amazes me how little people actually change. But that's your line of work, isn't it? Helping people to change?'

'Ewan idolized you. Vanessa looked up to you. Eva was scared of you. Sarah fancied you. I've only just learned that she died.'

'She killed herself. It was very sad. For those of us who were still her friends.'

'Yes. Then Jeremy – well, you didn't have that much to do with him, did you?'

'Your posh boyfriend? Not so much.'

'And Lewis . . .'

'Lewis was a druggy loser.'

'He was a young man who took drugs.'

'Look at him now.'

'He's not rich and successful, with an enormous

house on the beach. But he didn't let you push him around, did he?'

'You're assuming I agree with the notion that I pushed anyone around.' Chas folded his arms. 'Let's face it, Frieda. Some people are leaders and some people are followers. It's true in the playground and it's true in the workplace. The followers want their leader. They like being told what to do. They need it.'

'Is that so?'

'Why do you think I've done well?'

'Because you're a leader?'

'Right.' He took off his glasses and polished them on his shirt, then laid them on the table between them. 'But you still haven't explained why you're back. Thinking about the past is a very vague notion.'

'Something happened before I went.'

'Something *happened*?'

'There was an incident, at our house one night.' She sounded like a police officer: *an incident*. 'Someone broke in, or tried to break in.'

'I remember that. I was interviewed.'

'You all were.'

'A prank?'

'That's one way of describing it.'

'So you've come back because twenty-three years ago someone tried to break into your house and you want to know who it was.' He stared at her with his pale blue eyes.

'Do you remember that concert?' asked Frieda. 'Thursday's Children.'

'Do I remember! It was the biggest thing ever to happen to Braxton. They're still talking about it.'

'Did you go?'

'Of course I went. I was right at the front. Don't you remember?'

'I wasn't there.'

'Weren't you?'

'No.'

'I remember.' A smile broke over his face. 'You had the mother of all rows with Lewis, didn't you? It was almost as loud as the concert.'

'I went home.'

'So you missed the event of the decade.'

'I did. Who did you go with?'

'Who? You're asking me who I went to a concert with twenty-three years ago?'

'It was the event of the decade, after all.'

He pinched the top of his nose and closed his eyes. 'I can definitely remember Sarah being there, and some other girl, dancing away and wiggling their bums.' He suddenly sounded sixteen again, lewd and sniggery. 'And Vanessa and Ewan, of course, because that was the historic moment when they officially got together, never again to part. Snogging away to "Bring Me Luck".' He frowned. 'I can't remember anyone else.'

'Jeremy? Lewis?'

'I remember thinking it was odd that Lewis wasn't there, since he was such a fan. Jeremy was probably with the kids from his school. Though, come to think of it, we had a kind of scuffle with them, I seem to remember, or at least Ewan did. He was always hopeless when he was pissed. And Jeremy definitely wasn't involved in that. But, of course, there were hundreds of people. He could have been anywhere.'

'Lewis says he was at the concert.'

'Memory plays tricks, doesn't it?' He smiled. 'At our age.'

'Nothing else about the concert you remember?'

'Not a thing.'

'What time did you leave?'

'I have no idea. How would I remember that, after so many years?'

Frieda looked at the sea. The tide was going out and the wet pebbles glistened on the shore. 'Did you know Becky?' she asked.

'I was at the funeral an hour ago. Remember?'

'How did you know her? Through Maddie?'

'Why are you asking all these questions, Frieda?'

'I was just wondering.'

'I'm just wondering why you're suddenly so interested in all of us, after so many years.'

'I've taken up enough of your time. I should be going.'

'You'll be wanting a lift.'

'No. I'll walk.'

'It's miles!'

'I'll walk to the main road and get a bus.'

'It's no trouble to drive you.'

'I'd prefer to walk. Thank you.'

'Very well.' He stood up and picked up his jacket. 'So, I'll see you at the reunion.'

'You probably will.'

26

Frieda walked along the seafront. The cold, strong wind felt good in her face, scouring her skin, clearing her mind, whipping away the sense of unease she had felt sitting in Chas's house. She thought of what he had said. She thought of Jeremy and of Lewis. Chas had said that he had seen neither of them at the concert, but of course that didn't mean they hadn't been there. Just that she could no longer be sure they had. Jeremy, her ex-boyfriend; Lewis, who had been her boyfriend at the time. Surely, *surely*, if either of them had broken into her house and crept into her room to do violence, she would have known. However dark, she would have been able to tell from the smell of the skin, the feel of the body, the breath against her, the way they whispered those words. She shuddered and walked faster. There was rain in the wind now, stinging and salty, making her eyes water. The light was fading and the sea growing darker. Birds flapped slowly across its waters. She made herself remember again, in detail. The knowledge that there was someone in the room, his hand on her mouth, his fingers pressing and pulling, insistent, persistent, monstrous.

His body on top of hers, obliterating her. The pain. No.

She turned away from the sea and made her way towards the main road. Surely she would have known, and yet, even as she said this to herself, she couldn't be certain that the man in her room hadn't been Jeremy. Or Lewis. Or anybody. How old had he been? How do you tell a rapist's age in the silent darkness? She had simply thought of him as a man. How tall had he been and how heavy? She had no idea. She had always thought of him as huge and vastly heavy because he had overpowered her, but she saw now that he needn't have been either.

Now she was walking along the road. There was no pavement here, only a churned-up grass verge. Cars drove past and she was splashed with water from the puddles. She thought about Lewis. Why would the person she was going out with – having sex with – rape her? She knew the answer before she asked herself the question. It was about power. Domination. She had just had a violent argument with him, wounding and humiliating him. But Lewis had never been aggressive, only troubled. Jeremy was a different matter – and he had had a reason to be angry with her. She had left him.

Her suspicions were like a stain spreading across her mind. Once you started thinking about people in this way, there was no reason to trust anyone. Chas: he could be lying. Ewan: he could be pretending. Greg

Hollesley: she thought of his smile, the girls who had idolized him and the use he'd made of that. What else had he done?

A bus – the one she was meant to be catching further up the road – passed her in a dirty arc of water. Her mobile rang in her pocket and she scooped it out.

'Yes?' she snapped.

'And hello to you too.'

'Karlsson.'

'The same.'

'I'm cold and wet and walking along a road in the dark and I've missed my bus and I've had a horrible day.'

'Where are you exactly?'

'Why?'

'I could come and get you.'

'Don't be ridiculous. It's about two hours away.'

'I'm in Braxton.'

'What?'

'I left work early and thought, Why not visit the countryside? So tell me where you are.'

'I think this is the first time we've ever had a meal together,' said Karlsson.

They were sitting in a small brasserie on the high street. Frieda ordered sea bream with a green salad and Karlsson had quiche. He wouldn't drink any wine: he was going to drive back to London later, ready for an early-morning start.

'The first? Can that be true?'

'We've had plenty of whisky and a fair amount of coffee. You gave me a roll with honey once, and maybe some toast. But I can't remember a proper meal.'

'It's an odd place to start – Braxton high street.'

'How are things?'

'God, Karlsson, it's very nice to see you, though you look rather out of place here. In my mind, you belong to London. I don't know how things are. I don't really know what I'm doing here. I'm starting to think that everyone has a guilty secret.'

'Which, of course, they do.'

'Of course.' She smiled.

'But you still feel sure you're doing the right thing?'

'I just know I have to do something.'

'Have you made any progress?'

'It's like staring into a pond, trying to see past my own reflection to what lies beneath. I think all I've done is to stir up old memories, muddying the waters even further.'

'I've got something for you.'

'What?'

'Not much. Those names you gave me of the two men that the police interviewed.'

'Dennis Freeman and Michael Carrey.'

'That's it. You were right – they were both men who'd previously been in trouble with the police. Freeman you know about. He'd done time and he was later convicted of sexual abuse in another case and died in prison. Carrey was just a pathetic flasher in the park, frightening the kids.'

'And?'

Karlsson shook his head. 'Carrey was never really in the running. He was in a hostel at the time, had lots of witnesses who saw him being very drunk and ill that evening. You can rule him out.'

'I see. Thanks, anyway.'

'There's something else.'

'What?'

'I spoke to Crawford about Dean Reeve.'

'Ah.'

'It did not go well.'

'He doesn't want to reopen the case.'

Karlsson didn't reply.

'So that's the end of it.'

'I wouldn't say so.'

'What do you mean?'

'If you're right, then he's still out there. Doing whatever it is he's doing.'

'Well,' she said, 'thanks for coming all the way here to see me.'

'As I said, I had a spare few hours.'

'No. Thank you.'

'It's a pleasure.'

'Now tell me how you are.'

'I'm all right.'

'I need more than that.'

'It's all I can say, Frieda. I'm all right. Nothing more than that. My kids are still in Madrid. Mikey's grown about three inches and Bella doesn't lisp any more. They speak Spanish and have friends I've never met. They're starting to be polite to me.'

'Isn't that a good thing?'

'No, it's terrible. I get so nervous when I'm about to see them that I think I behave unnaturally as well. I over-plan everything so they won't get bored. And we make conversation. I even think in advance about things to tell them.'

'It's bound to be hard. When they come back, it'll return to normal soon enough.'

'Maybe.'

'So is that why you're just "all right"?'

'Part of it. Everything just feels a bit grey, I guess. I work too hard, I see my kids when I can, occasionally I meet friends.'

'I think,' said Frieda, 'that sometimes life can seem like a straight road that stretches ahead with no change in sight.'

'Yes, that's it.'

'And you're just trudging along.'

'Yes. Don't tell me I need to find a hobby.'

'I wasn't going to. I wasn't going to tell you anything. I was just going to say that it's hard and I'm sorry about it. Perhaps you need to make a change.'

'It feels impossible.'

'We're always freer than we know.'

'That's too deep for me.'

'Do you sleep properly?'

'I'm not going to talk to *you* about sleeping.'

'Fair enough.'

After Karlsson had left, Frieda had a coffee, then went to collect her coat and scarf from the coat stand in the lobby. Her coat was there but her scarf – the one she had had for more than fifteen years, that was exactly the right shade of red – had vanished. It mattered to her more than it should. She hated to lose things, and that scarf felt almost part of her, wrapped brightly around her neck on all her night walks through London over the years. She gave her mobile number to one of the waiters and said that if he found it he should contact her.

She walked back to Eva's in the icy drizzle. The path through the garden was muddy and her shed was cold and smelt slightly damp. She pulled down the blinds (she didn't want Eva staring in at her from the kitchen, hoping she would go over and pay her a visit) and turned on the electric radiator, then put water in the kettle. While she was waiting for it to boil, she checked her emails. There was one from Chloë that read simply – 'Frieda, everything's going wrong! Help!' There was also one from Tom Helmsley:

I've tracked down Stuart Faulkner. He took early retire-
ment and he's living near Clacton. His address is 48
Chesselhurst Road, Thornbury. I hope this is of some use,
Tom.

PS I get the impression his early retirement may not have
been strictly voluntary.

Frieda looked up Thornbury on her phone and saw
that it was about fifteen miles from Clacton, down a
B-road. It had no station. She frowned, considering
her options – and then, as if he had sensed that she
was thinking of him, her mobile rang.

'Josef?' she said.

'Is me. Hello, Frieda.'

'Hello. How are you?'

'Fine. All fine.'

Frieda waited but he didn't add anything. 'Is everything OK with Reuben?'

'All fine,' he repeated.

'Good.' She waited again. 'Are you ringing for any
reason, Josef, or just to say hello?'

'Just hello.'

'Well, in that –'

'And how you are. I wonder. I think of you.'

'That's nice.' And it was, she found. She pictured
Josef, his large hand wrapped around the phone, his
sad brown eyes. 'As a matter of fact, I was thinking of
you as well.'

'You were?'

'Yes.'

'Frieda. I help you.'

'Of course you do.'

'I mean at this moment. Tell me what to do.'

'Are you busy?'

'Now?'

'Tomorrow. I need another lift, I'm afraid. I could easily get a cab, in fact it would be much more sensible, but –'

'No cab, Frieda. I come.'

'You're sure?'

'I come early. Seven?'

'Definitely not. That would mean leaving at five.'

'Is good. Is fine.'

And she couldn't persuade him otherwise. She ended the call and spent an hour drawing shapes that turned into faces, faces that turned, without her wanting it, into the face of Dean Reeve. She tore out the pages from her sketchbook and crumpled them into little balls before throwing them into the bin.

27

Frieda was woken by a smell she couldn't quite recognize. Something was burning, but in a pleasant way. She looked at her watch. Quarter to seven. She pulled on her clothes and walked out into the yard. The light was on in Eva's kitchen. She pushed open the door and two surprised faces looked round. Josef was sitting at the kitchen table and in front of him was a plate of eggs and bacon and sausages and another plate with toast, and above them a mug and a glass of orange juice. Eva was standing with a frying pan out of which she was spooning potatoes.

'Frieda,' said Josef, in a tone of reproof. 'I let you sleep and then coming to wake you later with the coffee.'

'I've just been hearing all about you,' said Eva. 'In exchange for food.'

'I hope you got your money's worth,' said Frieda.

'I can't believe what a dramatic life you've been leading. I heard about your first meeting.'

'Yes, it wasn't the normal way of making friends,' said Frieda.

'What can I get you? Eggs? Bacon? Sausages?'

'I'm not really a breakfast person. And I thought you didn't eat meat.'

'I don't, but Josef does.'

'Is the main meal for the whole day,' said Josef.

Frieda surveyed the breakfast table. 'It looks like the meal for the whole of today and the whole of tomorrow.'

She settled for coffee and a piece of toast. 'I feel bad about this,' she said. 'I was fast asleep and you've driven down in the middle of the night and Eva's met you and made you breakfast.'

'I was glad to do it,' said Eva. 'Josef's been telling me things: about you, about his family. And he says he's going to have a look round the house. I was hoping he could do some work for me.'

'That's a good idea,' said Frieda, but cautiously. She wasn't sure she liked the way her two worlds were connecting.

'He told me he did your bathroom.'

'Yes. He . . .' She paused for a moment. There were many ways in which she could continue the sentence. He had done it without asking. And removed the old bath. And damaged the pipework so that she was without a functioning bath for weeks. Eva and Josef gazed at her expectantly. 'It was a very good job. Josef is someone you can rely on. At least, I find myself relying on him.'

'You'll probably curse me for stealing him from you,' said Eva.

'He's a free agent.'

'No,' said Josef. 'No stealing.'

On the way to Thornbury, Josef told Frieda about what he'd seen in his quick survey of Eva's house. The cracks in the outer wall, the damp, the missing roof tiles, the peeling window frames, the exposed wires. 'Everywhere you look,' he said, 'you see the bad things. If you have million pounds, you could spend million pounds easy.'

'Josef, I don't think Eva has a million pounds.'

'We talk. We make plan.'

'Make sure you see the money upfront.'

Josef's expression turned stern. 'Frieda, you be the detective and I be the builder.'

'I'm not being the detective.'

'What are you being?'

'I don't know. There's a darkness in my past. I need to find out what happened.'

Thornbury was near the coast but not actually on it. Josef drove past caravan parks and streets of red-brick council housing, an industrial estate. It felt like a town composed entirely of outskirts but with no centre. They stopped twice to ask people and were directed into a new housing development that had evidently been built on fields at the edge of the town. Frieda knocked at number forty-eight and a large woman opened the door. She seemed to be in her early sixties, dark hair tied up in a bun, and her clothes were just one size too tight for her, as if her obesity had been sudden and unexpected. Frieda felt a tug of recognition: there was something vaguely familiar about her, although she couldn't put her finger on it. She had an expression of concern, as if Frieda's appearance alarmed her.

'I was hoping to see Stuart Faulkner.'

'What about?'

'I was given the address by an old colleague of Mr Faulkner's.'

'Which colleague?'

'Tom Helmsley.'

'I know Tom,' said the woman, still wary. 'What's it about?'

'I met your husband many years ago. I need to ask him something. Is he at home?'

'He's gone to the supermarket.'

'I'll go and see him there. What does he look like?'

'Ordinary. But I thought you'd met him.'

'Briefly, long ago. I'll see if I can find him.'

Almost reluctantly, Faulkner's wife gave Frieda directions to Thornbury's retail park. When they got there Josef dropped Frieda off and went to the auto-part store.

It was a quiet day in the supermarket. Faulkner proved easy to find. There were a number of late-middle-aged men but they were all with their wives, a few steps behind, disconsolate, almost embarrassed to be there in the middle of the day. But there was one man alone, tall, distinguished, short grey hair, grey trousers and a green windcheater. He was at the till with his laden trolley. Frieda walked over and introduced herself. After a few suspicious questions, Faulkner led her to the supermarket café. It was almost full – women with children, women with other women, elderly couples.

'They do a nice lunch,' said Faulkner. 'In the summer you can sit outside.' They both looked through the giant plate-glass window at the parking area surrounded by other stores: pets, bicycles, DIY, furniture.

'It's not exactly the Mediterranean,' Faulkner admitted, 'but you get good value.'

Frieda bought a black coffee for herself, a cappuccino and a cinnamon Danish pastry for Faulkner. He peeled off part of the pastry and dipped it into his coffee.

'I'm impressed,' said Frieda.

'What about?'

'To see you doing the household shopping.'

'You met Lorna?'

'Your wife? She told me you were here.'

'Didn't you recognize her?'

'No. Have I met her before?'

'She taught biology at your school.'

'At Braxton High?'

'Yes. Under her maiden name, Miss Hopley.'

'Miss Hopley. Of course.' She had been thin then. Thin and cross.

'She's not well now.'

'I'm sorry to hear that.'

'She was always anxious, ever since we met. In the last few years it's got worse. Depression. She's got a diagnosis. She retired early. Now she doesn't really like leaving the house.'

'Is she getting treatment?'

'Are you some kind of doctor?'

'Yes.'

'She takes pills. They make her fatter. I don't know if they make her better.'

'It must be difficult for you.'

'I'm retired now as well. I've got the time to look after her. But we're not here to talk about my wife, are we, Frieda Klein?'

'You say that as if you know who I am.'

'I remember you, if that's what you mean.'

Frieda needed a moment to gather her thoughts. This was a surprise. 'It was more than twenty years ago. I was expecting you'd have forgotten all about it.'

'Our cases aren't just numbers. They're real names, real faces. I remember them all.'

'I've just read through the file.'

Faulkner frowned. 'Who gave you that?'

'Is it a problem?'

'It's unexpected.'

'It was arranged for me. You'll remember that I reported a serious sexual assault. I was interviewed by two young officers. Detective Constable Tom Helmsley and Detective Constable Kevin Locke. You weren't directly involved. What is clear, though, is that you took an interest at some point. You read through the statements, underlining, making notes, and then you stopped the inquiry. Is that right?'

'That's right.' Faulkner dipped another piece of pastry into his coffee and ate it. 'I suppose you're going to ask me why.'

'I was going to get around to that. But first I was curious about why you took an interest in the case in the first place.'

'It was my job.'

'But these were just the very preliminary interviews. It seemed a strange moment for you suddenly to read through the file.'

Faulkner scratched his left cheek as if he'd felt a sudden itch. 'I was doing a favour,' he said. 'I knew . . . well, I knew your parents.'

'What?'

'I was asked – by them – to have a look.'

'You couldn't have been asked by them.' Her voice was harsh. 'My father died before it happened.'

'Of course. By her, then.'

'My mother?'

'Yes.'

'You knew my mother?'

'Well, I knew both of them – before that unfortunate accident.'

'Before my father killed himself.'

'Yes.'

'How did you know them?'

'Braxton's a small world. I met your mother at a council event, I think. We knew each other.'

'Did you know me?'

'You?'

'Yes. Did you ever meet me?'

'I – I think I saw you. Yes.' He was speaking slowly and carefully, as if feeling his way along a ledge.

'I don't remember you.'

'I don't think we actually met. But when this happened, it was natural for your mother to contact me to help her out.'

'Lucky me,' said Frieda. 'Having a friend on the force. You stepped in and called a halt.'

'I thought it was the best thing. For everybody.'

'Based on what?'

'I would have to look at the file again but, from what I recall, there was no evidence of any kind.'

'Apart from my report.'

'Apart from your report. And even there, you provided no description.'

'It was in the dark.'

'You waited several days to come forward.'

'I was terrified.'

'You seem to have recovered.'

Frieda had to overcome a strong impulse to pick up her coffee and throw it over the retired detective. 'I'm fine,' she said finally, in a quiet voice.

'But I'm not sure you're the one to make the judgement.'

'I thought you'd left the area.'

'Yes, I had. But I'm back. For a while, at least.'

'Digging up the past?'

'It's not past, that's the thing. Anyway, I've other business. My mother's not well. But maybe you know that.'

'We've lost touch. But none of us is getting any younger.'

Frieda shook her head. 'It's not that. She's got a brain tumour. She's dying.'

Faulkner started to say something but he still had some pastry in his mouth and he began to cough. It almost looked dangerous. By the time he had recovered himself, his face had gone a flaming red. 'I'm sorry, I didn't know,' he stammered. 'She's really dying?'

'She's really dying.'

'Tell her . . . Send her my best wishes.'

Frieda looked Faulkner full in the face. Had she ever seen him all those years ago? Surely she would remember. In her mind she tried to strip away the signs of age, the streaked grey in the hair, the lines around his eyes and mouth. She felt an impulse to get away so she could calm herself down and think about all of this.

'You know,' she began, 'that my mother didn't believe me. She had a habit of not believing me,

284

but in this case she didn't believe me in a really big way.'

'Your mother –' He stopped himself and began again. 'I'm sure that your mother always had your best interests at heart.'

'That's one theory,' said Frieda. She had been playing with the coffee spoon, flipping it around between her fingers, and now she laid it down on the table. 'Thank you, Mr Faulkner, for seeing me.' She got up. 'By the way, do you still go to Braxton? To visit old friends, that sort of thing?'

'From time to time.'

'I heard you took early retirement. Do you mind telling me why?'

'It's a bit of a sensitive subject. But I'm sure when you ask around, people will tell you.'

Outside, when Josef saw Frieda, he slammed down the open bonnet of his van and wiped his hands with his rag. 'Now,' he said, 'we should see your mother.'

'That's a very good idea.'

28

Her mother was sitting in the living room, her feet in slippers, her hands in fingerless mittens decorated with little robins, and her face bare of its usual impeccable makeup. Her hair wasn't tied back in its normal loose bun at the nape of her neck, but hung loose and unwashed, making her seem both younger and older than she was. She wasn't alone.

'Hello, Frieda,' said David, looking up from the depths of the armchair, where he was occupied with the crossword.

'David – I didn't know you were here.'

'Where else would I be, once I knew our mother was dying?'

Juliet gave an artificial cough. 'The last time I checked,' she said, 'I was still alive.' She put a finger on her wrist, then nodded. 'Yes, as I thought. There is a pulse.'

'Aren't you going to introduce me to your companion?' asked David.

'This is Josef. You remember Josef, don't you?' she asked Juliet. She still hadn't decided on what to call her (Juliet, Mother, Mum?) so had settled on not calling her anything.

Juliet frowned. Her eyes seemed cloudy. 'The man from the council,' she announced at last, triumphantly. 'Pest control.'

'Do you have mice?' David frowned and glanced around, as though he expected to see them scuttling across the carpet.

'No, Josef is my friend.'

'I was here and make soup,' said Josef, encouragingly.

'How are you?' Frieda asked her mother.

'I don't know. You tell me. You're the doctor.'

'Hardly.' David gave a snort. 'Unless you want to talk about your past and all its secrets.'

'As a matter of fact,' said Frieda, 'there was something I wanted to ask you about.'

'Perhaps a sandwich for good health,' said Josef. 'And later Frieda can wash your hair. Yes?'

'Maybe we can be alone for a few minutes,' continued Frieda.

'I have nothing to hide from Ivan,' said Juliet, peevishly.

'Except I'm David.'

'If you want me to recognize you, you should come more often.'

'I'm here now.'

'Can we have a couple of minutes alone?' Frieda asked again.

'I don't think that's necessary,' said Juliet. 'Just say whatever you want. I would like a sandwich. No crusts.'

'No crusts,' said Josef. 'Very good.' He left the room.

Frieda took a deep breath. 'I wanted to ask you about Stuart Faulkner.'

For a moment the expression on her mother's face didn't alter. But then it gradually seemed to loosen and crumble. 'What?' she said at last.

'Stuart Faulkner.'

David laid down his paper and sat up straighter in his chair.

'What about him?' Juliet managed.

'You used to know him.'

'I used to know a lot of people.'

'He was a police officer.'

'So?'

'And you contacted him after I was raped.'

'What? What?' David stood up. 'What the fuck?'

'Don't swear,' Juliet said crossly. 'It's a bee in Frieda's bonnet.'

'You asked him to get the case dismissed.'

'I can't remember.'

'I don't believe you.'

'I'm dying. Is this the way you treat a dying woman?'

'You told him you didn't believe me and he helped get the case thrown out.'

'If I did, you should be grateful to me. That's all I'm going to say.'

'Rape?' said David. 'You were raped?'

'She said she was raped. It's different,' said Juliet.

'Why wasn't I told about this?'

'Because it didn't concern you,' said Frieda. 'You and Ivan were at boarding school, remember? We were that sort of family.'

David didn't reply. He looked so desolate that Frieda almost felt sorry for him. Almost.

'Why did Stuart Faulkner help you?' Frieda said.

'I think I should lie down,' said Juliet. 'I have a tumour in my brain, in case you've forgotten.'

'Police officers aren't usually so obliging to vague acquaintances, people they've met at a local council event.'

'Will someone please answer me?' David spoke loudly but neither Frieda nor Juliet paid him any attention.

'You were having an affair with him, weren't you?'

'It's none of your business.'

'You were having an affair with him and you asked him to intervene on your behalf.'

'Someone needed to protect you from yourself.'

'It began before Dad killed himself.' It wasn't a question but a statement. Everything had become clear-edged to Frieda. For a blinding moment she saw her father's face: he was gazing at her with his beseeching eyes.

'Jesus,' said David. He was walking up and down the room with heavy footsteps. 'Family reunions.'

Juliet lifted her head and glared at her daughter. 'Don't you dare,' she said. 'Don't you dare blame me for your father's death. Do you have any idea what it's like to live with someone who's depressed? Who sucks the joy out of your life as well as his own? Do you have any notion of what my life was like year after year, trying to hold everything together? What if I was having an affair with Stuart?'

'This can't be happening.' David stopped in his pacing and faced the two of them, his handsome face contorted with rage. 'I've been here for fifteen minutes and I've discovered that my sister claims to have been raped and my mother was . . .' He couldn't even say the words. 'No wonder I don't come and see you more often.'

He left the room, slamming the door hard behind him. Frieda felt suddenly and immensely weary. 'I don't think I am blaming you, really,' she said to her mother. 'Though, of course, it makes everything even more complicated. I'm just trying to work out what happened in this house all those years ago.'

'I thought you were delusional. I wanted to smooth things over.'

'Smooth things over.'

'Yes.'

'I was raped.'

'So you keep saying.'

'You still don't believe me.'

'What does it matter? It was twenty-three years ago.'

'It matters.'

'Only because you let it.'

A thought struck Frieda, and it was like a window opening in her mind. She squatted beside her mother and looked into her face. 'He was here that night, wasn't he?'

'I don't know what you're talking about.'

'Stuart Faulkner was here the night I was raped.'

'I don't feel very well. I want you to go away and leave me in peace.'

'Just tell me.'

'It makes no difference to anything.'

'It makes a difference to me.'

'Maybe.'

'Maybe he was here?'

'Yes. Maybe he came round for a bit.'

'Sandwich,' announced Josef, entering the room with a plate that he held out in front of him, like an offering. 'Goat cheese and little tomatoes and salad leaves and spice paste I found in cupboard. I also threw away all rotting things from fridge. Is good?'

Juliet didn't reply.

'It's perfect, Josef,' said Frieda. 'Thank you.'

'Who's that?' asked Vanessa, who was sitting with Eva and Frieda in Eva's kitchen, drinking tea.

'That,' replied Frieda, 'is Josef.'

'Who's Josef?'

'My friend. He's a builder.'

Wherever Josef went, he made a home for himself:

he'd done it at Frieda's house, at Reuben's, at the house of old Mary Orton, whom Frieda still remembered with anguish. And now he was doing it at Eva's. He was on the top floor, ripping out rotten planks and inspecting the damage behind them. Eva had taken him up a mug of tea and a plate of homemade biscuits, and had lent him an oversized pullover because it was cold and he had come unprepared. He was talking about staying the night and continuing his investigations the following day. Eva seemed taken with the idea. She would cook him and Frieda supper. Perhaps, she said, she should go to the late-night supermarket and buy food and a toothbrush.

'I always have toothbrush with me,' Josef had said. 'And clean clothes. The shorts. Just in case.'

Frieda didn't want to ask in case of what. Josef was in a relaxed and expansive mood. Eva took him up another mug of tea and more biscuits and it was several minutes before she reappeared. When she did, her cheeks were pink and her eyes bright. Vanessa looked at her friend with raised eyebrows, and Frieda's heart sank. She had the uncomfortable feeling of being sucked back into her girlhood, sitting here while Eva flirted with Josef and Vanessa rolled her eyes conspiratorially.

'So, what's it like?' Vanessa asked Frieda.

'What's what like?'

'Being here.'

'I'm not sure.'

'It's hard not to feel,' said Vanessa, 'that in some way those of us who stayed behind are regarded as the underclass.'

'Nonsense!' said Eva. 'Or maybe you're right. We're the ones who didn't get away.'

'Regarded as the underclass by whom?' asked Frieda. 'I don't know. You?'

'That's not how I think of you at all.'

'Ewan and I love this area,' said Vanessa. She seemed agitated, as if she was defending their entire way of life.

'Me too,' added Eva. She picked up a biscuit, examined it, then took a large bite. 'Though sometimes I think I should have left.'

'We don't.' Vanessa was almost aggressive in her vehemence. 'We feel loyal to Braxton. Other people come and go but this is our home. I don't understand why everyone leaves.'

'Some people need to,' Frieda said mildly.

'And then they suddenly need to come back?'

'You mean me?'

'It's a bit unsettling.'

'Why?'

Vanessa frowned. 'I don't know. When I heard you were here, I was thrilled. But you're not just here because you want to make contact with old friends, are you? We're not sitting around giggling about old times and discussing the scandal of getting older.

That's what I thought we'd do. Though you never really were a girly girl, were you?'

'Nor was I,' put in Eva. 'Maybe that's why we were such pals. People thought you were sophisticated, a woman-of-the-world, having sex and making out it was no big deal, but you weren't, were you? It was just a cover. You were probably as scared as me and just pretending to be experienced.' She put out a hand and touched Frieda's arm, as though she were in need of comfort.

'What do you mean?' asked Frieda, who was quite baffled by the last comment.

'Anyway,' Vanessa continued, 'it feels as though you want something from us all and we don't know what. Both Chas and Jeremy said you'd been asking them questions as well. And Maddie's hopping mad with you. You know that, don't you?'

'Yes. She blames me for Becky's death.'

'Poor Becky.' Vanessa's voice wavered. She looked close to tears. 'And poor Maddie. God, that was a distressing funeral, wasn't it?'

'Are your daughters all right? I saw them in the church. They knew Becky quite well, didn't they?'

'Especially Charlotte. She and Becky have known each other since they were babies – they were born only a couple of months apart. I can't tell you how horrible this has been for her. She's been in floods about it since it happened. We all have.'

'I'm so sorry about it all. Did Becky talk to her about what she was feeling?'

'It was a bolt from the blue. Of course, we knew Becks was going through a rough time. Her father leaving. Wanker,' she added unexpectedly.

'Did she have relationships?'

Vanessa looked at Frieda curiously. 'You see, this is what I mean.' She addressed Eva, explaining to her. 'She's *investigating* us all. Did she have relationships? I have no idea. Probably. But one of the things you discover when you're a parent is that there are things you don't know about your children. *You* had boyfriends when you were Becky's age, I seem to remember.'

'Boys loved Frieda,' said Eva, rather wistfully. 'Don't you remember? There was Jeremy, then Lewis. Poor Lewis.'

'And you and Ewan,' said Frieda to Vanessa. She was aware of how the atmosphere was endlessly shifting between hostility and a kind of matey nostalgia.

'My one and only.' Vanessa gave a laugh. 'Yes. He was my first boyfriend. God, I was so smitten with him. I still love him,' she added hastily. 'But love when you're fifteen or sixteen, that's something different. Everything was so intense.'

'Yes.' Eva sighed.

'But look at us all now. Me and Ewan, together for twenty-three years, with two daughters, elderly parents, a mortgage, a car, holidays in Spain or France. Chas with his terrifying trophy wife.'

'Vanessa!'

'Well, it's true, isn't it? Jeremy's rather porky now, the last I heard of him. He used to be so gorgeous. He and Chas have become quite matey,' Vanessa went on. 'I guess they're both rich – they've got that in common. And their thin, glamorous wives.'

'Jeremy's wife went to Braxton High,' said Frieda.

'That's right. Catrina. Do you remember her? Catrina Walsh. Very good at tennis.'

'Was she?' said Eva. She pushed a biscuit into her mouth and chewed it thoughtfully, her cheeks bulging. 'I remember her being Greg Hollesley's pet.'

'Really? Well, she married Jeremy and now she's got perfect teeth.'

'What were her teeth like before?' asked Eva.

'That's not the point.'

'Oh.'

'Then there's Lewis, all washed up,' continued Vanessa, blithely. Frieda winced and would have spoken, but Eva got in first.

'And me and Frieda unmarried and alone. Say it.'

'It is possible to choose to be alone,' Frieda said.

'Maybe,' said Eva. 'But it does get lonely, doesn't it?'

'And Sarah May dead,' said Frieda.

'Sarah May.' Vanessa repeated the name. 'Yes, Sarah May.'

There was a silence. Josef warbled in the distance.

'It's nice having a man in the house,' said Eva.

There was a loud rapping at the door and then it was pushed open.

'Hello!' a cheerful voice cried. 'Your chauffeur is here!' Ewan burst into the room, followed by three young people.

He kissed Vanessa, kissed Eva, kissed Frieda, knocked a couple of biscuits on to the floor with his sleeve, left muddy footprints on the tiles, beamed at them all.

'This looks very cosy,' he said. 'You've met my girls, haven't you, Frieda?'

'Briefly. Amelia and Charlotte, is that right?' They nodded, the younger Amelia shyly, while the older girl was cool, indifferent. 'I'm glad to meet you again. I'm very sorry about your friend Becky.'

Immediately, tears welled in Amelia's eyes while Charlotte nodded again and murmured something indistinct.

'And you'll never guess who this is,' said Ewan, gesturing towards the boy who was with them, a lanky teenager in low-slung tatty jeans and a leather jacket over a grey hoodie.

'I don't know your name,' Frieda said to him, 'but I know you're Lewis's son.'

'Yeah.' Even the voice was the same. 'I'm Max.' Max. Becky had mentioned him to her. 'Do you know my dad?'

'I used to.'

Ewan punched him playfully on the shoulder. 'Hasn't your dad ever told you about the mysterious Frieda Klein?'

'No.' He had Lewis's scowl as well, which he turned now on Ewan.

'Were you a friend of Becky's too?'

He met Frieda's eyes. 'I thought so,' he said. 'Though I had no idea. She shouldn't be dead.'

'You're right, she shouldn't.'

'I don't understand why none of us saw it coming.'

'No one understands,' said Vanessa, laying a consoling hand on his shoulder. 'And everyone feels guilty.'

'We should be going,' said Ewan, shifting from one muddy foot to the other.

The door opened again and Josef came in, carrying two mugs and a plate. He was singing to himself, just two or three words on a loop, but stopped when he saw everyone, making a comical gesture of surprise. He put the mugs and plate carefully on the table, then made a slight bow towards Ewan and his daughter.

'I am Josef,' he said.

'What were you singing?' Frieda asked him sharply.

'Singing?' He looked confused.

'When you came in just now.'

'I not know.'

'It was one of the Thursday's Children songs,' said Eva. 'It's been in my head, what with all the talk of that concert recently. And I was singing it when I took the tea up to Josef.'

'Earworms,' said Ewan. 'Irritating little things.'

'That's it,' said Frieda. 'I remember now.'

And she did. Although she had never listened to their music since leaving Braxton, it was still lodged in her memory. She probably recalled most of the words as well.

'We still listen to them sometimes, when we're feeling romantic,' said Ewan.

'They *dance* to them,' said Charlotte. 'It's embarrassing!'

Frieda grinned. She remembered the way Ewan danced, throwing his arms around wildly and bounding on the spot.

'I'll have you know, young woman,' said Ewan, 'that they have a special place in your mother's and my affections.'

'Yeah, yeah, you got it together at their concert. We know. We just don't want a replay.'

'You might not even exist,' said Eva, to Amelia, 'if your mum and dad hadn't gone to that concert.'

'I can even tell you the order they played those songs.' He closed his eyes in concentration. '"City Song", they always started with that. To get the crowd going. "Move In With Me". "Better Do It."'

'"Dylan",' said Vanessa. 'That was always my favourite.'

'And "Donny's Funeral". And they ended with

'"Tight Fit". And, of course, they did "Day Off" for an encore.'

'Dad, this isn't really very interesting,' said Amelia.

'My father plays them as well,' said Max. 'He doesn't ever dance, though.' He looked so forlorn that Frieda had to stop herself putting out a hand in comfort. She remembered Lewis like that. And then, from nowhere, she found herself thinking of Sandy – or, rather, picturing his face the last time she had seen him. She stared out at Eva's muddy garden and for a moment lost all sense of what was being said.

'Frieda?'

'Yes?'

'I said, we're on our way.' Vanessa was pulling on her thick coat. 'We must do this again. You should come and have supper with us.'

'Thank you.'

'I'll call you.'

'Yes.'

'And we'll see you at the reunion, of course.'

'Perhaps. I've not entirely decided.'

Ewan kissed her on both cheeks, then turned to Max. 'Can I drop you off?'

'No. I'll walk.'

'I'll walk with you part of the way,' said Frieda. 'I need a bit of fresh air.' She nodded at Josef. 'I'll be back shortly.'

'Is fine,' Josef said cheerfully. 'Isn't it, Eva?'

'Yes,' said Eva. 'Very fine. Time to open the *vino*, I think.'

Frieda and Max walked in silence for a few minutes, until Max suddenly asked: 'Did you know my dad well?'

'It was a very long time ago. Until now, I hadn't seen him for over twenty years.'

'What was he like?'

She considered. 'He looked like you. But you probably already know that.'

'People say so.'

'He was bright and thoughtful. But you probably know that too.'

'Not so much.'

'He took things seriously,' Frieda added.

'Was he – did he –you know?'

'Take drugs?'

'Yeah.'

'Yes. Like his friends. But maybe he was more susceptible.'

'He keeps telling me he's going to stop drinking and smoking and killing himself.'

'But he doesn't.'

'I've given up. I used to go on and on at him. I used to beg him and say he had to do it for my sake.'

'But that didn't work?'

'Greg says that in the end you can't change people, they have to change themselves.'

'He sounds like he knows what he's talking about.' A thought struck Frieda. 'Greg who?'

'He used to teach at the High, ages ago. He used to teach my dad. I met him at Maddie's a few times. I was a bit cut up about everything and he was nice to me.'

'Greg Hollesley.' Whom she had seen hugging Maddie ever so tenderly at Becky's funeral.

'Maybe.'

'He goes and sees Maddie?'

'He has friends in the area from when he was teaching here. I think he comes down because his mum or dad is in a home.'

'His father,' said Frieda, recalling what Greg had said to her. 'That's right. Did Becky know him?'

'She met him. I remember her saying she wished there were more teachers like him.'

'You don't want too many like him,' Frieda said.

'Here's where I go.' He gestured to the road leading off to the left. 'Were you Dad's girlfriend?'

'You should ask him questions like that, not me.'

'That means you were. You're well out of it.'

'It's tough for you, I know.'

'I really liked Becky.'

'Did you?'

'We were friends, proper friends. All the girls were so bitchy.'

'I'm glad she had you to talk to.'

'It wasn't enough, though, was it?' He glared at her wretchedly.

She walked back slowly, thinking about what Vanessa had said: that her return had unsettled people; about Greg Hollesley in Maddie's house; about Lewis and his angry, abandoned son. Music from Thursday's Children ran through her head. She'd never liked them. The night was dark and quiet. Once or twice she thought she heard footsteps but when she turned no one was there. She told herself she was imagining it. When she reached Eva's house she went round the back. Through the kitchen window she could see Eva and Josef standing close together. Josef seemed to be teaching Eva how to chop vegetables the way real chefs do. Eva was laughing. Frieda glimpsed her face, years younger and full of a merriment that took her back to the friendship of their teenage years. She turned away and went into her shed, shutting the door softly and pulling down the blinds.

29

The next morning Frieda walked into Eva's kitchen. Her head was still fuzzy from a night of turbulent dreams that still seemed more real than the dreary, hard-edged, unforgiving world around her. Then, quite suddenly, everything seemed to happen at once. Frieda was filling the kettle when Eva came into the kitchen. There was something different about her. Then Frieda noticed that lots of things were different. Her hair was rumpled and her face was flushed and her eyes were both bright and tired and there was a smear of mascara at the corner of one eye and she was wearing a checked shirt that was much too bright and looked strangely familiar.

At the very moment that Frieda recognized it as belonging to Josef – in fact, it was the shirt Josef had been wearing the previous evening – and had started trying to decide what her response was or ought to be, she heard voices. She turned round as the door opened.

'It's bloody cold,' said Jack.

'It's, like, about ten degrees colder than London,' said Chloë.

Frieda felt a wave of alarm. What could be the bad

news that would make them drive all the way here so early in the morning? 'What's happened?' she said.

Jack looked puzzled. 'Didn't Josef tell you we were coming?'

'No, he didn't.'

'We thought it would be good to have a day out. We've been really curious about this area – well, about you, really – and I went online and saw how close it was.'

'You should have told me,' said Frieda.

'Well, we did,' said Chloë. 'Via Josef. Where is he, by the way?'

Frieda avoided looking at Eva. 'I think he's still in bed,' she said.

'No,' said Eva. 'He's on his way down.'

And, indeed, before Frieda could say anything Josef came through the door, dressed in jeans and a T-shirt and with bare feet. When he saw Jack and Chloë, he gave a sleepy smile of greeting. As he walked past Eva, Frieda noticed that he touched her shoulder and Eva glanced round at him. Even though it was just a moment, it was the intimate gesture of a couple who knew each other well, who had secrets. Frieda was making another attempt at speaking, at establishing some sort of order, when there were more noises from outside and a knock at the door. Chloë opened it and Ewan stepped inside. He was wearing a bulky country jacket of the kind worn for shooting small birds. Behind him were his daughters, in hooded waterproofs, looking sullen and resigned.

There was a series of complicated introductions. Eva offered coffee to everybody.

'We were just going for a walk,' said Ewan, 'and we thought you might like to come along.'

Frieda looked at Amelia and Charlotte, who were checking their phones.

'That's kind of you,' she said. 'But these friends of mine have just come down from London so –'

'That's perfect,' said Ewan. 'They're welcome as well.' He raised his voice to include everyone in the room in the conversation. 'It's a lovely walk along the river to the pub by the old mill, then back along the railway track.'

'Sounds great,' said Jack. 'This is what you never get in London, people just dropping into each other's houses.'

Frieda seemed to be experiencing both claustrophobia and agoraphobia at the same time. Her old life, the world of Braxton, her childhood and adolescence, was like an organism that was trying to pull her back in. At the same time, the London world, the life she'd chosen, was unwilling to let her go. She looked across at Josef. Eva was leaning against him, whispering something in his ear.

'We don't have to,' said Jack, in a slightly pathetic voice. 'If it's a problem, Chloë and me can go off somewhere on our own.'

'That's all right,' said Frieda. 'We can go for a walk.'

'I've got some things to do in the house,' said Eva,

apologetically. 'And I think Josef needs to finish . . . you know, the job he's been doing.'

Frieda looked at Josef, who gave a helpless shrug.

'Work,' said Frieda. 'OK, fine. We'll head off.'

This turned out to be a complicated process. Eva offered coffee but Ewan said they could get a drink at the Perch. Jack and Chloë retrieved walking boots and windproof jackets from Jack's car. Josef hovered in the kitchen.

'I don't want to keep you from your work,' Frieda said, then felt guilty. After all, did she want Josef to be like her, always the onlooker, the one on the edge, observing, assessing, diagnosing? Wasn't it better to be the way he was, always seeming to swim with the current, to accept what was offered? Anyway, she was the one who had brought him.

It was a sunny morning, but cold, and there was a fierce, steely wind from the east. She thought again of the lost red scarf, but Eva gave her a heavy jacket and a furry hat. As the small group walked out of the house, Frieda looked back at Eva. She felt like a parent leaving two teenagers alone in the house. Ewan led the way over the road to the footpath across the field that sloped down to the river Char. He was with Jack and Chloë, and she could see him talking and pointing but couldn't hear what he was saying. As they joined the river and turned west, away from Braxton, she found herself at the back with Amelia and Charlotte. She explained to them that Jack had been a student of hers and that Chloë was her niece.

'Bit weird them getting together, then,' said Amelia, with a grimace.

Frieda did actually think it was a bit weird but it wasn't something she wanted to discuss with two Suffolk teenagers she barely knew. 'I think maybe they're just having fun.'

Amelia and Charlotte exchanged glances. They clearly considered her too old to have any knowledge about young people having fun. For a time, the path narrowed and they had to walk in single file. Hundreds of years ago, the Char had been a working river. There'd been a brickworks and warehouses further inland. The industry was long gone and the banks had been reclaimed by the woodland and lined with trees, but there were still weirs and locks and concrete embankments. Frieda liked it or, rather, she had a sense of how she would like it if she could walk there alone. It was her kind of nature, the sort of nature that had a history. They passed under an iron bridge and the path widened once more.

'So you were at school here?' said Charlotte.

'That's right. With your parents, and Maddie and Eva, of course.'

'And Lewis,' said Charlotte.

More exchanged glances. Charlotte and Amelia seemed to share a private, sarcastic language that made them impregnable.

'Yes.' Amelia pulled a face.

'And now you're friends with Max.'

Charlotte snorted.

'Why do you think that?'

'I met you with him, so I just assumed. Do you mean you're *not* friends?'

'He's a bit creepy,' said Charlotte. 'He just follows people around like some kind of little stray dog. I know you were together with his dad when you were a teenager, but have you seen what he's like now?'

'Yes, I've met him.'

'Well, there we are, then. You look at Lewis and you know what Max is going to be like.'

'There are worse ways to be,' said Frieda, thinking of Jeremy and Chas.

The girls didn't answer. They seemed impassive in a way they hadn't previously. Maybe it was just the cold.

'It's difficult when someone dies suddenly,' Frieda said. 'I mean for the people who are left behind. They wonder whether they should have done something.' She looked at the two girls. There was just a hint of a shrug from Charlotte. 'Did Becky say anything in the days before it happened?'

'No,' said Charlotte. 'She talked to Mum more than to us – she was always coming to see Mum when she was upset by stuff. It was a bit creepy, but Mum loves all that.'

'But you were her friends,' said Frieda. 'And she'd

been through a difficult time. She must have talked about her feelings.'

'We weren't really her friends,' said Charlotte.

'I must have misunderstood,' said Frieda. 'Seeing you at the funeral.'

'That was organized by the school,' said Charlotte. 'It was like an outing. When someone dies like that, everyone pretends they knew them really well, but none of us were affected. Not really, if we're honest. She'd gone weird.'

Frieda thought of the funeral, the mass sobbing. 'So you weren't close friends with her?'

Charlotte gave a soft-shouldered shrug.

'Not so much.'

'Are you saying you actually disliked her?'

'I didn't care much one way or the other. Becky just thought she was better than other people.'

'Do you mean she didn't have *any* friends?'

'She used to, but in the end people just got tired of her. She stopped being fun.'

'So you weren't friends with Becky and you aren't friends with Max. Were they friends with each other?'

'I don't know,' said Charlotte.

It didn't feel like anybody was friends with anybody, except for the two sisters: united against the world.

'So she was isolated.'

'In a way,' said Charlotte. 'But it was her own choice.'

'And how long was this going on?'

'I don't know,' said Charlotte. 'Most of the year.'

There was an electric chime and Charlotte took out her phone, then started sending a text. They walked on for a few minutes without speaking. Ahead, Ewan was standing with Jack and Chloë, pointing away from the river up the hill. Frieda looked to where he was pointing: the obelisk silhouetted against the grey sky. She turned to Amelia beside her. 'Do you know what that is?'

'The witch monument,' said Amelia, in an unimpressed tone. 'Dad keeps talking about it. It's his new hobby – local history.'

'It's completely boring,' said Charlotte. 'We did local history for GCSE and now Dad's doing it all over again and there's only about two things that ever happened in Braxton. They burned a witch, then they built a railway and then they took the railway away again.'

'Because who wants to come to a place like Braxton?' said Amelia.

The Perch stood facing an old mill with a large waterwheel. There were tables outside by the water but only one was occupied, by a group of people in thick parkas who were smoking. Ewan led them inside and found two tables by a window. He placed Jack and Chloë next to Amelia and Charlotte. 'I'm sure you young people have lots to talk about among yourselves,' he said. 'Things you don't want Frieda and me to overhear.' Charlotte and Amelia rolled their eyes. 'The funny thing is, when Frieda and I last met we were your age. Isn't that peculiar?'

Charlotte and Amelia rolled their eyes again.

'When you and Frieda last met, it was yesterday,' said Charlotte.

'All right, all right,' said Ewan, who seemed used to this treatment. 'You know what I mean.'

He went over to the bar and returned with a tray of drinks and packets of crisps. He sat down next to Frieda at the other table. He had a pint of local ale, which he clinked against Frieda's tomato juice. He nodded at the young people. 'They're better off without us,' he said.

Frieda wasn't so sure. Amelia was texting, Charlotte was saying something to Chloë; Jack looked distracted. She should have a word with him later. Ewan pointed out of the window at the mill on the other side of the pool by the weir. 'That was abandoned when we were at school,' he said. 'It was derelict for about twenty years. Now it's being turned into flats. Riverside properties. That's what people seem to want.' Frieda didn't reply. 'They're nice, Jack and Chloë. They speak very highly of you.'

'I'm glad,' said Frieda, 'because they mean a lot to me.'

Ewan took a gulp of his beer, then looked down into the glass. Frieda recognized the sight. She had seen it often in her consulting rooms, as people plucked up the courage to say what they had come to say.

'It's been funny, you coming back,' he said.

'How so?'

'It makes you look at yourself, think of the way others see you. And it's also made me think about the old days. It's like when you dig up one of those time capsules that's filled with random objects from the past.'

'What did it make you think?'

'I know what you think of me. It's a bit like the girls. For them I'm this loud sort of Scout master who keeps saying things like, "Let's go for a walk" or "Let's go to a museum." I'm a bit loud and a bit boisterous. But what I've been thinking is that when you were going through difficult times back then, some of us were a bit wrapped up in ourselves and maybe we looked the other way.'

'The other way from what?'

'I don't know. But don't you feel sometimes, looking back on teenage life, that it was a cruel time?'

'Yes, I do.' Frieda regarded Ewan with new interest – he had lost much of his cheeriness and seemed muted, thoughtful, much more appealing to her.

'There's an episode that haunts me,' he said. 'It happened years ago, but I keep thinking about it. I wake in the night and it's there waiting for me. Once when I was out with Vanessa, she was attacked. There was a group of drunk or stoned teenagers or young men, four of them or maybe five, and first of all they surrounded me and jeered a bit. Said stupid things about the way I looked, about how they bet I couldn't get it up. You know the kind of thing.'

'Nasty.'

'Yes, but that's not the point. It was just words. But they suddenly lost interest in me and turned on Vanessa. They pushed her around, and then one of them started touching her breasts. I remember her expression – terrified and abject. And do you know what I did? Nothing. I stood there and did absolutely nothing while they touched up my poor wife. Then we just left and went home. What made it worse was that she tried to comfort me. She told me it had been the wisest thing not to get involved and she understood perfectly and it was nothing to feel bad about. I've never talked about this to anyone because I feel so ashamed of myself. Even now, all these years later, it's a taboo subject.'

'And yet you're telling me.'

'Perhaps that's because in some strange way you're someone people want to talk to, unburden themselves. I guess that's your job. But also – well, it sounds stupid. I'd like to make amends. I can't do anything about letting Vanessa down, but if there's anything I can do to help you with whatever it is you're after here, then I'd like to think you could trust me.'

On the way back, along what had once been a railway track and was now a cycle path, Frieda made sure she was walking with Chloë and Jack.

'We've missed you,' said Chloë. 'You're never at home.'

'It's just for a bit. How are you both?'

'There's so much I want to tell you,' Chloë said, 'but not in front of Jack.'

Jack blushed. Frieda smiled and asked him some questions about his work. She still thought of him as the boy he had been when they first met. Now he was a man to whom people would confess their darkest fears in the hope that he would give them some kind of refuge. They could do worse, she thought.

'Ewan showed us the Mary Ames monument,' said Chloë.

'That's the spot where she was burned,' said Frieda.

'I did it in history once,' said Chloë. 'These women were tried and persecuted and burned for being different, for not being straight or for saying what they thought or being a healer. Don't you think that someone like Mary Ames just wanted the right to have autonomy?'

'Maybe,' said Frieda. 'Or maybe she just wanted the right to be a witch.'

She let them walk on, and waited until Ewan caught up with her. His face was blotchy with cold.

'Fuck,' he said.

'It was your idea.'

'It's what I do. Drag the girls away from their computers – though, of course, they bring their phones with them.'

'I wanted to say something to you.'

'Look, I didn't want to intrude.'

'Something did happen to me.'

'On the night of the concert?'

'What makes you say that?'

'I might not be Sherlock Holmes, but you've been interrogating us all about it, Frieda. Of course that's when it happened.'

'You're right.'

'Do you want to tell me what it was?'

'No.'

'Of course.' He put up his hands. 'I'm not prying. I'm really not.'

'I was attacked,' Frieda said.

Frieda had started to get used to the expression on people's faces as she told them: shock, bafflement, almost embarrassment, not knowing what to say.

'In your own house?'

'Yes.'

'What a terrible thing. Were you hurt?'

'Scared rather than hurt.'

'Why didn't you tell us?'

'I didn't want to.'

'Jesus, what kind of friends were we?'

'Teenage friends.'

Ewan looked troubled. He walked on a few paces, kicking at a small stone. 'Why are you returning to it now?' he said at last.

'It's unfinished business. I want to find out who did it.'

'After all these years?'

'I know. But I have to try.'

'Revenge?'

'Call it justice.'

'How can I help?'

'I need to work out the timeline for that evening: who was where when.'

'You really think it was someone you knew?'

'Yes, I do.'

Ewan nodded slowly. His normally jovial face wore a solemn, almost tragic, expression. 'If there's anything I can do . . .'

'It's kind of you.'

He shrugged, embarrassed. 'It'll be difficult. I have difficulty remembering what I did last night.'

'It's surprising what people remember.'

'A timeline?' said Ewan.

'I'm grateful for anything you can tell me.'

His face flushed. 'You're welcome.'

Chas was having lunch with Jeremy, in a London club that felt more like an eighteenth-century house. They met three or four times every year, sometimes with their wives, sometimes like this: the two of them over a good meal with a bottle of burgundy and a fire crackling in the little fireplace.

'So she's speaking to everyone,' said Chas. 'You, me,

Ewan, Vanessa, even Lewis Temple. She's staying with Eva.'

'What does she want?'

'I was hoping you could tell me.'

'I've no idea,' said Jeremy. 'She came to see me and asked me about the concert we all went to. It was twenty-three years ago! What does she expect?'

'But why is she asking?'

'God knows.'

'She's stirring things up,' said Chas. 'You don't live in the area any more. It's not the same for you.'

Jeremy nodded. 'I said I'd get back in touch with her,' he said. 'But I haven't yet. I went to her house but there was no one there.'

'She still looks good, doesn't she?' said Chas.

Jeremy swilled the wine round in his glass moodily. 'She's ageing better than my wife, I must admit. She's a bit intimidating, though. But, then, she always was. God, I was obsessed with her.'

'She cast a spell.'

'That was how it felt.'

'Do you remember being interviewed by the police?' asked Chas.

'Of course I do. I was bloody terrified.'

'She wants to know where we all were.'

'We were all at the concert, weren't we?'

'That's right,' said Chas. 'Suddenly everyone seems sure they were at the concert.'

Jeremy hesitated for a moment and gave a nervous

318

smile. 'Well, then.' He lifted his hand for the bill.

'It's just a bit disconcerting,' said Chas. 'Having her come back. It's like someone returning from the dead.'

'That sounds like a guilty conscience talking.'

Chas gave his bland smile. 'Everyone has something to feel guilty about.'

30

'We've got rid of our warts,' said Chloë, as they walked down the high street. 'Haven't we, Jack?'

Jack was seized by a fit of coughing.

'I've got to go and see someone who lives up this road,' said Frieda. 'What are your plans? When are you leaving?'

'We've hardly arrived.'

'We don't want to get in your way,' said Jack.

'Yes, we do. Is it an old school friend?'

'Someone I knew at school, at any rate.'

'Can we come with you?'

'No.'

'You're no fun.'

'We should go and visit your grandmother,' Jack said.

'I've only met her a couple of times,' Chloë said. 'And she didn't seem to like me much.'

'You know that she's dying,' Frieda said.

'That doesn't make her any nicer.'

'I'd like to meet her,' said Jack.

'I thought we'd be striding up steep hills,' said Chloë. 'Bumping into sheep and jumping rushing streams.'

'This isn't the Lake District.'

Chloë grimaced. 'Where does she live, then?'

Frieda started to give directions.

'Just show me on your phone.' said Chloë. 'I've left mine in Jack's car.'

Chloë held out her hand and Frieda passed across her mobile.

'What's the code to unlock it?'

'Why would I have one?'

'In case somebody stole your phone.'

'I wish somebody would.'

Chloë sighed and started tapping at it.

'You should think about passwords,' Jack said.

'I've got enough to think about,' said Frieda.

'I'm serious. I'll bet you haven't changed the password for your remote access number.'

'I'll bet you I don't even have a remote access number.'

'For getting your voicemails when you're using another phone.'

'I've never done it. Didn't know it existed.'

'Haven't you been reading the papers in the last couple of years?'

'Not if I can help it.'

'Without one,' said Jack, 'as people have discovered, it's easy for someone else to access your email. Like the journalists who've been hassling you.'

Frieda frowned. A thought had occurred to her. 'Or Dean Reeve.'

'Dean Reeve?'

She thought of the note she'd received, sent as if from Mary Orton. She thought of the scarf she had lost. She remembered footsteps behind her. And further back: back to Mary Orton's death, when someone had been there to save her. To Hal Bradshaw's burned house. To the sense that he was always one step ahead of her, anticipating her moves, understanding her secret fears. She took her phone from Chloë and stared at it. 'So what do I do?'

'Phone up your service provider and change your password. And not to your birthday or to something about you that someone could guess.'

'Frieda?' Chloë's voice roused her. 'We're getting a bit cold. Just give me my gran's address.'

She did so, still preoccupied with the new certainty that now gripped her. As the two of them were leaving, she took Jack's arm to hold him back. 'Keep an eye on her,' she said.

'She can be rather wild sometimes.' He sounded admiring.

'My mother could crush her.'

She watched them as they walked off together, Chloë taking skipping steps, bumping her hip against Jack's, seizing his hand and then dropping it. However hard she pretended, she was still a child and Frieda felt a pang at her ungainly eagerness.

Once they were out of sight, she walked up Mount

Street and took the little lane that ran out of the town beside a field that in the summer was yellow with buttercups. There was a rickety old horse by the fence, all its ribs showing, and when Frieda held out her hand to it, it drew back its lips and bared its long yellow teeth. A few hundred yards on, she came to the house standing back from the road, Georgian, with large windows and a raised round fishpond near the front door. Frieda peered into it and saw a single mottled carp nosing the bottom.

When Maddie answered the door, her expression was stony. 'I don't want you here.'

'I know. But I hoped we could talk for a few minutes. There's something I need to say.'

'You've got nothing to say that I want to hear.'

'Five minutes. If you still want me to leave after that, I give you my word that I'll go.'

Maddie stared at her, then shook her head slowly from side to side. But she said, 'All right. I'll give you five minutes. But I can't imagine what you've got to say that will make me want ever to set eyes on you again.'

Frieda stepped into the house and followed Maddie into the sitting room. The first thing that struck her was the sweet stench, even before she saw that there were flowers everywhere, lilies and hothouse roses, ornate mixed bouquets. Some were drooping and dying. There were cards on every surface too.

'Go on, then,' said Maddie. Neither of them sat down.

'Becky didn't kill herself. I don't have evidence that I can give to the police but she was killed.' Maddie started to protest but Frieda continued. 'She was killed by the man who raped her. I believe that he found out – somehow – that she was going to the police.'

Maddie shook her head. 'You're a liar. You just want it not to be your fault.'

Frieda paused. She hardly heard Maddie because she was preparing herself to say what she had come there to say.

'I know she was raped because twenty-three years ago the same man raped me.'

'What did you say?'

'When Becky told me about her experience, I recognized it as my own. The same scenario, the exact same words the rapist said to her. I know that the pattern of her behaviour leading up to her death made it seem clear to you, and to the police, that she killed herself. She didn't. There is a man out there who preys on vulnerable young women and who raped and killed your daughter.'

'No. No.' Maddie looked utterly baffled and disgusted.

'She wasn't making it up.'

All of a sudden, Maddie sat down on the carpet.

She put her arms round her knees and pulled herself into the smallest shape possible. Frieda remembered her as she'd been in her house in London, a few weeks ago: impeccably presented, carefully smiling, smelling of expensive perfume and smooth with makeup. Now she was dishevelled, unbuttoned and un-defended. She, Frieda, had led her to this. If Becky had not told her the story, if Frieda had not encouraged her to go to the police, the girl would still be alive and her mother would not be crouched on the floor, like a pitiful animal, her ordered life in shreds.

Frieda squatted beside her. 'Do you believe me?' she asked.

'She was in a mess. Everyone knew that. It was your doing. That's what you can't deal with.'

'She was troubled, it's true. But if I'm right, then the man who raped her always picks on young women he knows to be particularly vulnerable. He felt confident she wouldn't be believed.'

Maddie lifted her head. 'You say it happened to you?'

'Yes.'

'How can you know? How can you possibly know? It was twenty years ago. More than twenty years.'

'I know,' said Frieda, 'that it was the same man.'

'Why didn't you tell me?' She clambered to her feet. 'If you'd told me, I would have believed her.'

'I should have told you.'

'And then maybe she wouldn't be dead.' She stared around at all the dying flowers. 'This just makes everything worse. Now I have to live for the rest of my life with the fact that I didn't believe her.'

'He knew that no one would believe her because she was going through such a rough time. That's the point.'

'Who is he?'

'I don't know. But he isn't a stranger. He knew me. He knew Becky.' Frieda hesitated, then added, 'And I feel certain that he knew Sarah May.'

'Sarah May? Did it happen to her?'

'I think so.'

'Someone we know? Someone *I* know?'

'It must be.'

Maddie's head seemed to wobble slightly and her eyes had a glazed look. Suddenly she picked up a vase of lilies and threw it against the wall, where it shattered. Flowers and glass lay on the floor. She picked up another vase, this one full of tight pink roses, water slopping over the brim. But Frieda took it from her and put it back on the surface.

'Bastard,' Maddie said. 'Bastard. Evil, stinking bastard. My little Becky. My darling daughter. What have I done? Why can't I tell her I'm sorry?'

'Maddie –'

'Don't you talk to me in that calm voice. You don't understand. You'll never understand. You're not a mother. You're just a machine. You don't know what it feels like *here*.' And she punched herself hard in the chest. 'You should have told me. If you knew Becky was in danger, you could have saved her. I'll never, ever forgive you. I still think you're making it up. It's mad. You're mad.'

'Listen to me. I believe that whoever raped Becky found out that she was going to the police and that was why he killed her. We need to work out who knew about it.'

'It was you who told her to go to the police. You did it.'

'Did she tell you she was going?'

'Of course. I was still her mother, even if she felt I'd let her down.' Her face crumpled. Tears rolled down her cheeks, into her mouth, on to her neck. 'I let her down,' she whispered. 'That's the last thing she felt about me, that I let her down.'

'Did you tell anyone else?'

'I can't think. I can't remember anything. We have to go to the police ourselves.' She clutched Frieda's sleeve. 'We have to go right now.'

'I've already spoken to them.'

'Without telling me?'

'Yes.'

'I always thought you were a stuck-up fucking bitch. She was *my* daughter. Mine. Not yours. How dare you?'

She seemed to be stretching out for another vase.

Frieda took hold of her hand and held it. 'I need your help.'

'How?'

'First of all, and this is important, you mustn't talk to anyone about what I've told you. If it's someone you know . . .'

Maddie snatched her hand away and took a step backwards. 'You're just sick. And you spread sickness. If I hadn't asked you for help, everything would be all right.'

'I want you to think very hard about what happened to Becky in the last few weeks of her life, and talk to me about it, not anyone else. I particularly want you to try to remember who you told about Becky going to the police.'

'I never told anyone Becky had claimed to have been raped.' She heard her words and her face twisted; she was swinging wildly between rage and despair. 'Was she really raped?' she whispered to herself. 'My little girl? Raped and murdered. It can't be true.'

'You're sure you never told anyone?'

'I didn't want to. I thought it was best to keep it quiet.'

'But you might have confided in someone.'

'I can't remember. I don't feel very well. You have to go now.'

'You have my number and I want you to call me when you've thought things over.'

'Just leave.'

'Can I ask one more thing?'

'What?'

'It might seem intrusive.'

'What?'

'I saw Greg Hollesley at the funeral and I wondered . . .'

Maddie's face turned a flaming red. 'Get out of my house. Out of my life. Out of this town. We don't want you here. We never did.'

When Frieda reached her mother's house, Chloë was in the kitchen, making tea in a very angry, noisy manner, banging mugs down and slamming cupboard doors shut.

'Not a success, then?'

'She called Mum a slut. I can be rude about my mother, but no one else is allowed to be.'

'I'll talk to her.'

She strode into the living room where Juliet sat in her usual armchair, gazing vacantly at a manic cartoon on the TV. Frieda turned it off.

'I was watching that.'

'You were rude about Olivia to Chloë.'

'Who's Olivia and who's Chloë?'

'Olivia was married to David.'

'Oh, her.'

'And Chloë is your granddaughter. As you know.'

'I've got a brain tumour. Maybe I've forgotten.'

'She's your granddaughter and she's not got a particularly easy life –'

'Because her mother's a slut. Yes.'

'Stop now! Just because you're dying it doesn't mean you have a licence to be cruel to everyone.'

'She's got a tattoo and a nose ring and one of those horrible love bites on her neck that she doesn't even bother to hide. What makes her think she can come here with her lover-boy and pretend to care about me? She called me "Gran".'

'What is she supposed to call you?' Frieda looked carefully at her mother. Perhaps the brain tumour had made her so hectic with rage. Then something caught her eye through the window.

'What's Jack doing in your garden?'

'Weeding,' said Juliet, triumphantly.

'Why?'

'I told him to. He is a gardener, after all.'

'No, he isn't. He must be freezing out there.'

'I preferred that man from the council.'

'Josef.'

'I never really had any time for women.'

Chloë came in with three mugs of tea, which she set down on the small table. Frieda could see that she had been crying.

'I never had time for cosy girl talk,' continued Juliet, with a kind of relish. 'Why aren't you in New Zealand?' This was addressed to Chloë.

'What?'

'It's Ivan who lives in New Zealand. Chloë's father is David.'

'I hated being married,' said Juliet. 'That's my advice to you, young woman. With my dying breath. Don't marry and don't have children. And if you do marry, don't marry a man who is depressed day in and day out, week in and week out, so that you feel you're being sucked into a black hole and will never escape. Everyone else felt sorry for him. Poor, adorable Jacob.'

'What's she talking about?' whispered Chloë, to Frieda, urgently. 'Can we go?'

'Wait.'

'What did King Lear say about serpents?'

'I-I don't know,' stammered Chloë.

'Of course you don't. You failed your exams, didn't you? You see, I do know some things about you. David said he was disappointed in you.'

Frieda laid a hand on Chloë's arm and stooped down towards Juliet. 'Is this how you want your granddaughter to remember you?' she said. 'As a spiteful old woman?'

'I don't care about being remembered.'

They collected Jack from the garden. His shoes were clogged with mud and his face pale with cold. Frieda saw with satisfaction that he had pulled up several plants along with the weeds. 'You didn't have to,' she said.

'She's quite scary.'

'Some of that's her brain tumour. The rest is her. Come on, Josef's collecting us in his van at the bottom of the road.'

'Where are we going?' asked Chloë. She still looked dazed. 'What about Jack's car?'

'You can pick that up later. I thought you might want to go to the coast.'

'It's quite cold and it's getting dark.'

'That's when the sea is at its best.'

Frieda directed Josef until they were driving along the side of a broad and widening estuary where boats were tipped on the mud of a low tide. In the dying light, all colour seemed to have leached away. Eventually they turned into a gravel drive and drew up outside a long white building that stood alone, looking out on to the estuary as it flowed into the grey-brown sea.

'Sea View Nursing Home,' read Jack, from the sign. 'Well, that's true anyway.'

'Why are we here?' asked Chloë. 'I've had enough of old people for one day.'

'I thought you could go for a walk along the coastal path and I'll come and join you when I'm done here.'

'Who are you visiting?'

'The father of someone I used to know.'

'This day,' said Chloë, 'hasn't really turned out the way I was expecting.'

'There's a lovely little inn a couple of miles away, and after this I'll buy us all a meal there.'

'That sounds better.'

Frieda turned from them and went up to the main entrance. She was struck by how hot and clean and over-lit it was, and how quiet, almost as if nobody was there at all. Her footsteps rang out. She walked up to the reception desk and pressed a bell.

A woman came out of a side door, carrying a mug. 'Can I help you?'

'I was hoping I could see Mr May.'

'Robbie? Is he expecting you?'

'No.'

'It's quite late for visiting.'

'I won't stay long.'

'I'm sure it will be all right. He doesn't get many visitors, poor lamb. But now he's had two in one week! What did you say your name was?'

'I didn't, but it's Dr Frieda Klein.'

'Are you family?'

'I used to live round here, many years ago. I was a friend of his daughter's.'

They walked up the broad stairs and along the landing until they came to a door that the woman pushed open.

'Robbie,' she said, putting her head into the room. 'Robbie, there's a lady here to see you. That's right. Her name is Frieda.'

*

Robert May had a round pink face and a smooth bald head. He was wearing a soft green jersey and baggy trousers, with slippers on his feet, and had a blanket across his lap and a book of crossword puzzles on the table beside him. He looked very cosy.

He examined her in mild puzzlement. 'I don't think we've met.'

'It was many years ago. I hope you don't mind me coming like this, out of the blue. I was a friend of Sarah's.'

He gazed at her with his blurred blue eyes. 'You knew my Sarah.'

'I only just found out that she'd died.'

He gave a sad chuckle. 'You're a bit late with your condolences, dear.'

'I know. But I am sorry. Truly sorry.' Frieda pulled a chair from the side of the bed and dragged it across so she was opposite him. 'I liked her a lot,' she said. 'I went riding with her a few times.'

He smiled. Everything about him was soft and muted, as if he'd been rubbed away by time and grief. 'Sarah loved horses. Whenever I see one, I think of her.'

'You never married again after your wife died?'

'No. I was sixty-one when Sarah . . . did that. To be honest, I had all the stuffing knocked out of me.'

'Because she killed herself?'

'She must have known that by killing herself she would be killing me too.'

'Did you have no warning?'

'She got very sad sometimes. Weepy. About her mother, problems at school. But she was a teenager. I thought it would pass.'

'Were there people she talked to – apart from yourself, I mean?'

If Robert May was surprised by any of Frieda's questions, he didn't show it. He passed his fingers slowly across the gleaming dome of his head, then said, 'She had friends, of course. That girl with red hair.'

'Eva.'

'Eva, yes. She was nice. And there were others. I forget their names. Mr Hollesley was very good to her as well. Took an extra interest. He came to our house quite a few times to help her with her work. He told me he thought she would go far, with that extra bit of support.' He smiled to himself, not bitterly but sorrowfully. 'Go far,' he murmured. 'And now my girl's buried in the churchyard a few miles from where she was born, next to her mother.'

'Did you ever think,' asked Frieda, not knowing how to put it less bluntly, 'that she might not have killed herself?'

'That's what the man asked.'

'The man?' Frieda remembered what the woman at Reception had said about two visitors in one week.

'Just the day before yesterday someone was here asking about my Sarah.' He gave his soft chuckle. 'I'm quite in demand.'

'Who was he?'

'I'm not quite sure. I think he was from Social Services or something. Just checking up on me. I told him he'd arrived a bit late in the day. He was very nice.'

'But he didn't tell you his name?'

'He might have done but I can't remember.'

'What did he look like?'

He didn't seem put out by the questioning. 'I'm not very good at noticing things like that. Average. Not thin and not fat, not small and not tall. Short, greyish hair. Nice brown eyes. They reminded me of Sarah's eyes. He said I might have another visitor, and here you are.'

So Dean had got here before her. Dean, with his nice brown eyes. Sweat prickled on her forehead. He wanted her to know he had been here.

When she got up to go, Robert May stopped her. 'One thing you can do for me, if you'd be so kind.'

'Of course.'

'Their graves. I never get there now.'

'You'd like me to visit them?'

'Would you?'

'I'd be glad to.'

'Put some flowers there. Tell them they're from me. I don't want them to go thinking I've forgotten.'

Later, after Jack and Chloë had gone, Frieda went away to the shed with her phone. It took an hour and a half of being moved from person to person and waiting in virtual queues, but finally she was put through to someone who could help her. No, they couldn't tell her if her voicemail had been accessed. But, yes, she could change her password.

31

It was the middle of the night, three o'clock, maybe, or four, and Frieda was awake. It was a steely, clear wakefulness that was different from anything in the daytime. Sleep seemed impossible. It was as if falling asleep was a skill she had entirely lost. If she had been in London she would have got out of bed and dressed herself, gone outside and walked down to the river or up along Regent's Park or into the maze of streets that led east or west. Here in Suffolk, the lanes and footpaths were utterly dark. She would have needed a torch even to step outside. She could have walked into Braxton but it was too small, too familiar.

She had sometimes told her patients that the middle of the night was a bad time to think about your life and your problems. That was one reason why she got up in the middle of the night. The streets and lights and noises and smells of the city, the cold air of the very early morning, they were a way of controlling her thinking, of calming it, damping it down.

But now she felt as if she was walking in her own head, picking up ideas and memories, looking at them, examining them, arranging them, putting them aside.

She thought about what had happened to her in the dark in Braxton, less than a mile from where she was lying. And what had happened? She made herself name it. Say it aloud. 'Rape.' It sounded strange in the darkness, as if someone else was saying it.

Frieda had had two patients who had been raped. She started to think about what they had said about it, then stopped herself. She mustn't deflect it on to someone else, not now, not here in the dark. What did she – Frieda Klein – think about it? What had she thought about it at the time? She had been at that painful moment of having left her first boy-friend and being involved with her complicated, hopeless, lovable second boyfriend. And then this had happened, that strange mixture of violence and ghastly intimacy, of threat and monstrous desire. In a strange way, what was most important was not the act itself but what was in your head and what was in his head.

That was what had haunted her afterwards as well. It was like being loved and hated at the same time, caressed and assaulted. In fact the caresses, the sticki-ness between her thighs, were themselves the worst kind of obscene assault. And then, after seeing it through her eyes, seeing it a second time through his eyes: the sense of power, of having marked her, taken possession of her, taken something from her. Even if it wasn't true, the suspicion that he – that unknown he – would believe it, and believe it for ever. She could see that clearly now. But what had her sixteen-year-old self thought? Frieda suddenly felt as if she was in a room full of people and all the people were herself, at different ages. They shared memories and habits but, even so, they sometimes found it difficult to communicate with each other. And there, in the distant corner, was her sixteen-year-old self, the Frieda who had been raped, alone and in the dark, and then not believed. Frieda wanted to get to her to question her, reassure her, but it was as if there were too many people in the way.

Lying in the dark she thought of something, something she mustn't forget. She switched on the light and the sudden glare made her eyes ache. She fumbled in the pocket of her jacket and found a pen and a crumpled piece of paper. She wrote on it, then switched the light off and within a few minutes she was asleep.

At breakfast, Eva was in a blurry, sleepy, amiable post-sexual state. She needed to bubble-wrap several boxes of plates and bowls for a shop in Theberton but she seemed in no hurry to make a start. Josef was already outside, up a ladder, clearing gutters at the side of the house. Frieda was starting to feel like an intruder. Was it possible that this could turn into something serious? Well, what business was it of hers? She took a sip from her mug of black coffee. The mugs and the plates had all been made by Eva and had a pleasing roughness and unevenness, each one a slightly different shape.

But the mugs were awkward to drink out of, with little rough patches and sharp edges. She put her hand into the pocket of her jeans. She could feel the piece of paper she'd written on in the night.

'You said something, Eva,' Frieda began cautiously. 'I wanted to ask you about it.'

Eva was spooning her homemade marmalade on to two large slices of toast. She paused. 'What?'

'You were talking about me when we were teenagers. Apparently you have the impression that I was still a virgin when I left Braxton.' In her head she could still hear her own sixteen-year-old voice crying out that she was a virgin. Her futile effort to make the man feel sympathy for the girl he was violating.

'Everything seems to be about sex at the moment,' said Eva, cheerfully, and bit off a large piece of toast.

'Still,' said Frieda, 'it seems a funny thing to remember, after all these years.'

'I suppose it's the sort of thing that would stick in the mind. Most of us were madly trying to pretend we were more experienced than we were. We were saying we'd done things we hadn't done, and enjoyed things we hadn't really enjoyed and that we were in control of things that actually terrified us. So, if somebody in the group actually said they were a virgin, that was a big deal.'

'But I didn't say it because it wasn't true.'

'Well, no harm done. I'm not sure if I believed it or not.'

'Who said it to you? It wasn't me.'

Eva looked thoughtful and puzzled.

'You know how it was. We talked so much rubbish. Someone would tell someone something who would tell someone else and probably half of it was made up.'

'But in this case, who told you? I really want to know.'

'Frieda, it was more than twenty years ago. I can't remember who whispered what to whom.'

'You must remember something. Was it a girl? Was it a boy?'

'It was definitely a girl. I would never have talked to a boy about something like that.'

'So which girl?'

'Honestly, Frieda, I'm sorry this ever came up. I didn't mean anything by it. It was just girls giggling about each other.'

'Please.'

Eva looked flustered. The playfulness was gone now. 'I don't know. I don't remember. But it must have been Maddie or Vanessa or one of the girls. What I do remember is I was always scared about not being with the group because I knew how we talked about absent girls when I *was* there. It seemed funny then, but it doesn't seem funny now.'

Maddie looked as if she'd bitten something unpleasant. 'What are you up to, Frieda? In some strange way, is this all about you?'

'I know it sounds strange,' said Frieda. 'It's something that people were saying about me and I need to know where it came from.'

Maddie took a deep breath. 'Are you being serious? You've come here because you want me to remember what people were saying about your sex life when you were a teenager?'

'I've got a reason for it.'

'I'm sure you have.'

'I'll explain it to you later. But for the moment I need you to remember anything that you can.'

'The answer is no. With all due respect, your sex life was not a subject of discussion between me and my friends. Nobody told me that you were or weren't a virgin. I knew you had a boyfriend and I knew who he was and what Lewis was like, so I drew my own conclusions. Is that what you wanted to know?'

'Thank you. Have you thought any more about who might have known that Becky was planning to go to the police?'

Maddie nodded slowly to herself and drew a deep breath. 'I told Greg.'

'Greg Hollesley.'

'Yes.'

'You and he are lovers.'

'Were,' said Maddie. The fight seemed to have gone out of her. 'All of that's over now. I don't think it ever meant much to him. I was just convenient. But he was nice to me and made me feel good about myself at a time when I felt crap. Now – well, now I can't believe I'll ever want to look at a man again, or buy a pair of shoes again, or gossip with friends again.'

'He was at the funeral.'

'Oh, yes. He always does the right thing,' Maddie said drearily.

'How much time did he spend with Becky when you and he were involved?'

'No time. I don't think Becky knew anything about him.' She looked sharply at Frieda. 'If you're thinking it was him, that's just crazy.'

'Why?'

'Crazy,' repeated Maddie. 'He's a head teacher. He lives in London. He didn't know Becky. He's a successful, sane man who knows which side his bread is buttered and who's always in control. Of course it's crazy.'

But he comes to Braxton regularly and he lived here when I was a teenager, thought Frieda. 'You say he knew Becky was going to the police.'

'I think I told him.'

After she had left Maddie's house, Frieda had to lean against the wall for a few seconds to gather herself. Going to people she had known as a teenager, the people she had left behind, and asking them what they had been saying or not saying about her sex life was like being publicly flayed. But she had to make herself do it. It was almost all she had.

When she knocked at Vanessa's door it was even worse. Ewan answered. Well, why shouldn't he? It was his house. He greeted her warmly and led her through to the kitchen, and then Charlotte was there as well, apparently finishing off a late breakfast. Vanessa gave her a mug of coffee – the third or fourth she'd had that day – and sat her down at the rustic kitchen table, but the atmosphere was a bit constrained and awkward. Frieda felt like an intrusive relative who had got into the habit of dropping round just a little too often.

'You're going to ask me about the timeline,' Ewan said.

'I wasn't, really.'

'We can probably do something,' Ewan said doubtfully. 'But it was such a long time ago. And drink had probably been taken, among other things.'

'What timeline?' said Charlotte.

'It's just something long in the past,' said Ewan. 'It's not something that would interest you.'

Vanessa came and sat next to Frieda. 'Is this about anything in particular?' she asked.

'There was actually something I wanted to ask you,' said Frieda.

'What?'

Frieda gave the tiniest flicker of her eyes towards Charlotte. 'In a minute,' she said.

'Charlotte,' said Vanessa. 'Have you brought your washing down?'

'Are you trying to get rid of me?' said Charlotte. 'Are you going to talk about grown-up things that aren't suitable for me to hear?'

There was a terrible moment of silence, the sort of silence when you were waiting for a crash or an explosion.

'I did want to ask your mother something,' said Frieda. 'In private. But we can go somewhere else.'

Charlotte suddenly looked embarrassed and vulnerable. 'I'm sorry,' she said. 'I need to go anyway.' She picked up her mug and the remains of her muffin and left the kitchen.

'I assume I can stay?' asked Ewan, jovially.

Frieda flinched slightly in spite of herself but she was beyond that kind of shame now. So she asked Vanessa the question she'd asked Maddie. Vanessa looked at Ewan, who had turned red, shrugged and shook her head.

'What a funny thing to ask,' she said. 'No, I don't remember anything like that.'

Frieda stood up. 'That's all I came for. Sorry for intruding.'

'Any time,' said Vanessa. 'Let me see you out.'

Frieda started to protest but Vanessa walked with her to the front door, opened it, then stepped outside with her and shut the door behind them. It was a bright morning, but blustery and cold. Frieda looked with concern at Vanessa, only dressed in one of the thin, loose cardigans she always wore.

'I'll only be a minute,' said Vanessa. 'You know, Frieda, you've really stirred up old memories.'

'Sorry.'

'No, no, I didn't say it was a bad thing. It's just that . . .' She looked around. 'I never expected when I was young that the silly, awkward things you did would somehow stay awkward. You never really get over them.'

'I don't understand,' said Frieda.

'You're a therapist. I thought you specialized in people talking about their past.'

'No, I mean I don't understand why you're saying that now.'

Vanessa looked around again, as if she was worried someone might see her. 'The answer I gave you inside wasn't quite right.'

'What do you mean?'

'Things got a bit messy back then, didn't they? We got up to all sorts of things.'

'Vanessa, what's this about?''

'There was a party a week after the Thursday's Children concert. What I remember is that Ewan and I had had a tiff about something stupid and I was there on my own.' She paused. She seemed uncertain about how to continue.

'Yes?'

'It was all a bit vague. I was out in the garden with, well, with Chas.'

'Go on.'

'He was talking and talking. He was stoned. We probably both were. And he tried to get me to kiss him, he kept trying, wouldn't take no for an answer. I probably did kiss him a bit. It's not something I'm very proud of.'

'And?'

'I think he may have talked about girls who pretend to be experienced and aren't really. And he may have mentioned your name. I feel awful saying this to you, but you asked.'

'Yes.'

'And you can see why I couldn't say this inside.'

'Yes.'

'Not that it's a big, terrible secret but it wasn't my greatest moment.'

'So it was Chas Latimer who said it?'

'Yes.'

'Good.'

'Frieda, how can that possibly be good?'

32

She leaned against an old tree outside Vanessa's house, feeling shivery, took her mobile from her pocket, scrolled down to find Chas's number, pressed it and waited for him to reply.

'Hello?'

'It's Frieda. Are you busy at the moment?'

'Yes. I'm at work. You're not, I take it?'

'I'd like to meet you.'

'How nice.'

'What time do you finish?'

'I said I was busy, but that doesn't mean I can't fit you in.' Frieda grimaced at the phrase. 'Can you come to my office?'

'Where is it?'

'About two hundred metres from my house, on the esplanade. Number thirty-seven. You can't miss it – it's the old customs house, all spruced up. Why don't you come at –' There was a pause and an ostentatious rustle of paper and Frieda knew she was meant to be imagining Chas looking through his crowded appointments diary. 'Three o'clock any good?'

'Fine. What's the name of your company?' For it occurred to Frieda that she had no idea what

Chas actually did, just that he made lots of money from doing it. Had Eva said something about head-hunting?

'Just Latimer's,' he said airily. 'Ask for me at Reception and my assistant will come and collect you. Do you want to tell me what this is about — apart from the pleasure of my company, of course?'

'Not really. Not over the phone.'

They ended the conversation but for a few minutes Frieda stayed where she was, feeling the cold wind against her face, carrying spots of rain. She welcomed the anger that was hardening inside her; her heart was a clenched fist.

Josef said, of course, that he would take Frieda to Chas's house. They arranged to meet in an hour outside the little café where she had met Lewis. She didn't really feel like going back to Eva's house. She didn't know what to make of the affair that had sprung up between Eva and Josef, but she certainly didn't want to spend her time watching it.

So she sat at a small table near the window and ordered a bowl of butternut squash soup and a roll. Today she felt cold to her bones, in spite of her thick coat. She drank the soup and gazed out at the street, where people were now running for cover as the rain thickened then turned to a spiteful hail. The sky looked purple and swollen.

She thought about Greg Hollesley, who had known

that Becky was going to the police. Then she thought about Chas Latimer: his blue eyes with their small pupils; his habitual air of ironic humour; his love of power. When he was a teenager, he had tried to control everyone around him, even the teachers, and now he did the same. He manipulated people, then watched to see how they would react. Vanessa had said Chas was stoned when he kissed her, but Frieda felt sure it had been a deliberate act of sabotage: as soon as Vanessa had got involved with Ewan, Chas would have wanted to take her away; it would have amused him. And he had told Vanessa that Frieda was a virgin. The desperate lie Frieda had told her rapist when she was sixteen had found its way to Eva's kitchen table twenty-three years later and been traced back to him.

She finished her soup and pushed the bowl away. Chas Latimer. If he was her rapist, he was also Becky's and Sarah May's rapist, and their killer. She tried to connect him in her mind with the man who climbed into the rooms of vulnerable girls, called them 'sweetheart', violated them and ended their lives. She analysed her thoughts and she analysed her feelings. It was a sort of syllogism. The rapist was an awful man. Chas was an awful man. That didn't mean they were the same awful man. And it didn't mean that they weren't.

Josef's van pulled up and she went out into the gleaming street.

*

Josef's normally stubbly face was newly shaven and his hair was clean. He was wearing a shirt that Frieda didn't recognize. She wasn't going to say anything to him about Eva, it was no business of hers, but Josef had no such inhibitions.

'Eva was your good friend, yes?'

Frieda remembered Eva as she had been all those years ago, a red-headed tomboy, clumsy and straight-speaking and loyal to a fault. 'We were friends.'

'And now?'

'I don't know. It's been such a long time. It's hard to return to a lost friendship.'

'She likes you,' he said. 'Very, very much. She tells me she never had a friend like you, when you were gone from here.'

'That's sad,' said Frieda.

'If it's not OK, I stop.'

'You mean, with Eva?'

'I stop. Like that.' He lifted his hand from the steering wheel and snapped his thumb and middle finger. 'Say the word.'

'I don't want to say the word. It's nothing to do with me. But I would hate it if anyone got hurt.'

Josef stopped in the small deserted car park overlooking the deserted beach – just one young man and his barrel-chested dog on the wet sands – and Frieda climbed out of the van. 'I don't suppose I'll be long.'

'Long, short. All good.'

She walked along the road in the rain, feeling the

salt stinging her skin. Chas's office was easy to find – it was an old wooden building, beautifully modernized. There were only two small windows in its front façade, but when Frieda was buzzed through the double doors she saw that the back, looking on to the sea, was almost all glass. It was as though the rooms were full of liquid light. She could see the man with his dog from here, and now she could also see Josef, who was smoking a cigarette at the water's edge, stepping back occasionally to avoid the small waves that curled at his feet.

A tiny woman with a helmet of platinum blonde hair showed her up to Chas's office on the first floor. It was a large room that was empty, except for a huge curved desk with three chairs ranged round it and, in the corner, an equally huge terracotta pot containing very tall dried flowers. It was more like a stage set than a workplace.

Chas stood up and spread his hands, as if he owned not only the room but the sea outside as well. 'Welcome.'

'I won't be long.'

He took off his thick-framed glasses, then arched his eyebrows. 'Oh dear,' he said. 'You'd better tell me.'

'Many years ago, you told Vanessa that I was a virgin.'

His smile froze. 'I'm sorry?'

Frieda repeated her statement.

'I'm beginning to think you have a problem.' He

353

put his glasses back on, tapping them into position. 'I know what happened with your father. That would be enough to send anyone off the rails. I couldn't be more sympathetic.'

'Why did you say I was a virgin?'

'I don't have a clue what you're going on about. But you do realize that you sound insane?'

'You told Vanessa, when you and she kissed.'

'When we kissed? I'm sorry, am I trapped in some kind of teenage girl story? Are you going to start talking about prom dresses?'

'Don't you remember?'

'Remember kissing Vanessa? For fuck's sake, Frieda, I'm nearly forty. I might have kissed Vanessa – I kissed lots of girls. I don't know what I said to her. And, anyway, this isn't a Jane Austen novel. Nobody cares if you were or weren't a virgin when you were sixteen. Not me. I didn't care then and I certainly don't now.' He came round from behind his desk and stood in front of her. His glasses gleamed. 'What I do think is that you're in danger of becoming irritating.'

'Something happened here twenty-three years ago.'

'So I gather.'

'And it happened on the night of the concert. Thursday's Children.'

'This is clearly some kind of personal psychodrama.'

'I don't care what you think. But I don't give up and

I won't go away. Something terrible just happened in Braxton and you went to the funeral. I believe it started back in 1989 and you need to tell me about that evening. I know you were there at the start of the concert, but you weren't at the end. Where were you?' Frieda stepped forward. 'And do not fuck me around the way you fuck everyone else around.'

For a moment he looked uncertain. Then he took a step backwards. 'I went to hospital,' he said.

'What?'

'You heard.'

'I don't believe you. You didn't say that to the police when they interviewed you. I've read the transcripts.'

'You can believe me or not.'

'Why did you go to hospital?'

'Why? Why do you think?'

'I don't know. That's why I'm asking.'

'I was drunk. Not just drunk. Paralytic. Vomiting. Yes. That's why I didn't tell the police. I was embarrassed. If they'd pressed me, I'd have told them but they never got back to me.' He bounced slightly on the balls of his feet, as if testing the springiness of the pale carpet. 'I had my image to protect, after all. Very important for a sixteen-year-old boy.'

'How did you get to the hospital?'

'In an ambulance. Though I don't remember that bit. I was told when I woke up. What I remember is the headache and the IV drip.'

'Do you have proof?'

'No, I do not have proof. If I'd been expecting you, I'd have got my mum to write me a note.'

'I'm going to have to check this.'

'Do what the hell you want as long as it means you get out of Braxton and never come back. We don't want you here any more.'

Frieda left the building and walked out on to the beach. She gazed over the grey, wrinkling water for a while, her hair whipping against her face, then pulled out her phone and called Jack. It went to voicemail so she made her way back over the sand to where Josef was waiting. Just as she reached the van, her mobile rang.

'Jack? Thanks for calling back.'

'That's fine. If this is because Chloë's told you that –'

'It isn't. I want you to do me a favour.'

'All right,' he said warily.

'I want you to find some A&E discharge forms that would have been sent to Chas Latimer's GP in Braxton, or nearby at least, twenty-three years ago, on February the eleventh.'

'How am I going to go about that?'

'I don't know.'

Then she made another call. She gave her name and asked to be put through to Mr Hollesley.

His tone was polite but cool, the charm gone.

'You knew about Becky's rape.'

There was a pause before he spoke. 'Maddie told me that Becky had claimed to have been raped, yes.'

'She was raped. And you knew she intended to go to the police.'

'I believe Maddie told me that, yes.'

'You and Maddie were having an affair.'

'I don't have to answer to you.'

'How well did you know Becky?'

'Hardly at all. My thing with Maddie wasn't really public.'

'Were you in Braxton when Becky died?'

'I was in London. With my family. I was very shocked and distressed to hear of Becky's death and I don't know why you're intruding into Maddie's grief. I'm surprised at you.'

Josef dropped Frieda outside Eva's, then drove away to get some building materials. Frieda made her way round the back to her shed, hoping that Eva wasn't in the kitchen to see her as she walked through the little garden. She needed to be alone. Tomorrow she would go home, and the thought of her little house, the open fire, the quiet rooms, even the tortoiseshell cat that she was the reluctant owner of, gave her relief.

She opened her computer. There were two emails from Sandy, one sent the previous evening and the other that morning, which she didn't open. She knew that, very soon, she was going to have to face up to what she had done, let the pain flood in, but not today.

There was also an email from Ewan, which she did open. Under a message that simply read, 'See what you think', there was an attachment. She clicked on it to find a display of lines and colours that at first made no sense to her. Then she saw that he'd done it: he'd assembled a timeline of the evening of the concert. And it wasn't just one but a series of parallels: a line for each person whose movements he had tried to record, girls as well as boys – and there was a complicated colour code for time and for place. Frieda stared at it, trying to see the gaps and overlaps, trying to make a coherent picture out of fragments. It made her head hurt. She was almost pleased when there was a brisk knock at the door.

'Come in,' she called, but Eva already had. She was carrying a tray on which there were two mugs of tea and a plate of buttered crumpets.

'I thought you might need something warm,' she said. She looked warm herself, with her red hair, her flushed cheeks, her layers of bright clothing.

She's happy, thought Frieda, with a stab of anxiety. 'Thank you.'

'What's that?' Eva was looking at Ewan's timeline.

'Just research.' She hesitated for a moment. 'I'm trying to establish where everyone was on the night of that concert. Thursday's Children.'

Eva took a mug of tea and a crumpet and sat on Frieda's bed. 'Don't you think you should tell me why?'

'I said before, something happened that night and –'

'I'm not a fool, Frieda. I know your mother's dying, but that's not really why you're here, is it?' Eva's flushed cheeks had become even pinker. Her freckles stood out. Frieda couldn't work out if she was angry or simply agitated. 'You have to tell me. I'm your friend. I was.'

Frieda closed her laptop lid. She looked out on to the soggy garden, full of brown leaves and withered shrubs. 'All right,' she said. 'The night of the concert, I argued with Lewis. Remember?' Eva nodded. 'I couldn't face it all and I went back home. I went to bed. Someone broke into our house that night and I want to find out who.'

Eva didn't say anything, just went on staring at her and waiting. Frieda heard the phrase in her head, 'I was raped.' Why was it still so hard to say it out loud? This was what people who'd been raped confronted: not only the disgust and disbelief of others, but their own self-disgust, their own shame, so that they couldn't even say the words.

'I was raped,' she said. 'I was raped by someone who knew I was lying in my bed while everyone else was at the concert.'

'Oh, my God, Frieda, I'm so sorry.'

She stood up and put her mug on the floor, then came over to Frieda and hugged her, bending down awkwardly and folding her in her arms. She smelt of baking and herbs and clay. Good, clean, strong. Her breasts squashed against Frieda's body and her hair tickled her face. Frieda sat quite still, neither resisting nor responding.

'You should have told me,' she said, drawing away at last. 'You should have told me then.'

'Probably.'

'That's the reason you left.'

'There were other reasons.' She wondered how much she should say; how much she wanted to say to Eva, or to anyone. 'I did tell my mother, but she didn't believe me. It's OK. It was a long time ago and it hasn't ruined my life or defined who I am. But I need to know.'

She thought about Sarah May and about Becky. Should she tell Eva that they had been raped by the same man, then murdered? No. Eva could join up the dots if she chose.

'So your timeline,' said Eva. 'That's what it's for – to work out who could have done it?'

'There are people I can eliminate. They were there, had witnesses. But I can't eliminate Lewis.'

'But you were going out with him. It doesn't make sense.'

'We'd argued. He was angry with me. Really angry. And nobody seems to remember if he was actually there or not. I don't think he was.'

There was a silence. Eva went and looked out of the window. With her back to Frieda she said, 'He was there.'

'But you said before that you couldn't remember.'

'I know. But I do.'

'Eva?'

'What was that awful phrase? Lewis and I got off with each other that night.'

'You and Lewis?'

'I felt awful. We both did, really rotten and treacherous.'

'You said it was afterwards, after I'd gone.'

'That as well. It never amounted to much. Frieda, can you ever forgive me?'

'I haven't got any business forgiving or not forgiving,' said Frieda. 'What matters is that Lewis was there.'

'He was.'

Frieda nodded, took a gulp of her cooling tea. 'I'm glad it wasn't him,' she said at last.

She called the Shaw number and Vanessa answered.

'We've just been talking about you. I feel terrible we haven't had you round for dinner yet.'

'Could I speak to Ewan?'

'All right.' She sounded slightly crushed. 'I'll call him. He's not long in from work but I think he's on the computer. Surprise, surprise.'

Frieda could hear Vanessa calling his name and soon he picked up.

'Did you get what I sent you?'

'Thank you. You obviously put a great deal of time into it. How did you manage it?'

'I do a lot of presentations for work.'

'No, the actual information.'

'Mainly Vanessa and I remembered what we could.
I made a couple of calls. Braxton's a small world.'

'I'd like to go through it with you.'

'When?'

'How about now?'

Ten minutes later, he was sitting beside her at the
table.

'Some of it needs altering,' she said.

'What?'

'Chas wasn't there throughout.'

'I thought . . .'

'He was taken to hospital. Didn't you know?'

'No.' He looked sheepish. 'My attention was on
other things.'

'And Lewis was there, after all. Can you put that
in?'

He was busy typing, manipulating lines.

'There you are.'

'Does anyone know if Greg Hollesley was there?'

Ewan pulled a face. 'Greg Hollesley? You mean . . . ?
I'll ask around. Discreetly.'

'I think I'm a bit beyond discretion now.'

'I'll ask anyway.'

'And Jeremy.'

He gave a little whistle. 'This is all a bit close to
home, Frieda.' He paused a moment. 'But I feel I saw

him. At least, a great crowd from his school were there and I feel fairly certain he was among them. So,' he said, staring at the coloured lines and the gaps, 'Lewis was there, and Eva?'

'Yes, Eva was there.'

'Chas, but not all the way through.'

'Right.'

'I was there. Vanessa was there. Sarah was there.'

'But I need to find out about Jeremy and Greg.'

He nodded several times.

'Thank you.' She hesitated. 'You and Vanessa were there all the way through?'

'Yes. I mean, we didn't actually . . .' He halted, his cheeks pink, and gave a small, embarrassed laugh. 'I don't need to go into the details of our first sexual encounter. But we were there until the very end. You can ask her if you want.'

'All right.'

'Can I ask you something? Do you remember me as a schoolboy?'

Frieda turned to look at him. 'Of course I do.'

'I feel I was always on the edge, never at the centre.'

'Did you want to be in the centre?' Frieda asked, thinking that what he had said was partly true.

'Like Chas or Jeremy? That's never been me. Maybe that was why Vanessa and I got together. She felt the same way about herself.'

'And now?'

'Now it's different. I suppose that's one of the good

things about growing up, finding a partner. You don't have the same need to be part of the group.'

'We were an odd group, though, weren't we?' Frieda said.

'Looking back, I can see we were. But you weren't on the margins or at the centre.'

'Wasn't I?' She smiled, although she was feeling obscurely sad.

'No. You didn't follow or lead. You were just yourself. I admire that. It's like you always knew who you were.'

'I don't think that's true.'

Later, she walked along the dark, wet streets towards her mother's house. Her thoughts were slow and her legs felt heavy. Looking at Ewan's timeline had been like being trapped in a crowd of clashing voices, speaking over each other. She felt a queasy anxiety.

When she pushed open the front door, she saw there was a pair of men's shoes just inside. Stout brown brogues, polished but scuffed at the toes. They didn't look like David's style.

'Hello?' she called, walking into the kitchen. No one was there, but the teapot was warm and there was a large bunch of flowers in the sink, still wrapped in paper.

She put her head round the living-room door, then went up the stairs. The bedroom door was shut and she knocked before pushing it open. Her mother lay in bed, propped up by pillows. She seemed to have shrunk in the past few days; her features seem oversized and her face much older. But she was smiling.

She was smiling because a man was sitting on the chair beside her bed. He was, Frieda saw, holding her hand between both of his. The back of his head was familiar. He turned round, and it was Detective Chief Inspector Stuart Faulkner.

His soft expression faded and a slightly sullen one took its place. 'I don't think your mother was expecting you.'

'No,' said Juliet. 'I wasn't. You can't just turn up, you know, and expect I'll be lying here waiting for you.'

'I'm heading back to London first thing in the morning, so I won't see you for a few days.'

'I think I'll . . .' Juliet's face twisted as she made the effort to find the word, which came out slurred '. . . survive. Or maybe not.' She gave a hoarse laugh, sounding drunk.

The two of them looked at her, plainly waiting for her to go.

'Goodbye, then.'

'Shut the door after you.'

As she did so, she could hear them laughing.

'Frieda? It's Jack.'

'Any luck?'

'I got what you needed. Chas Latimer did go to

hospital late on February the eleventh, 1989. He was rehydrated and released the next morning.'

'So he told me the truth. How did you find out?'

'Do you really want to know? A friend of mine from medical school works in Colchester and his girl-friend —'

'All right, all right, that's fine. Thanks, Jack.'

33

Frieda walked slowly back towards Eva's house, her mind heavy with the sludge of memories. The rain had cleared and it was possible, through the chasing clouds, to glimpse pale stars. The wind was cool on her cheeks. She felt that she was gazing back through a fog at the figures in her past: Lewis, Jeremy, Eva, Ewan and Vanessa, Maddie, Chas, poor dead Sarah, but their young faces kept dissolving into the faces they wore today, creased by time, soured by disappointment, plumped by complacency. And she thought about Becky and her friends, who, it had turned out, were not proper friends at all: that great crowd of teenagers weeping in the church for a girl they hadn't really liked. A hot and bitter anger surged through her, but when it faded she was left with sadness. Poor Becky, she thought, poor, solitary Becky. And very faintly, like the merest aftertaste, she thought, And me too, the Frieda I once was.

As she turned the corner she saw a figure hesitating near to Eva's gate, and when he turned at the sound of her footsteps she realized it was Max, although for a moment her mind, preoccupied by the past, tricked her into thinking it was Lewis, they were so alike. She raised her hand and approached him, thinking as she did so of how Ewan's daughters had spoken of Max as slightly creepy: hanging around like a stray dog, they had said. Like his father, they had said. The cruelty of the young.

'Hello, Max. Are you here to see me? Or Eva, perhaps?'

'I've only just discovered that you're the therapist.'

'I'm *a* therapist.'

'I mean you're the one Becky told me about. I didn't know until today.'

She looked at him sharply. 'Becky told you?'

'Yes.'

'You'd better come in. We can go to the shed.'

They walked round the back of the house and through the garden, soft with fallen leaves. The lights were on in the house, and as Frieda closed the shed door and drew down the blinds, she saw Eva's face peering out of the bedroom window.

He took off his heavy jacket, under which he was wearing just a thin red T-shirt in spite of the wintry weather. He sat on the chair by the desk, obviously finding it hard to begin.

'Becky told you she came to see me,' she said, to help him.

'She said she trusted you.'

'Did she tell you why she came to see me?'

There was a silence, during which Max didn't meet Frieda's gaze. Then he said, 'Yes. She told me . . .' He swallowed hard. His face looked pinched and young. 'She told me she'd been raped.'

'So she did have a friend, after all. I'm very glad.'

'It didn't do her any good, did it?'

'When did she tell you?'

'A few days before she died.'

'Tell me about it.'

'We were up by the witch monument – you know it?'

'Yes.'

'She started talking about how witches were just women who were outsiders, who didn't fit in, so they had to be got rid of. She said she was like a witch. She said – she said she could talk to me because I was an outsider too so I knew what it felt like not to be listened to or believed. I didn't really know what she was talking about but I knew it was important to her. She'd been looking so limp and hopeless lately but then she seemed stronger.'

'Go on.'

'She said she'd met someone recently who had listened to her and believed her. She said this person had told her that she rang true. She kept saying that phrase: "rang true".'

Frieda remembered saying that to Becky, and how the girl had taken heart from the words.

'Then she blurted out what had happened and she started crying. Really crying. I'd never seen her cry like that before, or anyone actually.' Max seemed almost awed by the memory. 'She was snorting and gulping and her whole face was wet and slimy. Then loads of people arrived and saw us there. They were sniggering and making stupid comments because I was hugging Becky and she was crying and I think I might have been crying too, though I've no idea why.'

'Did you know them?'

'Sure. They were from our school. Even Charlotte Shaw was there, giggling and rolling her eyes.'

'Did you speak to them?'

'Becky just ran off along the river and I followed her. She wouldn't say anything for a while. Her face was all dirty and she'd got stung by nettles on her legs. I never saw anyone look so miserable,' he added. 'Not ever. When I think about her now, I keep seeing her like that.'

'Did she say anything more?'

'She said she was going to the police. She said she knew it was the right thing to do.'

'She told me that too,' said Frieda.

'She had something she was going to give them.'

'What?'

'She was going to go and collect it before going to the police station.'

'But what was it?

'I don't know.'

'But it's obviously important. Think.'

'I don't know. She didn't say. She just mentioned it

in passing. She was talking about going to the police, about how she was feeling, all of that.'

'But she didn't say where she'd left it?'

'She didn't tell me,' he said, 'but I knew she'd left it at Vanessa's.'

'Why?'

'She was really close to Vanessa – Charlotte's mum. Everyone likes her. I knew she was there a few days before she died because Charlotte was going on to me about how pissed off she was that Becky came running to her mother, rather than Maddie. And then, the day before, she went to Vanessa's again. I know that because Vanessa said so herself. She said that she was one of the last people to see Becky alive. So I figured Becky must have left whatever it was with Vanessa.'

'We should go there,' said Frieda, standing up.

'I already did. I thought it might be important.'

'And?'

'And she told me it was true Becky had given her something for safe-keeping and she had collected it again the day before she had died. That's why she'd gone round there.'

'So Vanessa gave it back to her?'

'Yes. She told me that Becky had come round with a little bundle a week or so beforehand and asked her to keep it safe. She said she wanted to keep it away from her mother's prying eyes. It was in a plastic bag and all wrapped round with masking tape. Vanessa

assumed it was something to do with a boy or something. She didn't see any harm in it. She always had
a soft spot for Becky – she felt sorry for her with
everything that had happened. I think she was really
upset when Charlotte started being so bitchy towards
her.'

'Did Vanessa know why Becky wanted it?'

'She said that Becky wanted to show it to someone.'

'Someone?' said Frieda. 'That doesn't sound like
the police. Did she know who it was?'

'No.'

'She must have taken it to give to someone,' said
Frieda. 'And then somehow it went wrong.'

'I think everything went wrong for her.'

Frieda walked with Max up the road.

'Did you love my dad?' he asked abruptly. He was
staring ahead and on his face was an expression of
stony acceptance, as if he was preparing himself for
another blow.

'I did. Young as we both were, we loved each other
once.'

'Why?'

'Why did we love each other?'

'Why did you love him?'

Frieda understood that Max was asking why anyone would love him, the son. 'He was the only person
I knew in all of Braxton who was true,' she said. The

words she had given to Becky – that she *rang true* – echoed in her mind.

'True?'

'Who was trying to be himself,' she said.

'I don't understand.'

'It's hard to explain.'

'I don't want to end up like him.'

'Just because you're like him it doesn't mean you have to have a life like his.'

'I wish Becky was here now and we could all three of us talk like this together. Making things feel less ugly.'

'So do I, Max. But we'll have to make do with finding out how she died.'

It was late now, and the streets were deserted, but she didn't return at once to Eva's. Instead she made her way to Maddie's house. She was thinking of the bundle that Becky had retrieved.

It was several minutes before Maddie answered the door. She had obviously been asleep. She was in a dressing gown and her face was creased from the pillow. Old makeup was smudged round her eyes.

'What are you doing here? It's the middle of the night.'

'I'm sorry to have woken you, but I'm going to London tomorrow and I needed to see you before then.'

'Why? What's happened?'

'Can I come in?'

She stepped into the house and Maddie closed the door behind them. She led Frieda into the kitchen.

'What?' she asked again, sitting heavily in a chair. She looked frightened.

'I've been talking to Max,' said Frieda. Maddie made an impatient gesture. 'Becky told him about the rape.'

'She told *Max*?'

'She also told him she was going to the police and she had something to show them.'

'I don't understand. What do you mean, she had something to show them?'

'I don't know myself,' said Frieda. 'But it seems clear that she left something with Vanessa, for safe-keeping, then collected it the day before she died.'

Maddie rubbed her eyes. 'What do you mean, left it with Vanessa?' she asked. She sounded like a small child. 'What did she leave?'

'Max described it as a bundle. Wrapped up in masking tape so no one would open it. Have you seen anything like that?'

'Of course not.'

'Have you cleared out Becky's room, been through her possessions?'

Maddie shook her head from side to side. 'Not yet. I can't.'

'So there might be something in there?'

'The police looked at her room. Afterwards.'

'But because they were sure she had killed herself, they wouldn't have conducted a thorough search.'

'I don't know.'

'I thought we could take a look.'

'Now?'

'If you don't mind.'

'If you think it's important.'

'We can do it together.'

'Can I pour myself a brandy?'

'Of course.'

'Would you like some?'

'Do you have whisky?'

'Yes. I think so. We can both have whisky.'

She found the bottle, nearly full, and poured generous slugs into two glasses; she took the bottle with them as they went up the stairs towards Becky's bedroom. The door was closed and Maddie stood before it with a face of terror. Then she turned the handle and they went in.

Becky had been nearly sixteen when she died, a disturbed and anorexic adolescent with a troubled history. But her room was the room of a girl, neat and bland. The walls were yellow, with a large corkboard above the desk covered with photographs and postcards. Frieda saw pictures of Becky as a little girl: Becky between her parents, Becky on a horse, Becky with groups of friends. There were several photo-booth strips showing Becky's face pressed against the face of one friend or another. One was Charlotte.

The girls were often pouting their lips as if for a kiss, or sticking out their tongues. It all seemed absurdly young and innocent. The bed was single, with a white, frilled duvet cover and several colourful cushions scattered across it. There were soft toys piled up on the broad windowsill, some worn and obviously going back to early childhood, but others newer, as if she was still collecting them. They stared at Frieda and Maddie with their glassy eyes.

'What shall we do now?' asked Maddie. She had already finished her whisky and now poured herself another.

'Just look for this package,' said Frieda, staring around her.

She opened the narrow wardrobe, in which there were bright dresses and shirts, a pile of shoes jumbled on the floor. She looked through each drawer in the chest, and in the padded pink jewellery box on its surface. She knelt down and slid out the under-bed boxes, where there were folders and files and school textbooks. She lifted up the duvet and the pillows. Maddie just watched her, drinking the whisky. She seemed unable to move.

'I don't know what I'm looking for,' said Frieda, at last. 'But I don't think it's here.'

Maddie wandered over to the window and stared down at the heap of soft toys. She picked one up and pressed her face into it. 'I don't know how to bear it,' she said.

'I'm so sorry.'

'I wake up in the morning and sometimes I don't remember and then I have to face it all over again.' She put the soft toy gently back in its place. 'She loved these,' she said. 'Even when she was going out in her stupid high heels or coming back reeking of tobacco and drink, she liked her little animals. They were her comforters. Stupid, isn't it?'

'Not stupid. Painful.'

'This one's called Rodney and this one's Wendy and this one's Lucy. I think I know all the names even now.' She sniffed, then poured herself a third slug of whisky. 'Where's Percy, I wonder?'

'Percy?'

'Percy is a red squirrel, missing half his bushy tail. She often used to sleep with him on the pillow.'

Frieda turned to the bed. 'He's not there now.'

'It doesn't matter.' Maddie's voice was dull.

'It might,' said Frieda.

'What do you mean?'

'We can't find the package, but we can perhaps work out what was in it.'

'I don't know what you're getting at.'

'This squirrel – Percy – is missing. What else?'

Maddie stared at her in anguished bafflement.

'What isn't here?' said Frieda. 'What's gone from Becky's room?'

'I don't know.'

Frieda took the glass from Maddie's hand. 'Shall we

try to work it out? You've already noticed that Becky's squirrel is gone. Is there anything else? Items of clothing? Objects?'

Maddie stared around her, then suddenly she nodded and went over to the wardrobe. She slid the hangers across one by one, murmuring to herself, frowning intensely in an effort to remember. She took out shoes and paired them neatly on the floor. Then she did the same with each drawer, lifting piles of neatly folded T-shirts and going through them, shaking out each pair of knickers and each balled sock. There was a stupefied expression on her face. Suddenly, as she was working her way through the large bottom drawer, she stopped.

'What is it?' asked Frieda.

'Her pyjama trousers. Stripy blue drawstring ones. A bit tatty, but she loved them. They don't seem to be here.'

'You're sure?'

Maddie went through the contents of the drawer carefully, then looked in the other drawers once more. She stood up and picked up the pillow on the bed that Frieda had already lifted. 'They're definitely not here.'

'They wouldn't be in the wash, anything like that?'

'No.'

'So we're missing a soft toy that Becky often had on her bed at night and her pyjama trousers.'

'And I can't find the T-shirt she often wore at night either. It used to belong to her father and she was attached to it. It's white with a red circle on the chest.'

She stood up and walked over to the bed, sat on it and looked around the room with eyes that had become like a camera, taking everything in. 'Hang on. Her mouth guard. To stop her grinding her teeth in her sleep. Where's that? She had it on her bedside table but, look, the box is empty.'

'In the bathroom, perhaps?'

Maddie shook her head but went to look, returning empty-handed.

'Could she have been wearing it when she died?' asked Frieda.

'You don't wear a mouth guard when you hang yourself,' said Maddie.

'Exactly. These are all night things.'

Maddie stood up abruptly and started rummaging through the jewellery box. 'She wasn't wearing her horseshoe pendant. I remember noticing that. She used to wear it all the time. I didn't really take much notice then. It seemed meaningless compared to everything else. But it isn't here either.'

'Did she wear it in bed?'

'Yes. In bed, in the bath. She hardly ever took it off.'

'All right. I think that Becky must have taken off every single thing she was wearing on the night of her rape,' said Frieda, slowly. 'Even her mouth guard and her pendant.'

'Why?'

'Because everything was contaminated. She took

them off and stuffed them into a bag because she couldn't bear to see them or have them anywhere near her. But later she would have realized they were evidence.'

'Evidence?'

'DNA,' said Frieda. 'Semen. Hair. It's almost impossible for there to be no trace.'

Maddie made a little sound and put her fist against her mouth.

'So she didn't throw it away but took it to Vanessa's,' Frieda continued.

'Why?'

'Perhaps she thought you'd discover it,' said Frieda, gently. 'And, given everything that had passed between you, she preferred that you didn't. But she collected it again, the day before she died. And the question is: where is it now? Who did she see that evening, Maddie? Do you know?'

'I know she met up briefly with a group of her school friends, down by the playground – it's a sort of gathering place for the Braxton youth. But I'm not sure who was there and who wasn't.'

'Was anyone here?'

'Greg,' said Maddie. 'He came for a couple of hours.'

'Greg Hollesley?'

Maddie nodded, her cheeks burning.

'Anyone else you can remember her seeing?'

'Eva popped round for a bit. She wanted semolina

for some shortbread she was making and the shops were closed.'

'Becky was killed because she had decided to go to the police.'

'Yes,' Maddie whispered.

'Your daughter was a brave young woman.'

'We have to find him,' said Maddie. 'Can we?'

34

Frieda and Josef left the next morning. When Frieda told Eva that she was going back to London for a couple of days, she felt as if she were leaving home all over again. Eva looked shocked and upset, then turned to Josef. 'Will you be driving Frieda back again? For the reunion?'

'I think.'

'Well,' she said brightly, and held out her hand to him, as if he were a taxi driver who had come to collect Frieda. 'Goodbye, then.'

'Hey.' Josef pulled her to him and gave her a hug. When they moved apart, Eva wiped one eye with a sleeve.

'Anyway,' she said, 'it's not really a goodbye, is it?'

The plan was to drive back into London, open the mail, check that the cat was all right, contact patients. She would clear the decks, then return to Braxton, to her mother and to the reunion. But as soon as she stepped through her front door she saw an envelope with familiar writing on top of the pile of letters on the mat. She picked it up. It didn't have a stamp. Sandy must have pushed it through the letterbox himself, today, after the mail had been delivered.

She tore open the envelope and read the few lines written inside. She felt an instant pang of guilt. She'd barely thought of him in the previous days, during her journey into the past. She picked up the phone and dialled his number. There was a very brief conversation. An hour later Frieda was standing at the top of Parliament Hill and saw Sandy walking up the path towards her from the Hampstead side. Frieda felt she couldn't just stare at him as he approached her so she gazed down at the blurry city in front of her. When she turned towards him, he was almost on her. He looked older, his face newly lined. They didn't kiss or shake hands.

'This feels like the sort of place where spies meet,' said Sandy. 'Neutral territory, away from any surveillance.'

'It's somewhere we never came together,' said Frieda.

'I'm sure you can tell me something interesting about it,' said Sandy. 'Is there an underground river here? Like the Walbrook, where you left me, the river you said was struggling to get free. Is this the spot where a famous murder was committed?'

Frieda looked at the angry face. Was this the man she'd loved? Was this what they'd come to? 'I'm very sorry about all of this,' she said.

'Which bit? In particular.'

Frieda wanted to say, Don't. Please, for everything that we've been to each other, let's not do this. But she couldn't. 'I'm sorry it was so sudden,' she said. 'I'm sorry I've hurt you so badly after everything you've done for me and been to me. And I'm sorry that I've disappeared and that I haven't been getting back to you.'

'Oh, that. I was thinking more of how when you were in terrible trouble, when you'd almost been stabbed to death, I gave up everything and moved back to England. How we made a commitment to each other and then how you suddenly ended it, just like that, with nothing leading to it, no warning, no discussion.'

'I owe you more than I can say. If I've done you wrong –'

'If?' said Sandy, bitterly.

'I feel terrible about that and I'm truly sorry. But it would have been worse just to have continued.'

'I've been thinking about this. Do you think it's a coincidence that this has happened when you've gone back to the terrible trauma in your past?'

'No, I don't.'

'So how's that going? Have you found him yet?'

'I don't want to talk to you about that.'

'Oh, I see,' said Sandy. 'I'm out of the inner circle now, am I?' Frieda didn't answer. 'You can't do this, Frieda. You can't just use me like this and toss me away.'

'It's not like that.'

Sandy started to speak and stopped. He was making a visible effort to control himself.

'What we need to do . . . what *you* need to do, is to get through this, do what you need to do in your home town, deal with whatever ghosts there are in your past, and then we can talk. We can get through this.'

At this, Frieda took his hand and looked him fully in the eye. 'Sandy, I want to say this clearly: no. We are finished. It's over.'

Suddenly a desperate expression appeared on Sandy's face. 'Frieda, you've got to tell me, is it something I did? Something I did without realizing it?'

Frieda waited before speaking. Explanations were what she did, but this she found almost impossible to explain, yet she was utterly sure of it.

'What I asked myself,' she said, 'is whether you and I should spend the rest of our lives together, and when I answered no to that, nothing else mattered.'

'That can't be true,' said Sandy, and Frieda saw a flash of suspicion and anger. 'Is there something you're not telling me? Is it someone else? Is it Karlsson? Or that builder? It's better if you tell me, because I'll find out.'

Sandy must have seen something in Frieda's face because he took a step backwards.

'And then what?' asked Frieda. She took a deep breath. She had promised herself, absolutely promised, that she wouldn't get angry with Sandy because that would just be a way of letting herself off the hook, but at that moment it took an effort of will. 'You should go back to the States,' she said.

'You won't get rid of me that easily,' he said. 'I'm still part of your life.'

'Oh, Sandy. Let all of this go. Let me go.'

It ended badly, with Sandy walking angrily away. As Frieda made her way down the hill, her phone rang. It was Reuben.

'Are you in London?'

'Why?'

'Have you talked to Sasha? She's been trying to reach you.'

'I've been away.'

'Away?' said Reuben. 'Haven't you heard? Phones still work at a distance.'

'It's been complicated.'

'Go and see Sasha.'

'Why?'

'Because she's your friend.'

'I'll call soon.'

'No, go and see her. And not in a few days. Now. This minute.'

Frieda had intended to return to London for a day or two almost incognito, seeing nobody. She walked down to Highgate Road and caught a taxi over to Stoke Newington. As soon as Sasha opened the door, Frieda knew why Reuben had called. Sasha's skin was always pale but now it looked almost grey, her eyes dead, her hair matted. Sasha was her friend, but Frieda had met her as a patient who was then suffering from the abusive treatment of her previous therapist. She had been in a bad way but now she looked worse. Her shoulders were slumped, she moved slowly, she didn't even seem to fully recognize Frieda.

'Where's Frank?' Frieda asked.

'Away,' said Sasha. 'A case.'

'Does he know you're like this?'

'He's working.'

'Where's Ethan?' Frieda asked, with a sense of alarm. But Ethan was in a baby bouncer hanging from the door frame of the kitchen, grubby but fine. Frieda gathered together everything she could think of, nappies, feeding bottles, the buggy, some of Ethan's clothes, then called a cab, bundled them all inside and took them back to her house. Sasha just allowed everything to happen, as if she were half asleep. Frieda laid her on her sofa, then made a simple meal of rice and mashed carrots for Ethan before she bathed him. He simply stared wide-eyed and solemn and accepting. She put a nappy on him (she had to look at the instructions on the side of the box) and laid him in her own bed, banking him up with pillows so that he wouldn't roll off. He was asleep within a couple of minutes, his two hands clasped beneath his cheek.

Then she turned to Sasha and did almost the same

as she had done for Sasha's little son. She led her up
to the bathroom and ran a new bath, then took Sasha's
clothes off, made her get in and helped her friend
wash herself. Then she dried her and dressed her in
some of her own clothes, which were too big for her.
She took her back down to the sofa, then ran out of
the house, worried about leaving her for even a few
minutes. She bought some bread and butter and milk.
Back home she made tea and toast with jam and fed
it to Sasha piece by piece, and made her drink the
warm liquid.

'I can't,' Sasha said finally.

'You don't need to say anything.'

'I don't know what it is. It just came over me so
suddenly and there was nothing I could do to stop it.
It was like a wave.'

Sasha's speech was slurred, almost as if she were
drunk.

'This happens,' said Frieda. 'It's difficult being a
mother. But you'll get through it. We will.'

Later, Frieda led Sasha upstairs and put her into the
bed beside Ethan. She couldn't think what else to do,
so she lay down on the bed beside her friend. For
some time Frieda thought Sasha was asleep but suddenly she spoke.

'What'll I do?' she said. 'What'll I do?'

'I'm going away tomorrow,' said Frieda. 'Back to
Braxton. Just for a few days. But I'll find someone to
look after you.'

Frieda saw that tears were running down Sasha's face. 'Can't you take me with you?' She sounded like a small child.

Frieda stroked her hair. 'Not this time, my darling,' she said. 'Not this time.'

Chloë arrived just before Frieda left. She looked self-consciously solemn and excited, and also apprehensive. 'What am I supposed to do?' she asked, as if she was volunteering for a dangerous military operation.

'Just keep an eye on Sasha. Make sure she eats and has enough to drink. A doctor friend of mine is coming to see her mid-morning and Reuben says he'll drop by as well. I've left plenty of food in the fridge. Make sure Ethan's all right.'

'I don't know anything about babies! They scare me. They always scream and turn purple when I pick them up and once one was sick down my neck. And I can't change nappies, Frieda. Don't ask me to do that.'

'You probably can, if you put your mind to it. But I don't think you'll have to. Sasha will be here. If Ethan cries, comfort him. If he's hungry, give him food.'

'What food? What do babies eat anyway?'

'I've put plenty of jars of baby food on the table, or you could always mash up a banana or something. I've made up several bottles of milk that are in the fridge.'

'Oh dear,' said Chloë.

'You'll be fine. You can do your revision and make

cups of tea for both of you. I just don't want Sasha to be alone at the moment. Frank's away but I've talked to him. He'll be back in a couple of days.'

'Can I ask Jack round? He's got little nephews and nieces.'

'OK.'

'Why me?'

'Because I trust you.'

Chloë's cheeks became pink. 'All right, then.'

35

A young man in a grey suit walked on to the stage and tapped the microphone. It sounded like the beat of a bass drum, which then turned into a spiralling howl. People in the hall put their hands to their ears.

'Could someone do something about that?' he said. He took a small pile of index cards from his pocket and looked at the top one. 'I'm Tom Cooke. I'm the headmaster of Braxton High School and I'd like to welcome you all back.'

Frieda heard a voice, so close to her ear that it almost tickled.

'He looks more like the head prefect.'

She looked round. It was Chas, standing at her shoulder, leaning in towards her. There was a terrifyingly thin blonde woman just behind him, wearing a purple silk dress and makeup that was a formal mask over her strained face. Her shoulders were knobbly and her arms all sinew and bone. Chas's wife, thought Frieda.

The headmaster looked down at his index cards. '"Born to serve",' he said. 'As you all know, that is the motto of Braxton High School. Someone once said to me that it sounded like the motto of a tennis academy.' He paused, leaving space for a laugh that didn't come. He swallowed, too close to the microphone, so it sounded like water in a pipe. 'But you here, you old Braxtonians, are living proof of our motto. Among you I've been told that there are people who have made their mark in business and in the retail sector, in the law and insurance and in the City. We've got a potter and someone who can repair your boiler. I might give him a call myself.' There was a pause for a laugh that, once more, didn't come. 'I've even been told that there may be a psychiatrist here tonight, so mind what you say to your neighbour.'

'Your fame precedes you,' Chas murmured.

'I'm not a psychiatrist,' Frieda said.

'I don't think they know the difference out here.'

Tom Cooke moved gradually through his pile of index cards. He talked of the refurbishment of the science building, of the challenges of the school's new academy status; he informed them about a special exhibition illustrating the school's history on display in the corridors, and he pointed out the location of the pay bar and the fire exits.

'In conclusion,' he said, 'I hope you'll all think of joining the Friends of Braxton High School and ensuring that we continue the school's great traditions and, in the words of our motto, continue to serve a new generation.'

There was another silence, then a sprinkling of applause as he walked away from the microphone.

Immediately, the atmosphere changed. The lights dimmed, and the murmur of conversation grew louder.

'This is my wife, Clara,' said Chas.

Frieda put out her hand and Clara gripped it in her cold thin fingers. 'I've heard of you,' she said. 'And I gather you came to our house.'

'It's beautiful,' said Frieda.

Clara leaned forward, her large eyes glittering. 'It's a gilded cage.' She gave a high laugh and turned away unsteadily on her spindly heels. She was clearly already drunk.

Chas looked after her and shrugged. 'I don't know why she insisted on coming,' he said. 'It'll only make her jealous all over again.'

'Should she be?'

'Women hate men to have a past.'

'I think it's more often the other way round.'

'What's your past?'

'Frieda Klein.' Frieda turned round. Two women were staring at her with amazed expressions and both gave a little scream of greeting. 'Frieda bloody Klein,' said one. 'You are literally the last person I thought would ever come to a school reunion. Paula and I were talking last night and the one thing we agreed was that you wouldn't be here.'

Paula, Frieda said to herself. Paula. The name meant nothing to her. She couldn't remember the faces either. But it didn't matter because the two women then caught sight of Chas, gave another little scream and hugged him. Chas glanced over their shoulders at Frieda with amused helplessness. She saw how he gave each woman a kiss just a little too close to her mouth. Frieda took the chance to slip away, jostled by crowds of men who had started drinking before they arrived, and women who'd spent too much time thinking about what they should wear to a reunion. How did they want to appear and who was it they wanted to be when they met all their friends and pseudo-friends from the past?

Beyond the people, the special decorations, the bunting and the exhibition, Braxton High School was both changed and utterly familiar, as if she were revisiting her past in a dream. She walked out of the main hall and along a corridor with classrooms on either side. An extension had been built at the end, jutting out into the old playground. All the classroom doors were new and brightly coloured. The whole space had been scoured year after year by new cohorts of teenagers but something remained, a smell, the feel of the wooden floor, so that she felt herself back there, and it was no longer a memory but a vivid, queasy sense of dread and darkness. She could hardly believe that she had come back but she reminded herself that there was a reason: she had a promise to keep.

Returning towards the noise of what now sounded like a boisterous party, she saw a couple walking along the corridor. Their faces were turned away from her towards a project on the wall. As she got closer, she recognized the man.

'Lewis,' she said.

He turned round and smiled. 'Hey,' he said. 'Looks like we couldn't keep away.'

The woman with him was tall, curvy and very dark, like a gypsy. She wore a knee-length black shirtdress, belted at the waist. Frieda saw what looked like a chain wrapped around one of her ankles but then recognized as an ornate tattoo. Lewis introduced her awkwardly as Penny, then introduced Frieda with a complicated and incoherent explanation of who she was, which made Penny look at Frieda with new attention.

'Max has been talking about you,' she said.

'We've got some interests in common,' said Frieda.

'He's being a bit mysterious at the moment. Is everything all right?'

'I think it will be.' She looked at Lewis. 'He's a thoughtful young man. I like him.'

His face relaxed. 'Good. In fact, he's here tonight.'

'Here?'

'A group of them are helping out with the catering. Roped in, volunteered, whatever. He'll probably offer you a cocktail sausage or a mini pizza. Though you might not recognize him – he had to put on smart trousers and a jacket.'

'I'll keep an eye out.'

'We're going outside for a smoke. Some things never change. You want to join us?'

'There are some people I need to see.'

'So one thing has changed.' He turned to Penny. 'We used to go out to the sports field at lunchtime.'

Penny slid her arm through Lewis's and smiled at Frieda. She obviously wasn't one of those women who Chas had said were jealous of their partner's past.

Frieda walked back into the hall, where she had to push her way through the crowd. Some still looked like children, others were her own age and a few were much older. This was where she had come from. Frieda felt a lurch at the thought, then saw Vanessa clutching two plastic glasses and looking around. She wore a dark silk dress with a flowery jacket. When she saw Frieda she gave a nervous smile. 'I was bringing a drink for someone but I've forgotten who they are and I can't find them anyway. Do you want it?'

'What is it?'

'White wine.'

'All right.'

Frieda took a sip. At least it was cold.

'Is Ewan here?'

'He's around somewhere.'

'He's right behind you,' said a voice, and she felt his arm around her shoulders. Ewan kissed her on both cheeks, then held her at arm's length. 'You're a sight for sore eyes,' he said. 'I've just bumped into Mrs Flannigan. You know, the old PE teacher. God, she terrified me. I used to pretend I was ill on days when we had PE. Cross-country runs. Do you remember?'

'Yes.'

'It was all right for you. You could run, which I couldn't, and also you looked great in shorts. Which I certainly didn't. Jeremy! Jeremy, over here.' He waved both arms in the air. 'I was just saying that Frieda looked great in shorts.'

'She probably still does,' said Jeremy. He was wearing a silvery-grey suit and a red bow-tie. Maybe that was the latest look in the City, thought Frieda. 'Where's Catrina?' asked Vanessa. 'Catrina was in the year below us,' she explained to Frieda. 'That's why Jeremy's here.'

'I think she's in some screaming huddle near the front door,' said Jeremy. 'It's really strange. As if people aren't just remembering the past but actually returning to it. Soon everyone will be snogging on the dance floor.'

'Speak for yourself,' said Vanessa.

'I won't be snogging anyone but you, honey,' said Ewan, patting her on the back as if she had hiccups.

'That's because it was Vanessa you were snogging then,' said Jeremy, with a laugh that took everyone by surprise. 'But who was I snogging?' He looked at Frieda, who turned away.

'Are you having a good time?' she asked Vanessa.

Vanessa took a gulp of wine. 'I'm not sure. I

suppose I must be. Have you met any old school-mates?'

'A couple.'

'Does it bring back happy memories?'

'My memories of the school are a bit mixed.'

'Max,' said Ewan, turning with a smile. 'What a transformation. Hey, watch out!'

Max, dressed in black and his hair brushed flat, was holding out a silver tray at a tilt. Several smoked-salmon blinis slithered to the floor and lay face down. A gaggle of teenagers, most of them girls, stood nearby, also carrying trays. They were giggling at him. Frieda saw Ewan and Vanessa's daughter, Charlotte, among them.

Vanessa stooped and picked them up. She was wearing a dress that was slightly too small for her, her breasts almost bursting out. Frieda saw Max glance down, then quickly away, mortified.

'How are you?' Frieda asked him.

'I don't know why I'm here.'

'I know what you mean.'

'Have you seen my dad?'

'He's with Penny. Who seems very nice,' she added encouragingly.

'Is he . . . you know?'

'He's fine. I think he's having a cigarette outside.'

'I'm a bit drunk,' he admitted. 'I can embarrass him for once. I finish at half nine. Could we have a talk before I go home?'

'Shall I meet you by the swings?'

'Hello, girls.' It was Chas again. He put an arm round Vanessa and Frieda. 'Are you meeting up with some of your old flames?'

'No.' Frieda stepped out of his embrace.

'I've only just arrived,' said Vanessa.

'I've already encountered a couple of my guilty pleasures.'

'I don't even want to know what that means.' But Vanessa giggled.

'I've had a couple of women of a certain age come up to me and, well, you know, it's funny the things you've forgotten about until someone reminds you.' He glanced at Frieda. 'I suppose you disapprove of the idea of guilty pleasures.'

Frieda was spared having to answer when she noticed Eva standing on her own and walked across to join her.

'Thank God,' Eva said. She was dressed in a brightly striped dress and had put on blue eye-shadow. 'Finally someone I recognize. I really thought I'd know more people but most of them look too young to come to a reunion. Or too old. You look nice, though – I love that scarf thing. Or is it a stole? Do I look like a tent? Is Josef with you?'

The last question was such a sudden change of subject that it took Frieda by surprise. 'You mean with me at the reunion?'

'He could have come. He said he might. People are bringing people.'

'He's got a job on a big construction project in London.'

'Good for him.'

'Look, Eva, if you want to talk about it . . .'

'Because that's your job, isn't it? But there's nothing to talk about. It was one of those modern adult sort of relationships. No commitment on either side. Just two people having a good time.' She raised her glass, then saw that it was empty. 'Can I get you another drink?'

'I'm fine.'

'Now, look over there. Do you remember Mr Hollesley?'

Frieda saw him talking to the two women she had failed to recognize earlier. They were gazing up at him adoringly. 'Greg. Yes. I met him the other day.'

'Greg,' said Eva, admiringly. 'I would never dare call him that. He'll always be Mr Hollesley to me. He's still so handsome. But there were some people who called him Greg even when we were at school. Do you remember Teresa Marland?'

'I remember the name.'

'Do you remember the school trip to Belgium?'

'I didn't go on school trips.'

'If Teresa Marland is here, ask her about the hotel room in Ghent and Mr Hollesley and see if she goes red.'

'I don't think I will.'

'Things were different in those days,' said Eva.

'They couldn't get away with it now.' She looked more closely at Frieda. 'Am I shocking you?'

'No,' said Frieda, slowly. 'It's just hearing you talk about what happened with you and Josef. It was painful for you. Then, hearing you talk like that about Greg Hollesley and that girl, as if it was just fun.'

'Well,' said Eva, 'we're at a reunion. We're meant to be laughing about the past. All of us have things we're not proud of.'

'Like what?'

'We just do. This isn't the evening to talk about it. Or then again, maybe this is the only evening to talk about it.'

From then on the evening was like a series of snapshots, flashes in a dream. Greg Hollesley came up to her and gave her a kiss on both cheeks, wine breath and aftershave. Max reappeared, and this time he was clearly drunk, swaying on his feet, his tray tipping and wine spilling over the brim of the glasses. Lewis and Penny came back into the room, looking blurry. He whispered something in Penny's ear and she laughed. Was he telling her something about what Frieda was like as a teenager? Was it funny? Then she saw Eva go up to them. She looked a bit drunk and she put her arms round Lewis's neck while Penny watched with a bemused expression.

She saw Vanessa and asked her where Ewan was. She wanted to ask him something about the evening, that other evening when they had been together, most of them, most of the time. So many alibis. So few opportunities.

'He went out with some of the gang for a cigarette. They're probably behind the bike sheds.'

'He doesn't smoke.'

'He did when he was sixteen, though.'

She saw Chas deep in conversation with one of the women she'd met early on, not Paula, the other. He raised a hand and pushed a strand of hair away from her face, and then touched her lip with his thumb, very gently. It was like watching him at work at a party many years ago. Where was his wife, rail-thin, wretched Clara? She found her in the Ladies. She was standing in front of a mirror, absolutely immobile, staring at her reflection as if she'd seen a ghost.

'Should I leave him?' she asked Frieda, as if they were continuing a conversation they'd started earlier.

'Leave Chas?'

'Yes. You tell me.'

'I have no idea. It's not something anyone can decide for you. And I don't even know you.'

'You know Chas, though.'

'Not really.'

'I think I have to leave him. But I know I won't.'

Eva and Vanessa burst in. 'Guess what?'

'What?'

'There's a fight going on in the playground.'

'Between who?'

'I don't know. Men with fists. It doesn't look like in the movies, though, more like a messy, undignified scramble.'

Frieda touched Clara's thin arm. 'You don't have to stay, you know,' she said, then walked back into the noise. The music had started up.

'Want to dance?' asked Jeremy, appearing at her side. His head was shiny with sweat. 'For old times' sake?'

'No.'

'Can't you even say, "No, thank you"?'

'I'll dance,' said Vanessa.

'Where's Ewan?'

'Probably talking about computers,' said Vanessa, with a laugh. 'He was never a great dancer. He just sort of bounced.'

Frieda saw that Maddie Capel had arrived, in a shiny, short red dress with red lipstick like a gash across her face. As she looked at her, Frieda thought, This is what this is all about, people coming here and dressing themselves up and performing in order to say, Here I am. This is what I've made of myself. This is what time has done to me. This is what I've become.

And then she thought, Someone in this room raped me, raped and killed Sarah May, raped and killed Becky Capel. He's here.

The music got louder, the lights were turned down lower, people were dancing, at first just a few pairs, then a thickening crowd. It was like a teenage party performed by a middle-aged cast. She saw Eva dancing with a man she didn't recognize, Greg Hollesley dancing with a woman she didn't recognize, then with Maddie, holding her close. Maddie's eyes were shut and her mascara had smudged: she'd been crying. She saw Jeremy standing at the side with his wife, who was saying something in his ear, angrily. His bow-tie had unravelled. She saw Chas walking out of the hall with the woman who wasn't Paula. She saw Clara leave, car keys in her hand.

'Aren't you going to dance?' Frieda looked around. Lewis was there, but not Penny.

'No.'

'Not with me?'

'Not with anyone.'

'Why did you come this evening?'

'Why did you?'

He shrugged. 'A trip down memory lane?' he suggested. 'Look at us all.'

'I like Penny.'

'You think she can save me?'

'I think only you can save you.'

'Same old Frieda. You shouldn't have come back.'

'People keep saying that.'

Eva broke away from her partner and made her way towards them. She'd taken off her shoes and her hair had come loose. She looked absurdly young. 'Come and dance, Lewis,' she said, holding out her hand to him.

'Not just now.'

'Please. Just once.'

He took her hand and let himself be led into the crowd. He'd always been a good dancer.

'All alone?' It was Vanessa again, breathing slightly heavily.

'Hello. Are you enjoying yourself?'

'Well,' Vanessa began, then stopped. 'Wait here,' she said, and disappeared into the crowd. A couple of minutes later she re-emerged. She was clutching a bottle of white wine and two plastic glasses. 'Let's go outside for a moment. I can't talk in here.'

The two of them walked out of the front entrance of the school, the one that was normally reserved for teachers. They sat down on a low wall. It was dark now and they could see shapes of people around them. Some had their arms around each other, kissing, murmuring. There was a glow of cigarette ends, the smell of smoke.

'How old are these people?' said Vanessa. She poured wine into two of the glasses and handed one to Frieda. Then she took a cigarette packet out of her pocket. She offered one to Frieda, who shook her head. She lit one for herself. 'For one night only,' she said. She took a deep drag, then coughed.

'I was going to ask you,' said Frieda, when Vanessa had got her breath back. 'Max told me about Becky giving you a package to keep.'

'That's right. He seemed very agitated about it.'

'Why did she give it to you?'

'I have no idea. I imagine she didn't want Maddie finding it.'

'Do you know what it was?'

'It was all taped up. She obviously didn't want anyone prying.'

'You weren't tempted to look?'

'Of course I was tempted. But she trusted me so I couldn't. One of the things you learn with having children is that they have to have their secrets.'

'There are good secrets and then there are secrets that are better told.'

'Yes.' Vanessa sighed. 'Now I wish I'd made her confide in me more, but at the time it seemed like she was just another adolescent. Like Charlotte. Or Max – he's another one I fear for.'

'He's very upset about Becky.'

'That's complicated, of course.'

'Why? They were friends.'

'Is that what he told you?'

'Yes.'

'He was more like her stalker. I think he scared her a bit. That's why I was a bit taken aback when he came storming round to our house asking for that bundle she left. It seemed odd.'

'What are you saying?'

'I don't think I'm saying anything in particular. Just that you shouldn't believe everything Max tells you. He's very like his father was, isn't he? I know you and

Lewis went out, but that was decades ago. He always was a bit of a strange one.'

'Who isn't?'

Vanessa laughed. 'That's true. Anyway, I feel sorry for the young ones. It makes me remember what it was like at that age. So intense. So easy to go off the rails.'

'You were close to Becky.'

'She was a sweet, vulnerable girl and she was friendly with my girls. I was fond of her. I wish I'd been able to help her.'

'I'm sure you did what you could.'

'I don't know.' Vanessa said. 'And I worry about the effect on others. I do feel anxious about Max, though.'

'In what way?'

'I think he let Becky's suicide get to him. He seemed distraught. I'm afraid he may do something stupid.'

'He seems all right to me,' said Frieda.

'He's so unstable, like his father. I talked to him this evening and something about him really scared me. It reminded me of her.'

Frieda started to say something but then a man stumbled past them, brushing up against Frieda so that her wine spilled.

'That was Jeremy,' said Vanessa.

'I know.'

'Where's he off to?'

Frieda just shrugged.

'You hate this place, don't you?'

'That's not right exactly.'

'You know, people can surprise you, even at their worst.'

'What do you mean by that?'

Vanessa drained her glass and refilled it. 'Doesn't this bring back memories?' she said. 'In the garden at parties?' In the dark, Frieda could barely make out her expression. 'People don't always stand by, you know. A few years ago I was out with a girlfriend – we had a meal or something, a bottle of wine, maybe more than a bottle. Afterwards I was walking back, looking to get a taxi, and I bumped into a group of young men. They started saying things and then it all got out of control. They started touching me, putting their hands on me.' She stopped while she took another drag on her cigarette. 'It was horrible, utterly humiliating, and then it became frightening. I thought that was it. Then, quite suddenly, a man walking past intervened. I thought they were going to kill him but he somehow managed to talk them down and take me by the arm and get me away and find me a cab. In the end nothing happened at all and I never knew his name. I sometimes think there's an alternative universe where that man didn't walk past and I'm dead and those men are in prison or maybe still walking free.'

There was a long silence.

'Ewan told me that story,' said Frieda.

'Really?'

'In a slightly different version.'

'That's the thing about a marriage. You have your fund of stories.'

Frieda looked at her watch: it was nearly half past nine. 'I'll be back in a moment,' she said. She made her way down to the playground, which was empty now apart from a man standing alone and smoking a cigarette. Max wasn't there. She waited a few minutes, then walked swiftly back inside and through the hall into the kitchen. It was full of teenagers. A couple was standing up against the wall, kissing; the boy had his hand up the girl's skirt, and Frieda recognized the girl as Charlotte. She tapped her on the shoulder.

'What?' said Charlotte. 'What are you doing in here?'

'I was looking for Max.'

'That creep. He's pissed.'

'Where is he?'

'I don't know and I don't care.' She stared at Frieda, wrinkling her nose. 'You're weird.'

Frieda went back into the hall and made almost an entire circuit of it, in the dim lights and grinding music, through the hot bodies and past the grinning, grimacing faces, before she found who she was looking for.

'Are you having a good time?' said Lewis. He seemed more sober than anyone else in the room. 'I've been talking to Penny about the old days.'

'Where's Max?'

'Max?'

'Yes, where is he?'

'I've no idea. Probably still in the kitchen. I saw him a bit ago. He was having a fine old time.'

Frieda felt she should stop worrying but she couldn't and at first she couldn't remember why, then suddenly she could. She remembered Vanessa's words: she had said that Max reminded her of Becky.

'Ring his mobile.'

'What's this about?'

'We don't have time: ring his mobile.'

Lewis pulled his phone out of his pocket and called.

'Straight to voicemail.'

'We've got to find him.'

'Won't you tell us what's going on?' This from Penny.

'I'll explain later. Come with me.'

She pulled Lewis after her and they ran outside, past couples and groups. The night air was cold and damp.

'He's not in the hall or the kitchen or the playground. Let's look in the car park. Keep calling his mobile.'

They hurried through the rows of parked cars. She stared around at the dark crouched shapes of cars, then back at the school where lights spilled out across the gravel driveway. They could hear the music from where they stood, but faintly.

'How did he get here?' she asked Lewis.

'With me and Penny. He's staying with us for the weekend.'

'Did he say anything about leaving early or going on somewhere else?'

'No.'

He could be anywhere. In one of those unlit classrooms, by the bike sheds, on the sports field, on the flat roof that was so temptingly easy to climb on to, in some clinch with one of the girls who'd been laughing at him earlier. He could be smoking with a group of friends. He could have gone on to a pub.

'We've got to go to your house. Where's your car? Have you got your keys on you?'

'Yes.'

Lewis wasn't protesting any more. He had picked up on her urgency. He ran over to a small, rust-spotted car and unlocked the doors. They both climbed in.

'Is it far?' Frieda asked, as they drove out of the school gates.

'Near the old barracks, up the hill.'

'I know them.'

'Can you tell me what's going on?'

'I think he's in danger.'

The car veered round a corner. Rain started to fall heavily; the windscreen wipers had frayed and the loose rubber slapped against the glass. Soon they were out of the centre of the town and were driving along the ridge of the hill, looking down at Braxton.

Here, the houses were identical, row upon row of small, flat-fronted buildings in an interlocking grid of small roads and cul-de-sacs. Frieda saw that all the roads were named after flowers: Hollyhock Close, Sunflower Street, Lupin Rise. It felt very quiet, no cars on the roads and no people; most of the windows were unlit, with curtains drawn. Lewis screeched to a halt outside number twenty-seven Campion Way.

At the front door, his hands were trembling and he couldn't get the key into the lock. Frieda took it from him. The door swung open and they stepped into the tiny hall. Everything was dark and quiet.

'There's no one here,' Lewis said.

They heard the screech of tyres coming from the road at the back of the house as a car drew away. Frieda called out but there was no reply and she ran up the stairs, two at a time.

One door was open and the room empty. One door was closed. She hurled it open and stepped inside, Lewis on her heels. She could hear him breathing, a ragged gasp.

Even before Lewis turned on the light she could see the shape in front of them. Above them. Legs moving slightly. The dazzle of the bulb brought his face into view, blue lips and open mouth. Open eyes staring. Strung from a rope.

'Hold him up,' she said. Lewis looked at her unseeingly. She wrapped her arms around Max's legs and pushed upwards, taking the weight from the rope.

'Do this. Hold him.' Lewis was staring at her, his face sweating. He looked like he was in shock. Could he do this? Then, like a man in a dream, he put his arms round his son's legs and Frieda stepped away.

'Just for a few seconds,' she said.

She ran down the stairs again, feeling her ankle turn on the bottom step, into the kitchen, wrenching open drawers until she found a serrated knife, and then upstairs again. She pulled a chair from the side of the bed and stood on it, then sawed at the rope until it gave and Max's body fell in a soft, heavy heap into Lewis's arms and toppled him; they lay on the floor together, father and son. Lewis was crying out Max's name.

She pulled Lewis away from Max, put her phone into his hand. She turned the boy over. He lay there in his ill-fitting black jacket. His eyes were closed now. White drool ran from his mouth. The noose was still around his neck.

She put her hands firmly on his chest and began pumping up and down, up and down. Behind her she could hear Lewis giving his address through retching sobs.

Chest compression. Pause. Mouth-to-mouth. Lewis's son, who looked so like the boy she used to love. Pause. Chest compression. His eyelids were blue. Mouth-to-mouth again. A bitter taste on his lips. She felt Lewis beside her.

'Is there anything?' Lewis was crouching at her side. She could hear his hoarse breathing.

She tried not to think or feel. Just to make her body into the machine that would bring Max back. For they had heard that car screeching off as they entered the house. It couldn't have been long – seconds rather than minutes, even.

'Feel his pulse,' she said to Lewis, and he put his thumb against the blue vein on his son's thin wrist.

'I don't know,' he said. 'I can't tell. I don't know. Frieda.'

They heard the sirens and then they saw the blue lights striping the ceiling. Lewis ran down the stairs. Frieda could hear him crashing, falling. Then the door was opened, and soon the room was full of people, calm voices, instructions, a stretcher. A mask over Max's chalky, spittled face. The rope removed from his neck. A blanket over his motionless body. She stood up, cramping in all her limbs.

'Go with him in the ambulance,' she said to Lewis. 'And call his mother on the way. I'll stay here to wait for the police.'

'Yes,' He stared at her wildly for a moment, his face a clench of horror, and then was gone.

Frieda could hear the police car coming over the hill. She went quickly into the bathroom and ripped off several sheets of lavatory roll, then returned to Max's room and to his narrow truckle bed.

Very carefully, making sure she didn't make contact

with it, she picked up the little red squirrel that had lost half its tail and had been Becky's favourite soft toy. It had gone missing but it was now on Max's pillow. She wrapped it in the toilet tissue so that no bit of it was exposed. Then she lifted up her dress and tucked it under the waistband, arranging her scarf so that it covered the bulge, before she went downstairs to let the police inside.

36

In those minutes of searching for Max and cutting him down and struggling to revive him, it had felt as if time was speeding up and slowing down, a wild night in which lights were flashing, sounds coming and going, loud and soft.

When the police arrived it felt as if normality was being restored, except that everything was slightly grey, everything was moving just a bit too slowly. There were three of them, two men and a woman. After they had introduced themselves to Frieda and taken her name, address and relationship to Max, they went upstairs in slow single file and into Max's room. They picked up the severed rope and put it into a plastic bag. Then they looked around, opening drawers and lifting up books.

'He didn't leave a note,' said Frieda.

'You can't be sure.'

'I am.'

She could see them exchanging glances.

'Have you moved or touched anything?' they asked.

'No.'

Frieda sat on the bed. It was hard to concentrate on anything while she didn't know if Max was alive or dead, but she needed to order her thoughts. She felt a weight on the bed next to her. The female police officer had sat down beside her. She had light brown hair tied back behind her head and an eager freckled face. She was young and nervous. She couldn't have been used to this.

'Are you all right?' she asked. 'Can we get you something?'

'I'm fine,' said Frieda. 'But thank you.'

'We're almost done here,' the woman said. 'We need to check that you're all right and that the premises are secure.'

'Because it's a crime scene?' said Frieda.

'Crime scene?' said the officer. WPC Niven. That was her name, Frieda remembered. 'He just tried to kill himself and it looks like he succeeded. Poor guy.'

Frieda knew that it was probably pointless, that it had all happened before. But she had to try.

'You need to treat this as murder, or attempted murder if Max survives.'

'What?' said Niven. 'What do you mean?'

'You need to do a few things,' she said.

Niven looked suddenly wary. 'Like what?'

'This hanging was staged . . .'

'We don't know that.'

'So Max must have been drugged. You'll need to organize a blood test. The sooner the better.'

'I'm not sure about that.'

'A member of the public has alerted you, which

means you need to investigate. You should write it down in your notebook. Just so you don't forget it.'

Niven's face had flushed. Frieda wasn't sure whether it was out of anger or embarrassment. But Frieda saw her write the words 'blood' and 'test'. Her handwriting was rounded, like that of a small child.

'Also,' Frieda continued, 'you need to talk to Ewan Shaw.'

'Is he a witness?'

'He did it. Go on, write his name down.'

Niven seemed paralysed, so Frieda took her notebook out of her hand and wrote Ewan's name, address and phone number, then handed it back to her.

'There,' she said.

'Is he a friend of yours?'

'I know him.'

'Why would he have done that?'

Frieda hesitated. The crucial evidence – Becky's toy – was no use at all. It would only incriminate Max.

'What it can't be,' said Frieda, 'is a suicide, or an attempt. Max was seen forty minutes ago at the party at Braxton High School. He was serving there, in good spirits. We found him here, unconscious, with no means of transport. When we arrived, I heard a car drive away at the back.'

'Did you see it?'

'No, but you could ask Ewan Shaw where he was in the last hour and who saw him.'

'I'm not sure we can do that.'

'I know how this works. I've notified you of a crime. I've informed you of a suspect. At least a witness. You need to respond. The more quickly you do it, the more likely you'll turn something up.'

'I'll talk to my supervising officer,' said Niven, standing up from the bed.

'Do it tonight, not tomorrow,' said Frieda. 'And while you're at it, ask him about the death of Rebecca Capel.'

Niven looked puzzled for a moment. 'The girl who killed herself?'

'She didn't kill herself. If it would be any help, I could come with you to see Ewan Shaw.'

Niven looked down at her notebook. 'Dr Klein,' she said, 'it doesn't really work like that.' She went across to the other two officers. Frieda saw them conferring, and the two young men glanced round at her. As she stood up, ready to leave, one approached her. He seemed almost resentful.

'I've been talking to my colleague,' he said. 'We always investigate occurrences like this. And we'll conduct interviews.'

'Including Ewan Shaw.'

'We'll talk to him. If you have any relevant information, let us know.' He wrote a number on a pad, tore it off and handed it to her.

'Is this a direct line?' Frieda said.

'You'll be put through to the right person.'

Frieda turned on her heel and walked out of the

room, out of the front door and into the slanting rain. Her phone rang and she snatched it out. Lewis: only when she saw his name on her screen did she understand how scared she was, clogged with fear for the young man who looked so like the boy she had loved once, and who had touched her heart with his rawness and his troubles.

'Lewis. Tell me.'

'He's alive.' There was a strangled sound at the other end, and she realized that Lewis was weeping. 'He's alive, Frieda.'

'I'm so glad.'

'I don't understand . . .'

'All that can come later. Go back to him now.'

'Yes. Yes. But, Frieda . . .'

'Go to your son. He needs you.'

She ended the call and stood for a few moments, letting the knowledge seep through her. Max was alive. She had discovered her rapist, Becky's killer. Her job was done now, although nothing seemed quite over. She walked through the maze of roads named after flowers, on to the road that looked down at the centre of Braxton, where the lights glinted in the darkness. Her mother was there, dying. Her school was there, with its corridors and classrooms and ancient, tainted memories. Her past was there, but not her future. She turned her back on the town and started to walk, pressing buttons on her phone as she did so.

'Reuben?' she said. She had left her coat at the school, and was wet and cold.

'Frieda?' His voice was thick with sleep.

'Have you drunk anything?'

'Sorry?'

'Tonight.'

'I was at the theatre. I had one glass of wine beforehand.'

'Can you come and fetch me?'

'Can't you get a cab?'

'I'm in Braxton.'

'Hang on. Wait.' She could picture him sitting up in bed, turning on his light. 'From Braxton?'

'Yes.'

There was a silence.

'All right.'

'Thank you, Reuben.'

'You're crazy. You know that, don't you?'

'Maybe.'

'But you're all right?'

'Yes. I really am.'

37

'When this is over,' said Reuben, 'you'll need to talk to someone about all of it.'

'It is almost over,' said Frieda, staring out of the streaming window of Reuben's shabby old Prius. 'And I don't think there'll be much to say about it.'

'Does that mean nothing much has come of all of this?'

She touched his arm. 'Reuben, I'm grateful that you've done this. I feel like you've saved me from something.'

'I think you've saved *me* from time to time. Saved me from myself. I had a feeling that at the end of your expression of gratitude you were about to say "but".'

'Friends are meant to be the people you can talk to. I was going to say that you're one of those friends I can be silent with.'

'That sounds like a funny thing for one therapist to say to another.'

'I've had some good sessions that were largely silent. Sometimes I'm pleased when my patients *stop* talking.'

'I'd be relieved if almost all of my patients stopped

talking,' said Reuben. 'But before we descend into silence, where do you want to go? Shall I drop you at home?'

'Yes,' said Frieda.

'You'll probably be glad to be alone in your own house at last.'

'Except I don't think I will be alone.'

Frieda opened the door as quietly as she could, but Chloë came down the stairs before she had time to shut it, rubbing her eyes blearily. She was wearing boxer shorts and one of Frieda's T-shirts. Her hair was tied up on the top of her head and her face, rubbed clean of any makeup, looked young and anxious.

'It's just me,' said Frieda. 'I didn't mean to wake you.'

'What time is it?'

'Late.'

'I didn't know you were coming back tonight.'

'It was a last-minute decision.'

'Your clothes are wet. And what are you wearing that dress for?'

'Never mind that now. I'm going to have some tea, but you should go straight back to bed.'

'I'll have some tea with you. Sasha and Ethan are asleep in your bed, by the way.'

'I expected that.'

'Me and Jack are in your study.'

'The sofa will be fine.'

To her surprise, the house looked all right but there was an unfamiliar smell of talcum power and something she didn't recognize in the air; Babygros and miniature cardigans were draped over the radiators.

'How's it been?' she asked, as they sat in the kitchen with their mugs of tea and the cat sitting at her feet purring loudly.

'I've made lots of tea,' said Chloë, 'and lots of toast and I've learned how to change a nappy – it's not so bad, really. Sasha's slept a lot. Jack was here after work and he's even washed the floor and the bath and he said he was going to clean the windows. But I don't think he got that far. Ethan's really cute but it's tiring having a baby around all the time. I mean, I know it's only been a matter of hours, really, but you can never just take time out, can you?'

'You can't. But you've clearly done terrifically,' said Frieda. 'I knew you were the person to ask.'

Chloë tried and failed to look modest and unresponsive. 'How are things in the country?' she said.

Frieda sipped her tea. 'I can't really talk about that now.'

'Why? I mean, that's fine. By the way, Sandy's been here. He said he'd come back.'

'Did he?'

'I like him. I don't see why you have to break up. Do you think there's a chance . . .?'

'No.'

Upstairs they heard a small wail, then a louder one. After a few seconds it stopped.

Chloë went back up to bed. Frieda crept into her room where Sasha lay sleeping in the bed, Ethan's small dark head beside her. They looked very warm and peaceful. She took her dressing gown from the door and went into the bathroom for a quick shower. Then she took a rug from the airing cupboard and lay on the sofa. What had just happened felt like some disordered, feverish dream. Was it really only a few hours ago that she'd been at Braxton High, surrounded by all the people from her past, or that she'd seen Max swinging from the girder in his room? She stared around at her familiar room: the hearth where tomorrow she would build a fire, the chess table where she would sit and play through a game, the pictures on the wall. She was at home, where she had longed to be, and yet it felt slightly strange to her. Or perhaps she felt strange to herself, only half returned. It wasn't over, but the end had begun. She knew at last.

She lay back on the sofa and heard the cat yowling as it made its way towards her. Its behaviour seemed to have changed while she had been away, as if it had to re-establish possession of her. It came into the room and she felt its weight on the sofa and it lay beside her, occasionally licking at her hair. It was quite dark outside, and silent, but it took her hours to fall asleep.

*

In the morning, she woke Sasha with a mug of coffee and took Ethan while she showered and got dressed. When she came downstairs, Frieda saw that although her hair was clean and her clothes seemed neat and well ordered, there was something askew. She felt as if she was watching a film where the picture and the sound were very slightly out of sync, just enough to make the viewer feel uneasy without quite knowing why.

'How are you feeling?' she asked.

'Better. Definitely better. I saw your doctor friend and she was understanding and helpful.'

'What did she give you?'

'Well, it's got a funny name and a picture of the sun on the box but it's citalopram. I know all about these things.'

'And you're taking it properly?' said Frieda.

'I'm doing what it says on the packet. Frank's coming to collect me today.'

'Will he take time off to look after you?'

'Don't worry. I'm going to be all right.'

'You know that the pills will take a couple of weeks to work?'

'I think the placebo effect has already kicked in. I'm really feeling a lot better than when you last saw me.'

'Did your doctor recommend therapy?'

'I told her I had friends who could help me with that.'

'I've been talking to a woman called Thelma Scott. She's very good.'

'I don't think it would be a good idea to see a therapist that you'd seen. I'd find it . . .' Sasha paused for a few seconds '. . . unsettling.'

'There's something else,' said Frieda. 'I've used your contacts in the labs before and I've got something. I want to know if there's any useful trace that can be recovered from it.' She reached into her shoulder bag and took out the little toy squirrel wrapped in lavatory paper.

At the sight of it, Sasha pulled a humorous face. 'Is there a reason why the police aren't checking it?'

'It's complicated,' said Frieda. 'I got this from a crime scene, but unfortunately it was the wrong crime scene.'

'I'm not even going to ask what that means. But I'll make a call.'

'It's urgent,' said Frieda. 'Really urgent.'

'I'll make it right away.'

Frieda felt like a ghost in her own life. She was going to have to start things up, properly see her patients, take on new ones, but on her first day back, she didn't call anyone and she didn't check her messages. Sasha and Ethan left before midday, and Chloë an hour later. For years the house had been her refuge, her escape; now it felt empty and abandoned. She needed to reclaim it. But for now she was waiting. Waiting for the phone to ring, for the knock on her door, for justice to be done, for danger to be over.

That day, she tried to work, contacting patients, going through her notes, preparing for a lecture she was to give in the new year. In the evening she took out her pad and pencils and sketched a bottle of water that was standing on a small table in a patch of sunlight. She went to bed early and lay awake with the thought scratching away at her that she was in the wrong place, that she should have stayed in Braxton. No, she said to herself, no. She had done what she could. She had rescued Max and she had told the police about Ewan and it was up to them now. They would interview Max. He might remember being assaulted by Ewan and that would be that. Or there were all the other things that police could do: CCTV, number-plate recognition cameras, tracing mobile-phone signals. He'd had to leave the scene in a hurry. He might have left something or Max might have left traces in his car. There'd be something. It wasn't much comfort, though, and it didn't help her to sleep.

The next morning she woke late, drank a black coffee, had a bath, drank another coffee and, almost on impulse, left the house. The day was grey and cold but it was dry, so she headed north into Regent's Park and walked to the boating lake. She sat down on a bench near the water and watched the runners and the children and the mothers or child-minders pushing buggies. A few yards away an old woman was throwing pieces of bread to a gaggle of Canada geese.

Frieda was suddenly aware of someone sitting next to her. She shifted away slightly on the bench.

'We should start eating them,' said the voice. 'They're pests, but they probably taste good.'

Frieda didn't need to look round. She knew the voice. She had heard it in recent days and she had heard it years ago, whispering to her out of the darkness.

'How did you find me?'

'It wasn't too hard,' said Ewan. 'Vanessa got your address from Eva and I came up to London with the commuters and waited in the street, then followed you. It's interesting looking at someone when they don't know they're being looked at. You see them in a different way.'

The idea of Ewan spying on her made her feel nauseous.

'Why didn't you see me in my house?' said Frieda. 'Wouldn't that have been simpler?'

'I wanted to make sure you were alone.'

'There are all these people around.'

'And the geese. When we were children, these geese were exotic and now they're shitting everywhere that there's fresh water.'

Frieda turned and stared at him. He was wearing a thick duffel coat. His hair was tufty and his face was red in the cold air. He looked like a nice, friendly kind of guy, the favourite uncle.

'Was it Rohypnol?' Frieda asked.

Ewan's smile disappeared, and a more wary expression replaced it. Frieda thought of Sarah May and Becky. That expression had been the last thing they ever saw. 'Have you got a phone?' he asked.

'What?'

'Show me.'

Frieda took out her phone. Ewan took it and examined it. 'I want to check you're not recording this.'

'I hardly know how to use it for making phone calls,' she said.

He handed it back to her. 'You're due for an upgrade,' he said. 'That one's an antique. Now, you were asking me a question.'

'Rohypnol.'

'You mean in the drink I gave poor little Max? No. There are better things than that. You wouldn't have heard of them.'

'GHB?'

'All right, you have heard of it.'

'Easier to get hold of, traces disappear from the body more quickly.'

'You should be doing my job,' said Ewan.

'A patient of mine used to take it,' said Frieda. 'Recreationally.'

'My turn to ask a question. How did you know?'

'Many small things that added up to one large thing. And you left evidence at the scene.'

'Oh, yes, you took Becky's touching little fluffy toy. It's funny how teenage girls decorate their beds with the cuddly animals they had when they were toddlers. How would you interpret that? I mean as a therapist.'

'I'm having it tested.'

'Good luck with that.' Ewan seemed utterly unconcerned. 'Is that all?'

'It was a sort of feeling,' said Frieda. 'That lying story you told me about failing to stand up for Vanessa. It showed you were constructing a persona for me. One you thought I'd like.'

'It's not exactly evidence.'

'I don't care about evidence. Everything was too perfect. Nobody else remembered the night of the concert properly except you. You remembered everything, and in the right order.'

'I always was a bit of a nerd.'

'Everyone else was suspicious but you wanted to help me, to get involved: you and your timeline.'

Ewan leaned forward and Frieda thought he was going to whisper something but instead he gave a sniff as if he was savouring the smell of her. He closed his eyes for a moment, as if he was thinking of something pleasurable.

'I can't tell you what that meant to me,' he said. 'It was like experiencing it all over again, being close to you, seeing your skin, your hair, those eyes. I know about you and your psychotherapy. I've looked you up. You're wanting to ask me why I did it.'

'No. I don't need to ask you that.'

'This is part of it. Following you, then sitting here

with you. The fact that you now know is even better. You know and yet you have nothing. It's like doing it all over again but better. Doing a thing like that to someone in the dark is never quite enough. You need them to know who did it. Really, it's almost like being in love, that special connection between two people. Very few people have it.'

'Becky was a troubled, vulnerable young woman. You terrified her, attacked her, raped her, and later you killed her.'

'Yes,' said Ewan, softly. 'Troubled, vulnerable young women are just the sort who make things like that up. No wonder the police have trouble believing them.' He leaned back and closed his eyes for a whole minute. Then he gave a long sigh. 'You can't imagine it.' He opened the fingers of one hand and looked at it as if he were holding something. 'It's like taking something and capturing it for ever. Now, I know what you're going to ask.'

'What?'

'Why am I here? Why aren't I being questioned by the police and charged with multiple offences?'

'All right, why aren't you?'

Ewan looked thoughtful for a moment. 'I'm not an expert on police procedure but I don't think that blurting out an accusation without any evidence of any kind is much use to anybody. A young police officer asked one or two questions about the reunion. She seemed a bit embarrassed about it. I was in and out in less than half an hour. The only irritating thing is that in the small world of Braxton, when something interesting like that happens, everyone seems to know about it.'

'They didn't learn it from me,' said Frieda.

Ewan continued, as if he hadn't heard, 'I went into the farm shop and someone asked about it. The barman at the Dog and Butcher mentioned it. Judy at the garage mentioned it when I was buying petrol.'

'That must have been embarrassing.'

Ewan's smile returned. 'You know what I tell them? I tell them that there was this strange woman called Frieda Klein who used to go to the high school with all of us. She left the area for some mysterious reason.' His voice changed to a stage whisper. 'I refer to rumours of a breakdown. Now she's back because her mother's dying and she's going around making wild accusations and we should all be understanding.' He grinned at her with satisfaction. 'That's what I tell them.'

'I'll never stop,' said Frieda. 'You know that, don't you?'

Ewan looked at a long-legged blonde runner loping past, then back at Frieda, as if he were about to deliver a punchline.

'The police aren't even very interested in Max. You never know what these young people are going to do after they've taken the wrong pill.'

'I mean it. I don't stop. I don't give up. I don't go away.'

'Neither do I, Frieda.'

Frieda looked straight at him, a giddy feeling opening up inside her. It was as if they were playing chess, staring at each other across the board.

'One day,' she said, 'when you've been in prison for months or years, mainly in solitary for your own protection, you'll realize that you were acting out of a pitiable fear and weakness. Then you can begin the journey of understanding what you've done and who you are. That'll be terrible, unimaginably terrible, but it'll be better than being you now, here.'

When he replied, he spoke more softly. 'None of us liked you, Frieda Klein. You thought you were better than us. You didn't even bother to look at me. You barely knew I existed, however hard I tried. Well, you had the smile wiped off your face.'

'You don't understand,' she said. 'You think you have power, but you should be dealt with mainly as a public-health risk, like a rabid dog. You're already being punished in the worst possible way, which is being you, living your life. Being in the hell of yourself. But I won't give up until you're stopped.'

Ewan smiled at her. She stood up and he stood up too.

''Bye, Frieda – I need to catch my train. But remember, I know where you live, in every sense. Are we going in the same direction?' Frieda looked at him with contempt. 'No? Pity.' He paused, then added, 'Sweetheart.'

434

Frieda sat back on the bench and stared in front of her, not watching him walk away and not seeing or hearing the geese. At last she took out her phone and dialled.

'Sasha? Did you hear back yet?'

38

Karlsson had a small, narrow, neglected garden behind his house. They took their mugs of coffee and stepped out into it. There was a hint of imminent rain and it was cold and nearly dark.

'You don't need to be polite about it,' said Karlsson.

'I wasn't going to be.'

'Some time soon I'll go to a garden centre and get some plants.'

'It could do with a bit of colour,' said Frieda.

'But not too many. Mikey and his friends need to play football here. I want to get a little toy goal for them. Or *un gol* as they probably call it now. Did I tell you that I'm learning Spanish? I'm going to a class.'

'That sounds good.'

'So I can talk to my children. Someone in the office said that Spanish was a really easy language to learn. I'm glad I'm not doing a difficult one.'

'You just need to keep at it.'

'Is that what they taught you in the Girl Guides?'

'I was expelled from the Girl Guides.'

'You'll have to tell me about that some time.'

'But if we could stick to this case for the moment? What do you think?'

'Do you want the good news or the bad?'

'The good news, I suppose.'

'There isn't any. I'm sorry, Frieda. I know this is . . .' He stopped. 'Let me go through it as I understand it. Stop me if I get something wrong. There's no active police investigation into any of the Braxton crimes.'

'That's right.'

'There was crucial evidence at the scene of the staged suicide but you removed it – committing a criminal offence in the process.'

'Ewan had put it there to frame Max. I had to take it away.'

'You don't have much confidence in the police, do you? Anyway, you had this evidence independently tested. Which meant that it would be inadmissible in any court proceedings. But, from what you told me, the said item had no trace evidence of any kind, except for the fibres from the toilet paper in which you stored it. Can I warn you that the next time you steal evidence from a crime scene you should wrap it in a clean plastic bag?'

'The toy squirrel was taken from Becky's room but it had no trace of her or any fibres at all. It had been cleaned in a washing machine. Doesn't that strike you as revealing?'

'It could be, but it's of no use in a criminal investigation. You say that you've met the alleged rapist and murderer and that he confessed to you.'

'Not confessed but confirmed.'

'But you have no evidence of this?'

'Unfortunately I don't wear a wire twenty-four hours a day.'

'You could have used your phone.'

'He checked my phone. Not that he needed to.'

'There are no witnesses. This boy who survived didn't see anything.'

'He was given GHB in a drink.'

'Is this based on the tox report?'

'The test wasn't carried out in time. Ewan told me.'

'Didn't Max remember being given it?'

'He thought it was one of his friends, but he was already very drunk.'

'So you have nothing.'

'Those were Ewan's exact words.'

'Why did he come and see you?'

'Partly to warn me off. But more than that, he was getting off on it. It was like he was doing it to me again, reliving it.'

'Frieda, there are two things I could do. I could go down to Braxton and try to get something going. But if it was me down there, I think I'd tell myself to fuck off. Or I could haul him in myself. It's not strictly legal but . . .'

'No,' said Frieda. 'You'd be risking your career. You're never going to do that again. And it wouldn't work anyway. I know him.'

'Which means that you need to let it go.'

'No,' said Frieda. 'Never. If I stop, he'll do it to someone else.'

'You may have scared him into giving up.'

'Or the opposite. I may have reminded him what it's like to have power over someone. I'll have to do something.'

Karlsson rapped against his mug with his knuckles so that it gave a little ring.

'Frieda, this is me. I don't know what you might possibly have in mind but, whatever it is, think very carefully before doing it.'

Frieda turned to him. 'What would you do?'

'Nothing.'

'I don't believe you.'

'Please don't be foolish.'

She met Josef in a small, crowded pub up the road from her house – and not so far from where he was working. Her head was ringing with tiredness and she wanted to be at home but he had sounded so eager. She drank spicy tomato juice and ate a bag of crisps; he drank a double vodka, in a few gulps.

'Eva is fine?' he asked.

Frieda thought of Eva's angry, defeated face when she discovered that Josef wasn't with her. 'Fine,' she confirmed.

'Nice woman.'

'Yes.'

'And you?' he said.

'What?'

'Do you know who is the man?'

'Yes. I know.'

He nodded. 'As soon as I saw your face, I was sure you had found him.'

'Were you?'

'I have the sense.' He tapped the skin under his eye in a mysterious fashion. 'Did I meet him?'

'Yes.'

'Wait. I will guess.' As if it were twenty questions. 'I meet many friends at Eva's but it is the man with two daughters.'

'Yes.'

'Ewan.'

'Yes.'

'From first I did not like this man.'

'Why?'

'I see the way he look at you.'

'How did he look at me?'

'He looked at you with big, big smile and cold eyes.'

'And you saw that at once?'

'Because I know many men like this man.'

Frieda put down her glass and considered him. 'Many men, you say.'

'Not liking women. Pretending, but underneath is this bad feeling.'

'Go on.'

'Scared and hating.'

'Scared and hating,' repeated Frieda. She leaned across and kissed him on the cheek. 'Thanks, Josef.'

'For what?'

'Just thank you.'

'Is he now in the lock-up?'

'Ewan? No. There's no evidence.'

'He goes free?'

'For the moment.'

'Frieda,' said Josef, solemnly. 'This is terrible.'

'I know.'

'What can I do?'

'You can do nothing at all.'

39

Supper was ready but Ewan hadn't arrived. Vanessa called him. No reply. Louder. Still no reply. She ran upstairs and looked in the bedroom. She knocked on the door of his study. Nothing. Then she heard his voice. It seemed to be coming from outside. She returned downstairs and stepped out through the French windows. He was talking on the phone. She started to say something, but he waved her away. She hovered and he gestured again, almost angrily, as if he was pushing her off.

She stood inside and waited. The girls were at the table. They had already started eating. After a few minutes, Ewan came inside. When he saw Vanessa he frowned.

'The food's on the table,' she said.

'I'm going out,' he said.

'What? Now?'

'I won't be long.'

'Ewan, we're eating supper.'

'I won't be long.'

'Who was on the phone?'

'I don't know. A man. He said he wanted to tell me

something about Frieda Klein. Something I'd find interesting.'

'What?'

Ewan looked at her with a flash of irritation. 'If I knew that, I wouldn't need to be told, would I?'

'Why can't he come here?'

Ewan put a finger over his lips, as if he were telling a small child to be quiet. And he had an expression on his face that suggested bad things would happen to the small child if it didn't obey. 'I haven't finished with Frieda Klein,' he said.

Frieda put a potato in the oven to bake, then set about clearing the house. She took the sheets off her bed and the towels off the rack in the bathroom and put them into the washing-machine, picked up various baby items (a wooden rattle, a tiny sock, an empty bottle that had rolled under the bed) and put them into a bag to give to Sasha. Then she went upstairs to her study where Chloë and Jack had been. That took much longer. There were mugs and plates, apple cores and empty crisps packets, a bottle of wine by the side of the bed. They had been there less than two days but it felt like the mess of weeks. Frieda put everything back the way she liked it, wiped the surfaces, vacuumed the floor, then sat down for a few moments at her desk. Her sketchpad was open and her last drawing had a circular brown mark on it from where a mug had been set. She ripped the page out and threw it into the bin. Her mug of soft-leaded pencils had been tipped over and she had to retrieve them. When this was over, she promised herself, she would give herself time in this garret room to draw, to think, to be herself once more. And, after all, she wouldn't have Sandy making claims on her time any more. She would be alone again, entirely her own woman.

The potato was overcooked. She put butter on to it and poured herself a glass of red wine. Her head hummed with thoughts, with pictures. Ewan was free. She knew he would not stop. Perhaps she'd given him pause or perhaps she'd given him encouragement. He had been both complacent and victorious this afternoon.

She ate the potato and drank the red wine, then stood up and wandered round the house but couldn't settle to anything. She was too pent up. She went out to her patio and stood for a while in the cold drizzle. Ewan Shaw, the clown, the sweet guy, the good guy, clumsy and helpful, everyone's friend. Ewan, her rapist. Becky's rapist and her killer. Sarah May's. Who had tried to kill Max simply because Max was a bit of a nuisance and a useful decoy. As if people were just things, as if lives were toys to be played with, broken and thrown in the garbage bin. Ewan, who would do it again. Who wouldn't feel guilt. Whose wife would let him get away with it over and over again because he was her husband and wives had to support their husbands, and because she didn't want to see, didn't want to know, would spend the rest of her life being motherly and concerned, looking in the opposite direction and pretending even to herself that something monstrous wasn't going on under her nose, with her complicity and tacit consent. She had always known. She must have known about Frieda, or why would she have given Ewan his alibi? She must have known about Sarah, about Becky. She must have handed over the package Becky had left in her care to Ewan, knowing, and told him about Max coming to retrieve it.

How Vanessa must have loathed her, thought Frieda. How hatred and fear must have risen in her like bile when she opened the door and saw that she had returned.

And not just Vanessa. Chas must have known as well. He had repeated the words that Frieda had said to Ewan that night long ago, when she had told him in her desperation that she was still a virgin, as if pity would restrain someone who had no empathy in his veins. Ewan must have told Chas. What was it to them? A dare, a laddish prank, a bit of a joke, something they could laugh chummily about, man to man: Frieda Klein, but she was asking for it anyway, thinking she was better than the rest of us; I took her down a peg or two. Was that it? But then the others: Becky and Sarah and nearly Max. Maybe others she did not know of. They were just children. She had to do something and she didn't know what, not yet.

She roamed through the house, turned the radio on, then off again, made herself coffee that she didn't drink, and then, when she couldn't bear it any longer, put on her coat, missing the comfort of her red scarf, and left the house. At first she walked without knowing where she was going, through dark side streets, the cold, cleansing wind in her face and lungs. Then she headed east, past Fleet Street and St Paul's and towards Whitechapel, on small deserted streets that ran between tall buildings and shuttered shops. Soon she was in an area of London she barely knew. There were lots of boarded-up houses, weeds filling the small front gardens. A mangy fox ran across her path. She turned south towards the river and Shadwell Basin. The Thames could take her home again.

By the time she reached her front door, it was two thirty in the morning and she had been walking for hours. She felt better; perhaps she was even tired enough to sleep at last. She hung her coat on the hook by the door and unlaced her boots, easing her sore feet out of them, then started to mount the stairs, thinking of her bed, clean sheets and a soft pillow, only the cat to disturb her.

'Hello, Frieda.'

She swung round. Sandy was standing at the bottom of the staircase. He was wearing jeans and a jumper that she had bought him, and was holding a tumbler of whisky.

'I hope I didn't startle you.'

'What are you doing here?'

'You look tired. Have you been on one of your night walks?'

'I've been walking and I'm tired and I want you to leave my house at once.'

'Are you back for good? Is it over in Braxton?'

She looked at him, so at home. There was no love left inside her. 'It was Ewan Shaw.' He deserved to know that at least.

'Your old friend?'

'Not my friend.'

'Has he been arrested?'

'No.'

'But . . .'

'I don't want to talk about Ewan. Or anything. I asked you what you were doing here, in the middle of the night.'

'I came to see you. We need to talk.'

'You let yourself into my house.'

'I've a key.' He held up the whisky. 'I hope you don't mind. You were rather a long time.'

Frieda came down the stairs and took the glass out of his hand. 'I do mind,' she said.

'I had to see you.'

'You don't have to see me. I'm not good for you, Sandy.'

'You know that I'm not just going to disappear out of your life.'

'Out, I said, *get out*. Give me my key and get out of my house.'

'Frieda. Please listen.'

'I don't want to listen to anything you have to say. How dare you let yourself into my house in the early hours?'

'I'm sorry if I've upset you. I thought –'

'Just go. Now. And don't come back.'

'You don't mean it.'

'If you aren't gone in the next minute, I'll call the police.'

'Oh, you mean your special policeman, Malcolm Karlsson.'

'Forty seconds.' She pulled her mobile out of her pocket. 'If this is the way you want it to be. And give me that key.'

He shrugged and handed it over. 'After everything we've been through,' he said.

Frieda didn't reply, just watched him as he opened the door and stepped out into the street. Then she pulled it shut on him and drew the chain across it. She could feel her heart hammering and the beads of sweat on her forehead. She went into the kitchen, poured Sandy's whisky into the sink and rinsed the tumbler. Soon it would be morning, and what was she going to do then?

But she never had the opportunity to decide. At a quarter past five her phone rang, waking her from a heavy mess of dreams.

'Yes,' she said.

'It's David. Your brother,' he added, as if she wouldn't know.

'She's dying.'

'Yes.'

'I'll come at once. Where is she?'

'In the main hospital. Hendry Ward.'

'OK.' She was out of bed, turning on the light, opening the cupboard for clothes. 'I'll get the first train out.'

She pulled on trousers and a shirt, slid her mobile into her pocket, took her toothbrush and toothpaste from the bathroom. Then she went downstairs, put on her coat and boots, then picked up her bag. She remembered to check there was enough food in the cat's bowl and then she let herself out into the November dark. It was very cold and wet; she thought perhaps the rain was turning to sleet. She walked swiftly to the Underground and got there just as it was opening. There were already a few people waiting outside, early risers or those who had been up all night and were at last going home to bed. She arrived at Liverpool Street in time to get the six o'clock train out. It was almost empty: most people were travelling in the opposite direction; soon they would be pouring into London from all directions.

Frieda sat back and looked out of the window into the darkness. She didn't think about her mother; she thought about her father, to whom she hadn't said goodbye, who hadn't said goodbye to anyone. Why was that so important? She had once had a patient who found it almost impossible to bring even a phone conversation to an end. She didn't know how to say goodbye or how to leave. There always had to be one more thing to say; endings were intolerable.

At the station, Frieda climbed into a cab. It was only a few minutes to the hospital, where she had last been with her mother for the brain scan. By the time she got there it was light – or as light as it would ever get on this day of low grey clouds and sleety rain. She went into the Ladies and cleaned her teeth before taking the stairs up to the second floor.

Her mother was in a curtained-off cubicle in a ward of six beds, all of which were occupied. David sat on a plastic chair beside her. Juliet Klein was asleep or unconscious. He was reading a newspaper, which he folded in half as Frieda drew back the curtains and stepped inside. He didn't get up, just nodded as she pulled the second chair to the other side of the bed, next to the locker.

'Have you contacted Ivan?' she asked.

'Twice now. The first time was when she was diagnosed, and he said that he would fly over when the time came – by which I take it he meant when she was on her deathbed. Now that she is on her deathbed, he says he wouldn't get here in time.'

'He probably wouldn't,' said Frieda.

'No. What a family we are.'

Frieda didn't answer. She looked at her mother, whose mouth was half open, as if her jaw had come unhinged, and whose skin was slack. Her breath rumbled in her throat and she smelt sour. There was an oxygen mask at the ready round her neck and an IV in her arm, which was thin and bruised. She would have hated to be seen like this, she who had always been so meticulously prepared for the world.

'Have you talked to her?'

'An hour or so ago she opened her eyes and told me I'd put on weight. That's all.'

'What do the doctors say?'

'That it won't be long. She might not wake up again and then we'd miss our grand deathbed reconciliation.'

Juliet Klein's eyes opened. 'What are you saying about me?'

Frieda thought about taking her mother's hand, then changed her mind.

'Why are you here?' Juliet's face pulled tight. 'Am I . . .?' She couldn't finish the sentence, but swallowed painfully.

David leaned over and spoke very slowly, as if to a child who was having trouble sleeping. 'Yes. You're dying, Ma.'

Juliet Klein blinked several times. Her arms, lying above the covers as if she was dead already, moved convulsively.

'Are you in pain?' asked Frieda. 'Is there anything you need?'

Her mother didn't answer. She turned her head to one side and then the other on her pillow and made a sound that wasn't a cry but wasn't a word either.

'Ivan sent his love,' said David, loudly, separating out each word.

'Ivan?'

'Your other son.'

'Tell me if you want anything.' Now Frieda did take Juliet's hand, for she saw that her mother was terrified.

'Must leave here.' She made a frantic flurried movement as if she would get up from the bed and try to escape, but remained where she was, her eyes glassy.

'She's not really of sound mind,' said David.

'Don't talk about her as if she wasn't here.'

'Who are you?'

'I'm Frieda, your daughter.'

'Daughter.'

'Yes.'

'Overrated.'

'What's overrated?'

'Never wanted to be a mother.'

'I know,' said Frieda. 'It's all right.'

'Wanted . . .' And again her words became unintelligible.

'What's she saying?' David leaned forward. 'What are you saying, Ma?'

'I think she's saying she wanted a different life.'

'Too late,' said Juliet Klein. Her face was very small

and pinched on the pillow. Her eyes glittered at them. Her breath rasped as if her chest was rusty and broken.

A nurse came into the cubicle and bent over the bed. She put the oxygen mask over Juliet Klein's mouth but the dying woman pulled it away, the elastic snapping on her cheeks. She tore her fingers from Frieda's grasp.

'No,' she said. 'No. I won't. I won't. No.'

She closed her eyes and after a moment was still. Her breath snagged in her throat. Frieda watched her intently. Her angry, unhappy, ironic, stubborn mother was leaving them.

'Is she dead?' asked David, after a pause.

'No,' said Frieda.

She wasn't dead but she didn't open her eyes again or speak, and then, at last, her breathing stopped.

'Now is she dead?'

'Yes.'

'So with her dying breath she told us she wished she'd never been a mother.'

'You probably already knew that.'

'No. No, I didn't.'

'Are you all right?'

'Actually, I feel good. I always thought it was just me she didn't like. It's rather a relief to know it was all of us.'

There was a pause. Frieda was about to stand up and fetch the nurse when David spoke again, in a quiet voice. 'That — that *thing* you say happened to you . . .'

'The rape,' said Frieda. 'It has a name.'

'Yes. Well. Are you — I mean, what's going on with that?'

Frieda looked at her mother, who had never believed her story and who now never would. 'I don't want to talk about it, David.'

'That's probably for the best.' He sounded relieved. 'I mean, it's all in the past and sometimes you just have to let sleeping dogs lie.'

Wake up those dogs, thought Frieda. Set them loose on the world.

40

After an hour of silences and muttered information, Frieda had the sense of being at a party where the hosts were still friendly and hospitable but really starting to wonder whether it wasn't time to go. So she left. The hospital wasn't designed for walking out of. Frieda made her way through a car park and along little driveways until she reached the main road. Her mother had died. Her father was dead and her mother was dead. She was an orphan. The hard fact of it was like a package in her mind that she very deliberately stowed away. Later she would retrieve and unwrap it but not now, not yet. That would be an obstacle.

Even when she had been by her mother's bed, holding her hand, she had been thinking also of that voice out of the dark, that voice beside her in Regent's Park. *You know, and yet you have nothing. Sweetheart.* Frieda thought of what she had gone through so often with her patients. You had to acknowledge the past and then you had to let it go. She had once seen an eighty-year-old woman who was still arguing with her father as if she were an angry teenager, a father who had been dead for forty years. But this wasn't the past.

She took out her phone and made a call. 'Are you at home?'

'No. But I can be.'

A little more than an hour later Frieda was walking along the seafront. She turned up the path and rang the bell. When Chas opened the door, he looked over her shoulder with a frown. 'Are you alone?'

'Yes.'

'How did you get here?'

'Bus, train, cab.'

'I didn't know that was even possible. Do you want some coffee?'

The thought of going into Chas's house, standing on his rugs, surrounded by his paintings, repulsed her.

'We can walk along by the sea.'

'It really isn't the weather for it.'

'Then put a coat on.'

Chas disappeared and re-emerged, wearing a long, bulky fawn overcoat, a navy blue scarf and a brown trilby hat. They crossed the road and they were on the pebbles. They turned north with rows of coloured beach huts on their left and the grey, foaming North Sea on their right. Chas pointed at one of the beach huts. 'That's ours,' he said. 'For the price of that you could buy a five-bedroom house up in the north. If you wanted one.'

Frieda pushed her hands into her pockets. The wind was blowing from the north, so cold that it made her face ache. She turned to Chas. 'You knew,' she said.

'What?'

'Vanessa knew. And you knew.'

'What are you talking about now?'

'It's the only thing that made sense. It always struck a wrong note that Ewan so accurately remembered the concert.'

'Is this the Thursday's Children concert? Back in 'eighty-nine?'

'Yes, we're still talking about that concert. When we remember real things, it's a mess, all in the wrong order, pieces missing, pieces forgotten. Police know that and therapists know that. But Ewan remembered it all in the right order, just the way we remember made-up stories.'

'Ewan was always the obsessive type.'

'Still covering for him?' said Frieda, almost in fascination. 'You and Vanessa placed him there all the way through. You gave him his alibi.'

'Frieda, this was all a long time ago –'

'Stop. There are things you can say, but don't just insult me.'

Chas turned away briefly. Frieda could see the edge of his jaw flexing. But when he turned back to face her, he seemed entirely calm. 'If you're making some kind of accusation,' he said, 'which you seem to be, then you need to talk to the police. But if you're going to pursue this . . .'

457

Frieda looked at the sea. A white-haired old woman was throwing a stick into the waves. A black dog, a Labrador, plunged in, disappeared into the breakers and came out again triumphantly, the stick clutched in its jaws. 'Then what?' she said.

'I don't know what you want from me.'

Frieda looked back at the dog, which jumped into the sea again and then again. 'Of course,' she said, 'there's a part of me that wants simply to look you in the eye and ask you what you were thinking. But I know what you were thinking.'

'You know nothing about me.'

'I know *something* about you. But that's not why I'm here. You can believe what you need to believe. People generally do. But I came here to tell you this. It may have seemed funny when you were sixteen, that a boy put a mask on and raped a girl to teach her a lesson . . .'

'I don't know anything about that.'

'Just listen to this and I'll go. Ewan came to see me in London. He acknowledged what he'd done, but he said I had nothing on him, which is about right.'

'I don't know why you feel the need to tell me this.'

Something peculiar was happening to his face. His habitually bland, amused expression kept breaking up and re-forming. It was as if Frieda was seeing another Chas behind the mask, someone not so in control, not so self-satisfied.

'If you're going to be in a state of denial, I want to

be clear about what it is you're denying. I don't know how well you've kept up with Ewan.'

'We occupy different worlds now.'

'In 1991, he raped Sarah May. But something went wrong and he killed her.'

'And you know this how?'

'Ewan has an instinct for girls on the edge, the isolated ones, the ones who won't be believed. Like Becky Capel.'

'Which was suicide.'

'Becky started to find the strength to stand up for herself. I'm partly to blame for that. Unfortunately the person she turned to was the person who had spotted her vulnerability in the first place.'

'Ewan?'

'No. Vanessa.'

'You're telling me that Ewan raped Becky and Vanessa covered for him as she had covered for him in the past? That they were acting as a team?'

'She was always good at looking the other way, not seeing what she wasn't meant to see, not knowing what she wasn't meant to know. The human mind is good at that.'

'Yes.' He turned away from her and stared out at the great grey waters.

'When Ewan knew I was back in Braxton and that I wasn't going away, he had the idea of framing Lewis and Max.'

'Are the police investigating this?'

'I don't think so.'

'Why are you telling me?'

'You can do the right thing.'

Chas's cheeks were flushed now. Frieda couldn't tell whether it was from anger or shame or just the cold wind.

'And what's that, Frieda?'

'You can tell the police everything you know. Ewan is a rapist and a murderer and he could, probably will, do it again.'

'He knows you're watching him. He's not likely to do anything again.'

'That's what you're relying on?'

'What you've said about me isn't right,' he said, but in a different tone, almost thoughtfully.

'You could make amends,' she said softly. 'It is in your power.'

Again Chas turned away to study the sea, his hands thrust into his pockets and his shoulders hunched. After a long time, he turned back.

'Tell me what to do,' he said quietly, almost in a whisper.

Then Frieda's phone rang.

'Wait,' she said urgently. 'Let me take this and then I'll tell you.'

'Is that Frieda Klein?'

'Who is this?'

'This is Detective Inspector Craigie. We've already met. Where are you?'

'Why do you need to know?'

She repeated the question and Frieda gave her Chas's address.

'Stay there. I'm sending a car for you.'

'Why?'

'We need to talk to you.'

'What about?'

'Don't you know?'

'You were the one who called me.'

'We'll discuss it when you get here.'

There was a pause after Frieda rang off. Then Chas spoke. 'All right,' he said. 'I will tell the police.'

Frieda stepped forward and took his arm. 'That is the right thing to do,' she said. 'And it's also a good, brave, hard thing to do. Thank you.'

'I'm not doing it for you. I'm doing it for myself.'

'I have to go to the station. I've no idea why. Do you want to come with me and get it over with?'

'No. Not quite yet. Give me a bit of time to compose myself.' He gave a bitter smile.

'I'll call you later this evening. All right?' She was anxious that he would think better of his pledge and he sensed it.

'I won't back out, Frieda.'

'OK.' She hesitated. 'You don't need to hang around for me here.'

'I should get back to work. Do you want to wait at my house?'

'No. Thank you.'

So he left, and for half an hour she walked up and down the beach until she saw a police car arrive. There were two uniformed officers who said they had come to take her to the police station. She asked them what this was about and they said she would be told when they arrived.

'What if I don't want to come?'

They looked at her as if she had said something rude. 'Why wouldn't you want to come, Dr Klein?'

It all seemed too much trouble, so Frieda just got into the back of the car and nothing was said to her the whole way to the police station. The two officers seemed constrained even when talking to each other. They drove into a car park and one of the officers led her to a back entrance, which looked almost unused, then up a staircase, littered with empty cardboard boxes. The officer left her in a bare, windowless interview room. After a few minutes DI Craigie came in. She was accompanied by another detective, a bulky man with unevenly cut hair. She introduced him as Detective Constable Pearce. As they sat down opposite Frieda, both of them looked at her with curiosity. But there was no small talk, not even a greeting.

'Something's up,' said Frieda. 'What is it?'

'You made an accusation against Ewan Shaw,' said Craigie.

'He raped at least three women,' said Frieda. 'Including me. He killed two of the women: Rebecca

Capel and Sarah May. He also attempted to kill Max Temple.'

Craigie and Pearce exchanged looks.

'Does anybody share this view?' Craigie asked.

'What does that matter?'

'Have you convinced anyone else of this?'

'I don't see the point of the question.'

Craigie flapped her hands in a gesture of exasperation. 'Does anybody else know what you know? Or believe what you believe?'

Frieda thought for a moment. 'Ewan Shaw's wife, Vanessa, knows about it. I'm not sure of the full extent. When you called me I was talking to someone I knew when I was growing up here, a man called Chas Latimer. He knew about the original rape. I mean when Ewan raped me. I think he'll confirm this.'

'What about Ewan Shaw's knowledge of all this?'

'Clearly he knows what he did.'

'I mean about what you know.'

'He knows.'

'How do you know?'

'He came to see me in London.'

Both of the detectives sat up with a start. 'He did what?' said Craigie.

'He tracked me down in London and followed me.'

'And?'

'He told me I had nothing on him. That he was safe.'

'That he was safe?'

'Yes.'

'He used that word?'

Frieda paused for a moment. 'What are we talking about here?' she said. 'Why are you asking these questions?'

'Did he say he was safe?'

'I don't remember him using that exact word.'

'So why did you say it?'

'I think it conveyed in a fair way what he was trying to get across.'

'And how did it make you feel?'

'Is this some kind of joke?'

'How did it make you feel?'

'That's a difficult question to answer.'

'Did you think he was taunting you?'

Frieda thought for a moment. 'Yes,' she said. 'I think that was part of it.'

Craigie leaned across the table, her elbows resting on the top. Frieda recognized the body language: confrontational, intimidatory.

'You accused Ewan Shaw of raping you,' Craigie said. 'Do you feel he was demonstrating his power over you?'

'I think *he* felt he was, which is a different thing.'

'And that made you feel angry?'

'I think he's a mixture of self-pity and rage, which is a dangerous combination.'

'Did you feel angry?'

'Yes. And other things.'

'Like what?'

'Determined that he would never do it again.'

'I see. And what did you want to do about that?'

'What I wanted – and what I want – is to get him. Since the police don't seem very interested in doing anything about him.'

'You wanted to get him?'

'Yes.'

'And what do you mean by that?'

'I want to stop him.'

'I see. How did your meeting with Ewan Shaw end?'

'Inconclusively.'

'What did you do after the meeting?'

'What do you mean? Immediately after?'

'Just tell us what you did between then and now.'

'I went to see a friend of mine, a detective in the Met, and talked things over with him.'

'Was he sympathetic?'

'I wasn't looking for sympathy. Then I went home.'

'Can anyone confirm that you were there last night?'

'Yes,' said Frieda, thinking of Sandy's visit. 'Then very early this morning I came back up here to go to the hospital.'

'What for?'

'My mother was terminally ill. She died earlier today.'

'Oh,' said Craigie. 'I'm sorry.'

'I went straight from the hospital to see Chas Latimer. And then I was driven here.'

Craigie sat back in her chair. 'You were in the hospital?'

'Yes.'

'Fuck,' said Pearce, under his breath. 'I don't fucking believe it.'

Craigie shot him an angry glance and turned back to Frieda. 'With family members?'

'One of my brothers was there.'

'Can you tell us when you arrived?'

'I caught the first train out of Liverpool Street, just before six this morning. I arrived at the hospital at about seven thirty, I suppose. And I was there until early afternoon – I'm not sure what time, but I'm sure you can find out from my brother or the nurses. Or CCTV.'

'Fuck,' Pearce said again, louder this time. 'This is a farce.'

'I went straight from the hospital to Chas's house, which is where you picked me up.' She saw the way they were staring at her. 'Are you going to tell me why you brought me here?'

The two detectives exchanged glances.

'You know the obelisk just outside Braxton?' Craigie asked.

'The witch monument?' said Frieda. 'Of course.'

'Ewan Shaw's body was found there at just after seven thirty this morning.'

'His body?' said Frieda, slowly. 'Do you mean his dead body?'

'That's right. He failed to return home last night and this morning his body was found by an old woman walking her dog. She's currently in hospital herself. She didn't react well to it.'

Frieda felt almost dizzy with the shock of it. She thought back to Ewan's tone at the end of their meeting. 'Did he kill himself?'

'Oh, no,' said Craigie. 'His throat had been cut. It was all very clever. It was certainly premeditated. It was done in a place with no CCTV. And at the same time, we can rule out financial motivation. His wallet was still in his pocket, with a hundred and twenty pounds in cash inside. And then there were extensive injuries suggesting a prolonged assault. Injuries that might have been motivated by a sense of anger or revenge. Do you have any comment to make about that?'

'No.'

'Don't you think he deserved it?'

'No, I don't.'

Craigie leaned in close again. 'You said he raped you, that he raped and killed two other young women.'

'Yes.'

'And he told you to your face that he wouldn't be caught.'

'He would have been caught, though. Somehow.'

'How many people know what you know? Or what you think you know?'

'Know for certain? Just me,' said Frieda.

'How many people know what you suspected?'

'By now, quite a few. Things spread fast in a town like Braxton. Ewan told me that almost everyone in Braxton knew about him being interviewed by the police. He seemed to think that someone in the police might have gossiped about it.'

'That's a serious accusation.'

'I don't care. And Chas Latimer knew.'

'Can you think of anyone who might have wanted to do this?'

'Dr Klein,' said Pearce, 'Ewan Shaw's widow has told us in a statement that the last time she saw him he was going out to meet a man who claimed to have information about you.'

'What kind of information?'

'She didn't know. Clearly this man is someone we're anxious to interview. Have you any idea who he might be?'

'No.'

'The purpose may have been to lure Ewan Shaw out of his house. And it sounds like someone who knows you.'

'Or knows of me.'

'Any ideas?' asked Craigie.

Frieda thought of Lewis, and she thought of Josef and Sandy. 'No,' she said.

'Something was found with his body. I wonder if you can help cast any light on it.' She bent down and lifted up a plastic evidence bag, which contained the ripped half of a red woollen scarf. Frieda's red scarf, which she had owned for so many years, wearing it every cold autumn and winter day.

'No,' she said slowly. 'No. I can't help you, I'm afraid.'

41

Frieda walked along the empty street, carrying flowers. Sasha had dropped her off. She and Ethan were waiting in the little café where – it seemed years ago – Frieda had met up with Lewis again. It was a little before seven in the morning and Braxton barely seemed to be stirring. In London, there would be people, cars, the sounds of radios and doors slamming. Here it was a dark, still dawn, only the street lamps lighting her way.

The churchyard was a dim space of huddled gravestones and ancient trees. The spire of the church rose through the fog. The moisture on the ground seeped through her shoes; she could see her breath curling into the air. She could only just make out the names of the dead as she walked between the graves and the carved angels. It took many minutes, bending down to trace inscriptions, clearing moss away from letters, before she found them both.

Bethany May, 1947–1983
Dearly Beloved Mother and Wife
And under it, in newer stone,
Sarah May 1973–1991
She lives in the hearts of all who loved her

Frieda cleared the weeds away from the small plots and then she put the flowers on the graves, in the little vases that were there. She would ask Eva if she would come once a month just to see that everything was tidy and put new flowers there. That was the kind of thing Eva would like to do. She would pick blooms from her own garden when it was spring and come here, in her long bright skirts and with her red hair blowing, and sit and weep for the friends she had lost.

The flowers had gone from Maddie's house. Only a red cyclamen on the table remained. Maddie sat opposite Frieda and they drank tea together. She was wearing an old brown cardigan and faded jeans, no heels on her shoes, no makeup on her face.

'I don't know whether to hate you.'

Frieda considered this. 'Would it make you feel better to hate me?'

'I'm beyond feeling better. My daughter, my only child, is dead. I keep remembering her when she was tiny and happy, and then I remember all our rows, terrible, terrible rows. And I remember not believing her. I wake in the night and I see her face when she told me what had happened to her and I didn't comfort her and hold her tight and tell her I would help her through. After that, what's left to me? I have a failed marriage behind me, no job or real purpose, my so-called loved affair is over, my friends – well, look what's happened to people I used to call my friends. But nothing really mattered, except Becky.'

'I'm very sorry.'

'You're sure it was Ewan?'

'Yes.'

'The Ewan I've known since I was thirteen, who sat in my house, ate my food, rubbed my shoulders, made stupid jokes, mended my computer and fixed up my shower curtain, who comforted me when Becky died, cried at her funeral, whose children I know, whose wife is one of my closest friends?'

'Yes. That Ewan.'

She closed her eyes and opened them again. 'What happens now?'

'You'll be interviewed by the police. They've got busy now that it's all too late. There'll be journalists as well. Careful what you say to them.'

'I don't want to speak to any journalists. He tried to kill Max?'

'Yes.'

'And he raped you when you were sixteen?'

'That was when it all began.'

'And he has daughters of his own.'

'That means nothing,' said Frieda. 'It may be that his own daughters becoming young women triggered him again. We can't know. But don't worry, there'll be plenty of instant experts in the media explaining it to us.'

'What will Vanessa do?' said Maddie. Her face

changed. 'Do you think she knew? How could she not have known? But she was my friend, I trusted her – did she know, Frieda?'

Frieda hesitated. Should she say what she knew about Vanessa? 'I'm not sure,' she said at last.

'Braxton,' said Maddie. 'This nice, safe town. Who would ever have believed it?'

Frieda thought of the witch who had been put to death a few hundred yards from here, all those centuries ago, in the place where Ewan had also been slaughtered. All those women over all the years, the vulnerable, the ones who didn't belong, the outsiders. Punished for being different.

'I never found it so nice,' said Frieda.

Frieda had one more call she had to make, repelled and attracted at the same time. There was no answer at the front door, so she walked around the side and there she was, in a sturdy grey jacket and gardening gloves, cutting with secateurs at the ivy that covered the wall of the shed. Vanessa looked round. She gave no sign of surprise or shock. 'I should call the police,' she said.

'I've just been with them.'

'The girls are out with their aunt. They're in a bad way. You'd better not be here when they get back.'

'I won't be.'

'Did you come to gloat?'

Frieda looked at Vanessa and felt, This is what it

473

was all about. This is why I came back. 'You know,' she said, 'what really scares me is not what people like Ewan do. It's what people like *you* do. He had these wires crossed, where sexual desire got fused with violence, but you let it happen. You enabled it and cleared up afterwards. There'll always be people like Ewan. What makes it worse is that there'll always be people like you and Chas and Jeremy, too, who stand back and let it happen.'

'You don't understand,' Vanessa said.

'Can I ask you one thing?'

'What?'

'Take your jacket off.'

'My jacket?'

'I was thinking about you, about sitting at your kitchen table, at the reunion party, and I realized that I've never seen your arms.'

Vanessa looked at Frieda steadily. Then she put the secateurs into her pocket and took the jacket off. Underneath was a rough green cardigan, which she unbuttoned and removed. She was wearing a long-sleeved grey shirt. She unfastened the buttons at the cuffs and rolled the sleeves up above the elbow. She held her arms towards Frieda, as if making an offering. Frieda stepped closer and took hold of Vanessa's wrists. Both arms were streaked with scars. Some were red, some raised off the surface in welts. Frieda could see from the wrinkles in the skin that some were years and years old. The faded scars were crossed and tangled in the more recent ones.

'It won't work,' said Frieda. 'It won't make the pain go away. Or the guilt. In the end, they will overwhelm you.'

When Frieda left, Vanessa had rolled her sleeves back, put on the cardigan and the jacket and was hacking once more at the ivy, as if her life depended on it.

Frieda went back to London and to her house for a couple of days. She saw five patients, including Joe Franklin, and no friends. She sat for a long while in her quiet study, drawing, thinking, pondering. She tried to draw Becky's face but it became her own face when she was younger. She tried to remember Sandy's face but it warped into Dean's. She talked on the phone to Reuben, Sasha and Karlsson about what had happened but nobody could really understand how she had gone back to her past and found herself still alive in its rubble.

42

'Are you sure you don't want her diamond earrings?'

'Quite sure.'

'Or this gold chain.'

'I don't want it.'

'There's a moonstone bracelet.'

'I don't want anything.'

'Can I give them to Trudy, then?'

'Sure. And ask Chloë what she wants, and Ivan.'

'I don't see why Ivan should have anything. He couldn't even be bothered to come over for the funeral.'

'There wasn't a funeral.'

'Yes, and the idea of leaving her body for medical research was like the final slap in the face.'

'There are worse slaps in the face.'

'I'm surprised anyone would want it. What about this picture?'

'No.'

'I'm duty-bound to inform you that it's probably worth quite a lot of money.'

'I don't want it.'

'Just don't come complaining to me after.'

Frieda and David were in their mother's bedroom,

sorting through her possessions. Outside, the skip that Frieda had arranged was already half full, and in the drive was the van that David had rented. They had already been through her clothes. David had taken a few dresses, a good coat, some jackets that he thought his young wife might like. Frieda had taken nothing.

The doorbell rang and David frowned, his hands full of jewellery.

'Who can that be?'

'I'll go.'

She went downstairs and opened the door. Lewis stood there. He looked as if he'd lost pounds in just a few days, and his hair had been cut very short. His eyes were red-rimmed, sore.

'How's Max?' Frieda asked

But he just tumbled over the threshold and stood in front of her. 'It was Ewan?' he asked.

'Yes. And he killed Becky.' She didn't want to talk about everything that had happened to her, all those years ago.

'You saved him.' He started to cry, not putting up his hands to wipe away the tears, letting them course down his weathered cheeks.

'I'm glad he's going to be all right.'

'How can I ever repay you?'

Frieda put her hands on his thin, trembling shoulders and looked into his eyes. 'I owed you,' she said softly.

*

477

After Lewis had left, David and Frieda went into the living room. Soon the van was full of the furniture and paintings that David would take away with him. Frieda had refused even the framed photograph of her father, squinting into the glare of the sun. She had his face stored away in her mind, and that was all she needed. She didn't want the food mixer, the silver cutlery, the glasses and soup tureens and teacups, the serving dishes, spice racks, rugs, throws, cushions, bottles of wine and spirits, jars of marmalade and pickles and jam; not the novels or books on gardening and politics and medicine; or the towels, umbrellas, digital radio, pot plants . . . She wanted to walk away empty-handed and free.

The bell rang again.

'Now who?' said David, angrily. 'Another ex-lover? Can't you leave well alone?' This was his only reference to the turmoil that had been caused in Braxton over the death of Ewan.

'It wasn't well,' said Frieda, leaving the room and going to the front door.

'Dr Klein?'

'My mother, Juliet Klein, doesn't live here any longer.' Or anywhere.

The man frowned, looking at the bulky envelope in his hands. 'I have a delivery here for a Dr Frieda Klein.'

'That's me.'

She signed for the package and went with it into the empty, echoey kitchen. Her name and her mother's address were on the front, written in large capitals. There was a nudge of memory under her ribs. Sliding her finger under the gummed flap, she pulled out a length of material. Red wool. The second half of her red scarf, whose first half had been left with Ewan's body, at the witch's memorial. She held it between her fingers very delicately, as if she would be able to feel the trace of the person who had stolen it from her, and then she felt that it was wrapping something. She unfolded the scarf and removed a greetings card. On the front was a photograph of daffodils in full flower. She opened the card and saw the message written in the same capital letters: 'HE CRIED WHEN I SAID YOUR NAME. REALLY CRIED.'

Frieda had a flashing sensation, like a waking dream. She suddenly imagined what Ewan had been through when he realized it had all gone wrong, when he understood it was his turn to be assaulted and tortured and killed. Where would Dean have done it? Somewhere remote, a shed, a lock-up, in the woods, where screams wouldn't be heard. That was what happened to enemies of Frieda Klein. Bad things. Frieda examined her own reaction, testing herself, as if she were her own patient. Was it what she'd wanted? Did she take pleasure in the idea of

Ewan knowing that there was nothing he could do or say to make it stop? After what he'd done to those girls.

No, she told herself. No. All it did was make a bad world worse. Dean had sent her this message because he wanted to tell her that he was still looking out for her, still in her life, like a lover, like a stalker, like a shadow and a ghost come back to haunt her. She remembered her own words to Ewan: *I don't stop. I don't give up. I don't go away.* Neither did he. He would never leave her. He'd done this for her: butchered Ewan on the witch's ground as a tribute and a sacrifice.

She laid the red scarf on the table. She would never touch it again. She slipped the card into her pocket. Then she rang Karlsson's number.

'Dean's here now,' she said, although, of course, he'd never been away.

Karlsson put the phone down. He thought about Frieda, and tried to picture her, but although he had seen her in Braxton he found he could only imagine her in London. He saw her walking along a street with the wind in her face and he saw her sitting beside a fire, her head turned towards him. Never quite smiling. Listening. Attending. The thought of her filled him with an emotion he struggled to identify: it was neither happiness nor sorrow, but something strong and deep. He wanted her to come home because he could talk to her in a way he couldn't to anyone else, and even though he was often inarticulate, abrupt, he felt that she understood the meaning behind the clumsy words.

Two years ago, he hadn't believed Frieda when she had told him that Dean was still alive and was both protecting and terrorizing her. Now he believed her, not because there was evidence but because Frieda had told him it was true. For better or for worse, she was a truth-teller. He sighed and turned back to his work.

Chloë rang Sasha.

'I just wanted to tell you that Frieda is going through all of Gran's stuff with my dad. But I think she'll be back soon.'

'Yes. She rang me. But thanks for telling me, Chloë.'

'I know you must miss her.'

Several miles away, in Primrose Hill, Reuben and Josef were cooking, or at least Josef was cooking and Reuben was pretending to help him while smoking cigarettes and drinking beer and leafing through a newspaper.

'Cardamom – you want to remove the seeds?'

'Sure,' said Reuben, vaguely.

'And I peel the potatoes and then while they cook I make *golubtsi*.'

Josef was very happy. He had already made the

wheat soup. Now, wrapped in his apron, he chopped onions, crushed garlic, fried mince, boiled rice and steamed cabbage leaves. He kneaded dough for the *pierogi*s, rolled it out into neat circles that he filled with poppy seeds, raisins and prunes, folding them into small semi-circles. He prepared a raw salad of beetroot and celeriac. He poured himself a shot of vodka, then started on the spiced honey cake that his mother used to bake for him and that reminded him of his homeland, the music and the mountains of his past.

'She would like this.'

'Yes,' said Reuben, holding out his empty glass. 'And she'd want some more vodka.'

The house was empty; the skip and the van were both full. The day was fading and David was anxious to be gone, pulling on his leather gloves and his tailored coat that made him look, Frieda thought, like an expensive hitman.

'Can I give you a lift?' he asked reluctantly.

'I'm going to walk.'

'Where to?' Frieda merely shrugged. 'Well, that's your business.'

They didn't hug or kiss. He climbed into the laden van and drove away.

Frieda put on her coat and then she closed the front door of the house where she had spent the first sixteen years of her life, where she had found her father dead, where she had been raped, where she had not been believed. She double-locked it and slid the keys back through the letter flap, hearing them clatter on to the boards. She walked to the gate and then turned. The house looked dead. All the windows were dark, like blind eyes.

When she had left Braxton as a teenager, she had run from it. Now she walked at her own pace. The afternoon was dull and cold, the sky a pewter grey darkening into winter dusk. She went down the lane, past Tracey Ashton's old house, past the mock-Tudor one that had once belonged to the Clarkes, then Mrs Leonard's cottage where, for a moment, Frieda expected to see the old woman in the garden, calling to her cats in her high, crooning tones. She went by the ancient chapel, and the bus stop, and at last was on the high street.

There were three police cars parked near the tattoo parlour. She walked past them without slackening her pace. A cluster of people stood nearby, and when they saw her, they nudged each other and gaped at her openly. She saw them whispering but couldn't hear the words. A man coming in the other direction stared at her. News spreads fast, a network of facts and rumours and lies. Did you hear? Did you know? Look. Look at her. Can't you tell? Stand aside. Evil eye. No smoke without fire.

On the other side of the road she saw a woman

she recognized as Liz Barron, a journalist from the *Daily Sketch* who had written about Frieda before. She was talking to someone, notebook in hand, nodding ever so sympathetically. In the distance, there was a television crew. The media had descended on Braxton.

Frieda didn't alter her pace. She passed the baker's, whose shelves were almost empty now, the shop selling cheap drink and DVDs, the newsagent's. A group of teenagers stood at the curve of the road. For a few moments, she saw Chas, Jeremy, Lewis, Ewan, Vanessa, Eva, Sarah, Maddie. She saw herself. All of them so young, just starting out, not yet sure of the roads they would take, trying on different selves. And then their faces faded, and they were just strangers, jostling on the pavement, staring at her avidly.

'That's her,' she heard one say, as she walked by. 'That's the woman.'

That's the witch.

A figure approached from the distance, dressed in a bright long skirt with vivid red hair. Eva. Who had been her mate, her best friend in a different world. But she was on the other side of the road and was talking animatedly into her mobile, at the same time fishing in her capacious bag for something. She didn't see Frieda. Frieda didn't stop. Indeed, she couldn't stop. She was leaving.

Over the brow of the hill ahead lay the witch's burning ground, now a crime scene and taped off. On the other side of the valley was Lewis's house, where Max had nearly died. To the left was Eva's, filled with pottery, herbs, the smell of biscuits, and waiting for a companion. To the right was the house where Maddie had lived and Becky had died, and also the house where Ewan and Vanessa had raised their daughters and never spoken out loud to each other of what they had done together. Behind her lay the house that had been her childhood home; her broken past and her bitter memories; the formation of the woman she had chosen to become. But now her road lay ahead, as shops petered out, then houses thinned, and the clear, shallow river marked the way from the town.

Her steps quickened as the town fell away and the darkness grew thicker. Soon she was on the brow of the hill and only then did she stop and turn to look back. Braxton lay spread out beneath her. The street lamps and the lights of houses glittered in the darkness, under the sprinkling of stars. The church spire pointed upwards, sharp and admonishing. Small coils of smoke diffused in the night sky. She would never return, and as she stood there she almost felt the town's power weaken, as if a weight was falling from her.

At last she turned away; the town was at her back. Perhaps Dean was walking beside her, out of sight but always there, her shadow. Yet for now she wasn't thinking of Dean. Or of Sandy, or her dead mother. She wasn't thinking of the murdered girls, of Ewan, of Vanessa, of any of those who had wrenched her life out of shape. She was thinking of the place she was going to and of the people who waited for her there. She was loved and she was alone and she was free.

THE FIFTH THRILLER IN THE FRIEDA KLEIN SERIES

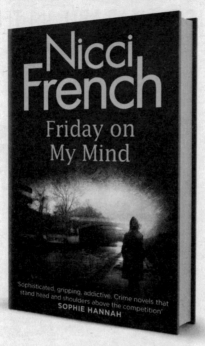

When a bloated corpse is found floating in the River Thames the police can at least be sure that identifying the victim will be straightforward. Around the dead man's wrist is a hospital band. On it are the words Dr F. Klein . . .

But psychotherapist Frieda Klein is very much alive. And, after evidence linking her to the murder is discovered, she becomes the prime suspect.

Unable to convince the police of her innocence, Frieda is forced to make a bold decision in order to piece together the terrible truth before it's too late either for her or for those she loves.

Rich in intrigue, intensity and atmosphere, *Friday on My Mind* is classic Nicci French – a dark, gripping and sophisticated masterclass in psychological suspense in which nothing is quite what it seems . . .

Coming July 2015

ALSO AVAILABLE IN THE BESTSELLING FRIEDA KLEIN SERIES

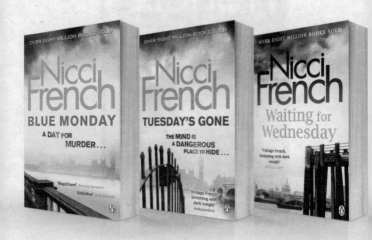

Available as Paperbacks
and eBooks